A dark fantasy of trust, loyalty, sacrifice, and courage in the face of adversity.

Cameron Mitchell

PO Box 221974 Anchorage, Alaska 99522-1974
books@publicationconsultants.com—www.publicationconsultants.com

ISBN 978-1-59433-211-1
Library of Congress Catalog Card Number: 2011922883

Manufactured in the United States of America.

Dedication

For James, because I promised. I would still be a blithering idiot without your help.

To Katharine,
Hope you enjoy the book!

Acknowledgements

Lots of people to thank, chief among them are Evan and Marthy. Evan, you took a chance on me when no others would, and words cannot express how much I appreciate that. Marthy was the best editor anyone could ask for. I also thank my friends. There are too many of you to list, but you all know who you are. Hopefully. You guys helped me out more than you know. Nancy definitely deserves a mention here, for her incredible help with my school. And thank you to the anonymous reader who left me an encouraging note with my very first rejection notice. That was the very first time I realized my writing was worth something.

And last, but certainly not least, I thank my mom, Terri. Cheesy as it sounds, I would be absolutely nowhere without you, with the book or anything else. Thanks for having me.

Contents

Dedication 3

Acknowledgements.. 5

Chapter One .... Twenty.. 9

Sub Chapter One .... Nolan 35

Chapter Two .... A Light In The Darkness................ 39

Sub Chapter Two 50

Chapter Three .... Greater Discipline........................ 51

Sub Chapter Three 64

Chapter Four................... Departure 67

Sub Chapter Four.. 83

Chapter Five................... The Wandering Blade.................... 85

Sub Chapter Five... 97

Chapter Six .... A New Arrangement 99

Sub Chapter Six 128

Chapter Seven .... Jaden Harves............................ 133

Chapter Seven 159

Chapter Eight .... Three Days Out Of Busby 161

Chapter Eight 179

Chapter Nine .... Escape From Fort Torrence 181

Chapter Ten .... A Very Cold Walk..................... 189

Chapter Eleven................. Another Hasty Departure 207

Chapter Twelve .... Deyrey Baaish 213

Chapter Thirteen............. Daylight................................. 225

Chapter Fourteen .... The Temple Of Immortals........... 235

Chapter Fifteen .... Four Went In, Three Came Out.... 249

Chapter One
Twenty

Halas Duer rubbed his blistered hands together and stood, his back protesting loudly against ache. Halas had been working for the better part of nine hours, but despite the soreness he was in high spirits; his family's potatoes were almost ready to be dug up. A warm wind blew in from the sea, stealing away the autumn chill that had recently settled over the city. The day was bright, the sky blue and inviting. All in all, it had been a good day. As Halas straightened, he felt a sudden sense of vertigo that banished the good and made him reel. The ground rushed up at him, and he fell to meet it.

And very suddenly, before the young man and the ground could collide, Halas Duer was somewhere else. The *where* around him was a terrible blur, but he could see the *who* just fine: Cailin. Her beauty shone pure through the gloom. Halas reached out to touch her, trying to lead her to safety, but he was hit with another sickening wave of nausea, punishment if ever he'd known it. This girl was not Cailin, he realized. She was bad, and Halas was not to go near her. She looked similar to Cailin, but the eyes—they did not belong to her. They were piercing and yellow, dark and savage. She smiled at him, and all resemblance melted away. The smile sent shivers down his spine. It was an evil smile. He was on someone then, his hands were wet, he could smell the stink of his breath— and he was back in the potatoes, lying on his back in a cold sweat. His head drooped to the side, allowing him to notice that the grass had turned an alarming shade of brown. Winter, it seemed, was arriving in a hurry.

He stood up and walked into his father's cottage, shaking his head. Already the daydream was fading, though he still felt dizzy, as if he were a child again, twirling with his friends in the fields until they were ill. Halbrick was in the kitchen chopping onions. The smell brought a smile to Halas' face. Onions were a favorite of his. "We have onions?"

"Bought them this morning," Halbrick said. "Your friend Desmond gave me quite a deal."

Halas didn't bother to correct his father. Halas likened poor Desmond Mallon to a roach: try as you might to be rid of him, it never quite worked. It wasn't as if he hated Des—just, when it came down to it, he much preferred the company of others.

He instead looked out the window, seeing the Cordalis Gate in the distance. Cordalis was the capital city of Ager, and certainly the biggest and busiest north of the Inigo River. Dozens of people moved in and out all day long, be they farmers, merchants, or even travelers from distant lands come to see the legendary place, a city that had survived a dozen sieges and two thousand years, a city that was surrounded by its walls but never constricted. Garek was somewhere in there, Halas knew. His younger brother was supposedly looking for a buyer for this year's harvest, but more likely than not he was drinking. Probably with Desmond.

"Have you been to see Conroy this week?" Halbrick asked.

"No Father, not yet."

"Halas, your studies are still just as important as they ever were. I don't want you slacking off."

"I'm not slacking off. I'll see him later today, after supper. I promise."

"Good," his father said. "After tomorrow, it will be harder to tell you what to do." He laughed. After a moment, Halas laughed with him.

———

The sun was setting when Halas left the cottage. He'd forgotten about the daydream. It was dark when he reached the Gate, but he knew he had over three hours before lockup, another sad result of the oncoming winter. A caravan moved past, the lead driver looking surly at the fact that he was getting out so late in the season. For everyone, it seemed, this summer had seemed all too short. It felt like it had been mere days since the Duer family planted their crop, and already they were ready to find a distributor.

The crowd of folks amassed in the Gate pavilion was calming, as the men and women gathered there grew tired of the place and went home for the night. Halas and Cailin had a game involving this crowd. They would sit in the grass and watch, then choose a person at random and create a story for why that person was here. Whoever told the most creative tale won the game, but after a while each tale was the same, because the people at the Gate were always the same: gossip mongers, more interested in who came and went than even their own families. Even in the winter months, when no new faces came through, there seemed to be a crowd. Some people, it seemed, just had nothing better to do.

Halas walked quickly through the city toward the house of his teacher. A few citizens still milled about in the streets, taking care of the last of the day's errands. One man in particular caught Halas' eye. He wore an unusually frilly and unusually purple robe that billowed about his feet. Two young girls chased behind him, carrying the tail of his robe and tripping over their own feet, but the man was oblivious. Halas watched him, amused, even turning around and walking backwards until the man disappeared. *I must tell Cailin about this,* he thought.

Conroy lived close by, and soon Halas, still laughing about the man in the robe, arrived at the manor, knocking twice on the thick door. It opened, and Conroy's gnome stood before Halas, a look on his face matching that of the earlier caravan driver. "I'm here to see Mister Conroy," Halas told him.

"Of course you are," the gnome said. He stood just slightly taller than Halas' waist, with a well-groomed beard and red cheeks, rosy from near-constant irritation. The gnome—Halas had never bothered to learn his name—led him through the house and into Conroy's study, all the while grumbling to himself. He had always been an unpleasant creature. Halas didn't know why Conroy kept him around.

Towering bookshelves lined the walls, filled with dusty tomes both ancient and new. It was a library, a study, and something like a tomb. The room smelled musty and dead. Dull yellow assaulted Halas from all directions. The study was easily his least favorite room in the Conroy manor. Being in it made him uncomfortable. Being in it for prolonged periods of time made him sick.

Mister Conroy sat behind a desk piled high with books and scrolls. Halas could remember when his hair was brown, though that had been a long time ago. It was now a shade of deep gray, with flecks of color here and there. He looked over his spectacles—another irritant—at Halas. "Ah, hello there!" Conroy said cheerfully. "I did not expect to see you this evening. How is your father?"

"He is all right. Our potatoes are ready to be harvested. I'm sure he's excited about that."

"Halbrick always is. I'm afraid I don't have much for you to do today, but I wonder if you could perhaps translate something for me." Conroy then lifted a scroll from the pile, showing it to Halas. "Tell me, Halas, do these symbols mean anything to you?" Halas looked from Conroy's wrinkled face to his wrinkled finger, pressed tightly to a piece of parchment. Strange symbols stared up at him from the page. They were jarring to look at, round but squared, each letter seeming to contradict and yet mirror itself. Halas frowned at the characters.

"They are unlike anything I have ever seen," Conroy continued, making Halas feel a little less foolish. No one was as well traveled as Mister Conroy. The man had been all over Aelborough.

"I do not understand them," Halas said. Conroy nodded, as if he had expected that answer. Of course he had. "Sorry," he added, unsure of what else to say.

"Nothing to be sorry for, dear boy. Nothing at all."

"Where did you find these?"

"That is unimportant." Conroy gave the usual answer, and Halas was not surprised in the least. "However, if you do not understand them, I'm afraid you cannot be of any use to me today. You may go home. Give my regards to your father. Good night."

"Good night, sir."

The gnome ushered Halas to the door and on to the street before he could even mention his birthday, a little irked that the old man had not done so. The night bit into him, chilling him through his cloak. He shoved his hands into the pockets and hurried home.

———

The Duer cottage was not a very large one, but it suited the family just fine. A round building with a slanted roof, it appeared to be larger than it really was. Inside were only three rooms: a kitchen that also served as a living and dining area, a bedroom belonging to Halas and Garek, and a bedroom belonging to their father. No one could call the Duers wealthy, in any sense of the word. The cottage walls were barren, devoid of the art Garek so often pined for. Each bedroom was sparsely furnished, one chair and one bed for each occupant. The walls were peeled and cracked. Yet despite all this, the cupboards of food in the kitchen were always well stocked; Halbrick never failed to see to that, and Halas owned plenty of his favorite books. Out back behind the cottage was a richly cultivated field, perfect for their potatoes.

The Duers were what most people referred to as quarter-farmers, meaning their field was relatively small and yielded little crop. The area around Cordalis was surrounded by these quarter-farms. They were reserved for either the very poor, who could not afford more space, or the very rich, those who viewed farming as a hobby rather than a life's work. Halbrick was proud of his potatoes, however, and did not mind the title. Between the house and the field was an enclosed privy, hidden from the city and any farmers with unusually keen eyesight. If Halbrick was anything, he was private.

Halbrick sat in the kitchen, chewing a wad of tobacco. He grunted at Halas as he entered, and Halas went straight to his room, tossing his cloak into the corner. Garek sprawled out on his bed, bouncing his coin off the ceiling. He looked upset.

"What's wrong?" Halas asked.

"Father's angry with me," Garek responded. The coin dropped to the floor, and Garek didn't bother to retrieve it.

"What for?"

"I came home late. I didn't find a buyer. I didn't shine his boots and build him a castle before he woke up this morning. Take your pick."

"Sorry," Halas said for the second time that night, for the same reason. He crawled into bed and fell asleep. It was a long time coming.

⸻

Halas awoke the next morning to the chirping of songbirds and a warm swatch of sunlight streaming across his face. He rubbed his eyes and wandered into the kitchen. Garek sat at the table, devouring a bowl of porridge. Halbrick was nowhere to be found. "Where's Father?" Halas asked.

"Out," Garek said cheerfully through a mouthful of food. Some of it trickled down his chin. "Happy birthday."

Less than an hour later the two marched up toward the Gate, laughing and joking. Though there had been little to threaten Cordalis for many years, the city wall was a relic of its origin, when war was frequent and demons loomed over the realm. At sixty foot-lengths high and near twenty thick, it had never been breached. Cordalis was a city built to last, it was said. The Gate pavilion was a broad pentagonal courtyard rimmed by the wall. Stairs cut into the stone led to the top. Beyond the courtyard there was a second, smaller wall, and through that a tunnel. This tunnel led to the city itself. The crowd had returned in full force. Halas and Garek wandered the courtyard, waiting for Cailin. Garek juggled his coin from knuckle to knuckle. He flicked it at Halas. Halas snapped it out of the air. For a moment he looked at the coin, feeling quite proud of himself for catching it. Garek grinned. Halas offered the coin, but when Garek moved to take it, Halas pulled his arm back. "Stop throwing it at me," he said.

Garek frowned. The coin was a gift from their father. Neither remembered how long ago it had been given. "Yes, yes, fine," he said.

"Good." Halas tossed Garek his coin. Garek tucked it away.

Cailin approached, breaking into a run when she saw the two brothers. She wrapped her arms around Halas' neck and kissed him. Halas grinned when it was over. "Happy birthday," she said. "When are you moving closer to me?"

"Soon."

"Soon?"

"Soon. I promise." He laughed.

"Good. Plenty of lots are open. I think my neighbors are all leaving the city. Most are awaiting buyers for their homes. Some haven't bothered."

"Why are they leaving?"

Cailin shrugged. "I don't know; it's the most curious thing. Folks are just… up and leaving."

That was troubling to Halas, but not too much. It was just too good to see her again. It had only been a day, but that day felt like weeks. He smiled and took her hand, saying, "Maybe it's your smell." Laughing, she pushed him, and that was the end of that.

He turned to Garek. "Now what? Olan? He wanted to walk the wall today."

Garek spread apologetic arms. "I promised Des."

Halas groaned. "Desmond? Come on, Garek, must you?"

"Oh, come on. You've never taken issue with him before."

Cailin gave a dramatic sigh. "I suppose we'll just have to endure." She cracked a smile at the brothers.

"Well, no Olan then. All right, let's go get Desmond."

Halas told them of the man in the purple robe as the three walked to a nearby neighborhood, stopping at a house with a roof made of thatched sea grass. Taking care to avoid the broken step and the enormous cat lying above that, they advanced up the porch and knocked on the door. A man just younger than Halas came out of the house, the beginnings of a goatee forming at his chin. Garek flicked the loose end playfully, but Desmond swatted the second attempt away. Natives to the northern land of Springdell, Desmond's family had moved to Cordalis when he was ten years of age. He still managed to retain bits and pieces of his old accent. It gave his speech an odd quality that Desmond absolutely adored. The accent made him quite popular with strangers, and Desmond relished every moment of the attention. Things became particularly irritating when the boy was drunk, and Halas frequently had to restrain himself from punching Desmond in the face.

As always, Desmond was drawn to Halas as if by tether. "So Halas," he said, "what is it like?"

"What is what like?"

"You're of age!" Halas had turned twenty that day, and as such, he was officially an adult in Aelborough. *Well, in Ager, anyway.* He wasn't sure how many years it was outside the country. "You can finally move away from this horrible place!"

"No, I can finally move *into* this horrible place." Desmond laughed.

But it was something to consider. Halas could move into the city and do what he wanted. No more farming. As much as Halas loved being outdoors, he *hated* farming. Farming was the avatar of the mundane, and Halas hated the mundane more than anything else. He had a few hundred detricots saved up, perhaps enough to buy a small place somewhere close. *One of Cailin's empty lots, perhaps.* "So, what today?" Des asked.

"Tavern?" Garek suggested.

"Let's stop by the marketplace first," Cailin said. "Mother wants me to pick up a few things." They started walking.

Halas stopped at the gallows. Earlier in the week, a man called Martin Broadbent had been paraded through the streets to be hanged in this very spot. Citizens and soldiers alike pummeled him with stones and rotten food as they cried out for blood. That sort of public display was reserved only for the worst of criminals, and Broadbent certainly ranked among them. He was said to be responsible for at least four rapes and six murders, three of them children. Captain Onath Cullough of the Badges had finally tracked Broadbent down after a lengthy chase. His trial was brief. Both Cullough and Broadbent were heavily discussed subjects amongst the people of Cordalis. The churches, who so rarely came to agreement on what should be done, had come together to fund a statue in the brave captain's likeness, to be raised in the city center, near King Melick's own keep.

Today, however, things were far more tranquil. There was an auction on. The auctioneer was a tall man, with blue-rimmed spectacles and a wide hat. He danced across the scaffold with the grace that was expected of him, rattling off prices of the gnomes sitting in the dirt before him, blank looks on their flush faces. Citizens crowded the stage, calling out offers and holding their cards. Some rattled packages filled with jingling coins. "You coming?" Des asked him.

"I'll be along in a bit."

A gnome would be a good thing to have once Halas purchased a house of his own. He would be able to spend his days searching for employment while the gnome tended to the place, keeping it in a state of utmost order.

Unfortunately, the cheapest at this particular auction was three hundred fifty detricots. Halas moved on.

As he attempted to find his friends, a dark-skinned man in a gold suit tried to sell him several things, including a goat that could speak and a dagger sharp enough to pierce dragon scales. The possibility of a talking goat was almost too much for Halas. He hesitated when the man threw out his offer.

Fifty detricots. You could not buy a *normal* goat for that amount of money. At the very least, it was a bargain in that regard. Halas would have followed the vendor if his friends hadn't been waiting for him. He excused himself to the man and left. He ducked between two booths, moving toward where he knew Cailin liked to shop. Several more salesmen harangued him, each item peddled more outlandish than the last. Halas had always hated the market for precisely this reason—there was never a moment's peace. It was common knowledge not to trust a seller unless he was parked firmly behind a booth. Booths were trustworthy; men who kept their wares elsewhere were typically cheats. Halas hated the market.

But Cailin liked it, and sure enough, Halas found her in Maryl's booth, Garek and Des in tow. She was inspecting two blouses, though both she and Halas knew she had no intention of buying either. Cailin had her routine with the market—say her mother wanted a few things, look at the garments for a while, and then leave. It was a pastime. A crowd of like-minded women pawed through the stacks of clothing. Maryl was an interesting woman and she sewed fine clothing (something even Halas could admit) but her prices were outrageous. She belonged in a store of her own, not some dismal booth in the market. Garek and Des looked sheepishly at Halas.

"Three fifty," he explained to his brother, who had seen him looking at the gnomes.

"Ah."

They finished Cailin's errands and left the bazaar. Garek suggested the tavern again, and this time no one had any objections. They arrived at The Jealous Duchess shortly after and found a table. The bar was rather empty, save for a few other patrons and an entertainer. The bard's name was Chase, and he was a regular throughout Lord Bel. He told stories and occasionally poems. Chase was quite popular with the younger folks. Halas had chosen a table close to the bard, wishing to hear what he had to say. They dug into their food, but Halas listened to the storyteller as he told a tale older than Cordalis, than Ager itself. It was one Halas always enjoyed.

"Gather round, ladies and gentlemen. Gather round to hear the tale of Aeon the Great, youngest son of Aelworth, hero and savior to all of mankind.

"Aeon was born in the year of 14, fifteen years after the great Captain Aelworth discovered this very land and settled in this very city. As a youngster he was a prodigy; at two years of age, he was capable of complex speech and knew his written letters. Yet no matter what he did, poor Aeon paled in comparison to his elder brother. Bakunin was the light of their father's eye. He represented hope for the kingdom that was to come, you see. Aeon himself was simply there. Aelworth loved him as a father loves a son, but he loved Bakunin as a king loves a kingdom.

"So Aeon grew up. He was a handsome boy, yet Bakunin was handsomer. He was a smart boy, but Bakunin was smarter. He was a strong boy, skilled in archery and swordsmanship and mathematics and navigation and everything else that makes for a good captain and a good king. Yet, with all his incredible accomplishments, he was nothing when competing against his brother. His brother was the *kingdom*, after all.

"Despite all this, it was not in Aeon's character to despair. Instead he thrived, taking all challenges head-on, and always besting them. He was unstoppable. None could defeat him in combat, armed or otherwise. None thought faster than Aeon the Great, none scribed better, or possessed more charm.

"In the year 34, Aeon was away at a jousting tournament, where he met Kristaeanna, his soon-to-be wife. With her favor in hand, he took the tournament trophy with ease, and fell madly in love with the girl in the process. The two were married just before returning to Cordalis, and Aeon, now betrothed and with Bakunin unwed, became heir to the throne.

"At this news Bakunin was pleased; he had discovered the joys of farming and wished to make his living there instead of as king. He wished for his tools to be a plow and hoe, not a sword and shield. King Aelworth would have nothing of this, but when Aeon presented himself as heir, he was secretly pleased. For nearly a year he denied this pleasure before embracing it on his deathbed. Beloved King Aelworth passed from the realm of the living in January of thirty-six, at the age of seventy-three. There was no question as to which of his sons would rule in his place; the honor was awarded strictly to Aeon.

"For two years they lived in peace, and the kingdom prospered. There were no wars, no plagues, no famine, no poverty. Aelborough was, for all intents and purposes, the perfect place to live. But the golden years of King Aeon's rule were short, because in April of 38, the Infernals came.

"Sayad was the first to fall. The people were reduced to nothing, nearly eradicated in the brutal genocide that followed. Before King Aeon could send aid, the southern kingdom was lost. The Infernals struck out across the land, burning what they could and slaughtering people and animals alike. The Sayad refugees fled to Cordalis and shelter. Aeon's army met with that of the Infernals on the Fields of Shankhara, in what is now the Burning Desert. The armies were massive. It was a bright morning. Aeon rode along the columns. His armor was white, and his blade shimmered in the sun. He bore his own standard, and planted it in the grass.

"'We will not be defeated this day!' Aeon cried. 'We will endure, and punish this new evil that has so wronged us! Let no demon pass these ranks!'

"And they charged, five thousand horse and twice that on foot. King Aeon led the assault. They raced across the field, but the Infernals remained unfazed. They held their ground, and Aeon's army broke upon their formation. As the men grew closer, they wailed in fear, for the Infernals were indeed demons, twisted and blighted, like nothing any man had ever seen.

"Aeon himself was unscathed in the battle. He rode among the Infernals, and his sword sang with their blood. King Aeon cut them down as if they were nothing. His brother fought at his side, and together, they slew many. The brave fought on, but it was a hopeless battle, for too many had fled, and Aeon's army was shattered. He and they limped back to Cordalis and sealed the gates. The Infernals were breathing down their necks.

"Aeon gathered together his most trusted advisors, including among them Kristaeanna, Bakunin, and his friend of many years, Nebi. While Aeon, his brother, and wife were legendary heroes, Nebi was no such thing. He was, in fact, a sniveling coward with little hair and a hunch in his shoulders." Chase hunkered down on his stool in his best impression of Nebi. Very few entertainers dared to portray the man as anything less than despicable. Halas had seen one try to make Nebi out as a misunderstood, if not pathetic, creature, but that bard had been doused with a bucket of water by several drunks and dunked in a sewer trench.

Chase continued. "'My friends,' Aeon said, 'we must find a way to destroy these abominations. They are a stain on the face of this fair world, and I shall not stand for it. Enough is enough.'

"'But what can we do, my lord?' asked the advisors. It was Kristaeanna who decided on the plan."

Here, the bard lapsed into such an eerily perfect impression of a woman's voice that Halas and the other patrons could not hold their laughter. Cailin shrieked it, doubled over, slapping her knees. Halas loved it when she found something truly humorous. Her laugh was wonderful, a cool glass of mead on a hot summer day.

"'We have discerned that these demons come from the south, correct?' 'Correct,' was the response. She continued. 'So we must lay great and powerful wards, as far from their origin as we possibly can. We must journey north of the Frigid Peaks.'

"Aeon and the others agreed. That very day, he, Bakunin, Kristaeanna, and fifty others set out from Cordalis, bound for the Frigid Peaks and the arctic beyond. Nebi would not go, but Aeon, out of some devotion to the man, insisted. He wanted to protect his friend, and knew that Cordalis would soon have to hold out against all forces. Nebi relented, but not due to Aeon's urgings. Two days following, the city was besieged by the Infernals.

"Aeon's journey across what is now Nesvizh was almost entirely uneventful. They were supplied and aided by the natives, some of them going so far as to join him in his all-important quest. It was when they came to the foothills of the Frigid Peaks that they first encountered troubles. For you see, Aeon the Great lived in a time when there were still goblin tribes roaming the mountains. The goblins were many, and they had united under the banner of the Infernals.

"Aeon's party had nearly doubled in size during their trek across Aelborough, and a great many battles were fought. The goblins were inexperienced at combat and lacked the tools to wage war. They had no horses, no metals; only their dim wits, wooden clubs, and of course, fire. It was the fire, many believe, that allowed them to whittle Aeon's forces down to almost nothing.

"During their third night through the Peaks, the goblins struck. They came from the snow like phantoms, dragging several men into the drifts, never to be seen again. Bakunin woke the camp and Aeon led the charge. The goblins were not prepared for such ferocity, and fell back into hiding. Aeon looked about the campsite, seeing the corpses and drag-marks in the snow, and he nearly wept. Nebi attempted to convince Aeon to go back the way they had come, but Aeon would have none of it. Whenever things escalated to violence, Nebi could be found cowering behind the king, and these times were no different. His whining counsel clouded Aeon's vision, but the good king was able to overcome.

"'We can stay here no longer,' he decided. 'We must be free of these dreaded mountains by sundown tomorrow. These final hours shall be grueling ones, but if you trust me and follow my word, we shall persevere, and overcome any and all challenges. These beasts are nothing compared to what awaits us back home should we fail. Come, then!'

"So they ran. They ran through the night and day. The goblins were unseen, hiding in the snow and trees. They launched great bundles of fire at Aeon's men, cutting through them like so many bits of paper. Aeon's men continued running, leaving their dead behind, and when it became clear to the goblins that they could win, they came in full force.

"Nearly five hundred of the things came upon Aeon, whose forces were already fighting exhaustion, grief, and the tremendous cold. Perhaps it was their grief that allowed them to stand fast and fight. Ever since Shankhara, they had suffered a brutal string of defeats, and had finally had enough. No goblin survived the battle that day.

"In the end, twenty men and women emerged into the Arctic Wasteland, battered but not beaten.

"They'd left the goblins behind, but there were still more dangers ahead. The Stoneacre Crags lay before them, great chasms in the earth capable of swallowing entire armies whole. Aeon the Great and his band were forced to abandon their mounts, and any extraneous gear. They crept across the crags with the carefulness and trepidation of tomcats. They rested between each major crevasse, and during one of these rests, Bakunin rolled over in his sleep and was nearly lost. Were it not for his brother, he would have been.

"It took a week to pass the crags, and as they progressed, Nebi grew nervous. He had been approached by the Infernals before Aeon left for Sayad with his army, and given his task. He was to kill Aeon and prevent him from casting his wards. Nebi had not wished to kill his best friend of many years, but in the end, coin had been his downfall. He was promised the king's treasury.

"He moaned all through the journey, complaining of physical hardship and fatigue. Because of his cowardice, he could not even bring himself to look his friend in the eye when he killed him. A day after having left the crags behind, Nebi plunged his knife into Aeon the Great's back, again and again. Aeon's blood sprayed. When he was finished, Aeon disarmed him with the ease unbecoming a dying man.

"'Nebi,' he breathed, 'my friend. Why have you done this to me?' 'They promised me the kingdom,' Nebi said, and it was a lie. Even in Aeon's final moments, Nebi could not bring himself to speak even the smallest of truths. Aeon nodded, as if he accepted this, though clearly he saw through the falsehood. 'It is all right,' he said. 'I forgive you, my friend. I love you no less than I did before, I love you as I love my brother, as I loved my father. You will forever be a brother to me, Nebi.'

"Nebi was so overcome with grief at Aeon's proclamation of mercy that he flung himself into the crags. Aeon could hardly speak, but he told Bakunin to assemble the party.

"When his men were before him, King Aeon spoke. 'Build a great temple here,' he said, 'of ice and snow. This is the greatest task any of you have ever faced, but I know that you shall prevail. You are the best men that I have ever known. It was an honor being your king. Build the Temple here, and my spirit shall do the rest.'

"Bakunin led the men off to begin construction, and Kristaeanna sat with Aeon as he died. She never told his final words.

"For weeks, the men labored over Aeon's temple. They slaved over it with precision, tending to each block with the care you would show an infant.

Even still, their pace was hurried, and when they finally completed the temple, they buried Aeon within it.

"Kristaeanna spoke to the men. 'My husband shall live on!' she declared. 'His spirit is immortal, and he shall dwell here forevermore, to protect against the deadly threat. Let him defend the Temple of Immortals, and let the Infernal menace never rise against us while these walls last!'

"With that done, Aeon's spirit set to work. The Inigo River sprang up from nothing, and the Infernals were turned to sand and banished to the deserts of the south. What damage that had been done could not be undone, but further mayhem was averted. Prosperity was restored and a new king set in place.

"That king was not a blood relative of Aeon the Great, for Kristaeanna, who would have been queen, decided not to return to Cordalis. No one knows if it was fear of the Peaks or a desire to remain close to the Temple of Immortals, but she, Bakunin, and the rest of Aeon's party decided to settle north of the mountains. She and he were married, and the village was named for Bakunin, eldest brother of Aeon the Great.

"That village is still there to this day. The long war was over, and it ended in the marriage of Bakunin and Kristaeanna."

What few patrons there were in the tavern applauded before returning to their meals or their drink. The bard gathered his things and retired.

Halas and his friends were finished with lunch, so they took to the city, wandering the streets and acting upon every dull whim before inevitably returning to the tavern that evening. The sun was low, and the Duchess had filled considerably since the morning. The four took up a booth near the bar. Halas went up to order the first round. "What'll it be?" asked Bert. "Mead?"

"You know me too well, Bert," Halas said with a grin. He held up four fingers. "Four, please."

Bert went to fill their pints. Halas glanced around the barroom. He saw several courtesans in the far corner, and saw Desmond watching them. Halas chuckled, wondering idly if Garek's friend had ever been with a woman. Bert handed Halas the mugs, and he returned to their booth. He thought of remarking to Desmond about the women, but decided against it. That seemed far too mean-spirited.

"Mead?" Garek asked, sniffing at his mug. "Have we not learned yet that Halas is not to go to the bar alone?"

"If he pays, I will stomach whatever he brings, just as long as it gets me good and drunk," said Desmond. "Just as long."

"I like mead," Cailin whispered to Halas.

"Thank you." He smiled and kissed her on the nose. "Tell me, Garek, what would you prefer? I have seen you drink Bert's *frogswallow*, and that smells like death itself. You are certainly braver than I, or stupider."

"Garek would drink horse piss if he found it laid him out properly," said Des.

"This coming from you, Des? Oh, what a treat!" Garek lifted his mug. "To frogswallow!"

"I cannot drink to that," said Cailin, sipping at her own pint. "Ever."

Garek and Desmond clashed their mugs and began chugging. Halas turned to Cailin and raised his own. "To not drinking to frogswallow?" he suggested. She tipped her glass against his, laughing.

Garek lowered his mug, already nearly empty. He winced as the alcohol coursed through his system. "Not good," he said, "not good. Desmond, get the next."

"Ale?"

"Something good and cheap."

"Cheap is good. I can do cheap." Desmond hurried off. Halas and Cailin were still on their second pint when Garek finished his fourth and Desmond his fifth. Garek burped. His ale sloshed out of the glass and over his hand. Garek didn't seem to notice. Halas watched him, bemused, his arm slung casually over Cailin's shoulders. Desmond's mother was distantly related to some king or lord or duke. He was in the process of trying to explain the complexities of this relation when Rufus entered. Halas saw their friend standing at the bar and waved him over.

He greeted them each in turn. "How much has he had?" Rufus asked Halas, indicating Garek.

Halas shrugged. "I haven't been keeping count."

"Next pint makes five," said Cailin.

"You've been paying attention?" They all laughed.

"What? I may catch him eventually. I want to be sure."

"Of what?" Halas asked. "He'll be long dead when you reach those numbers."

This time it was Cailin who shrugged, holding the pose and looking innocent, adorable. Halas wrapped her in a hug. He couldn't get enough of her. She laughed into his neck. "May not be a good idea to hold me here much longer," she breathed so that only Halas could hear. "Who knows what I could do?" Cailin stretched her own neck a bit and began to nibble on Halas' ear. He glanced at his friends, but none seemed to notice. "I've got liquor in me."

"Hardly."

"You never know." She pulled away, giggling. "You may be blessed, Halas, but you're not *that* blessed, birthday or not."

"Well in that case, I'll need more liquor. Anyone for whiskey?"

"Shots!" Garek and Desmond cried in tandem. Rufus nodded, handing Halas a stack of coins.

"That should pay for the round," he said.

The shots were pleasant fire in Halas' gut. He had one, but when Desmond insisted on a second round, Halas declined. Garek took two instead, and wobbled in the booth. Spittle began to pool down his chin. "Halas," Des warned, but Halas was already up, taking his brother by the arm. The three hurried into the street.

"I'm fine," Garek muttered, but shortly after he retched. Halas and Desmond got him to the nearby sewer trench just in time. Garek leaned over the side and vomited. Halas held his shoulder so he would not fall in. It had happened before.

Halas and Desmond waited for Garek as he expelled the alcohol from his stomach and into the trench. Two drunks out for a smoke of something heavier than tobacco watched, burping raucous laughter. Desmond shouted some very rude things to them, but the drunks had already moved on.

Garek, finally done, rolled on to his back and groaned, wiping the back of a sleeve over his lips. He looked up at Halas and Desmond. "Ready for round two?" he asked.

Halas rolled his eyes. He looked to Desmond. "Have you ever seen Garek be drunk this early in the evening?" he asked.

Desmond pursed his lips. "A few times, yeah. He'll be fine."

"If you say so."

They hauled Garek back into the tavern and settled him into the booth. Halas knew his brother would regret everything come morning, but for now, he had no intention of aggravating the situation. Garek was known to become unruly when drunk, to say the least. Once he'd even flung a glass at Halas for suggesting he pace himself. Halas had nearly knocked the younger Duer unconscious that night. They'd fought often, but that was in their younger years. Now Garek was bigger, and Halas afraid their fights would not be so one-sided as they used to be.

Rufus had a third round of shots ready. Garek downed his instantly. He sank a little on the bench, and belched. Halas was ready to rush his brother outside once again, but Garek recovered. "Come on, new round," he said.

"This never gets old," said Rufus.

They were rushing things, and no good ever came of that. Halas found he did not wish to deal with Garek in such a state, not on his birthday. "Cailin, I'm suddenly feeling a walk. Care to join me?"

"If we hurry," Cailin said, "we can catch the sunset."

Halas smiled and took her hand. They stood. "Leaving so soon?" Desmond asked.

"I'm afraid so." He turned to Rufus. "Try not to kill him."

"No promises." They were already having at another pint.

"Where are you off to?" Desmond asked, half-rising from his seat.

"We're just going on a walk."

"I could join you?"

"No, thank you Desmond," Cailin said, smiling sweetly. "That's quite all right."

"All right then. Bye." He hiccupped and lowered himself.

"Good night, Desmond," Cailin said. "Ready?"

"Let's get out of here."

They did, running through the Gate and toward Jim's Forest. Their favorite knoll wasn't far, and they settled in, Cailin curling up in the crook of Halas' arm. The sun cast an orange and purple glow over everything. It was a beautiful sight, the land a cascade of red and orange in the fiery ball's last moments. Combined with what was in his arms…

When darkness had set in, Cailin turned to face him. Their lips were inches apart. The smell of her favorite mead was strong, but no deterrent. She leaned in and kissed him. Halas had come to like the taste of it on her.

"Happy birthday."

———

The sun was but a faded memory when they raced toward the Gate. Halas didn't know quite how much time they had until lockup, but he knew it was soon.

They skirted the forest closely, too closely for Halas' liking, but Cailin didn't seem to mind. She ran along the edge, dipping in and out of the foreboding timber. Halas was worried; he continually glanced toward the dark veil that seemed to cover the woods from within, terrified that something would come out of there and take them both.

His worry seemed to make Cailin want to go even farther in. Halas managed to pull her away, and they ran for the Gate. He and Cailin reached the two guards. "Cutting it a bit close, are we?" one said with a reassuring wink.

"Good night," Halas told Cailin, giving her a chaste peck on the cheek.

"G'night."

She disappeared into the city. "You too?" the guard asked. Halas shook his head, pointing toward his father's cottage and explaining that he lived there. The guards took on a surlier demeanor then, dismissing him with a curt grunt.

"Wait!" All three men turned toward the voice. It was Desmond, supporting Garek with one arm, leading him along. Halas grinned. "He lives out there, in the cottage over yonder," Des explained. "Howdy, Halas."

"Hello Des. You two have fun?"

"We always do. Take him from here?"

"Mm hmm."

It was an awkward exchange, as Desmond was still slightly drunk, but they managed to shift him around without dropping him. *Garek is heavy,* Halas realized, practically dragging him home. *When did he get so fat?*

———

Halas had settled down in the kitchen to read a book by Nathanial Asselin. It was his telling of Aeon the Great's story. Halas owned many different versions of the same tale, but Asselin's was his favorite. The bard earlier in the day had piqued his interest, and he'd wasted no time in tracking down the book when he was finished putting Garek to bed. He was nearly to the Fields of Shankhara when his father returned. Halbrick did not bother to stomp his boots clean of the mud or hang up his traveling cloak. He walked quickly to the back of the house, snatching his poke from the table as he passed. "Where have you been today?" Halas asked.

"Happy birthday," Halbrick mumbled as he disappeared. Something was wrong.

"Father?"

Halas followed him into the yard, where Halbrick was busy trying to light a cigarette. His hands shook, chasing the cigarette around in little circles. Most unnervingly, he didn't seem to realize he was doing so with an unlit match. Halas took a careful step forward. He had never seen his father like this. Halbrick was deeply perturbed. He was *scared.* Seeing him so made Halas feel frightened. Something gripped at the inside of his chest. So far as Halas could remember, his father had never been afraid, not like this. Halbrick continued to chase the cigarette.

Halas struck a match for him, igniting the tobacco. Halbrick inhaled deeply, and almost immediately seemed to relax. He would move quickly to the pipe, likely before Halas even left him.

"What's the matter?" Halas asked.

His father said nothing for a while. They stood like that in the yard, Halbrick smoking and Halas anxiously awaiting a response. "It's nothing. Nothing at all. Go to bed," Halbrick finally told him. "I've a present for you in the morning."

Disturbed, Halas obeyed. He lay awake for a long time, watching the glow of his father's pipe in the corner of his window. What had happened? Deep down, he did not wish to know. It frightened him to think that something could affect the man like that. Halbrick was indomitable, and it must have taken something truly terrible to upset him in such a way. Halas could not even begin to imagine the horror, but he tried to all the same. His curiosity was as powerful as his worry. He wanted to go to his father and make sure things were all right. Maybe Halbrick would explain.

Right, and maybe he will buy a goat to help him tell the story. Halas knew the idea was silly. Halbrick kept his own counsel, and even if that were not the case, Halas would never expect him to confide in his sons. Halas rolled over and looked at the doorway, hoping to see his father pass by, into his own bedroom, but Halbrick was still outside. How long had it been? There was no way of telling in the dark. He frowned. What seemed like several hours slipped by, and Halbrick remained outside, relighting his pipe every so often. When the match flared, Halas would catch a momentary glance at his face, and each time it shocked him. Halbrick looked gaunt and pale. Something was truly wrong in the world, and Halas did not know what it was. He only knew that it had frightened his father, and that was the worst thing of all. Eventually, Halas forced himself away from the sight. Garek's loud snoring interrupted his thoughts, allowing him to find rest.

A week passed, and then two weeks. Each morning, Halbrick would leave before Halas awoke, and return well after the sun set. To make matters worse, Conroy would have nothing to do with him, citing various excuses occasionally, but more often than not he would just shut the door in his face.

One day, Halas awoke to find that his father had not left. It was time to dig up the potatoes. Halas thought it would be his chance to find out what was happening, but Halbrick spent the day keeping his two sons busy. Whenever Halas attempted to ask him about what he was doing in the forest, Halbrick would dodge the question, sending Halas to do a more laborious task than the last, and often the menial things he often set Garek to.

He soon quit asking.

Halas became so lost in his work that the day passed him by quickly, and after supper his thoughts caused the night to do the same, the sun edging its way into the corners of the sky as he pondered. He stood up and went to the window.

There was Halbrick, hurrying away from the house as if he didn't belong there in the first place, a burglar in the night. Instinctively, Halas ducked down, peering just over the lip of the window, watching his father. Where was he going?

The forest.

He watched his father walk into the trees, apparently unafraid once he disappeared from the view of every house except his own. *Is he mad?* Halas thought. *I have to go after him!* He bolted from the cottage, grabbing his own cloak and boots, pulling them on along the way and accidentally stomping a few potatoes in the process. They were stored in piles and barrels in front of the cottage, waiting to be sold. He tripped on one of these, and they tumbled into the grass like stones from a barrow. Halas ignored them.

There was something in those woods, something wholly evil. Halas knew it. Everyone in Cordalis knew it. Jim's Forest, unofficially named for the first boy who had foolishly ventured into it hundreds of years before, never to return, was not something people dealt with lightly. Everyone had their own personal tale of what happened to poor Jim. Halas thought he'd been devoured by spiders; Garek figured he'd been swallowed up by a hole in the ground; Des reckoned he was lost in the trees and went mad; Cailin was of the opinion that the whole thing was a farce. Now that Halas thought about it, he realized that Halbrick had never spoken of his beliefs on the matter.

Halas reached the Treeline (like the Gate, its status as a proper noun had never been contested by the citizens of Cordalis), and the frozen fist of fear gripped his heart and squeezed, becoming a tendril of fire somewhere near his groin and legs. It took a mighty effort for him to will his feet forward. Then he was past the first spruce, standing in a thick moss covered with the remains of rotten leaves. He drew in unsteady breath, took a few timid steps forward, and leaned on a knot as he looked for his father. It was cold to the touch. The feeling of the bark against his skin made him think of corpses. Halas had never actually seen a corpse before, much less felt one, but the trunk reminded him of one all the same. He pulled his hand away, looking at the tree. A feeling of revulsion rose in his gut. The knot remained indifferent. He forced himself away.

"Father!" Halas called. Nothing, only the far-off hooting of an owl. He contemplated turning back. The owl certainly seemed to beat this message into his head. The call was a warning; surely no normal birds lived in the wood. *Surely.* He was so positive that this was the case that he realized his legs had carried him back out of the trees, into the fields again. Halas glanced back at his cottage; it dwindled in the distance, but it was there. It was safe, and the idea of hiding under his covers for the night was not an unappealing one.

No. His father was in here, somewhere, and thus was in danger. Halas had to do something to help him. He swung back toward the forest, walked forward, cried out again.

But Halbrick had many years of experience under his belt, years that Halas did not possess. It would be foolish to think he could *rescue* his father from anything. He remembered a story from his childhood.

There had been a terrible Fire. Whole cities, whole *worlds* had burned. Fire raged for many centuries, until brave young Sea decided to put it out. Sea knew that he alone could extinguish Fire, so he set to work. But Sea's friend Forest had tried to save him, saying that Fire could not be defeated. Forest had nearly died, but Sea had extinguished Fire just in time to save his friend.

He felt like Forest, and the irony was not lost on him. But irony aside, what could he do against this menace that Halbrick could not?

Something. Perhaps just being there could save his father's life. Perhaps he could serve as a distraction long enough for Halbrick to get them both to safety.

"But if Father needs to be saved, why did he go in there in the first place?" Halas wasn't aware he spoke aloud until the word *did.* The noise startled him, and he threw his hands over his face to protect against whatever had come to protect its territory. The rest of the sentence slopped out of his mouth.

But there were only the trees, wavering slightly in the breeze. Their leaves rustled against each other, sounding like a million bugs scurrying across brick. Halas could almost feel them on his flesh. He scratched at his arms. *They're not real,* he reminded himself. *It is just the wind. They are not real.* A light mist swirled gently about the ground. It reminded Halas absurdly of a fence.

But the more I watch it, maybe the idea is not so absurd.

He took a step. One step and he was through the Treeline. The mist covered his ankles, and for a moment he was sure that something would jump from it and take him. A gnarled creature of the undead, perhaps, his skin patched in scabby growths and his teeth worn down to brown stumps of nothing. But no creature did, so he took another hesitant step. Then he was clear of the mist, surrounded by the springy moss. A third, and he collected the courage to call for his father. It took every ounce of willpower Halas had.

Now even the owl was silent; even the tree's leaves had stopped rustling. All that remained was the wind, and that was rapidly dissipating. The crushing silence swept from the forest, urging Halas to make himself hidden. He felt a million eyes settle upon him, watching his every move, waiting to strike. His skin crawled, and the lump in his gut solidified even further.

Halas Duer walked farther into the forest and tried to retain his courage, for his father's sake. Against all logic or reason, he pressed forward into the dark.

There. A flitting movement in the trees to his right. Halas spun to face them, and caught a quick glimpse of something large moving through the brush. It grunted and began to paw the ground. This was no imagined creature, no monster of the mind. This was a living, breathing beast, with teeth and claws and a taste for warm blood.

Any shred of bravery left Halas then, dissipating into the thin mist that had begun to reach from the border and gather about his knees. With a high scream, Halas ran. He vaulted over a high root, scrambling to keep his feet. The creature, whatever it was, followed, a series of guttural noises still coming from it. Halas screamed again. He could see what appeared to be the Treeline. Safety. Salvation. Home.

But his foot snagged on another root, and he fell face first into the moss. Immediately, he began to feel weary, as if all the will was drained from his body. He was more tired than he had ever been in his life, and he happened to be on a very comfortable surface.

Halas closed his eyes, and his breathing began to relax. Nothing could hurt him here. Not while he slept. The moss was far more comfortable than his bed had ever been. Why not sleep here? He was so tired, in any case. *Why am I even awake? It's late. I'll just lie down for a bit and rest.*

Something moved past his head.

He bolted for the Treeline, clearing it and running toward the cottage, slamming the door and throwing himself down in his bedroom, covering his head with a blanket, shivering madly and not from the cold. The old boyhood rule came to him then: blankets protected you from monsters. It was silly, especially with Halas so recently becoming an adult, but now it seemed to make all the sense in the world. As long as he could not see the monster, it could not see him, and he was safe.

Halas stifled a groan. He could hear coarse breathing nearby. The beast, whatever it was, had followed him home, was now waiting just inches from his bedside, waiting to devour him.

But that was ridiculous, and even though Halas knew it full well, it still took him almost an hour to muster up the courage to poke his head free. When he did, he expected to see a monster that stood from wall to wall, slavering hungrily over his next meal.

But there was only a sleeping Garek in his own bed. Halas laughed at his own ludicrous reaction. It was a tired, nervous sound. *Well, Garek's snoring certainly* sounds *monstrous.* He sighed.

Halas crawled toward the window, looking out toward the forest. There was nothing, only the swirling mist.

What had happened?

It all hit him then, and Halas started to cry. He cried because for all he knew, his father was dead. His father was dead and Halas couldn't do a thing about it, because he was too afraid. He cried because he hated himself, and he cried even more because he knew nothing could make him go back into those trees. He didn't leave the house that day, desperately waiting for Halbrick to come home so he could explain a few things and assuage Halas' guilt.

But Halbrick did not return.

"It has been two days since my father went missing. Please, I need your help." Halas stood at the headquarters for the Badges, trying to persuade a captain to send a patrol out after Halbrick. The Badges served wherever needed. Their business was safety. They were your friends from fire and foes. The rhetoric was printed on their banners.

"What's your father's name?"

"Halbrick Duer."

The captain nodded to himself, but Halas doubted that he was going to remember the name. Already he knew how this would turn out. He bunched his hands into fists.

"Right, Halback Duer. And what did you say your family does?"

"We are farmers. We own a cottage just outside the Farm Gate. Finest potatoes in the city." Guilt, terror and sleeplessness couldn't prevent the pride from showing in Halas' voice, pride he himself had no recognition of.

The man scoffed. "Well, forget it then. I won't endanger my men, especially over a stupid quarter-farmer who got his self lost. That forest is not worth the trouble. Move on."

"Move—move on? *Move on?*" Halas was fuming. Move on? How could they suggest such a thing! He almost took a swing at the captain. It was a tremendous feat that he managed to get himself under control.

"Listen here, kid. There are twelve men in this building right now, and each one of them will do more for this city than your entire family ever has, or ever will. Got it? A thousand farmers sell crop to Cordalis, and one less won't make no difference."

"And you—you actually want to…to go out there?"

Halas stood outside the cottage with Desmond and Garek. It was Garek who had spoken, after hearing Halas' plan, if it could be called that.

"Yes, I do. Our *father* is out there somewhere, and he needs our help!" Halas was shocked at Garek's reaction. For two days, he had not seemed worried for Halbrick at all. In fact, he seemed rather happy. He knew Garek and Halbrick rarely got along even in the best of times, but Halas still hated his brother for his attitude. Halas needed all the support he could gather to find his father safe and sound, and he was not getting it. Not nearly.

"I want to go as well," Des said, nodding to himself. "There's still a few hours fore the sun sets. If we leave now, we can look around. Test the defenses, so to speak."

"With *what?*" Garek demanded, a bit of color coming to his cheeks. "We have, what, a bow and a few arrows? Some knives? Whatever lurks within those trees is not going to be stopped, or even frightened, by a bow and some knives!"

He had a point. Even still, Halas wanted nothing more than to strike his brother, to hit him and keep hitting him. *It is as if he does not care! Am I going mad?*

An idea came into his head. Mister Conroy had traveled all across Aelborough, collecting a great many things. Halas had spent many hours wandering his manor while Conroy related to him the stories behind every artifact.

Some of which were weapons.

———

"No."

The word stopped him in his tracks. He paced—stood, now—in Conroy's study, watching as the old man leafed through some tome or another, regarding Halas with barely a passing interest.

"No?"

"No."

Halas lost it. Weeks of pent-up rage flowed from him then, right on to the old man who sat less-than-innocently in the comfortable armchair before him. "Conroy…I…I have had it with this, and I have had it with you!" he cried. The old man lowered his spectacles down the bridge of his nose, looking up at the sudden outburst. "For weeks now, you have…you hardly even acknowledge my existence anymore, writing me off with a few words and the slam of a door. It's unfair! I want to know what is going on, and I want to know now!"

Conroy observed him quietly with the hint of a smile on his lips. *What right does he have to be amused?* Halas cried to himself. *I need him right now, more than anything. The guard won't help me; my own brother won't help me! Why won't Conroy help me?*

What is happening?

Finally, the old man sighed, removing his spectacles and placing them on the desk in front of him. "Perhaps you should sit," he said.

"I'm fine," Halas said through clenched teeth. He was starting to feel embarrassed, aware of the fact that he'd just thrown his first tantrum in fourteen years.

"Very well then," Conroy began. "Your father is safe. It is true, he is in the forest, but he is safe. Halbrick can take care of himself. I would not have you and your friends traipsing about the forest in such a manner as you would like. That would only serve to endanger your life as well as your father's mission. Going after Halbrick would require him to break away from his goal to rescue you. You would accomplish nothing, Halas. Your father is a master swordsman, and well-versed in anything those trees could throw at him. He will be safe. You, however, would not. I wish I could tell you more, but I cannot."

"You cannot? Why can't you? Tell me!" Conroy's tone was so patronizing. Halas was no longer a child to be coddled and protected. He wanted more than Conroy's word as to his father's safety.

"You mustn't get so angry. It's not healthy."

Halas settled his breathing, attempting to calm himself with little success.

"Your father and I are working on something of great importance. I do apologize for keeping you at a distance, but I am quite busy these days."

"What are you working on?" Halas was mildly interested, and he used this to distract him from the anger.

"As I said before: I cannot tell you."

"You can't..." Halas cut himself off, not wanting to have another outburst. Part of him did, but he managed to contain that part. *For now.* He held a clenched fist to his forehead and drew breath through his nose. Halbrick called it the bull. He'd taught the exercise to Halas many years ago. It usually helped to calm him down, but now all Halas wanted to do was punch Conroy in the nose. Halas relaxed the fist and put it over his mouth. "Did my father leave any messages? Anything at all?"

"Why yes, he did. I'd forgotten until you reminded me. Not as young as I used to be." Hope filled Halas with a sudden warm sensation. Could there actually be an explanation? Could it be that simple? Conroy chuckled, standing up and moving to another table that was just as cluttered at his desk. Rifling through the papers, he finally lifted a small scrap of parchment. Conroy adjusted his reading glasses, holding the paper up to the light from the window.

"Ah yes. He says 'Don't forget to sell the crop. No less than five thousand.'"

Halas ran his hands through his hair and gnashed his teeth with frustration, and stormed out of the house. Des loitered in the street. He hurried to Halas as he emerged.

"Well?"

Halas pushed past him. He wanted to be alone.

———

Several days passed, and Halbrick still did not return. Conroy rarely called upon Halas anymore, and Halas had given up trying to speak with the man at all. The feeling of it was awful. Conroy was more than just a teacher, he was a dear friend. Halas spent nearly as much time at the manor as he did at home, running errands, doing his studies, or simply talking with the old man. Things had changed so much in the past month. Halas found that he no longer enjoyed his life. The only thing that brightened his spirits these days was Cailin. When he was with her, he found he could focus on other things than Halbrick and Conroy. They still lurked at the back of his mind, but he did not feel as disheartened. Cailin was a joyous presence in his world, and he was incredibly lucky to have her. He sat, leaning against the front door of the cottage, gazing off toward the forest. *Those trees. Those stupid trees.*

Halas contemplated inviting Cailin into his home. After all, his father was not exactly there to catch them. He would never know. Their relationship was very improper, and while Halas did not think Halbrick would mind, he would feel honor-bound to tell Cailin's parents. Halas knew they were unaware of his entire existence, but he did not fully understand why. Halas had every intention of marrying Cailin someday, and he did not think it would be at all difficult to conceal the extent of their physical relationship for the time being. They had first made love over a year before, lying on their knoll in the middle of the day. Halas remembered it well; it had been the best day of his life. Afterwards, however, Cailin seemed out of sorts. She rarely spoke to him for several days, and seemed awkward and quiet when she did. Halas finally got it out of her that she was worried her parents would find out. "They're very proper," she had said, "my father especially. They will be furious if they find out I've…you know, before marriage."

Those were the days when Cailin was still shy on the matter of sex. Halas smiled, remembering it. He had promised to keep their relationship a secret amongst the adults in their lives. Only Conroy knew fully, and Halas knew he could be trusted.

Now everything was different. Back then, Halas had trusted the old man with all his heart, but now he was unsure. The trust was severely damaged, and knowing that hurt Halas more deeply than he could imagine.

The door thumped him in the back, and he fell forward. Garek came out of the house, giving him an embarrassed smile. He apologized several times as he slid down the wall next to his brother.

"What're you thinking about?" he asked.

Halas mulled it over. "It's been over a week, Garek, and he's still not come home. A whole week!"

"Conroy said…"

"I know what Conroy said. But what if he's wrong? What if he doesn't know what he's talking about? What then? Do we just sit here and leave him to die? Is that it?"

"No. I'm not…I'm not saying that. Believe me, I'm worried about him too. It's just…things have been nicer around here, y'know?"

"How can you say that?" Halas demanded, getting to his feet, his fists curling up at his sides.

"Listen to me—I'm sure Father is all right. I trust Conroy on this. I do."

"You don't even like Conroy. The only thing he's ever taught you are foreign swear words."

"True," Garek conceded with a chuckle, "but there's something…I just trust him this time, okay?"

"No you don't," Halas said. He could see right through his brother. "You're a horrible liar, and you're not helping. Stop trying."

"Is that necessarily a bad thing?"

Garek's poor attempt at humor only served to anger Halas further. He stormed off, leaving Garek to go into town to search for a buyer. At least it would get him away from Halas for the day.

He cast himself down on his bed, watching the trees outside. Small drops of rain pattered quietly on the window. Halas closed his eyes. He opened them to a downpour, the heavy drops hitting his window like stones. He must have fallen asleep. He heard muted voices outside the cottage. Opening the door, he saw Garek standing with the auctioneer from before, with the blue-rimmed spectacles and wide hat, holding a sopping wet cloak around his slender frame. They were standing over the potatoes, exchanging offers.

"Won't you come inside?" Halas asked the man, politeness winning over the anger he felt toward his brother. "I'll make tea, or coffee, if you'd prefer." The man was strange; it was entirely possible that he preferred coffee.

"Well that's quite all right," the auctioneer said, bowing his head slightly at the gesture. "Young Garek and I have already come to an agreement. What was it, Garek?"

"Seven thousand."

"Ah yes. Seven thousand. To be paid upon transport of the supply. And 31 per cent through the season."

Seven thousand! Halbrick had said no less than five, but seven was unheard of. How had Garek done it?

"You're going to have to shut your mouth sometime." Garek's voice snapped him from his reverie, bringing him back into the present. The buyer was marching off toward Cordalis, undoubtedly to locate a few good laborers.

"How did you do it?"

Garek grinned. "Secret's mine to keep," he said, going into the cottage and shutting the door. "Wet out there."

"It is," Halas said, remembering his feelings. He wanted to stay angry, even though he knew he wasn't anymore. "Moving them into town today?"

"Yes," Garek said.

———

Halas had never been so wet—or so cold—in his life. He, Garek, and several laborers spent hours pushing carts through the mud into Cordalis. It became easier past the Gate, when the road became an actual road, shoddy and uneven though it was. Finally, after six loads, the auctioneer approached Halas, standing in the man's warehouse. "I'm calling it off for today," he said. "Tell your brother to make this the last trip. We'll resume when the rain ends."

"Right. Yes, sir," Halas told him, rushing off to find Garek. He helped him with the last cart, and the two hurried home. They came in together, collapsing on their respective beds. Though his mattress was about as solid as a slab of granite, Halas had never been so comfortable. He'd helped move the crop before, but never in the rain, and never so much at a time.

Halas fell asleep right then, steadily soaking the bed with rainwater. It was the one night he did not think or worry about his father.

Sub Chapter One: Nolan

Nolan whistled a quiet tune to himself as he fingered a small coin. He sat in a plain wooden room somewhere in Cordalis, looking up at two brutish thugs. They were Dar's cronies, and he assumed that they had recently dragged him in here. Nolan didn't know for sure, because his last memory was running away from them. Then the bigger one had stepped out in front of him, and he'd woken up here, in the plain wooden room somewhere in Cordalis.

Not that he minded; it had only been a matter of time. Dar was Patriarch of Wentworth family, and they were not to be trifled with.

"Any of you chaps have something to drink?" he asked, but they remained statues. Nolan rolled his eyes and went back to his tune and his coin.

The door swung open, and a tall, lanky man entered. He sat down before Nolan, who had dropped his coin. This was no mere enforcer, not even an interrogator. The man who had entered Nolan's cell was *Dar himself*. Such a thing was unprecedented. Dar never oversaw personal matters such as this.

In matters such as this, matters with which Nolan had become well acquainted, there was a process. Protocol. Dar's outfit was organized in layers. For lower-level interrogations, you were locked in a small room, a room much like the room Nolan currently resided in, and greeted by a lower-level thug.

The thug worked you over, and he did his job well, before releasing you into the wild to beg and pilfer.

For *higher*-level events, the thugs were just there as an intimidation piece. They'd touch you, they'd hurt you, but the real hurt came from the designated inquisitors. Big, brutish men whose brains matched their muscle. Nolan had once had the pleasure of meeting an inquisitor, and he'd been out of the game for weeks, had almost starved to death, and would have if not for Leon.

There had never been any third-tier interrogations, until now. Nolan figured it appropriate that he was the first. But then, he didn't really know if he was or not—perhaps those who reached this stage did not survive to tell the tale. Nolan had no intention of dying, especially not in this rat-hole.

No, he was going to escape. No one would even lay a hand on him.

But Dar—Dar *himself*—that had been an unexpected blow all of its own.

Nolan tried to swallow, but his throat had gone dry. His tongue was pasted to the roof of his mouth. "Hello there, Dooley," Dar said.

"Can't say I'm pleased to see you," Nolan said. Dar chuckled.

"Nor I you. You've become a nuisance of late. I cannot believe the audacity you display, freelancing in my part of the city! The gall!"

Nolan was afraid, but even more afraid to show his fear. So, worried that his voice might betray him, he said nothing. Dar snapped his fingers, and the cronies were on him, pinning him to his chair with giantlike strength. A third entered, taking Nolan's hands and holding them to the table. Nolan struggled, but the three men were all much bigger than he was.

"There is a punishment for what you've done. I'm afraid I'm going to have to take your hands, one finger at a time. I can't say I'm disappointed. You would have done yourself a favor, turning yourself in to the Badges. A shame my people got to you first."

"A big shame," Nolan said, his voice shaking. He still struggled. Dar stood, a dagger in his hands.

"You've one last chance, Dooley. Tell me where the gems are, and I'll make it quick. Three thousand detricots is no small amount."

"No, it isn't," Nolan agreed. He looked frantically around the room for some way out. There was none; he'd have to fight or lose his hands, and Nolan was no fighter. Gritting his teeth, he planted his feet at the bottom of the table. Dar was taking his time, making sure that Nolan really took in the knife that would do the punishing. Fear was the man's greatest weapon, and Nolan could hardly let himself give in to that. If he was afraid, he was dead. Nolan exhaled.

He uprooted the table, throwing both it and Dar to the ground. He snapped his head back into one thug's groin. The man fell to his knees, and Nolan's left hand was free. He smashed it into the second man's groin, rolling across the table, but their cohort grabbed him by the back of his tunic. Nolan tore the fabric getting free, kicking the man in the chest and knocking him over. Dar nearly knocked *him* over then, standing on the table as he was. He sprang off. He'd been able to catch the men by surprise, but they were quickly recovering. *Time for a quick getaway,* Nolan decided. This went beyond his hands now. He'd be fast or he'd be dead.

"Sorry about the nethers, gentlemen!" he said, and ran out of the room.

Chapter Two
A Light In The Darkness

Desmond lounged in the sun, eyes closed, basking in the warmth. Halas sat up against the cottage, fiddling with a small knife and watching him. He wondered how anyone could be so relaxed when he himself was so agitated. The idea of peace was beyond him. His chest was in a knot. He couldn't remember the last time he had eaten, and yet he did not feel hungry. His sleep was more fitful than ever before. Halas crossed his arms across his stomach. Halbrick was in trouble; there was no doubt about that. He no longer believed Conroy. There was no way the old man was right. Not after three weeks in…in *there*.

"Would you make up your mind already?" Des asked. Halas frowned. They both wanted to go into the forest, but Halas suspected that Desmond just wanted to explore. "I've been inside before, you know," he added. "It isn't that scary of a place."

What Halas *really* wanted was for Desmond to go away. He willed the thought to him, and was not surprised, though mildly disappointed, when Desmond did not react.

"No you haven't! You stepped past the first tree on a challenge and ran out." He neglected to mention his own previous foray into the wood. *Go away,* he urged. *Leave me alone.*

Desmond grinned. "That doesn't count?"

Halas closed his eyes and sighed. Desmond was not leaving, Halbrick was still lost, and the trees had not spontaneously decided to erupt in flame. He supposed there were no other real choices. "Fine," he said. "Let's go. While the sun still shines."

Des was on his feet in a flash. He smiled as he drew a knife from his pocket. "Come on then."

Halas gestured to the blade. "You had that with you?"

"Of course."

"Oh. All right, then."

The two ran toward the forest, not wishing to waste any time. But even Desmond was wary. When they neared the Treeline, their movements slowed. Then both greeted the trees. Making the decision to go after Halbrick had been just fine in the safety of the cottage, but what was it now? Halas thought it was something like idiocy, but he said nothing. If he backed down now, he would never get another chance. Feeling very much like boys rather than men, Halas and Desmond exchanged a sheepish glance before stepping inside together. They were immediately cast into darkness unmatched. The canopy was thick and did not allow for much light to shine through, but once his eyes adjusted Halas could see there were gaps where beams of it came through like spotlights. Halas resisted the urge to grab Desmond's hand. Desmond led the way, creeping softly through the padded moss. Halas forced himself to follow. It went against every instinct he had. There was no noise in the forest. Though their boots were heavy, their footfalls were very nearly silent. Halas touched Desmond's arm.

"Don't slip in this stuff," he warned. "It makes you sleep."

"Right." Desmond didn't ask how he knew that. Perhaps it did not occur to him.

Halas took a moment to look around. There wasn't much to see. The forest was a mix of trees, mostly tall oak and willow and ash, but with the occasional marauding black spruce mixed in. There was also the moss, white scraggly stuff that felt like a cloud beneath their feet. A cage of red vines had formed around a dead stump nearby. Desmond was well ahead of Halas, and he hurried to catch up. They pushed their way through the thick black boughs.

The faint sound of a child's laughter drifted through the air, wafting about their heads. Halas glanced around. Were there children here? The child sounded as if he were playing merrily, unaware of the terror that surrounded him. The laughter changed partway above them. It became a shrill cackle, that of a madman. It sent shivers down Halas' spine, causing his skin to erupt in gooseflesh. The cackle did not fade, as Halas would have expected, but disappeared abruptly. It was replaced by a growl.

Halas saw two red eyes in the shadows. They were rimmed by the silhouette of a great wolf. Halas had seen wolves before, and this one was far too big. It was the size of two wolves, or possibly even three. He knew beyond the shadow of a doubt that this was the creature that had chased him before.

It growled and started forward, pawing the ground with thick, broad feet. Its tail flicked absently, and its fangs dripped with a dark liquid that was not unlike blood. Halas clutched Desmond's arm in fear. Desmond himself took a few steps back. "Run," Halas whispered. He realized that he should probably take his own advice, and turned to Desmond.

"*Run!*"

They ran. They sprinted through the forest, arm in arm, tearing great big gouges in the moss with their boots. Tufts of it flew up behind them. Halas was in the lead, pulling Desmond along. They flew past the trees, all the while chased by the wolf. It gave a bone-chilling howl as it went, loping along close to the ground, its shaggy head bent forward until it was nearly parallel to its knees. It snarled and snapped at the air.

Neither Halas nor Desmond considered their knives, knowing instinctively that the puny things would not even scratch the great beast.

Flecks of spittle struck their backs. The wolf was close now, so close it could almost taste them. Halas lowered his own head and willed his legs to go faster. He felt only fear. There would be no escaping this thing. How could they? Desmond pulled ahead. The trees were thickening, growing closer together. It seemed to Halas that they were doing this of their own accord, working together with the great wolf to slow its prey. The walls were closing in. Halas and Desmond had to grip each trunk and pull themselves along, as if they were swimming. And still the wolf gave chase. It plowed through the trees that gave Halas and Desmond such trouble as if they were nothing, splintering them in its wake.

Branches clawed at them, scratching at whatever they could take hold of. Halas could not believe what was happening. These trees were *alive*, and just as deadly as the wolf that pursued them. They tore at his face and chest. Fresh bursts of pain blazed to life all across his body. Halas' breath was pounding. Already his legs burned. Already his side was enveloped in a dull throb. He could not run for much longer.

If they did not find sanctuary soon, the monster would kill them.

But luck was on their side in that evil morning. They came to a sharp drop. Roots and trees twisted up and down the hill. At the bottom was a river. The water was surprisingly clear. Halas had only a moment to take this all in, for he had not seen the drop, before he and Des went over the side. Desmond managed to keep his feet as they slid, but Halas floundered on his back, groping madly for purchase. In his panic, he found Desmond's trouser leg, dragging the younger man down with him. They rolled bodily down the hill. Halas' tunic pulled up over his head. The world became muffled through the thin fabric.

His descent was stopped suddenly by a root that stuck a few inches out of the dirt. His foot had caught in it, or *it* had caught his foot. A terrifying suspicion assured him it was the latter. Desmond continued rolling, bellowing curses. Halas lay backward on the slope, looking up at the top. He tried to sit up, but the stitch in his side was too sharp. He yelled and lay back, yanking his shirt down.

The wolf was at the top of the slope. Halas was still close enough to see why it had not caught them: its left forepaw was mangled and bloody. It limped to the edge of the hill and growled. Froth spewed from its teeth.

The root was tighter than it had been moments before. Blinding pain shot through Halas' leg, and he screamed, but pain seemed to be the tree's ultimate goal, not death or capture. Halas' foot came free, and he slid slowly down the rest of the way, settling to a rest with his shoulders against a pine tree. It beamed down at him and he shied away, crawling over to Desmond. He looked up at the top of the slope.

The wolf was gone.

"Are you all right?" Desmond asked.

"I think so," Halas replied. He was breathing heavily, and sore all over. He felt as if someone had worked him over with a club. "And you?"

"If that is the last cliff we fall off of, I'll live happily ever after until the end of my days."

Halas breathed nervous laughter. Desmond helped him up. Halas tested his foot. It hurt to stand on, but he could walk. He'd had worse. "Where are we?"

He looked around. The moss was gone, replaced by a far more normal looking bed of old leaves. Little bits of grass and ferns poked up here and there. Behind them, the stream gurgled happily along. Halas didn't like the stream. He felt as if it were mocking him.

"I don't know. I know that I do not like it. This place is far too pleasant."

"I agree. We should…"

He was cut off by a snarl as the wolf flew through the air. Desmond pushed Halas aside at the last second, accepting a nick on his left arm just above the elbow. He threw himself toward the stream. "Halas, come on!" he yelled.

Halas was just behind him. The two splashed into the water, which moments ago had been only knee-deep. But the stream was deceptively deep and deceptively wide. Before they knew it, it was up to their chests. Still they waded, and Halas dreaded the rest. He reached out for Desmond's hand and took it. "I cannot swim!" he yelled.

Desmond pulled him along.

Water was everywhere. It came at Halas from seemingly all sides. A moment ago it had been a calm, peaceful stream. Now it was a raging river, trying desperately to pull Halas all ways at once. The current tore him from Desmond's grip. Tall waves crashed over his head, forcing him under. He clawed out ahead of him, scrambling for a hold. If the river had its way, it was going to keep him there forever. He'd stopped moving.

No! Stop it!

A hand touched his and retreated. Halas was granted a brief moment of clarity. (*That's enough!*) He suddenly felt like he was not under the water, but above it, in a warm and dry meadow. He looked around, stumbling forward. Dead grass stretched in all directions, covered in something Halas' brain could not immediately identify. He stared at a peculiar looking mound, and gaped.

Bodies. Bodies everywhere, corpses, a graveyard absent of its grave digger. Some were mere skeletons; most were still fleshy, with pale, taut skin and scabbed muscles and an abhorrent stench that put even the worst of Cordalis' sewer systems to shame. The hand that had touched him belonged to a small girl of about four years. She cocked her (*Stop!*) head to the side and looked into his eyes. He could see maggots writhing beneath her skin, little moving bumps just under the surface. The sight filled Halas with sick dread. He wanted to vomit. He wanted to scream.

Let him go! You're killing him! He'll die!

But to scream, he'd have to breathe.

That thought made him instantly aware that he was drowning. The façade meadow melted away, replaced by the bottom of a riverbed. Everything was different, except for the girl. She clutched his shirt with cold, dead fingers, wrinkled patches of flesh stretched across her bones. For a moment Halas could do nothing but gape.

This was real. It was all happening, and he would die if he did nothing.

He kicked the little girl aside. Her skin rotted away as she drifted, and she was nothing but a smiling corpse, grinning an evil grin, leaving deadness in her wake. Halas began to pull madly for what he thought was the surface.

Stop it stop it STOP!

The water receded. It trickled slowly around his legs, and he stood up in a daze. Des stood halfway to the bank, bent partially over with his hands resting on his knees. He had stopped shouting. The river was once again a stream, and both were glad for it.

Desmond watched Halas. His mouth was open in a noiseless wail. "Bodies," he gasped as he staggered ashore. "There're bodies in there!"

He stumbled out of the water and tripped. Mud from the bank caked over his hands and knees. He felt something touching him. It was the girl, he was absolutely sure of it. A great sucking sound echoed into the trees as he tore his arms free of the mud. There were bugs on his hands! Slithering things of all sizes. Caterpillars, spiders, flies, worms. They crawled over his skin and made it move along with their rhythm, made his stomach churn. Again Halas wanted to vomit, and this time he gave way to the feeling. He shook his hands in the air and thrust them into the chill waters. The bugs were washed from his skin, but the awareness of them remained. He could feel the things scuttling across his flesh, a million tiny legs coating him like a second shirt. He shuddered, and Des helped him away from the bank. He retched again, falling into the grass, heaving up his breakfast.

Coming here had been a mistake. Conroy was right. Trying to collect himself, Halas rose and took a deep, steady breath.

The wolf had disappeared. Halas got a look at Desmond's arm. The sleeve was a shredded, bloody mess. He took Des by the forearm and tried to examine it. "Later," Des said. Halas nodded brusquely.

"Right. Thank you, Desmond."

"My pleasure. That's twice now." He grinned. Halas forced a smile of his own. It wasn't as hard as he would have thought, however, for he found himself genuinely happy to see Des. Who would have thought?

"Where is the wolf?"

"It slunk into the woods after you went under. I do not doubt that it will be back."

"Nor do I."

"What do we do now?"

Halas looked around, taking in the slope. Cordalis was somewhere up there. Garek, Conroy, and Cailin were somewhere up there. *But Father's in here,* he thought, his gaze going deeper into the trees. Wherever Halas looked, his eyes inevitably wandered back to that stream. There was a dead little girl in there, floating forever along with countless others. How many lives had this place claimed?

He dragged his foot through the dirt unconsciously, unsure of which course of action to take. "We must find my father," he said after a time. Halbrick would know how to get them to safety. Halbrick would make things okay again.

"Halas…" Desmond began. His eyes were steady, grim, resolute, but Halas could see his brow wavering ever so slightly.

"Go back if you must. I…I cannot abandon him out here."

"And I cannot abandon *you,* you fool. I have no choice but to follow you."

Halas smiled sadly. He looked at his feet, suddenly ashamed of himself. He could not be responsible for Desmond's death. He wouldn't be.

"Never mind," he said quietly. "Father can fare for himself. I do not wish to cross the river, so let us find a way around. I know that this stream comes in from the east, and does not come out. If we were to go west, we would find its end."

"A good plan. Lead on, then."

Halas looked up. The sun was high in the sky, having only begun its daily cycle a few hours before. He frowned, unable for a moment to tell where west was. He followed the sun's arc and nodded to himself. "This way," he said.

They went west, and soon came to the end of the Inigo River Tributary. Their footfalls were heavy and tired, their faces drawn tight. The river came to rest in a small pool, but Halas harbored no doubt as to its true depth; it was probably well beyond any sense of normalcy. "How is it that you cannot swim?" Desmond asked. "There are a hundred streams and ponds near your farm."

"Father never let us," Halas explained. He did not know why.

He and Des skirted the pool and came around at the base of the slope. It was just a few foot-lengths to the top. Desmond helped Halas up.

Once they stood at the top, confusion set in. There were three broad directions in which they could go. Cordalis lay in one. He supposed that each direction would take them out of the trees, but how far were the edges? Certainly at least one path would lead them deeper in, and Halas had no desire to cross the forest in full, even in daylight.

He found himself longing for the mother he'd not had since he was young. Younger than the little girl in the river.

The dead little girl.

No time to give up, he told himself. *Just set a direction and follow it. You'll not be alone; Des is here. You just have to trust your luck.*

Halas took a few steps forward on quivering legs. Behind him, Des squatted by a tree, lifted a twig and poked at something. "Halas," he announced, "I believe that this mushroom is talking to me."

"What?" Halas went to his friend. Desmond sat before the biggest mushroom Halas had ever laid eyes upon. He'd had seen smaller dogs. Its surface was a pale white that was somehow inlaid with purple. Its pores sucked in air and gushed faint, odorous green fumes. Des watched it studiously. "Desmond, it's fungus. Mushrooms cannot speak."

"I can hear it."

"Desmond, you're…"

"Just listen!"

Halas gave in, and listened. He couldn't hear anything. With a grunt of impatience, he pulled Desmond away, back to the pool.

"No more communing with plants. We're getting out of here." After a bit, he decided on a direction that he was fairly certain led back to Cordalis. Due in part to the incredible stress both boys were under, it never occurred to either of them that they could just follow the river out. If they had thought of that, they would have found that it was less than a mile's walk. It would have taken them minutes.

But they didn't think of that, and so they stumbled upon the cabin.

It was dark and old. Dim light came from the windows. Racks of tanned hide and drying meat stood silent sentinel before the doors. Halas also saw a rack of weapons. The roof was made of sod, and it looked newer than the rest of the building. Halas threw himself down and pulled Desmond along. Together they stared at the cabin. Someone was inside, they knew that much. There were footsteps from within, and shadows.

Neither one wanted to find out who lived there. Halas' mind wandered. Who would take up residence in such an evil place? Surely it could only be some dark sorcerer, feeding off children and death and anguish. He had heard tales of such men, but not since boyhood. They were mere fairy tales with no substance to them.

But now, Halas was not so sure.

Halas gestured back behind them, and Des nodded. They started to crawl, heaving themselves forward with their forearms. Halas realized that they had left the leaves and were back on the moss. He began to feel weary and, with great difficulty, clambered to his feet. He grabbed Desmond by the back of his jerkin and brought him up.

"Bloody hell, Halas! *Why?*"

"The moss makes you sleep. Just run!"

And so they ran. They ran until they could not run anymore, and then they leaned against the trees and rested.

As if it had been waiting for this, the world went completely dark.

Halas nearly lost control of his bladder then, and he would have had the lights not suddenly appeared. These lights were not from the sun, but from an independent source. Halas was reminded of crystal balls Conroy had told him of. Blue. Yellow. Green. Purple. Many different colored orbs hovered above their heads, flitting about between the trees. They cast a soothing glow, painting the forest in a new, pleasant light. How could he have been afraid of such a place? It was truly wonderful to behold. Halas watched the lights with awe. Where had they come from? One second, it was dark, and the next— well, there they were. It was as if someone had flipped a switch. "Can you see them?" he asked Desmond.

"I see them."

Desmond lifted his free hand, reaching up toward a white one. *The only white one,* Halas thought. He could see only the one amidst the myriad of colors above their heads. It hovered in place, as if waiting for Des. His finger touched it tentatively, and then Desmond sprang back as the white light darted away. "Ow!"

"What is it?"

"I think—I think it bit me."

"It *bit* you?"

"I think it bit me!"

A red orb spun around Halas' head before darting back toward the trees. The others kept their distance, floating lazily through the air. "Just don't touch them anymore," he told Desmond.

"I can't help it," he replied. "They're so pretty. Come on, Halas."

Desmond was drunkenly shambling away, pursuing the white orb. Halas felt compelled to follow his friend, until one zapped his neck. He jumped into the air with a curse unbidden. A green light hovered in the air before him. *Come with me*, the air whispered. "So pretty…" Halas slurred. He saw no reason why he shouldn't follow it. It *was* very pretty, after all.

So he walked in the opposite direction, following the beautiful green light. He knew that wherever this light took him, great fortune would follow. It was so pretty. The most beautiful thing Halas had ever seen. Why hadn't he done this before? Stupid, stupid! So intently did he watch the green orb, he didn't pay attention to his feet, and fell on his face.

Immediately, he realized what was happening, and yelled a louder curse. *The lights!* Halas got to his feet, feeling sleepier than before, and looked around. There was Desmond, off in the distance. "DES!" he screamed. "DESMOND! *STOP!*"

Halas ran after his friend, leaping over twisted and gnarled roots. One of which was moving. *It was moving!* He jumped over it. The whole forest was alive now, the spheres buzzing around in angry little circles, the trees shifting in place, strange noises coming from everywhere at once. Halas felt the sting as another of the lights touched his skin, again and again. They were coming at him in swarms, like gulls seeking a meal. He swatted them aside, but only succeeded in singeing his hands and arms. "Desmond!"

Desmond was close. Halas reached out and grabbed him by the shoulder, spinning him around. "Halas? What's wrong? Why aren't you following the lights?"

There was something terrifying about Desmond. It was his eyes. They were devoid of life, a dull, gray color. His skin had turned a pallid yellow, and little streams of spittle trickled down his chin.

Desmond Mallon looked dead.

Had Halas looked like that when he'd fallen? Gods, he hoped so. He cocked his fist back and hit Desmond in the face with all his strength, and that was what saved his life. The fire returned to Desmond's eyes, and he glanced around with confusion.

"Oh, *damn it!*"

The things were attacking both of them now, darting in and out. Halas and

Desmond ran, but neither of them had any idea of where they were going. One of the orbs struck Halas directly on the nose, knocking him on to his back. Blood pooled across his face, blurring his vision. Desmond sucked his hands up into his sleeves and grabbed the sphere, hurling it against a tree. The tree shook, but the light buzzed away, making a strange, moaning sound, almost as if it were grumbling. Halas was up, and they were running, hand in hand.

This only seemed to anger the lights further. They increased their attack tenfold, whizzing about and darting in ceaselessly, pummeling Halas and Des with a previously unknown fury. Halas landed on his face and felt one burning into the back of his neck. Desmond grabbed him and hauled him to his feet before being borne down himself. One of the things pressed against the small of his back and purred softly.

It's enjoying this! Halas thought as he lunged and kicked it. The light refused to give ground, burning through Halas' boot in an instant. He cried out and grabbed Desmond under the arms. Before he could lift, an orb struck him across the lips. Halas stumbled and fell over Des, landing on his bottom. The moss cooled him through his clothes, distracting him from the burns, even those on his face and neck. Another orb struck him on the forehead, and blood continued to pool down over his eyes. In that moment, for a brief instant, everything became clear.

He felt them settling on his flesh. He heard them purring. He smelled burning meat. He tasted blood.

He knew he was dying.

And then a voice cut through the air. It was not that of a child, or a madman. It was a familiar voice, one that brought comfort to Halas' ears.

"*Nagh lior kael jo*! Leave them alone, lest you incur my wrath! Leave these two be!"

Halas recognized the voice, though he had never heard it spoken so…elegantly. "Father?"

———

The lights withdrew and the trees were still. Halbrick strode toward them. He'd never looked quite so elegant either. Halas could not think of a more adequate word to describe the man. *Kingly, maybe. Heroic.* A cloak fluttered behind him in the light wind. None of his skin was exposed, aside from his face, and even then he had his hood up. He wore a pair of faded green gloves with his sleeves tucked tightly into them. There was a sword at his hip and a bow in his hand. Halas could see the fletching of an arrow sticking up over his left shoulder. It all looked very out of place. Halas wrapped his arms around him.

"Father!"

"What are you doing here?" he demanded. Halas pulled back in surprise. He glanced at Des, who was looking over what he could see of himself. He was covered in purple sores.

"I thought you would be in trouble. I've not seen you in weeks! You would fault me for thinking such things? No one comes in here! I was worried."

Halbrick's features softened, but only for a moment. He looked around cautiously and then embraced his son. "Come with me. Hurry!"

They emerged from the forest shortly after. Halas was beginning to feel incredibly tired. His limbs were heavy, and his head lolled on his neck. Halbrick supported him and Desmond, ushering them across the field and into the cottage. Few of their neighbors saw them. Harri Cormack, a man Halbrick was frequently at odds with over prices, happened to look their way and scowled. Halbrick offered a weak smile. Halas, meanwhile, had lost control of his legs. He sagged in his father's arms and fell. Halbrick cursed and scooped him up, lifting him gently and quickening his pace. Desmond followed behind, his hand clutching Halbrick's shoulder. They cut through Dennis and Patty Carlyle's field and hurried to the cottage, ignoring Patty's yipping questions. Once inside, Halbrick sat them down and tore off his gloves, reaching into his pockets and withdrawing a small flask. "Drink this," he said. Halas obeyed, as did Desmond. It burned his throat, but quickly turned cool and soothing. As it spread through his body, he felt warm, oddly enough, but awake. Minutes before, his body had been falling apart piece by piece. He'd not lost feeling, but his brain insisted on telling him his arms and legs were simply gone. Halas knew they were there, he could see them, feel them, but could not move them. Now he was regaining control. He shivered at the sensation.

"Are you both all right?" Halbrick asked. Halas nodded. He still felt itchy, and imagined he was covered in the same blotches as poor Des.

"Think so," Desmond said.

"Good. I am thankful. But what in Aelworth's Good Graces were you doing in that forest?"

"We were worried about you, Father. I should ask the same question."

"It does not concern you. Did Conroy not tell you I was safe?"

"He did, but you were gone for three weeks! I could not believe his words any longer."

"Has he ever led you astray? Has he ever lied? Has he ever even been wrong?" He had not, as far as Halas could remember.

But that was not the point.

"I was terrified!" he said. "What if you had died in there? What if those—those things—got to you? And there must be other dangers in that forest."

"There are," Halbrick said. "Beasts of unimaginable evil. What you saw were the willowisps—beacons of light created by the forest in an effort to spy on travelers and lead them astray. They are the least of your problems, should you ever return to those trees. Had you gone deeper in, you would encounter creatures that would rend you limb from limb with claws and teeth so sharp they could split even iron."

"Created by the forest?" Desmond asked, intrigued.

"Yes," Halbrick said. "The forest is entirely sentient. He, too, is dastardly. To cross one of his trees would be dire."

"Why were you in there?" Halas asked again. "For what reason?"

Halbrick sighed. "My reasons are my own," he said. "Perhaps, someday, you will come to learn, but until then this must remain a secret. What I do in there is extremely important, and I cannot have you going off and speaking of it. Just, please, do not follow me in there, ever again. When I pulled you from the Treeline, sopping wet and half dead, I…I would die with you. Such a thing would cripple me. When people ask about your blemishes, tell them that you stumbled upon the poison oak plant. Otherwise, do not speak of today again, even amongst yourselves. It never happened. Promise me."

"We promise," they said in unison. Halbrick smiled.

"Excellent! Who wants supper?"

Sub Chapter Two

The bed he awoke in was the softest he'd ever known. Nolan could smell fresh bread. His stomach was pleasantly full. Where was he? When had he eaten? He couldn't remember anything past crawling through the gutter.

He looked around the room and discovered he wasn't alone. A beautiful girl sat next to his bed. She was the most beautiful girl Nolan had ever seen. Her hair was jet black, contrasting her creamy white skin. Her body was tight, and firm. Nolan could imagine himself doing a great many things to that body, but as great as it was, the girl's best feature was easily her eyes. They were gleaming yellow, full of intelligent fire. Nolan took it all in, stunned into silence. She smiled at him, and all semblance of pain melted away. Nolan grinned.

"Hello, Nolan," she said.

The girl, still smiling, faded into nothing. Suddenly Nolan was on a ship, on someone, could smell blood and decay, struggling on the ground.

Nolan opened his eyes. He was still in the gutter.

Chapter Three
Greater Discipline

Six miserable days later, the sores were just beginning to fade, and Halbrick had not returned to the forest. Halas was glad for that, though he suspected that his father would soon take up the mysterious errand once he was certain that Halas was all right. For Halas' part, he had stuck to his word and not discussed it with Desmond, even though he was burning to do so. Desmond was clearly sharing the same desires, and the two had decided without words to not be near each other for fear of breaking their promise.

Halas had never liked Desmond until now, but his brother remained oblivious to this fact. For several days, Garek did not notice the change. Then he began to wonder. After a week, he came out and asked. "Look at what he did!" Halas said, running his left hand along his right arm, pointing out the sores. "If he had not convinced me to go with him, none of this would have happened. As if I enjoy needing your help rubbing Mister Conroy's salve on my back."

"Nor do I," Garek chuckled, satisfied with the answer. Halas, of course, was not mad at Des, but what else could he say? He was actually a little proud that he was able to make up a story on the spot as he had.

And the salve was *very* cold.

"Garek, leave your brother alone," Halbrick said as he entered the room. He had not heard the words, only the tone Halas had spoken them with. "He has enough on his mind without you pestering him all the time. Why don't you make yourself useful somewhere?"

"Sorry, sir," Garek mumbled, looking at his feet. Halas frowned.

"I want to speak to you about my father," Halas said. Conroy's eyes darkened. "I will not discuss his task in the forest."

"I understand that, sir. This has to do with Garek."

"Ah, all right then." Conroy smiled. "Gnome, fetch us some tea."

"Of course, Master." The gnome scurried out of the room.

"Halas, please sit down." He did. "What is it that troubles you?"

"Father does not treat Garek as he should. He does not deserve to be looked upon as a delinquent, as Father does. I know the two of you are good friends, and I hoped that you might speak to him about it."

"I am afraid it is not my place, dear boy. Halbrick is a father and, for better or worse, he is Garek's. Though I do disagree with the way he handles that boy, it is entirely within his power to do so. Nothing I say or do can change that, even if I wanted to put my nose where it does not belong."

"Then what is it you two are doing in the forest? Surely that is putting your nose where it does not belong."

Conroy sighed. "Please, Halas, do not involve yourself in this matter. Leave it be."

"I cannot! Every day, I do nothing but dwell on it. Do you know what it is like to have something this strange going on, and yet you are unable to do anything about it? It concerns my entire life! What if Father *dies?*" He whispered the last word. "All I can do to distract myself from it is try to help Garek. Would you deny me that?"

"Yes, Halas. I would."

Halas stormed out, pushing past the gnome with his tea tray.

He didn't want to go home, but he could not stay near Conroy's. Halas wanted desperately to reconnect with the man. He did not understand why his teacher was so forcibly pushing him away. He had nowhere else to go, so he went to The Jealous Duchess, and drowned his sorrows in the cheap ale.

———

Halas slept late the next day, for no better reason than he did not wish to look at his father. He opened his eyes to a giant pounding an equally giant hammer into a just as giant drum. The songbird's whistle was a piercing shriek. Shuffling into the kitchen, he cursed the bird.

Quietly, of course.

Garek sat at the table next to a steaming bowl of porridge. Garek smiled. "Best way to cure a head-ache," he said. Halas mumbled his thanks and slowly ate. His mouth was dry, but he forced it down. Having probably returned to that dreadful forest, his father was nowhere to be seen. Halas did not ask.

Both brothers heard a knock at the door. Garek shrugged and rose to answer. Halas continued to eat, watching his brother. He wondered who was outside. No one knocked; everyone who knew the Duers knew that it was acceptable to simply walk in. Garek opened the door and was faced with five Agerian soldiers. They were dressed in fine silver chainmail, with gilded helmets. Buckler shields were strapped across their backs, and each man bore a sword at his hip.

"Garek Duer?" one asked. Halas hurried to the door and put a hand on his brother's shoulder. A lump formed in his throat. He tried to swallow it down, but could not.

"Yes?" Garek answered. His voice wavered.

The man unfurled a scroll, reading from the top. "Garek Duer, you have been appointed by King Melick's court to serve a six month sentence aboard the naval transport, *The Wandering Blade*. You will report for duty to Captain Brennus at four o'clock in the afternoon on September the sixteenth. If you choose to desert, you will be hunted down and punished to the full extent of the law. Do you understand?"

Someone had to say something, and it was not going to be Garek. Halas' brother was speechless, his mouth agape. "What is this?" Halas asked. The pounding in his head picked up. He felt dizzy.

"I am not speaking to you, sir, but to Garek Duer. He does not have the option of refusing. Mister Duer, do you understand me?"

"September the sixteenth? That's only eight days from now!"

"I know full well what today is. Please, stand away. Garek Duer!"

"Um." Garek's mouth was still open.

"I asked you a question. *Do you understand?*"

"Yes. Yes, I suppose I do. September sixteenth?"

"That is correct. Do you know where the Naval Offices are?"

"I believe so," Garek said. Halas could tell that he was barely keeping himself together. "If not, I will find them."

"Very well."

The soldiers marched off. Garek closed the door after them. He sat down on the floor and began studying his hands. Halas looked at his brother, unsure of what to say. The silence was a chasm between them, and suddenly Halas was sure that he never wanted to be apart from Garek again.

"Was I just drafted?" Garek asked.

"I…I think so."

"What do I do now, Halas?"

"Where is Father?"

"I do not know. How could this happen? I'm not yet twenty. I cannot own land, work for anyone but my family, nor can I marry. How is it that I am allowed to do this?"

"Every citizen of Ager becomes eligible for military service at fifteen." Halas swore. How could this have happened? He knew about the draft, certainly, but could not remember the last time it had been put into action. *Keep it together,* he told himself. *Who would know what to do?*

It was only the second time Garek had been to Conroy's house and, despite the way Garek had treated him the first time, Conroy seemed more than happy to see him again. He beamed at the sight of the brothers, practically dragging Garek to his personal collection to see a new artifact he had bought from the marketplace that day. Conroy seemed astounded that he had even found it. He claimed the vendor obviously did not know what he had. Halas followed along more than eagerly. It was the first time in a long time Conroy had actually seemed happy to see him. After the tour, he settled them down in his study, sitting down behind his desk. "What troubles you?" he asked.

"Garek's been drafted," Halas said quickly. Conroy frowned.

"Drafted?"

"Is that even legal, anymore?" Garek asked.

"I fear it is, though rarely used. There are more than enough soldiers and sailors who serve the king with far more loyalty than a draftee. How very strange."

"Is there any way to get out of it?"

"No. King Melick has made it so such a thing is impossible. I'm afraid you are stuck, my boy."

Garek put his head in his hands. Halas put a reassuring hand on his brother's shoulder. "Is there nothing you can do?" he asked. Conroy shook his head. He truly did look upset.

"I am sorry."

They left Conroy's house and wandered the city in silence. There had to be something Halas could do. Something, anything. There had to be a way to help his little brother. Conroy had once taught him that in the days before King Melick, you could file a formal appeal against the court. That would no longer work.

Maybe he could hide Garek somewhere. Halas could purchase a home under another name, and move there with his brother. No one would find him—it would require the king to order a search of every home in the city, and that was out of the question.

Or it would be as simple as someone seeing him.

Garek would not live inside a cramped house forever. He would have to leave eventually, and if a Badge or an informant saw him, he would go to prison.

What other options were there? He and Garek could leave Cordalis—leave

Ager! There were other lands out there, lands that tolerated deserters. There had to be. But the world was dangerous. If any of Conroy's tales were true, it would devour them. Aelborough outside Ager was filled with wild beasts and monsters, highwaymen who would rob you blind and leave you stranded in the wilderness, corrupt warlords who would decapitate you for the joy of drinking your blood. There were even dragons! Conroy had said that dragons were rare but entirely real. Ages before, a band of adventurers calling themselves the Candlewood Trio swept through the territories north of the Frigid Peaks, slaughtering dragons by the dozen, but they were killed before they could complete their mission. Dragons were creatures of Equilibrium, evil incarnate created to fight all that was good and pure.

In other words, creatures that would eat all three boys without even tasting them.

No, he was being silly. But what else could he do?

"Halas?"

"Yeah?"

"I think…I think I want to go."

Halas stopped, looking at his brother. "What?"

"I think I want to go. There's no challenging the draft. Besides, I could do with getting out of here for six months."

Halas knew Garek was right, but was angry with him all the same. He was angry with a lot of people. Still, he forced those thoughts from his mind. Garek needed his help. "Father won't stand for it," he said.

"Please, Father will love this. He's been wishing me gone since I learned to speak." Halas smiled. It was a sad smile, not one of mirth. "He will be all the happier, especially if I do not return."

"Do not say that!"

"Sorry Halas, but you know I am right."

"Then I'm going with you."

"No, Halas, don't do that. Stay here with Cailin. Buy a house, marry her, have a dozen fat children. You deserve better than the navy."

"You make it sound like it is a permanent post. I don't care what you say, Garek. You will not go alone."

"Desmond will go."

"So will I."

———

Halas and Garek went to tell their friends. Halas had a faint hope that someone, maybe Rufus or Olan or even Gale, would want to accompany them. He had no right to expect it, of course, but still he hoped. Olan was the first they found, rooting around in a park. He beamed when he saw them, puffing out his chest with the false enthusiasm that he summoned whenever there were greetings in order. "Ho there, Brothers Duer! How may I be of service to you on this fine, if not slightly overcast, day?"

Olan burst into giggles at the statement, much as he always did. He had aspirations of becoming a bard, and maybe even working his way into the Royal Theatre, but he never could help but laugh at his own folly. Halas and Garek pulled him aside.

"What's the matter, chums?" Olan asked. He still retained that foolish accent, though he was beginning to sense the serious mood the brothers were in. Garek sighed; Halas spoke.

"Listen, Olan, I've bad news. Garek's been drafted."

"What?"

"It's true. He's to leave on the sixteenth, and I'm going with him."

"*What?*" Olan's jaw dropped. Halas nodded solemnly. Olan shook his head. "Are you out of your bloody mind, Hal?"

"I think so. I just wanted to tell everyone before…well, I don't know. I just felt you all should know."

"Well, I'm glad you told me, I suppose. Who else knows?"

"No one," Garek cut in. "You're the first."

"I'm honored." Olan's eyes clouded, and then he looked around, almost frantically, as if he were looking for a way out. An escape.

Garek didn't catch it. "What's the matter?" he asked.

"I've…erm…I've just remembered what I'm supposed to be doing. I'll see you later. Goodbye, fellows."

He ran off without waiting for an answer. Halas and Garek found, throughout the day, that this was common. Some of their friends expressed their condolences, some shed a tear or two, but all found they had important things to attend to. And just before they ran off, they said goodbye.

To Halas and Garek, those goodbyes sounded awfully final.

No one offered to come along. No one even joked about it.

Except for Desmond Mallon.

"Well of course I'm going," he said. "You can't stop me, either."

"Can't we?"

"Not a chance. I wouldn't miss this for a million detricots!"

"Told you," Garek said.

Halas shook his head. In the span of just a few days, Desmond had gone from slightly above a roach to one of Halas' dearest friends. He wondered how he ever could have disliked him. "Des, we have got to be the stupidest people in this city."

"Probably," Desmond said, "but I wouldn't have it any other way."

———

Garek did, in fact, know where the Naval Offices were. He led Halas and Desmond there, and they wandered until they found a door labeled *Brennus*. Halas knocked. A man answered, short, stout, and balding, with a round belly and cheeks. He looked almost like a gnome! "What is it?" he said gruffly.

"Captain Brennus?" Halas had not expected someone of this man's sort to be a prestigious naval captain. Brennus was supposed to be somewhat of a legend on the Inigo. Halas chewed on his bottom lip for a moment, and raised his eyebrows. Did sailors really follow this man?

"Nuh uh. Cap'n's not here. I'm his First Mate, Cloart. Whaddya need?" A sort of relief hit Halas at the confession. It burned inside him, making him feel ashamed. Cloart's speech, though not exactly eloquent, was soft. Halas knew immediately that he was a kind man. He felt embarrassed. Halbrick had always taught him never to judge others by their appearances, but Cloart just seemed so much like a gnome. It was eerie.

"My name is Halas Duer, and this is my younger brother, Garek, and our friend, Desmond Mallon. Earlier today, Garek was drafted."

"Right, yeah. Yer not supposed to be here till September sixteenth."

"We know," Halas said. "But I wish to sign on."

"As do I," said Des.

"Why the infernos would you do something like that?" Cloart asked, scratching his head, flecks of something coming off with each stroke.

"I won't let my little brother go this alone, sir." Garek frowned. He hated it when Halas referred to him as his little brother. It sounded so very patronizing. Halas knew it just as well as Garek did, and for the most part he managed to avoid the phrase. Sometimes, however, there were slips. There were always slips.

"Eh, sure. There's always deckhand spots to fill. Yer main jobs'd be cooking and cleaning the decks. Ye okay with that?"

"Of course."

"Then welcome aboard."

———

Desmond skipped off the stairs, spinning in the dirt to face the Duer brothers. Garek grinned. Only Halas was unhappy. He didn't want to go at all, but who else was going to keep Garek safe? He watched as Garek grabbed Desmond's waist and tackled him to the ground. They rolled away from the stairs. Desmond hopped up, pushing Garek over. They ran to catch up with Halas.

"What do we tell Father?" he said morosely.

"I was forced into this," said Garek with a grin. "You're the one he'll be angry with."

"He's right, y'know," Desmond said, his own grin widening. He shoved Halas. "Not now."

"Oh, all right."

He didn't have to worry much about telling Halbrick over the next few days, as he did not return. Halas wondered if he would before the sixteenth. He surely hoped so.

———·———

The sun was brilliant when Halbrick came home, casting the wrong mood for such a conversation as the one that had to be held. Halas and Garek watched grimly from the table as Halbrick sat down across from them, stuffing a wad of tobacco into the corner of his lip. He looked up at his sons, a questioning look on his face. "What is it?" he asked.

Halas immediately decided that he wasn't going to tell. Not here, not now, not ever. He looked at Garek, who seemed to understand. The junior Duer brother nodded, then looked at his father.

"Father," he began, "A few days past, some men came to the door. Soldiers." At this Halbrick stiffened, as if he knew what was coming. "They… they spoke of the draft. I am to report to Captain Brennus at the Naval Offices on the sixteenth." He said the last part in a single breath, in his rush to be free of his no longer secret burden.

The only sound was the gentle wind outside the cottage. At last Halbrick spoke, though it was barely a whisper.

Halas thought it was a swear.

———·———

They had finally moved the last of the crop to their buyer's warehouse. Covered in sweat and dirt, Halas and Garek dumped out the last cart, letting the buyer's gnomes sort them out. They walked to the man, now wearing a magnificent green suit with a yellow cloak. He looked strange indeed, but that was not their concern.

"Here you are," the man said. "Five jewels, equal to three thousand detricots." They had received the other gems after earlier loads.

"Thank you," said Garek, brushing his hands off on his trousers before taking the bag. "It's been good doing business with you."

"And yourselves. You're fine men; you take after your father. Good day, sirs."

"How does he know Father?" Halas whispered as they left. Garek shrugged. They decided to take a shortcut through Desmond's neighborhood to get to Amelia Gelbert's bank. Halbrick had an account there, and Halas was authorized to deposit funds into it. The gems would go to Gelbert, who would give Halas and Garek official notaries for three thousand detricots. Halas would then take the notaries downstairs to a teller, and have them deposited into Halbrick's account. It was a process that would take the better part of the afternoon. Desmond lived roughly in the center of Lord Bel, the mercantile district of Cordalis. The bank was only a short ten minutes from his house. Walking through an alley between a tailor shop and Mort's Delicatessen, Garek tripped and dropped the pouch. Halas grabbed for it, but stopped cold. A young man stepped out of the shadows. He looked oddly familiar, though Halas could not place him.

"Good morning, boys," the man said, casually scooping up the bag. "I trust you're enjoying this fine day?"

"Put that down!" Garek yelled as he got to his feet.

"I don't think so. These lovely gems are now property of Nolan Dooley, Thief Extraordinaire. Tell your friends about me, will you?"

Halas rushed at the thief, but Nolan quickly spun around to the left, hitting him in the ear with the bag. Halas fell to his knees. The man kicked him in the side of the neck. Halas' breath exploded from him, and he toppled. Garek started forward, but the thief had a thin foil in his hand. "Do not try it, young man. Step back."

Garek ignored him, clenching his fists and closing the distance. Halas struggled to his knees. If they were going to take this man, they would take him together. Nolan seemed surprised at the resistance. "Stop!" he cried. Garek kept on. Nolan swiveled on the balls of his feet and pressed his blade to Halas' chest. "If you don't stop moving, you fat little cow, I'm going to impale him!"

Garek took a wounded step back, the anger on his face quickly turning to fear, fear that Halas thought he could match blow for blow. Nolan's sword had pricked a hole in his shirt. It was cold on his skin.

The thief's words played quickly through Halas' mind, and he discovered that Nolan Dooley wasn't lying. He truly would kill Halas, if he thought he had to. After the forest, such things should have seemed laughable, but Halas couldn't bring himself to think that way. The point of the foil was too cold; it kept him barred in reality.

Garek stepped back, his fists clenched. "Make no mistake, thief," he said. "I will kill you."

Nolan Dooley, Thief Extraordinaire glanced at Halas with a smile. "We will see about that." And with that, he ran off. Garek chased him to the end of the alley, but the man was gone. He ran back to Halas.

"He took it all!"

Halas coughed and let himself fall over. Garek sat next to him and held his hand. It was several minutes before Halas could breathe easily again, much less speak. He burned where the sword had touched him. He thought he might have been bleeding. "It's all right."

"No, no it isn't. That was nearly half our money, Halas. And he took it. He took it all." Garek put his head in his hands. "What's Father going to think?"

"The man had a blade," Halas said. "Father won't think any less of you for that."

"So you say. You tried to get it back."

"Yes, and he put me on the ground." Halas coughed, but immediately stifled it, fearing Garek would think it forced to emphasize the fact that he had been *kicked in the neck*, and then stabbed. If he was bleeding, he'd been stabbed. That realization came with an odd sort of vertigo. His head swam. He'd never been stabbed before.

Garek didn't seem to care. He helped Halas up, and supported his older brother until he could walk by himself again as they headed home. As luck, or the opposite, would have it, Halbrick was inside the cottage when the brothers returned. He saw the bruise that covered the side of Halas' head, from the top of his ear to the middle of his cheek, and went to him, taking him gently by the chin and angling his head toward the window and the light. "What happened?" he asked with concern. "Are you all right?"

"I'm fine," Halas said, pulling his head away. "We were attacked."

"Attacked? What?" He briefly glanced at Garek, looking him over for any visible wounds. Satisfied, he turned back to Halas.

"He called himself Nolan Dooley, Thief Extraordinaire," Garek mumbled. "Stupid name. He tripped me with something, a rope, or twine or something, and grabbed the bag."

"What bag?" Halbrick hadn't known that they were collecting the last of the payment, but from the look on his face, he suspected.

"The payment for the harvest."

Halbrick held his breath, obviously trying to contain his anger. Halas looked from brother to father, ready to extinguish the flames before things became too out of hand. "How much of it? How much was lost?"

"Three thousand. Five gems."

In a rage, their father flung his chair into the wall, breaking it in two. He snarled and rounded on Garek. "You lost *three thousand?*"

"Father," Halas said, "it was not his fault! The man had a weapon."

"Yes, but that obviously did not stop you! My *good* son. You, at least, tried to get our hard-earned money back. How will we last through the winter, Garek? How will we eat? Did you even consider that, or are you too weak, too stupid to do that?"

"Father!" Halas said, putting a hand on Halbrick's forearm. His father shrugged it off.

"Halas, stay out of this!"

"I'm sorry," Garek whispered.

"Of course you did not think! Why should you? You're leaving for most of the winter. You selfish pig!" Halas' eyes widened. "Did you not consider your father's welfare, or your brother's? Of course you did not!" He sat down, rubbing his temples, and muttered to himself. "My son is a *laosboc*. What have I done to deserve such a burden?"

Garek was sullen, his stare burning holes in his own feet. Halas closed his eyes, wishing he had not gone after the thief. Maybe father would not be so angry with Garek then.

But he knew that was not so. Halbrick would react the exact same way, but he would have chided Halas first, doling out a meaningless slap on the wrist. Halas was an adult now, but he knew that had no bearing when under his father's roof. He had always received preferential treatment over his brother, something both Halas and Garek had learned long ago. Neither spoke much of it. Halas felt ashamed, and had ever since they were children. Halbrick did raise a good point, however. How would the two manage through the winter?

Oh dear.

Halas could not bear to watch. Halbrick was angry with Garek often, though rarely did it come to such intensity. He knew what would deflect his father's rage. Garek deserved better, so Halas steeled himself and spoke up.

"Father, I have something I need to tell you."

"Halas, no…"

"*Shut up!* What is it?" Halbrick demanded. He was breathing heavily now.

"Yesterday…I signed up. I leave with Garek on the sixteenth."

Halbrick looked at the ceiling and bit his upper lip. After what seemed like an eternity, he looked back at Halas. "Well then. I certainly do wish you had asked me about this beforehand." His voice was steady, but Halas knew he was just barely controlling it.

"You were not here."

"I see. Well!" He stood up. "I'm going into town, see if I can get something out of that buyer. Maybe he will take pity on my worthless son."

And with that, he left. As soon as the door had closed, Garek broke down and wept.

———

There was little Halas could do for his brother. He cleaned his newest wound. It had already stopped bleeding. After that they went into Cordalis together, and Halas left Garek at the nearest tavern. They were plentiful in Lord Bel. He had a few things to take care of. The thought foremost on his mind was Cailin. How would she take his leaving? She had been eager for Halas to move into a house near her own, but now he came to her with news that he would be gone for six months. He found her outside her house, sitting in the yard with a book. Halas had taught her to read over a year ago. She was a fast learner.

Cailin looked up when he approached and smiled. The smile fell when she saw his bruised face. She rushed over to him. "Halas, what happened? Are you all right?" She pulled him against her and hugged his chest. Her cheek pressed painfully at the prick Nolan had made with his foil, but only for a moment. Halas kissed the top of her head.

"I'm all right, Cailin. Garek and I were robbed today. The man hit me."

"We should tell someone, report this! The Badges may be able to…"

"The Badges have no interest in farmers. They proved that when they decided to write my father off." Speaking of his father, Halas felt miserable. For the first time, Halas thought that maybe Halbrick would raise his hand against Garek. It had never happened, never even come close, but today, Halas was not so sure.

"Halas, what's the matter? I know something bothers you."

"A lot of things bother me." He did not like speaking of personal problems, even with Cailin. It was not that he felt uncomfortable with her knowing, it was just something he did not regularly do. His thoughts were his own.

"Walk with me, please," she said, and took his hand. Cailin led him down the street. Halas watched her appreciatively. Her dark hair glimmered today. It flowed down her back. "Talk to me, just this once."

"The man called himself Nolan Dooley. He took our money from the harvest. Three thousand detricots."

Cailin let out a low squeak. "Three thousand? Surely the Badges would look fairly upon such a case."

Halas shook his head. "It's pointless. The money is gone."

"But that isn't all that troubles you, is it?"

He said nothing. They passed into a park. A group of children played on the far side, dueling each other with sticks. Two men sat near the pond, tossing bread crumbs in for the ducks. Cailin sat in the grass. She took both of Halas' hands in hers and squeezed them. "You can talk to me, you know. You always can."

"I know…"

"Then why don't you? It helps, you know. It's helped me time and time again."

"It's just…Father scared me today. He could hardly control himself when he found out that we had lost the money. He blamed Garek. I thought he would strike him, or worse."

"Has he ever hit Garek before?"

"No. At least, not that I can remember. He always says that he doesn't believe in it, that it's wrong. 'You should never raise your hand against someone unless you intend a fair fight,' he says."

Cailin stared at her lap. "My father felt differently. He said it built character."

Halas looked up at her. Cailin often spoke of her father with apprehension, but Halas had not expected this revelation. "He's *hit* you?" he demanded.

"Not for many years, but it used to be fairly frequent. My mother, as well. I suppose I grew used to it, but I remember long nights where I would listen to them argue from my bed. I could hear him become violent, and I heard her cry. Now the most he does is shout."

Halas had suddenly forgotten all about the day's events. She looked on the verge of tears. He took her in his arms and held her. "I'm so sorry," was all he could say.

"It's all right," she whispered. "Now it's only a memory, is it not? He never truly hurt me, like he did my mother. I was lucky in that respect."

"And he never will. I promise you that."

"Look at me!" She started to laugh. "Here I am, blubbering in public about something that happened years past, when you've had such an awful day. I'm sorry, Halas. Forgive me."

He smiled, and tapped her on the forehead with his middle finger. "Nothing to forgive. What is your book about?"

Cailin looked at the book with surprise. Halas thought she'd forgotten that she had even brought it along. "Some Nesvizhite princess. Jaenelle lent it to me. It really is quite silly; I don't think I'll be reading much more of it."

Halas sprawled on his back, dragging her with him. Cailin laughed. They watched a gull swoop lazily through the sky, calling for anyone willing to listen. Halas was content to lie there like that forever, but he knew it was not to be. He had to tell Cailin of the draft. Today was a sad day. Cailin had looked so blissful, sitting in her yard with her book, and Halas hated himself for taking her joy and stomping all over it, first with dredging up her past, and now this. He felt like scum, but it had to be said. He could not wait.

"Cailin, there is something I must tell you."

She had reached over him and was now picking apart a blade of grass with two fingers. She did not look up. "What is it?"

"Garek was drafted into the navy, and I'm going with him. We leave on the sixteenth, and will be gone for six months."

At first, she was quiet. Halas hated to see grief on her soft features. Nothing seemed more wrong. Hers was a face that was supposed to happy and cheerful.

"It's not right," she whispered. She was looking at her feet, her head pressed against his chest. He held her tight.

"I know. I'm sorry."

She looked up, her eyes wide and accusing. "Why are you doing this? Am I that much of a chore, that you must abandon me?"

"No!" He was a little startled by the comment. "Cailin, I am *not* abandoning you. I would never do that. I love you." She finally blinked. It was something Halas had never said to Cailin before, but he meant it. With all his heart, he meant it. "I do. But Garek…Garek is my brother, and he needs my help. I had to do it."

"Do you really love me?"

"Yes. Yes, Cailin, I love you. And when I come back, you will be of age, and I will marry you. We will buy a nice, big house, and have a dozen children. We'll even buy a dog. How does that sound?"

She smiled through her tears, and wrapped her arms around Halas' neck. "I'll hold you to your promise, though I do not like dogs. My father's are cruel beasts." Halas playfully rolled his eyes. "Halas, I want you to be safe."

"Nothing will happen to me. It's only a boat ride. Everything is going to be fine."

"I know. I love you Halas."

"I love you too, Cailin."

Sub Chapter Three

Nolan stood at the deck of the warship. He thought about the Western Isles, about how Raazoi had calmly walked past the guards right up to Li-Sun, Admiral King. They had stared after the two Easterners: her with her coal black hair and her stiff posture, him with his nervous glances and shuffling steps.

Just as calmly, Raazoi had explained to the Admiral King why it was in his interest to join forces with the queen's corsairs. She had stared at him with those eyes, and he had agreed.

Now they were well on their way down the river. If the winds were favorable, which Raazoi assured them they would be, they would catch up to *The Wandering Blade* in a matter of weeks. Nolan had no clear idea of why Raazoi was so interested in capturing what she would only refer to as 'the son,' nor how she had gotten the full support of the royal navy. He had no idea what she wanted in the Frigid Peaks. Every time he asked Raazoi, she simply told him that everything would be all right, and he believed her.

They quartered on Admiral King Li-Sun's flagship, a sleek boat with a name Nolan was still unable to pronounce. The sailors were at work all around him, hard, slanted faces sweating in the cold air. He gathered his cloak closer about him, wishing Raazoi were here to watch the sunset. However beautiful she was in the daylight, she was twice that at night, and even moreso in between.

She had told the truth when she'd said that the winds would be favorable. Not only were they harsh and furious, but the ship was always blown in the proper direction, never once veering off course. They crossed the waters back to Aelborough in less than a month, coming into the mouth of the Inigo River near Cordalis. Nolan looked off the stern, to see the distant gleam of one of Anaua's own cruisers. He frowned.

There was a strange tingling sensation at the forefront of his mind. He could feel something, but what? It itched inside his forehead, seemingly just beneath the skin. Nolan touched it, scratched it, but the feeling remained. He wondered if he'd been bitten by a tick, but knew instinctively that was not the case.

No, Nolan had a good idea of what this strange sensation was. Images of battle flashed through his head: triumph and glory, death and blood. Contrary to what he would have thought mere weeks previous, he liked it.

Nolan Dooley licked his lips in anticipation.

Chapter Four
Departure

They spent a lot of time together after that. Halas and Cailin walked every inch of the city and every inch of the surrounding grounds, hands locked firmly together always, and lips locked firmly together more often than not. Then they went to their knoll and watched the sunset, which came a little earlier with each passing day.

With a few days left before the sixteenth, Halbrick woke Halas early. He and Garek were discussing something, casual smiles on their faces.

Halas smiled. His family was so rarely at peace, and it made him feel relaxed when so few things did.

"Halas," Halbrick said. "Good morning. I was just telling Garek…well, I'll show you. Follow me."

He did, following Garek and their father out back, behind the cottage. It was cold, and the skies were grey. Halas wished he had bundled up. Three sticks were propped against the wall. Halbrick picked one up, and brandished it like a sword. His father had fashioned crude cross guards on each stick, roughly ten inches from one end. "Pick them up," Halbrick instructed. Halas tucked his hands into his sleeves before doing so. Once Garek had done likewise, he continued. "Hold them with two hands, near the bottom, like I am. Good. Now, put your sticks up, in front of your face. That is your default position."

"Default position?"

"Yes. Aelborough can be a dangerous place, and before you go out into it I would see you both prepared. It is important that you keep your sword in tight at all times. Never leave yourself open. Move your arms quickly, and never stay in one position. Garek, I will attack you. Try to defend yourself." Halbrick sidled in, swinging his stick. Garek blocked the first stroke, but the second left him in the grass, his own weapon pinned beneath him. "Now you, Halas." Halas missed the first, and Halbrick struck him across both forearms. It stung in the cold air. Halas hissed sharply. His breath crystallized. He longed for his cloak, but so long as Garek and Halbrick remained uncovered, he would do the same.

"Good attempt! I do not expect anything out of either of you yet. Come, let's try that one more time."

They continued on into the afternoon. It was hard, intensive work, and Halas no longer felt the day's chill. For hours, the Duer brothers attempted to hold back their father, who constantly shouted instructions as he attacked. "Move your feet! Twist your arms!" They stopped for a light lunch of apple sandwiches and went back to it. This time, Halbrick pitted them against each other, telling them to apply whatever they had learned. Halas wiped sweaty hands on his shirt, and Garek attacked, jabbing at Halas' chest. Halas clumsily sidestepped the blow, allowing Garek to step in close. Had he been wielding a real blade, Halas would have been sliced from end to end. Halbrick nodded. "Very good!"

Garek helped his brother up. Both were beaten, bruised, and tired. Halbrick told them they were done for the day. After supper, Halas draped a blanket over his shoulders and followed his father outside. Halbrick was once again looking at the stars, smoking his pipe. It was something he often did, moreso lately than normal, Halas realized. "Are they not amazing?" he said, aloud. "Millions of them, in places we will never see." He turned to look at Halas. "I want to give you something."

He led Halas back inside, into his room. He knelt down before the chest at the foot of his bed and produced a key from his pocket. It slid easily into the lock and twisted with a loud *click*. Halbrick opened the chest and reached inside. His hands came out with a bundle of black cloth as long as his arm. He balanced it on his palms.

"This, Halas, is very dear to me."

"What is it?"

Halbrick unwrapped the bundle. It was a sword, and a very fine one at that. Even Halas, who had seen many beautiful swords in Conroy's museum, was taken aback. Halbrick twirled it in his hand, admiring the blade. "This is Silvia, the sword I received when I was in the military. I named her for your mother, before we were betrothed. I want you to have her."

"Truly?" He could tell there were tears at the corners of his eyes, but he didn't care. This was not something he would have expected from his father.

"Yes. She'll keep you safe, as she did me. This sword and I have been through a lot together, and now it is your turn."

"I don't expect to face much excitement." A thought struck him, one he felt was worth bringing up. "I feel I must ask…do you have one for Garek, Father?"

"I only wish I did. Promise you will keep him safe?"

"Yes Father, I promise."

"Thank you. Now, go to bed. You need your rest."

———

Halbrick showed Halas how to clean and sharpen the blade, and several ways in which he could practice alone. He continued their lessons the next day, and the day after that. On that third day Desmond joined them, and Halbrick went into Cordalis, leaving the Duer brothers to teach him what they had learned. Halas realized that they had gotten quite good under Halbrick's tutelage, something he had not expected. In fact, he'd thought they were getting nowhere at all. He wanted to show Garek and Desmond the sword, but decided against it, so they went at it with their heavy sticks.

Halbrick returned several hours later to three battered young men. "I'm afraid," he joked, "that you enjoy hitting each other so much, you are not getting any better!" They laughed.

"Now show me what you can do."

They set to it, but Halas quickly saw that they were not alone. Harri Cormack, Patty Carlyle, Franz Eden, and Wesley Farthington stood on the outskirts of Cormack's field. Halbrick glanced at them as he approached. "Do not mind them," he said. "They're only flies on the wall. This is likely the most exciting thing a quarter-farmer will ever see."

As he spoke, Halas watched Cormack lean over to Patty Carlyle and whisper something that made her blush a deep red. Desmond raised his eyebrows. "Can we practice against them?"

Halbrick smiled. "I'm afraid not. Just ignore them. They will go away soon enough."

This seemed enough for Garek and Des, but Halas felt suddenly very silly. What good would swordplay do them? Nothing bad was going to happen. The flies, as Halbrick had dubbed them, had every right to laugh. Halas felt like a child at play, and at twenty, he was beyond such things.

Still, he couldn't very well cry off from the lessons. It took quite a bit of willpower, but Halas turned back to his father. "Okay," he said. "Ignore them."

As the sun set, the four, tired and sore, sat down to supper. Halbrick prepared a meal of potatoes, onions, cornbread, and had even found pork. Halas grinned at the sight of it. "How did you get all of this?" he asked.

"Conroy gave it to me. He's very generous."

———

They trained long and hard for days on end, sparring back and forth across the field. Against Garek and Desmond, sometimes Halas won, sometimes he lost, though the duels with his father were always brief. Halbrick was indomitable, and a fierce fighter. He often set all three boys against himself, and won every match. Still, he never seemed disappointed. "It takes time," he'd said. "More than I should like, I think. Yes, I should have started this much earlier. Again!" And so they went again, smashing the heavy sticks together. Several times they had broken the weapons, and yet Halbrick never seemed to run out. He showed them how to whittle chunks of kindling into crossguards. Garek especially took to it, and soon his stick resembled an actual sword, hilt and all. Halbrick smiled appraisingly when he showed him but said nothing.

When the sun fell each day, Halbrick dismissed them. Halas made his way into Cordalis to find Cailin, but his time with her was not as joyous as it had once been. He spent every moment dreading lock-up, knowing that the few hours a day they had was not enough. Since signing up, Halas, Desmond, and Garek had spent less and less time with their other friends, preferring their quaint little fellowship. There was a sort of camaraderie that had not been there before. Now Cailin dominated his time. When not training, he was with her. He wondered what Garek and Des were doing. He wondered how Desmond managed to train with them. Desmond's parents were merchants, and quite well-to-do. They had their own store in Lord Bel, and maintaining such a place was, to hear it told, very difficult. With Desmond's mother being as she was, Halas didn't know how Des was able to get away.

He looked over at Cailin. They sat together near one of the green-glass gardens, huddled together for warmth. Many such places failed come winter, but this one seemed no worse for wear. Halas had picked her a blue forget-me-not, saying it was a stern message. She held the flower to her nose to smell and let out a tremendous sneeze. A tendril of snot coated the flower, and her eyes watered. "Well, I certainly won't forget that!" she declared, laughing. "It's beautiful. Do you think this will preserve it in the winter?"

Now she was quiet, and somber. The time seemed so short, but already it was the fifteenth of September, and Halas was to leave early on the morrow. He took her hand. "Are you going to miss me?"

"I should hope so. Are you?"

Halas chewed on his lip, pretending to look deep in thought. Cailin smacked his arm, and he laughed. "Do you think I will?"

She reached before her and began to absently tear at a blade of grass. "I think you will. Garek and Desmond have bland imagination. They won't be any fun."

"Desmond is always ready with some quip or another, and he brings it out in Garek. They'll suffice."

Cailin nodded. "I suppose you're right. But do they do this?" She leaned over and kissed him, opening her mouth for his. He put a hand on her breast, and she grinned. "If only it weren't so cold out here." Halas' hand had drifted down to her thigh. She clamped her legs over it. "I have an idea."

"What's that?"

"Let's get an inn. Come on, up with you." She took his hand and dragged him down the street, leading him out of Lord Bel and into the Drifts. They had only two hours before lock-up, and Halas was wary of going so deep into the city. The Drifts were not the safest place to be even in daylight. He felt the prick of Nolan Dooley's blade, and shuddered.

"Are you sure this is a good idea?" he asked.

"Absolutely. I mean to give you a fantastic send-off, and rooms here cost next to nothing. Jaenelle told me Rufus once took her to a place called Rough 'N Tumbler, and they paid three coppers for two whole weeks. Paid for the room *and* service."

"Would that we had two weeks."

"Don't be so melancholy, Halas. Not tonight. Let tonight be *our* night, before I must give you over to King Melick. I want to enjoy it."

⁘

The next morning Halbrick walked with Halas and Garek into the city, and to the Naval Offices. They marched up the stairs to Captain Brennus' office and knocked. Cloart answered. "Oh, hello there. Guess it is the sixteenth."

"Is the captain here?"

"Nope. Just me again."

"Oh. All right then."

The first mate led them inside. Desmond was already there, sitting on a sofa against the far wall. Lazily, he bent his wrist in a sort of half-wave and winked. Garek grinned and sat down beside him. Aside from the sofa, the room was richly furnished. Paintings and documents hung on all sides, framed with cherry and silver. Opposite two armchairs was a desk much like Conroy's, though unlike the older man's this one was clean and tidy. Only a few pieces of parchment were visible on its surface, and those were neatly stacked and organized. An oil lamp sat in one corner. Cloart took care to avoid this as he put his boots up on the desk. Halas immediately decided that they were the foulest smelling things he had ever known.

"So, let's get started then. Ye'll be setting off with the *Blade*, eh? Today I'll be assigning ye your uniforms, signing your waivers and whatnot, all that technical stuff. We're leavin' in two days."

That came to Halas as a surprise, who thought they were leaving today. He blinked pointedly, and Cloart laughed. "I wondered why ye had your packs!" the man guffawed. "Didn't ye wonder why ye came *here*, stead of the docks?"

They hadn't. Desmond grinned sheepishly.

"Well let's get started, then. Here are your uniforms." He scuttled over to the corner, hefting four boxes. "Ye don't need ter keep them clean, really, or wear them much. We only wear em when we leave and when we arrive somewheres. Gotsta look your best then, ye do. We also wear em in battle. It helps to know who's who in one of them, ye know."

"Very true," Halbrick said.

"Battle?" Halas looked at Garek; his brother's face had gone white.

"Dontcha worry bout that," Cloart said. "Nobody ever sees battle. Ain't nobody's got the wrong sense to attack us anymore. Here, we'll start with your oaths." He indicated Desmond. "You were here first, so we may as well keep to that. Get up, raise your hands to your heart, and say your name."

"Desmond."

"Surname, boy. Say *I, Desmond,* and then your surname."

"Oh, sorry. I, Desmond Mallon."

"Now repeat after me. Solemnly swear to uphold the King's Peace, and the King's Law, within Ager and without. So long as he does not order me to any action which should dishonor myself or the law, I swear to serve my captain faithfully up until the end of my contracted service, where…upon I return to Cordalis and resume my normal life and duties. I will not desert, disobey, or question my king or my captain, within Ager or without. Without, my captain's word is law. I will serve him as I serve the king, loyally and dutifully." Apart from the one slip, Cloart said the words easily; it was likely he had long since lost count of the new sailors who passed through this office.

Desmond repeated the oath with Cloart, as did Halas and Garek. They all signed a sheet of paper bearing the oath on it, after Halbrick read it over and determined that nothing was out of place. Cloart folded the print and tucked it into his belt. "Now, on to the matter of payment." To Garek, he said, "You're to receive a sum equal to one thousand detricots for time spent aboard ship, paid direct from the coffers of King Melick himself. Upon returning, in six months or so, Captain Brennus will give ye a note which ye can take to Lord Straub, the king's Lord Treasurer. He will see to it that you're paid."

"We get this when we return?" Halas asked. A thousand detricots was no small amount. From their crop, it was still a loss, but Halas thought their father would be relatively pleased.

"Your brother does. That's your Draft Fee. You're also set to make a few crowns direct from Brennus. During the journey, the captain takes note of your service. Eight hundred is the base sum. Beyond that, what ye make depends on how well ye perform aboard ship. Bonuses will be awarded for potential hazards ye might face. Storms, pirates, what have you. Should ye be any trouble, payment is docked. Brennus is hard with that, so watch out, but he's fair. Anything bad happens, he'll get to the root of it."

"Now, is there any way we could receive some of this payment before departure?" Halas said, thinking of his father.

"Halas," Halbrick warned.

"No, it's okay. Lot of folks ask about that. It's not happening, boy. I'm very sorry, but more than once we've had men try to collect and disappear. You'll be paid for your services, after your services. Not before. Are ye their father?"

He pointed at Halbrick, who nodded. "And you," Cloart said, again indicating Des, "where're your folks?"

"They would not come," he said.

"Then I s'pose they void this right." He turned back to Halbrick. "This may be tough to hear, but in the event of death or serious injury, ye have the right to seek financial recompense from the Lord Treasurer, in funds up to, but not exceeding, a sum equal to one thousand and five hundred detricots."

Garek looked worried again. Halas felt the same. *Death. Could we die out here? Surely not, we're to be surrounded by sailors and soldiers. We'll be safer than ever.* Unconvinced, he put a hand on his brother's arm. "Don't worry, Garek, it's just a formality," Halbrick said.

"A what?"

"Nothing bad of any sort will happen. You'll both be all right."

Halbrick signed something, and Cloart made this slip disappear as he had the other. "As for belongings, you're allowed as much as ye can carry in one pack. In the event of an attack, weapons may be provided, but they're shit, so bring your own. Bring armor as well, if ye have it. Ye don't have any armor, do ye?"

"I'm afraid not," Halbrick said.

"No one ever does. Good armor's hard to come by these days. In any case, bring your uniforms, clothes, foodstuffs, that sort of thing." He rolled back in his chair and ticked the items off absently on his fingers. "Oaths, payment, provisions, uniforms, conduct—I think we got everything, fellas. I'll see ye at the docks."

"Well," Halbrick said. They were back at the cottage. Desmond had followed. "Since you won't be leaving for two more days, I'd like to get some extra training in. But first, let's have a look at your uniforms. Come on then, open them up."

They each held one of the three boxes Cloart had given them. Halas had his opened first. Inside were four identical uniforms. They were a silvery sheen with light trim and curved hats. Emblazoned on the breast of each tunic was the sigil for the Agerian Navy, a simple crested wave. Halas pulled his on. It was warm, warmer than his own clothes were, anyway, and fit snugly around him. How had they managed to get it fit? Taking the shirt off, he tucked it back into the box. Garek kicked his own box over to the cottage walls, grabbing his stick.

Halbrick had encouraged them to attack him whenever possible, when appropriate, of course, and now Garek did so. Halbrick faced him and threw himself at the ground, but Garek hurled the stick at his father, bouncing it off of his shoulder blades. Halbrick hit the ground awkwardly, rolling to his feet and lunging at Garek. Halas and Desmond had their own sticks in hand, but Garek was in the grass, facedown, Halbrick's elbows keeping him in place.

"Had enough?" he said, letting Garek up. He came up spitting dirt, and struggled to his feet.

Halas and Des glanced at each other before they attacked. Halbrick was still behind Garek, and when the boy tried to jump out of the way, his father grabbed him by the shoulders and held him as a shield. Try as they might, wherever Halas or Des attempted to strike, Halbrick would jerk Garek to block, always keeping them at bay. Desmond slowly stalked around toward Halbrick's back, but Halbrick threw Garek at his brother, rolling away and coming up with his stick, twirling it as he struck. Desmond hit the ground, knocked dizzy, and Halas' stick actually snapped in half as Halbrick smashed through it, dropping him to his knees.

"Very good!" he shouted. He was surprisingly kind about their shortcomings—at every moment, Halas expected him to scream at them, or at least Garek, for failing.

They went inside for lunch. Halbrick heated a thick stew of cabbage and rabbit, which they all hungrily devoured. Halas was grateful for the two-day reprieve, though he was far from sure it was the best thing for him. What if he had second thoughts and tried to run? It certainly seemed like the sensible thing to do. Why the blazes had he signed up for this dreadful trip in the first place? What was he thinking? All through the meal he silently berated himself. "We should be careful," Halbrick said, "and eat sparingly. No telling when we will run out."

Garek ignored the comment and kept eating. Desmond coughed.

That evening Garek and Desmond went into the city. Halas waited until they were gone before he took out his father's sword. He couldn't bring himself to call it Silvia. Halas had been nearly old enough to remember his mother when she passed, and thinking of her still pained him. She had been sick, Halbrick had later told the two boys. Halas only wished he knew more of her, instead of just a blurry face and a distant feeling.

He walked outside, drew the sword from the sheath Halbrick had also given him, and lifted it high in the air as he had been shown. Halas swung the sword down, practicing several stances and moves, though only for a few minutes. He sheathed the sword when he heard voices. Walking to the wall of the cottage, he went around back. There was Halbrick, talking to someone. The men's backs were to Halas. "Hello there," said a familiar voice.

"Hello, Mister Conroy."

Both men turned. Conroy was smiling, but Halas thought he looked sad. Halbrick's face was, as usual, unreadable.

"And how are you this lovely evening?"

It was strange, Halas thought. He'd never before seen Conroy anywhere but his own home, and now he was here, walking the grounds with Halbrick. Everything seemed very surreal, very out of place. Halas smiled politely. "I'm fine, sir. You?"

"Your father and I were discussing his plans for the winter. I thought it prudent that he stay with me, until he should come into some money. However, he refuses to accept my charitable offer. Try to persuade him, will you?"

Halas thought about it for a moment. "Do it for me, Father. I will worry about you through the entire voyage, hungry and cold and alone. Please?"

Halbrick frowned. Halas had hit a soft spot. He thought he could see a momentary twinkle in Mister Conroy's eye, but then it was gone. "I will consider it," said Halbrick. "For you, Halas."

"Thank you."

"Excellent! I'll have the gnome prepare you a room. Good night, you two."

"Good night," they both said. Conroy trotted away, and Halbrick lit his pipe, inhaling deeply.

Halbrick had very few things of value, and the next morning, he, Halas, and Garek carried three cases to Conroy's manor. The gnome had made up his spare bedroom, a room almost as large as the whole Duer Cottage, with a mattress and pillows of soft down and a private washroom. They set the cases down and Conroy ordered the gnome to put their contents away. Halbrick seemed uneasy, but Halas and Conroy assured him that this was for the best. Garek wisely said nothing.

Conroy cooked them lunch. Halas had never seen someone prepare a chicken like he had. He explained that that was how they did it in the country of Nesvizh, and they left it at that. After the meal, he led the three into his museum, where a sword was laid out. It was an iron broadsword, a simple and plain thing completely unlike the other weapons of Conroy's that Halas had seen. Conroy handed it to Garek. "This is for you," he said. "It came into my possession first in Arvid, out in Springdell. I left it behind shortly after, but confound it all, the sword came to me again in King Melick's own Red Hall. I know it shall find its way to me once more, and I want you to take care of it for me until that time."

"Really?" Garek said, dumbfounded. He took the sword gingerly, holding it aloft. "Are you sure?"

"I am. Keep it close."

"Thank you! But what of Halas?"

"I already have a sword," Halas muttered, feeling a little ashamed. He had asked his father about a sword for Garek, but hadn't even thought to ask Conroy.

"Oh," said Garek, not looking at his brother, still admiring the sword, dull though it was. "All right then."

They stayed the evening there, and soon Halas grew tired. He asked where he and Garek would be staying. "The gnome has made up a room for you two, as well," Conroy said. This house was far larger than Halas had ever thought; part of it even went underground. The gnome led he and Garek through carpeted hallways lined with paintings and other artwork until they came to their room. All their possessions were still at the cottage, however, and once they knew where there room was, they left the manor and the city. Passing through the Gate, Halas remembered something. "Cailin!" he yelled. "She thinks I've gone! I have to go see her, Garek. Would you bring my things to Conroy's for me?"

"Course I will. You owe me, though."

"Thank you!" He made as if to run off, but stopped. "That sword I spoke of—it is under my bed."

With that, he left, racing through streets and alleyways. The sun was setting when he arrived at Cailin's home and knocked on the door. A portly old man answered, scratching his belly with one hand and holding a cheap cigarette in the other. He cocked his head at Halas. "Who're you?"

"Is Cailin here?" Halas asked.

"No. She's out. Who're you?"

"Where is she?"

"*Who the blazes are you?*"

"My name is Halas, Halas Duer," Halas stammered. "Please, sir, I need to know where Cailin is."

"You and me both, son," said the man. "If you see her, tell her that her father wants her home, *now*. Just wait till her mother gets hold of her, the little brat," he muttered, slamming the door behind him.

Halas turned around, half expecting to see Cailin standing there, her beautiful black hair flowing in the dim light. He looked around, and realized then why she had kept their relationship a secret. She was afraid of her parents, of her father who had spent many long nights hurting her mother. Halas clenched his fists, but there was nothing to be done, so he sat down on the porch and waited. He wanted to find his father's sword and put it to good use. After having heard of what Cailin's father did to her and her mother, he felt it would be justified. He imagined himself bursting in just before the man could strike her, and tearing him apart. She would see him as a hero. He had often dreamed of rescuing Cailin from bandits, monsters, and the like, but they were idle fantasies. It disturbed him to think now that she may have been in actual danger, and he could do nothing.

It was hours after the sun had fallen below the horizon when he left, and that was only because Cailin's father set his dog on him.

He went to Desmond's house, where there were still lights on inside, so he knocked instead of going to Desmond's window. Des himself answered, rubbing his face sleepily. He frowned at Halas. "Halas, it's late. Go home, go to bed. We've got to be at the ship first thing in the morning."

"Have you seen Cailin?" Halas asked, ignoring him. Desmond shook his head. "Why do you ask?"

"Her father said she's not at home. Then he sicced his dog on me."

"He never was very nice," said Desmond.

"Desmond!" came a shrill voice from inside, "who's that out there?"

"It's Halas, woman!" Des shouted. Turning back to Halas, he rolled his eyes. "I've got to go," he said. "Good luck, though."

"Thank you. Sorry about Ema," said Halas, meaning Desmond's mother, Emaline. She was a constant nag. Desmond shrugged.

"She's just Ema," he said. Halas snorted. Desmond closed the door, and Halas walked down toward the street. He reckoned Cailin was probably at the Duchess. Hurrying down the porch, his foot went through the broken step and he fell on his face, landing squarely in the mud. Like his brother earlier in the day, he came up spitting, and clambered to his feet, cursing and grumbling. He pulled up his torn trouser leg and saw that he was bleeding. Halas swore loudly and walked away.

It did not hurt, but made him angrier than ever. All he wanted was to find Cailin and say goodbye before he left. *Is that so much to ask?*

Apparently it was, because when he got to the Duchess, Old Bert the barman had just closed up and sent all the patrons home. Halas, his breath hard coming now, ran back to her house, only to find the doors shut tight and all the lights off. A dog growled from somewhere in the yard. Sulking, Halas wandered back to Conroy's. The gnome let him in, looking him up and down. "Are you all right?" he asked, genuinely concerned. Halas shook him off.

"I need a bandage," he said.

"I'll get the master."

———

"Thank you for taking father in," Halas said minutes later. He sat in one of Conroy's reading rooms, his leg propped up on a stool. Conroy was cleaning his wound.

"It was my pleasure, Halas."

Conroy dabbed a wet cloth over the cut. It burned, and Halas hissed. "I am very sorry to see you go," Conroy said. He dried Halas' ankle and set to wrapping it.

"I am as well. Mister Conroy?"

"Yes?"

"Did I make the right decision? I am of age now. I could have moved into the city—I *wanted* to move into the city. In three months, Cailin turns twenty. She was to move in with me. What if I am throwing it all away?"

"You're not throwing it away, Halas." Conroy tapered off the linen bandage and sealed it to one of the folds. "Over the past few years, I have witnessed you grow into a wonderful young man. It is true you have changed much, yet you have always been a good person, and always will be. Kind, generous, loyal. Garek needs protection sometimes, and I have never seen you back down from that role.

"I know that, if you chose to stay here and something were to happen to Garek on that ship, you would punish yourself for the rest of your days. You will keep him safe, and you, both of you, will be back in six month, with many stories to tell."

"It just seems like such a long time. Six months! I have to spend the next six months apart from Cailin." Halas shook his head and rested his chin on his fist. His eyes were cloudy once again.

"Life is a very long affair. In fact, it is the longest thing you will ever have to do, and six months, even serving in the navy, is just a tiny thing. Cailin will still be here waiting for you, and then you will both move in together, start a family. I know this. I know that she will love you until the day she dies, Halas, because it is impossible not to. Your father will still be here, and life will be as it was. Six years from now, you will have forgotten all about it."

"What if I can't give it up? What if I am like you? You were my age when you first left home, and you did not settle down for many years."

"Dear boy!" Conroy laughed. "You are not like me. You will be able to give it up, when you find that adventuring is not all it is made out to be. You do not wish to live a life like mine. No one truly does."

"You once told me that no one chooses such a life."

Conroy sighed. "Very well.

"There is indeed a chance that you will not be able to settle down, to live out your life rooted in one place. Few receive the call, and fewer still are able to ignore it. It is a great and terrible thing, one that may very well consume you, as it did me. But I know you will resist. People do not choose to return to the wild; it is thrust upon them like a knife. Circumstance piles up until the journey is impossible to resist. Those that return to it deliberately are fools.

"When you return to Cordalis you will have had your fill of adventure. I will be here, your father will be here, Cailin will be here. There will be no urgently pressing matters that call you away. Your life is here, Halas, within the walls of this city. In my days, I had no one, but you have people who love you. There are many who love you, and that, you will find, can give you strength, strength enough to deny the call, to allow you to settle down.

"I know this, Halas, because I have faith in you. And you must as well, or else everything you work toward will be for naught."

There was something strange on Conroy's voice, Halas thought, but he did not know what it was.

The old man seemed pained.

———

There was no time to see Cailin in the morning. Conroy had a wagon ready when Halas awoke, and the gnome had prepared breakfast. He wolfed his eggs down quickly and went outside to Conroy's stable. Two white mares were hitched to the wagon, shifting from foot to foot and whinnying quietly. It was an open wagon, a cart designed to fit several people. There was room left after everyone on the small company had boarded, baggage and all. Conroy drove the horses, whistling a quiet tune to himself as he went. Halbrick smoked his pipe. Halas and Garek were quiet, which was a good thing, because Halas was sure that if he spoke he would lose his breakfast, and last night's supper as well. His stomach felt like it would soon explode, and his heart was heavy.

He was leaving. He and Garek, and Desmond, were going to be away for six months. Six whole months. Halas wished he hadn't signed on for this terrible voyage, that he and Garek and Halbrick could just be a family together, with no disputes or issues.

But that was not to be. Halas swallowed. To say that he was nervous was an understatement. Halas was on the verge of panic. What things would happen to him out in the world? From all the tales Halas had heard before, Aelborough was not a place for the weak. Dragons, warlords, malevolent sorcerers—he closed his eyes and took a deep breath.

Relax, he told himself. *Everything is going to be all right.*

Is it?

Halbrick smiled reassuringly at him, and patted his hand. That helped his nerves, a little. But it was enough to take him from his thoughts.

After leaving through the Shoreline Gate, the wagon stuck to the cobbled road, and Halas admired the open fields all around. He'd never been to Aelworth's Dock before. The road twisted and turned through the hills, and as they got closer to their destination, Halas wished he could go home. They passed by many farms and groves, some men and some women waving happily, others ignoring their presence completely. Past the hills and past the farms, they came to the Red Hall. A fortress of brick and iron, it looked very strange to Halas. Halbrick and Conroy paid it no mind.

Halas wondered if his father would be okay. He'd lost over half of his money, and now both of his sons. Aside from Conroy, he was utterly alone.

Six months!

Despite the chill breeze, it was a fairly nice day. The sun was shining, with only a few shreds of cloud dotting the sky. Halas could see green patches in the dying grass and leaves, little bits of nature struggling against the oncoming winter. If there was one good thing about this voyage, it was that Halas, Garek, and Des would miss winter entirely. He'd studied a few maps, and they were going all the way up the Inigo River to the city of Earlsfort. Halas wasn't sure where they would go from there—no official charts said. They all ended at Earlsfort. *Perhaps that is when we turn around.*

They stopped for lunch by a little stone bridge that arched across a brook. Here was the Bramford Intersection, Conroy told them, leading away in four different directions. Going north would eventually lead you to the Frigid Peaks. South took you to the Inigo River, and then even as far as Sayad. West were the docks, and east Cordalis. Home. Tethering the horses in the grass, the four men ate their sandwiches. No one had said much of anything since leaving Cordalis. In truth, no one knew what to say. All four were worried for each other, and all four had no words for their fears.

"Howdy there!" called a voice. Looking back down the lane, they saw a cart approaching, driven by Desmond's father. In the cart was Des, wearing his uniform proudly, his long black overcoat above it, and a skull cap to keep his ears warm. Beside him sat his mother, looking cold and sad. His parents were not very happy with Desmond's decision to sign on. Garek, finished with his lunch, rose and walked down to meet them. Desmond's father dismounted and tethered the mule near Conroy's. "Thought I was going to beat you folks there," Desmond said with a grin.

"I suppose not," said Conroy. "Come, sit with us for a bit."

They did, and had a lunch of their own. Halbrick and Conroy tried to make conversation with Desmond's parents, but they were not in the best of moods, and nibbled on their food in silence. Halas could see Ema's face beneath her veil, speckled with little bits of frozen tears. Halas and Garek changed into their uniforms. Halas was still curious about how his fit so well.

After lunch, they all moved out together, the Mallons riding beside Conroy's wagon. Conroy, ever the entertainer, tried to occupy them with songs and poems and tales, lighting up his pipe as he did so, but they were unreceptive. Desmond, however, listened intently.

The road and brook were almost parallel now, winding through the fields together. Crossing a second bridge, they came into view of the docks.

———

Shabby wooden buildings dotted the coast, but only one really stood out. That was the lighthouse. A tower of stone, it stood higher in the air than anything Halas had seen, even higher than King Melick's palace. He could not help but stare. A great beacon shone from the tip, one of the mysteries of this ancient place. No one knew what powered the light, or how to replicate it, and it never went out. The secret had died with Captain Aelworth. Piers stretched out to smaller boats and skiffs, and in the distance, Halas could see larger ships with broad sails. Sailors milled about near the lighthouse, talking with family and lovers, giving their final farewells. They all wore the silver uniform. Looking at the ships, Halas wondered which one was *The Wandering Blade*. They hurried down to the sailors.

A porter met them with a long list and a pencil in his scarred hands. "Garek Duer, Halas Duer, Desmond Mallon?" he asked. How he recognized them, Halas did not know. They nodded. "Very good. First Mate Cloart is by the lighthouse. He'll help you with whatever you need."

"Thank you," said Halbrick. They dismounted, and the porter led their horses off to a stable. They found Cloart inside the lighthouse, speaking with two other sailors. He walked over to them. Watching the sailors, Halas was a little surprised by the informality of it all. The men were just milling, like horses out to pasture. He'd expected rigid formations and the captain shouting orders. Halas had imagined it many times: the captain barked commands and the men moved efficiently onto the ship.

Halas had really just expected the captain to be *there*.

"Hey there," Cloart said. "Yer runnin a little late."

"Sorry," Halas said.

"No problem. Better late than never, I s'pose. We'll be headin over to the *Blade* any minute now, once everybody else gets here. Who's that?"

"Darius Conroy." Conroy bowed and shook his hand.

"First Mate Cloart. Just Cloart, thank ye."

Desmond's parents had led him away somewhere, Halas noticed. As Cloart left them, he exited the lighthouse and looked around. He saw them then, both hugging their son tightly. Halas turned to his father. "Goodbye, Father," he said. Very suddenly, Halas felt four years of age again, and rushed his father, embracing him tightly. He felt Halbrick's arms tighten around his back, and buried his head in the man's shoulder. He didn't care if the others were watching.

"Be careful," Halas whispered. "Please, Father, be careful. I love you so much."

"I love you, too." Halbrick pulled away. He gave Halas another smile and clapped him on the shoulder. "Goodbye Halas, Garek. See you in six months."

"G'bye," said Garek. Halbrick put an affectionate hand on his arm.

"I have a friend," he said, almost as an afterthought, "in Earlsfort. If you're there for very long, you should pay him a visit. His name is Jaden Harves; we served together. He'll help you with anything you need."

"Yeah, we'll do that. Thank you."

Halas turned to Conroy, and they, too, embraced. "Have a safe journey," Conroy said. "May your luck shine, bright as the stars." Halas cocked an eyebrow, and Conroy laughed. "It is an old saying," he explained. "Though it is a little silly, I think."

Desmond's family met them, and they walked out to the end of the pier, where the sailors were piling into rowboats. They stood near a towering man, with broad shoulders and deep blue eyes, a heavy sword at his back. With him was a boy. The boy was much younger than Halas, only fifteen years or so. He wore his hood up. Garek touched his forearm lightly. "Who're you? Your face is familiar to me."

"Aeon the Great," the boy responded with a sneer.

"No…really?"

"No you moron, I was being facetious."

As the two moved away, Garek leaned into Desmond's ear. "What's that mean?"

"Sarcastic," Des answered.

With that, Halas, Garek, and Des said another round of goodbyes, and climbed into one of the boats, struggling to get their baggage to fit. Older men rowed toward the bigger ships. *The Wandering Blade*, they discovered, was a huge galley, with three masts nearly as tall as the lighthouse, white sails and Agerian flags flapping in the wind. Webbed netting was cast over the side of the ship. The sailors climbed up it like spiders. The ropes were cold and stiff. Halas, Garek, Des, and the boy they had seen earlier had trouble, but made it. Setting their things down on the deck, they looked back toward the coast.

"Well," Desmond said, "that's that."

Sub Chapter Four

"Why are we doing this?" he asked, overcome once again by his curiosity. Raazoi lay naked up against his chest. The rich moonlight shone through their window. It made her raven hair and pale skin glow in sharp contrast to each other. Her eyes seemed to shine brighter than ever before.

"It is important," she answered, and Nolan suddenly felt very sleepy.

Pain's a funny thing. After a certain point, you stop feeling it, and yet you feel nothing else at the same time. It pervades your entire body like a cruel flood. Nolan was at that point. He couldn't imagine a world without pain. Time was gone, rational thought was gone. There was nothing else but the faceless thug and his club.

After an eternity it stopped. Nolan flopped on his back. His clothes were torn nearly away, but what was left clung to him, matted with blood. He wanted to groan, wanted to do something to convince himself he was alive, but he could not. A dull gray blur pressed closer to his face, and he heard filtered words. "Have we learned our lesson?" the Inquisitor asked.

Nolan nodded.

"Good. Next time you steal in this city, you'll do what?"

Nolan opened his mouth. He coughed blood. He tried to find the words, and they were there, he could feel them, but he couldn't speak but for one: "Dar."

"What? You'll have to speak up."

Nolan coughed again, but this smug bastard wasn't going to get the best of him. *Getting the living hell beaten out of me wasn't bad enough? Now he wants to be arrogant about it?* Nolan would have sneered if he'd been in control of his face. Still, he managed to speak, and was glad for it. It made him feel in charge. "I'll give to Dar. I promise."

"Good!" The thug scooped Nolan up. Nolan yelped, and things were dark for a while.

He opened his eyes. It was dark still, but Nolan thought that was because it was night. He tried to sit but could not. His back was on fire. From his position, he looked around. Buildings were on either side. He was in an alley. He'd been dumped. *Lovely.*

Nolan rolled over on to his belly through sheer force of will. His muscles cried out against him, but the bastards wouldn't mutiny, not until he was indoors somewhere in a warm bed. He wouldn't let them. He reached forward, felt the cold pavement, and crawled. Inch by inch, Nolan crawled down the alley. There was no breath with which to scream.

Nolan didn't know how long it took him to reach the street. He knew he'd blacked out a few times. When he was there, he slumped against what he thought was a tree and rested. It wasn't a bed, but it would do, for just a few minutes. He swore it would be just a few minutes.

The thundering of horses brought him to. Nolan rolled over and looked. Two children stared at him from the back of a carriage. Their parents drove on, oblivious to the poor dying man. Nolan managed a yell, but the carriage kept on. How late was it? Certainly there were few carriages out and about during the late hours, but how many of them carried families? People wandered the city at all hours, but once the taverns closed they were few and far between. If the hour was that late, Nolan's life rested in the hands of the drunks, an idea that did not appeal to him in the slightest.

So he crawled. It was agonizing, but he had to find someone, because no one was going to find him.

But the pain was overwhelming, and soon Nolan was unconscious.

Chapter Five

The Wandering Blade

Spray from the sea showered the deck, and Halas struggled to keep his feet. They sailed along the coast, well on their way to the Inigo, already ahead of schedule.

The Inigo River was not an ordinary river. When Aeon the Great banished the Infernal creatures, the Inigo had sprung up from nothing to be a great border between the Burning Desert and the civilized world. Fifty miles wide and many hundreds long, it did not conform to the normal standards of a river. To begin with, it did not actually run, save for when it wanted to. One minute it could be as still as a calm lake, and the next, thirty foot waves could drag you beneath the raging rapids and keep you there. Cloart assured Halas that that was just a myth—he said that the river was quite like the open sea, but incredibly calm, for the most part. In all his voyages, he himself had witnessed very few storms.

Cloart approached them, scratching himself as he went. Garek noticed him first. "Hello, sir," he said.

"Hey there. Cap'n Brennus wants to see ye. Follow me."

They followed across the broad deck and into the belly of the ship. The captain's room was one of modest size, with a bunk, a desk, and a private washroom. The four stood, waiting for the captain himself to appear. He came into the room after they did, surprising all but Cloart. Halas turned to regard him.

Captain Brennus was tall, thin, and muscular, as one would expect from someone of his profession. Also expectedly, his skin was a deep tan, from all his days spent in the sun. What seemed out of place, to Halas at least, were the man's eyes. They were gentle, not rough, and kind. "Good afternoon," he said. "I am Captain Brennus."

They introduced themselves, and Brennus made a point to put faces with names. "I trust Cloart has told you of your duties?"

"He has, Captain," said Des.

"Good. I thought it a good idea to meet the new members of my crew before we got too far out. Cloart, pray excuse us. I would like to take them to the kitchen."

"Aye, Cap."

The kitchen was larger than the captain's quarters, with shelves and cupboards filled with food and spices. Brennus then showed them to the storage area just behind it. Much of the supplies were fresh, though Brennus also showed them a large quantity of a thick, tough meat. "Never spoils," he said. "This is a special sort of jerky. That weird fellow up in King Melick's court came up with the recipe. He called it *spódhla*. We run out the fresh stuff quite quickly and live off this. Lucky for you there are plenty of ways to cook it, but you needn't worry about that right now. For supper, I would like something with chicken. Can you boys cook?"

"Yes," Desmond said. "For two summers I was tutored by Chef Merzio himself."

"Were you? I have had the occasion to meet Merzio. A fine man."

Halas had heard otherwise, and often. He wanted to laugh, but kept his composure. "Yes he was," Desmond offered.

"I would like to hear your stories, Mister Mallon. In any case, I'm afraid I have duties to attend to. I'll assign a guide to take you around the ship." He led them back to the deck, and called over a tall man with green eyes and a pronounced limp. "This is Martarey," he said, introducing them next. Martarey bowed his head. "Take them around the ship, will you?"

"Course," said Martarey.

The Wandering Blade was a very big ship. A *trom* class galley, its hull was unusually thick. The deck was open, with the exception of five ballistae and several smaller scorpions that were positioned around the perimeter, and the many passenger cabins, designed for people who, in either a moment of unrivaled bravery or stupidity, would book passage on such a ship. These cabins were together as a single structure, one story high in the middle of the deck. A single door led below to a beehive of cramped hallways and small rooms. The more senior crewmen had rooms to themselves; junior sailors had to share with one or two others. The galley was the largest room on the ship, with rows of cabinets and stoves in one section and tables in the other. Every surface of every room looked the same: bland, dark wood—and it was very easy to get lost. Luckily, Halas had a good sense of direction, and already a rough map was forming in his mind.

"So," said Martarey, "you're the draftees, eh?"

"I'm afraid so," Halas said. Did they not know that he and Des had actually volunteered? *It might be better to keep it that way,* he decided. "How long have you served on this ship?"

"Ten years," was the response. "And it'll be eleven 'fore we get to Earlsfort. She takes some getting used to, I gotta tell you."

"Who?"

"The ship, the *Blade.* Cap'n Brennus'll make sure and do right by you, though. He ain't the prettiest or the nicest, but he's sure the best there is. He takes care of us, see. Don't like no one coming in and mucking up what he got. So take care."

Halas closed his eyes and fought back a deep sigh. It was clear that Martarey resented them. He wondered if it was a common feeling, and suspected it was.

"We don't mean to step on any toes here," Garek said.

"Course not," said Martarey. "Just keep it in mind. Cap'n Brennus'll look out for ya, but you're low priority. Not crew, not even guests. Draftees. Ain't right, doin that. Lotsa people'd rather serve by their own will than the king's."

They were back in the open air. The waters had settled down for the time being. The sun was shining, but it was still cold. "Tomorrow," Martarey said, "wrap up. It's gonna get mighty cold fore it gets warmer."

That night they, along with the assistance of twelve other sailors, cooked a thick stew. Des seemed disappointed. Halas thought maybe he had anticipated something more challenging. "Take it to our guests, would you?" ordered the Absolon, the Head Chef. Halas took a tray with two bowls up to the deck. Sailors were scurrying around, busy at work. Wishing he knew what it was they all were doing, Halas walked to the guest's quarters. The big man answered. Inside, Halas could see the young boy.

"Hello," he said, "I was told to bring you supper."

"My thanks," the big man grunted, taking the tray and closing the door.

It snowed that night, and every day after for two weeks. Halas soon discovered that keeping the deck free of ice was an incredible chore, one where he, Garek, Des, and the other deckhands spent nearly all day on their hands and knees with sharp blades, chipping away at the frozen wood. They were given bags of salt and crushed stone to hold things over, but were encouraged to keep the deck entirely free of ice.

The gravel sat in the hold, unused.

———

It was nearly a week into the voyage. Halas stood up and rubbed his sore arms. He'd broken his blade. Cloart was nearby, shouting at two sailors. Suddenly curious, Halas moved closer to where he could hear. "Cut that out!" he heard. The two sailors looked at the diminutive man. One shrugged, and they both laughed as they walked away. Cloart went below, muttering to himself.

"What was that about?" Halas asked a sailor nearby.

"We don't like him much," the man answered. The two shoved roughly past Halas, turning separate ways and getting back to work.

Halas' own shift was finished, so he went below to find supper. He ate with Des and Garek that night, as they did every night. Desmond looked annoyed. "What's the matter?" Garek asked him.

"Absolon," he answered.

"What about him?"

"He's stupid. Doesn't know what he's doing in there. He's spent too much time cooking *spódhla*, and not enough time with real food."

"So teach him," Garek offered.

"He won't listen! The oaf is so obsessed with his *authority* that he won't take my advice."

"Then," the younger Duer continued, "do it without his knowing."

"I may have to. Not sure I can stand to eat like a beggar for so long."

The next morning, Desmond diced up several peaches and slipped them into the porridge, along with more than a little sugar. Halas savored every bite. He had only eaten peaches once before; they were rather expensive in Cordalis. But he was not alone in noticing the improvement. After breakfast, several sailors walked up to Absolon and praised his cooking. Absolon took these compliments to heart, boasting about this and that. He had not even seemed to notice the peaches as he ate, but that didn't matter. Desmond was the only one that morning who seemed unhappy. He had worked in secret, and Halas had forgotten that the one thing Des loved more than food was attention. He glanced at his friend, who ground his teeth and clenched his fists in anger.

Winter was quick to fall behind. The snow fell less, the sun stayed in the sky higher and longer, and best of all, it was warm. Each sailor wore less and less fur as the days went on, until finally they stopped altogether. After every meal, Halas took a tray of food to the strange passengers, but was never allowed inside. Walking back to his room after one of these excursions, he felt a pair of hands press against his shoulder, and then he was sprawling on the deck, his breath driven violently from his lungs. He rolled over on his back, gasping up at the stars. Raucous laughter echoed across the deck. Halas looked around, trying to see who had pushed him, but it could have been any of the crew.

He saw the big man still standing in the doorway, watching with a solemn look etched on his features. It was an expression that looked well at home. He gave a subtle nod, indicating a crewman Halas didn't know, and then closed his door. The crewman blurred. Halas covered his face with his hands, trying with a stun induced stupidity to hold his breath in that way. It didn't work.

This was the first of many assaults to come. Halas knew that he and his friends were on their own. They'd just have to put up with it, he supposed. *Six months isn't that long.*

Yes it is.

Six months.

---—·—---

If Captain Brennus or Cloart, or indeed any of the officers onboard, seemed to notice the attacks, they did nothing to prevent them. Halas hoped that they were just ignorant to the goings on, but Brennus was highly involved with his men. He played cards and darts in the hold at night, he ate with the crew each day, he broke open casks of beer and ale for even the most minor of occasions. They were a family. How could he not know?

It was the middle of the night, and Halas did not hear Garek's snoring. His brother was awake, then. *Well, good,* he thought, *so am I.* "Garek?"

"Halas. Why're you up?"

"Can't sleep. Are you all right?"

"I'm fine." He heard Garek roll over in the bunk below. Halas felt pained, as if the whole mess were his fault. He should have been able to prevent this. Garek never should have been allowed to leave.

"What do we do about these sailors?"

"Desmond likened them to schoolyard bullies. I wouldn't know."

"Nor would I, but he's likely right. How often are you pushed?"

"Least once a day. Mostly more. I think it's getting worse."

"What do you mean?"

Garek whistled through his teeth, thinking of what to say. "It's just a feeling I have. They don't like us. I don't really know why. It's not my fault I was drafted, after all. That's kind of the whole point of it."

"It doesn't matter much to them. We're outside their group. We don't matter. They think we've all been drafted. Perhaps we should keep it that way."

"Why?" Garek asked. "Maybe they'll like you and Des better if they find out you signed on willingly."

"Maybe," Halas conceded, "but you're not going to go it alone."

---—·—---

He broached the topic with Cloart the next day.

"Yeah," Cloart said. He stood at the railing, gazing off into the blue. He'd just released a falcon, and his leather gauntlet hung about his arm, momentarily useless. Halas leaned against the wall of the cabin behind him, hands in his pockets. The wind was chilly. "They're bad about it. We've been out here for nearly a month; the men get bored, restless. I've been the butt of their pranks for years now. 'S why the cap'n made me First Mate, so they always know there's a line they can't cross." The falcon circled above them for a bit before disappearing. Cloart turned to Halas. "Did you know my father was a gnome?" he asked.

Halas shook his head. "I did not. Is that why the crew treats you as they do?"

"Aye. Lots of people hate gnomes, and half gnomes are even worse. When I was a boy, my folks took me out to the theatre for the first time. We never got there. Know why?"

Halas shook his head. This story had a bad ending. Halas felt nervous, as if it were his fault. These days, he felt responsible for a great deal of things.

Cloart continued. "We made it almost to the doors, when some rich ones decided we weren't fit to enter. They called over a dockworker, gave him ten detricots. The dockworker had a bag of fertilizer. Now, my da was a free man, but that didn't mean much to anyone there. The dock man dumped the bag on my da's head. Called us 'shitty little shit people,' and laughed. Everyone laughed, even the patrolling Badges that passed us by."

Halas looked at his feet, suddenly feeling very ashamed, for himself and people in general. "I'm sorry."

"No worries," Cloart said. "Not your doing, and it's long past. I'm well over it. Never saw that dock man again." He turned back to the rail. His falcon had become almost invisible. "But it happens. For some it's worse than others. Folks don't like what's not theirs."

They stood in silence for a time, watching Cloart's falcon circle overhead. "I don't suppose Captain Brennus can make us officers as well," Halas mused, only half joking. Cloart smiled wanly.

"S'pose not. Anyhow, we'll be on naught but *spódhla* here soon. Some of the men are gonna take sick. Fair warnin."

———

Martarey was on galley duty when he happened to glance in Desmond's direction, just as Des, looking about as conspicuous as can be, slipped a fistful of spice into the cooking pot. Martarey lunged across the kitchen with the speed unbecoming a cripple and grabbed his wrist, twisting his arm behind his back. "What do you think yer doing!" he demanded, pushing Desmond to the counter. No one else moved. The room was still with confusion.

"What is going on?" Absolon asked.

"He's poisoning our food!"

That got to them. A few men drew what weapons they had on them: knives and small hammers, mostly. Others put up their fists. One wrapped a short length of chain around his knuckles. All shouted for blood. Desmond looked around, confused, and then laughed. He laughed until his face was red and he couldn't breathe. Martarey shook him and Des flopped like a rag doll. "What? What's so funny?"

Through the laughs, Desmond managed to get out: "It's cinnamon!"

A few of the men muttered, "We have cinnamon?"

When Des had finally stopped laughing, he wiped tears from his eyes and spoke. "There's quite a lot of spice in the hold. You ever use it, Absolon?"

"Of course I use spices! I'm a chef," Absolon stammered.

Garek was at the back of the crowd. "Then why's he have to put them in secretly?" he asked.

Desmond grinned devilishly at the chef. "I know how to cook *spódhla*, too," he said.

For this, Absolon had no words. But from then on, he let Desmond help him, and the food was better. Even the *spódhla*, when they eventually ran out of fresh stuff. Though they warmed to Desmond, it was not enough to satisfy the bitter dislike the sailors had for the draftees. Halas and Garek were still only spoken to when absolutely necessary and ignored when not. At best.

While most of the sailors began to like Desmond, others had a reaction that was the polar opposite. Absolon was a trusted member of the crew, and having a draftee show him up was embarrassing. A bunch of the cook's best boys gathered together one night and hatched up a plan.

———

Garek was alone when this plan was put into action. One of the best boys came from the aft deck and told him someone had defecated there. Not surprising, as Captain Brennus had allowed the sailors a drunken night. Garek had wanted quite badly to join in, but restrained himself. Drinking with these men would not end well. Now it was late, and most of the crew would be dead asleep. So, grumbling, Garek took up his mop and followed the boy to the mess. The only light was that of the stars; the lamps had been extinguished. Garek set his bucket down and soaked the towel, slapping it down into the mess, grimacing as he did so. He, again, wished this whole thing had never happened.

Of the three draftees, the only draftee was the smallest, therefore he was naturally the first. Two boys about Garek's age came up behind him, locking their arms around his and dragging him to his feet. They had thought Garek to be an easy target, and did not expect resistance. Garek surprised them.

He twisted free immediately, grabbing the first boy and shoving him into the second. They stumbled away, but a third had appeared on the deck. He grabbed Garek by the neck. Garek knocked his arm away and kicked the boy in the gut. The boy doubled over. Garek hit him again and turned to face the first two boys. They grabbed Garek's shoulders, driving him backward and into the bulkhead. Garek's arm struck the heavy wood awkwardly and sparked with pain. He hissed. One of the boys had dark red hair. He held his face too near to Garek and suffered for it. A cut opened on the Garek's forehead, but he hardly felt it. He was in a fury. His arm ablaze, he kicked free of the second boy, only for the third to rejoin the fracas, moving low and wrapping his arms around Garek's waist. Garek slammed his elbow against the top of the boy's head. The boy dropped.

Garek had been in dozens of fights over the years, he and Halas both. Had it been just those three boys attacking, he would have won with little trouble, and slept in his own bed that night. By morning he would not have even felt his injuries. But the best boys had friends, friends who were late to the party, but friends nonetheless. Three more came around the side of the cabin. They grabbed Garek and held him steady. He struggled, managing one last good hit on a newcomer, but one, one of the first who had appeared that night, struck him just under the collarbone, driving his breath away.

They had him. The red-hair boy grabbed Garek's own hair and yanked his head back, exposing his neck. A fourth and fifth stood watch in the aisles that led from the back of the ship, around the cabins, to the front. A sixth, the biggest, approached from the left aisle, cracking his knuckles. Garek moaned. At least he wished he could see their faces; it was too dark.

"What is this about?" he asked after mustering up the courage and regaining his breath. He felt a strong need to urinate. His breath came rapidly. His throat was dry. His toes curled against the soles of his boots.

"I think you know," said the boy. His voice was high, so much so that Garek didn't quite believe it was real. *I must be imagining things,* he thought. *These are children!* And then he started to giggle. This was all just so absurd.

"Shut up!" said the high-pitched voice. Garek complied. At six to one odds, he did not wish to anger these boys further. "Don't call out. If you cry out, we'll toss you over the side."

So Garek didn't cry out, he didn't yell, even when the first fist connected solidly with his gut. He stifled it, grunted and cried instead, trying to curl up into a ball. The second hit was harder and higher on his chest. The three boys held him in place as the heaviest hit him again and again, sometimes in the chest or gut, sometimes in the face or crotch. Pain replaced blood in his body as the latter substance splattered over the deck and the clothes of the boys closest to him in a hot spray. His nose ran blood and snot down his face. He could taste the foul mixture, and gagged.

This was it. These boys *did* plan to kill him, right here. They planned to hit him until he was dead. He wished he could see his friends. A dozen faces flashed through his mind. Martin, Olan, Tay, Rhic. Even Cailin, though she and he had never been close. More than that, he wanted to see Halas and Des. He wanted to apologize for bringing them out here, on this awful trip that was going to end in his death. His death at the hands of a bunch of sissy kitchen boys who had managed to overwhelm him with little fight.

The one name that never crossed his mind was that of his father.

What if it wasn't just him? What if these kids went after Halas and Des next? Surely they would, they were out for blood, rabid with the taste. The hitter probably couldn't even see for all of Garek's blood that had been spilt, but he still continued pummeling. Garek coughed and choked. Blood poured into his mouth. A sharper pain blazed as a tooth exploded.

It would end in the deaths of all three young men if he did nothing. Let them kill him here; he was in such pain that he didn't see much point in surviving. He'd never not feel pain again, he knew that much. It pervaded his very sense of being, and he knew it would always be a part of him, a second, terrible skin.

So Garek screamed. He opened his mouth and let out a great roar that awakened the whole ship. The scream brought every crewman to his side, weapons in hand.

At least, he tried to. Garek was so badly hurt that all that came out was a weak yelp. He heard the boys laughing. One released his arm he laughed so hard.

"That all you got?" said the hitter with the girl's voice. Garek wanted to snarl, but he wasn't sure he had any teeth left. "Nobody but us's gonna hear that, you rat scum. You'll be paying the punishment for trying!"

But the girly boy was wrong; help *did* come, in the form of one man. One man the size of two, and ample help on his own. The mysterious man, the ship's guest. He'd heard the cry and came running from his cabin, veins standing at attention on his neck and bare chest. He saw the attack and clenched his fists.

Garek dropped into a puddle of something that he tried to roll away from but failed. His vomit was added to the spill shortly after. Blinded by the mess, he could only hear the ensuing fight. It sounded like the boys were really in for it.

Halas couldn't sleep, and when Garek stumbled into their berth later that night, his face a mural of cuts and bruises, he jolted to his feet.

"Who did this to you?" he demanded.

"Some of Absolon's boys," Garek said. "They jumped me, beat me pretty bad."

Something took hold of Halas. He'd been angry plenty of times before, but never like this. What he was feeling wasn't anger, but something beyond that. It was pure rage. "I'll kill them!" he snarled, and he meant it. "Where are they?"

"Tormod took care of it," Garek said. He sank down on to his bunk. "He hit them worse than they hit me, put three or four in the infirmary. The others won't be goin nowhere for a while, neither." He smiled.

Halas sat beside him. "Who is Tormod?"

"Our guest. The bigger one."

"Are you hurt?"

"Little. Tormod gave me something for the pain. Think it's whiskey." He grinned. "If you still feel like killin them, they're just down the hall. Punch or two ought to do it."

Halas wanted to smile, but could not. He was trembling. Someone had hurt his brother, and they would pay dearly for it. *I should have been there with him. How could I have left him alone as I did?* He had to say something, had to reassure his brother things would be all right, but it seemed as if things already were. The big man had saved Garek. Halas owed him. "I will give Tormod my thanks in the morning when I deliver breakfast."

They sat like that for a moment, Halas with his hand on his brother's arm. He was opening his mouth to ask about the fight when the door to their berth swung open. Brennus strode in, Cloart and another sailor at his side. Halas saw that they were all armed. He glanced at his footlocker. His sword was buried inside, wrapped in its scabbard and an old shirt.

Brennus lifted a single finger to Garek and beckoned for him to approach. Garek looked cautiously at Halas. Halas gave a slight nod. Before Garek could rise, Brennus spoke.

"Don't look at him. Look at me. Come here."

Garek slowly stood and crossed the berth. His legs were shaking. Halas wanted to hurt the boys who had done this to him. Garek was a mess. Brennus looked him in the eye, awaiting an explanation. Garek said nothing. Finally, the captain broke the silence.

"Would you care to explain to me what happened tonight? Why three of my chef's best boys are confined to the infirmary and three others their beds?"

"Have you spoken with Tormod, sir?"

"It doesn't matter. I would like you to tell me what's happened."

"They attacked me while I was cleaning the aft deck. They attacked me and Tormod saved me."

"I knew that oaf was going to be trouble," said the sailor at Brennus' side. Garek took a clumsy step toward him.

"He is not an oaf! Those boys meant to kill me, and they would have had Tormod not been there. Tormod saved my life!"

Brennus raised a hand between Garek and the man. "Calm down, son. Flanagan meant no offense. He won't speak out of turn again, nor do I expect you will. Is that clear?"

Brennus' voice had changed that night from its usual friendliness, bringing a chill to the room. Halas felt momentarily frightened by the captain's sudden threat, but he said nothing. Brennus was in charge here, and nothing Halas said or did could change that.

"What did you say to them?" the captain asked. "Why do you think they attacked you?"

"I was just cleaning, sir, like I said. Someone defecated on the aft deck."

"Prolly the boys themselves," Cloart mused. "Listen, Bren, Absolon's aren't the brightest folk by a mile. They're bout as ornery as a family of angry badgers in heat. Member last year, with Batty?"

Brennus nodded. "Those boys are apt to stir up trouble, I know. I only wanted Garek's side of the story. What did Tormod do to them?"

"I didn't see," Garek said. "I was out of it."

"You seem to be doing fine now."

"Tormod gave me something, some sort of drink. I feel much better."

"I see. Everything seems to be in order here, but Garek, I want you to promise me something. Based on your account and several others, this incident doesn't appear to be your fault, so I will likely be pursuing judgment on the boys, and not you or Tormod. But I want you to promise me that you won't seek any sort of retribution. Let me deal with these boys."

"All right, I promise."

"Good. Halas, is it?"

"Halas."

"Halas, I want you to promise the same. Your brother doesn't seem to be much worse for wear, if what he says is true, and those boys will be dealt with. Do not make things worse. Your word?"

Halas clenched his teeth. He would not lie to the captain, but he wanted to make the best boys suffer. He wanted to beat them as they had beaten Garek, but that could not happen. "You have my word," he said.

"Good. If I catch any sort of hint that either of you are planning something, or if any harm comes to those boys, you will regret it. I don't expect they will bother you, and they *will* be tried. Is that clear?"

"Yes, sir," Garek said.

"I will leave you to it, then. I'm sorry about all of this. Good night."

"Night, sir," Halas said.

Brennus and the other man left, but Cloart stayed behind a moment. "Ye sure you're all right?" he asked.

Garek smiled. "I'm just as I was this morning."

"Yer face says otherwise."

Garek reached up to touch his cheek. The bruises seemed to have faded slightly even since the captain had arrived, but Garek's face was still a mess. He winced. "It stings," Garek said, "but I think it could be worse."

"Good, I'm glad. Listen, what the captain said, about dealin with Absolon's boys, he meant it. Don't go about seekin any sorta revenge, okay? That'll only make things a might worse, violence begetting more violence and all that."

"I won't," Garek said. "Tormod did more to those bastards than I ever could."

"Good night, Cloart," Halas said. He wanted to be alone with his brother, but immediately he regretted sounding so harsh. To soften the blow, he added, "I'm glad you're here." It was paltry, but he did mean it.

Cloart looked touched at the remark. "Eh, night," he said, and left the berth. Halas rose and checked the hallway outside. It was empty. He closed the door and turned back to Garek.

"Are you sure you're all right?"

"Really. Whatever Tormod has in that flask of his does wonders. Will you still take him breakfast in the morning?"

"I will."

"I'd like to go with you."

———

There were messes to clean up before breakfast. Halas and Garek were scrubbing heartily at the deck when Tormod's cabin opened, and he and the boy walked out toward the rail. Halas got a good look at him then. The boy was maybe fifteen or sixteen years, with dark hair and sharp features. He looked familiar, but Halas could not place him. Garek did not have the same problem. Unbeknownst to Halas, he had pondered over the boy's face ever since they departed from the docks. And now, finally, he came to a conclusion. "That's Prince Aeon," he whispered, bowing his head.

Prince Aeon was the son of King Melick and Queen Anaua. The two royal leaders were separated, each struggling for a piece of the city. There were rumors that poor Aeon, named for The Great One, was in danger.

Apparently those rumors were true, Halas thought. He wanted to rush over and swear service to the young boy. Garek noticed, and put a hand on his brother's. Halas shook his head to clear it. Was it really that easy to be seduced? It was as if just being in the presence of royalty sent shivers of fealty through his blood. He went back to cleaning, deciding it best to ignore the boy completely. "Look at them," Garek said.

"I don't want to."

"No, not them. The crew. Look at the crew."

Halas did. The crew looked at Prince Aeon and his—what, his bodyguard?—with disdain. They passed near a man called Gustava. Gus was responsible for the late night card games in the cargo hold. Halas had only heard of these games in passing. As Aeon and the big man passed, Gus spit. They pretended not to notice. "Least we're not alone," Halas said. Garek snorted.

"Guess they hate everybody then. He's coming!"

Halas looked up. There was the big man, standing over them. "Hello," he said.

"Hello," whispered Halas. Garek said nothing.

"My son and I would be honored if you would sup with us tonight. Would you join us in our quarters?" the big man asked. He sounded hopeful, almost nervous. Halas thought of the first time he had tried to kiss Cailin. He'd been so terrified, terrified that she would reject him, or laugh, or that she would accept him and he would be awful at it. The big man—Tormod—reminded Halas of that moment. Halas would not have taken the man for a timid one. "All three of you?"

"Sure, I suppose. Captain Brennus may not let us, though."

"Let me deal with Captain Brennus."

Garek laughed nervously, but Halas hit him to quiet him down. "We'll come with the food," he said. He had a hard time taking his eyes off the prince.

"Excellent! Come along now, Ennym." The boy reluctantly followed him back into the room.

Sub Chapter Five

A storm rocked them that day, tumultuous rain pummeling the ship like a rockslide, powerful gusts of wind blowing the craft side to side, back and forth. Nolan was on the deck. A cable snapped, zipping across the wood, taking the legs out from under a sailor. Nolan dove, grabbing the man by the wrists just before he could slide overboard.

The man thanked him in his own language. Nolan nodded in return. He staggered into his cabin, wiping a waterfall from his face.

"Raazoi? Are you all right?" he asked.

She was sound asleep, but he thought he heard her whispering something.

The storm continued to batter them. More cables snapped. Six men were lost to the river. Li-Sun himself went over the side, disappearing into the frothing waters beneath. As one, the men seemed to feel his death. They fell to their knees and wept, screamed and cursed to the heavens.

Every so often Nolan would go to check on Raazoi, yet still she slept. He worried for her safety, but her regular breathing and slight whispers told him that she was all right.

The weather lasted long into the night, finally clearing up just before dawn. Nolan wiped sweat and water from his brow, looking about. The deck was in shambles; crates and barrels overturned. What little livestock they had left was gone. Another four men were lost; no one had noticed them go in the panic and sorrow. They anchored.

Chapter Six

A New Arrangement

Halas and Garek brought Desmond and a tray of food to Prince Aeon's room. Halas balanced the tray on his hip as he reached up to knock on the door. Garek and Des stood resolutely behind him. He looked at them, at the tray, the door, and then back at them.

"Why am I the one doing all this?" he asked.

"What?" Des asked.

The big man let them in. The room made Halas miss his own back home. It had two beds, a table, and several chairs. The chairs were packed wall-to-wall around the table. Halas thought Tormod had had them brought in special. A single lantern hung on the far wall. "Please," the big man said, "have a seat." They did. Prince Aeon sat on one of the two beds.

"I am Tormod," said the big man, "and this is my son, Ennym. I'm glad you are well, Garek." He took a bite of the meat. Poor Desmond was doing his best with the *spódhla*, but it was still tough and hard to swallow. Tormod stopped talking, as if he were waiting for something. The three friends looked back and forth between each other. Finally, Desmond knelt. Halas and Garek followed his lead.

"My prince," Des said. "If there is anything that I may do for you, I shall. You have my service."

"I thought as much," said the prince. "Rise, you three. It would not do for us to be seen in this manner."

Desmond stood, looking embarrassed. Tormod directed them to the chairs. "Well," he said once they had each taken a seat, "thank you for not exposing us. Aside from the captain and first mate, no one else on this ship knows about my charge. I am his bodyguard, and it is very good to know that you are on our side."

"Who says we are?" asked Desmond. This time it was Tormod who smiled.

"Aside from the vow you just swore, and my saving your friend and *his* brother, you mean? The crew hates you almost as much as they hate us. I do sympathize; they were all looking forward to their leave before we commandeered the ship. Poor fellows." Prince Aeon grunted. "Anyways, the reason I asked you to join us this morning…"

"Tormod wants you here because he's worried one of these fools will try to hurt me, though I am more than capable of taking care of it myself. I am not a child, Tormod."

"It's showing," the bodyguard said. Garek choked back laughter. "But yes, he is right. It would not hurt to have three extra sets of eyes and ears on our side. In turn, you would stay in the guest's quarters right next door, instead of with the crew. The captain has also promised to lessen your custodial—cleaning—duties. What say you?"

"We'd be glad to," said Garek quickly.

"Excellent!"

"I do have one question, though," Halas said. "Why are you out here? You said you commandeered the ship. Why?"

"I am afraid that I cannot tell you," Tormod said. "Troublesome though that may be, it will have to remain a secret, even from friends. I do apologize."

"No worries," said Garek. They finished their meal and moved what few possessions they had up into their new room. There were four beds in this one, with a larger table and another lantern. The beds, unlike those the crew slept on, still maintained some semblance of softness and comfort, not to mention cleanliness. Halas slept very well that night.

———

The three friends spent a lot of time talking with Tormod. He was the Arms Master of the King, and had been for twenty-five years. Halas was amazed that the man was over fifty—he didn't even look thirty. He had traveled all over Aelborough, and told them fascinating tales about ghosts and goblins and hoards and treasure. But Halas' favorite was about the Shifters.

"Some say that the Shifters are the sentinels of Equilibrium, but I believe them to be men, like you and I," Tormod began. "But not. For the Shifters have the ability to shift their shape, to change into animals. No one knows how or why, or what dictates their changed form, but they know that there is a price. Each time the Shifters change, their human form warps, changes. They become uglier than anything else, even ogres and trolls. The longer they are in their animal form, the more hideous their human form will be."

"Then why do they change?" Desmond asked.

"If they do not, they are limited to the life-spans of normal humans. But, should they change, they extend their life to far beyond that. Many Shifters have been known to live for centuries.

"I once traveled with a group of Shifters, on the banks of the Inigo. They took the form of a pack of hyenas, wild dogs that used to live where the Burning Desert is now. No one has been to the Shifters' true home, but some suspect that it is in the desert itself. In any case, I only needed to travel with them for a few days, but two days into our journey, they robbed and abandoned me."

"What did you do?"

"Nothing. They proved impossible to track."

Prince Aeon snorted. "I could do it."

"Possibly." To Halas, he said, "Aeon here is a wonderful hunter."

———

Aside from the stories, Tormod was also improving their swordsman techniques. When he asked where they had learned what they knew already, Desmond responded, "You have your secrets, we have ours." Tormod was a better fighter than Halbrick, not much, but a little, and none of the three friends even came close to his skill.

"Do not be afraid to think during a fight. Not all victories come from physical prowess," Tormod told them one afternoon as they worked. Garek and Prince Aeon watched from the rail. "It is important to keep your wits about you, and not act on instinct alone. You must be mindful of your surroundings. Say, for instance, there is an icicle, or a chandelier above your head. Try to knock it down on your enemies. If the floor beneath them is flimsy, break it. If someone attacked us here on this ship, I would throw them overboard." He glanced almost imperceptibly at Garek, but Halas noticed. His stomach did a flip. "Using your surroundings can turn the tide of even the most difficult battles.

"It is crucial that you know your opponent, even moreso than the area around you. Know his moves, his rhythm. A truly difficult foe can only be defeated if you know him as well as you know yourself. You must be able to anticipate his every move.'

He and Halas sparred then, and Halas went nearly a full minute before being disarmed. He beamed. Tormod congratulated him with a warm pat on the back. "You did well, but know that there is no shame in flight. A very wise man once said, 'We fight so that we may win, we flee so that we may live, and we live so that we may fight.' Do not think it cowardice."

"Gallienne wrote those words, did he not?"

"You know of him?"

"I was taught several of his poems, though I could not recite any, I'm afraid. He was disgraced by King Robin IV, right, for chastising his decision on all of those beggars?"

"Where did you hear that?" Tormod asked, sounding angry. Halas did not wish to give up Conroy's name. He felt suddenly uneasy.

"My mentor."

Tormod's face softened. "I'm afraid you were misled, Halas. Gallienne was a plagiarist. He had been stealing his poetry from a regular performer in the riverside district. I am surprised your mentor did not know that."

Halas shrugged. "I suppose there are probably several accounts. You know how rumors get around."

"This is true." He smiled, all hint of his previous anger gone. "In any case, that should be the end of today's lessons. Come along, Ennym."

He led Aeon back to his cabin. Garek hopped off of the railing. Tormod's smile had made Halas feel safe, somehow. It radiated warmth. In fact, Halas was suddenly sure that he had mistaken something far more innocuous for anger. Perhaps Tormod had been irritated by an insect, or a brief change of wind. No sense in dwelling on it. "What did you two talk about?" Halas asked.

"Absolutely everything. The prince would not stop talking; I couldn't get a word in edgewise."

"Really?"

"No, I was being facetious. He's not a friendly person."

Halas smiled. They walked past Martarey, staring off into the distance, smoking a cigarette. It seemed everyone onboard the ship smoked, even more than Halbrick. "Storm's comin," he said. "Good luck stayin safe in yer warm and dry cabin."

It was enough to wipe the smile from Halas' face.

———

Even in their cabin they were cold and wet. The rain fell in sheets, and immense winds buffeted the ship. Water flowed under the door, soaking everything it could reach. Halas' feet were bare. The cool water on his toes felt amazing. Even still, he found himself pacing back and forth, nervous and anxious for the storm to pass. Des and Garek sat on their beds.

"How do you think it's going out there?" Garek asked.

"We're not sinking yet," Halas said. "At least, I don't think we are."

Garek nodded. "I spoke with Cloart this morning. He said that the boys will stand trial in a few days."

"Oh?"

Before Garek could speak further, there came a cry of, "Man overboard!"

Halas flung open the door and ran outside. Tormod was just ahead of him. The two ran to the railing, where more than a dozen sailors were gathered, including Captain Brennus. "Throw them a rope! Throw a damned rope!" he screamed. Garek and Des joined Halas, but they did not get closer to the railing. With sailors slipping and sliding all around them, it was amazing that Tormod managed to keep his feet. Halas himself was barely moving. Everyone seemed to approach the rail with some apprehension. Balance was precarious at best, and no one else wanted to go overboard.

"Who fell? *Who fell?*" someone was screaming. "Boyd! Boyd went over!" another voice called. "I'm here!" shouted Boyd. "It was Steph that went in!" One of the sailors stumbled into Halas. Both went to their knees. The man was gone before Halas could see who it was.

Tormod looked around before picking a heavy rope and tying it to the rail. He took several more and began looping them around his arms and legs. One went about his chest. He tied this one tight.

"Hold on to these!" he shouted to the crew. Clutching the one at the rail, he disappeared into the water.

"Tormod!" Prince Aeon cried, rushing forward. Already the rope Halas held was sliding toward the edge of the ship. He wrapped it around his hand, trying to hold on despite the burning pain it caused him. Looking around, he could see many of the others doing the same.

Then Garek fell.

Halas dropped his line and dove for his brother. Just as Garek went under the rail, Halas grabbed his wrist, digging in with his fingernails. His heart was racing. He felt strong hands on him, holding on to his back and arms, but he himself could not hold on much longer—the rain made things slick, and Garek was very, very heavy. Halas held him by the fingertips. Sacrificing his own hold on the rail, he took Garek's wrist with both hands and pulled, sliding forward until only half of him was on the ship.

Garek's feet kicked wildly beneath him, desperate for a place to stand. They scraped against the hull of the ship, but to no avail. Halas couldn't pull him up. Tormod would have been able to, but Tormod was somewhere under the waves. Halas stared at the roiling waters and was enraptured.

It all seemed so familiar. His mind was yanked back to the day he and Desmond had first entered Jim's Forest, searching for Halbrick. The river there had tried to kill Halas, normally a silly assumption, but true all the same. He had tried to cross it, and it had swallowed him. These waters now, they wanted to do the same. Swirling black waves splashed against the ship's hull, and every crash was accompanied by a cry of blood lust. The Inigo River sent tributaries all through the realm, and one of these went into the forest just outside Cordalis. The water wanted him.

He tore his gaze away, looked behind him and called for help. Desmond lay on Halas' back, his arms wrapped around his chest, a cable tied around his left arm. If Garek was going over, Halas was going over, and he suspected Desmond would go right after them. And they were slipping. The Inigo wanted him, and it was probably going to get him. After that, he did not know.

"Desmond!" Halas screamed. "Let go of me! Garek! GRAB GAREK!"

Desmond couldn't hear. Halas adjusted his grip. Garek would not stop thrashing, making it nearly impossible for Halas to even retain his hold, much less lift his brother up. His arms had caught a fire that even the downpour could not extinguish. Much more of this and he felt they would pop right off like dead branches.

Halas coughed, spewing water. He had to accept it. Garek was going to fall.

He couldn't allow that. Thinking those words—*Garek is going to fall*—caused him to do…something, granted him a strength he didn't know he possessed. Halas gritted his teeth and pulled. Garek rose away from the water, toward the deck. He wasn't going to die today, or ever. Not when Halas was around to stop it. Halas got to one knee, hauling his brother up over the side. Desmond grabbed Garek's shoulders, and together, the two pulled him away from the rail and stumbled toward the cabin.

The other sailors held their ropes tightly, but everything was a mess. None of the men could keep their feet. Only Captain Brennus seemed impervious to the harsh wind and slick rain. The brave captain stood at the edge, one foot perched up against the rail, holding a line as if he were reeling in a heavy fish; a statue against the tides. Other sailors looked on helplessly, unable to abandon their duties else the whole ship perish.

"*PULL HIM UP!*" Captain Brennus cried, and began steadily marching backwards. Halas left Garek and Des to pick up the slack between Aeon and another sailor. Other men moved in, taking the ropes nearer to Tormod and the men who had gone into the water, everyone heaving as one. Eventually, a man appeared over the side, followed closely by a second, and then Tormod, carrying the third over his shoulders. The sailors dropped the cables, hurrying forward to carry the four away from the side.

"Are you all right?" someone asked Tormod, the only conscious one of the four. He nodded, gasping for air. Everyone was soaked from head to toe, but Tormod seemed none the worse for wear. Halas repeated the question to his brother. Garek was on his back, eyes closed, but he murmured a very quiet yes.

"Let's get these men below," said Captain Brennus. "You'll be all right?" he asked Tormod.

"I will."

The sailors carried the three unconscious men down below, and Tormod walked on his own back to his cabin, carrying Garek. Halas and Desmond hurried along behind. Tormod laid Garek on a bed, and then sat at the edge. Aeon wrapped his arms around his neck. "I was so worried you'd be hurt," he said.

"It's all right," Tormod said, "I'm all right."

———

"Your shoulder is dislocated," Halas heard Tormod say. He opened his eyes. Garek and Prince Aeon sat on one bed, Tormod and Desmond on the other. Des was quite obviously in pain, lying on his back, breathing heavily. He had a large burn around his elbow. "This is going to hurt. Here, bite down for the pain."

Halas looked himself over. He was still very wet—they all were—though it had obviously been some time since he'd fallen asleep. His feet were torn in places, and he had a burn like Desmond's on his hand. Garek was covered in bruises, as was Tormod, though Tormod did not seem to notice his. He took hold of Desmond's arm. Halas looked at his friend—there was a length of rope in his mouth.

"What are you doing?" he asked, startling Garek.

"Halas!" his brother said, "are you all right?"

"I'm fine." He was on the floor, against the wall. He stood up, the pain in his feet flared, and he quickly sat down again. "Maybe not. What are you doing to Des?"

"He's dislocated his shoulder. I have to put it back in place."

"What does that mean?"

"His arm is out of alignment. Garek, hold him down. Desmond, try not to move." Desmond's eyes were wide, and Garek tried to avoid his gaze when he pressed him to the bed. "I'm going to count to three," he said. "One…two… three!" Tormod jerked Desmond's arm forward. Halas heard a loud snap. Desmond screamed briefly, bucked in Garek's grip, and passed out.

"He'll be fine," Tormod said. "And he'll have a new trick to show off. I think Desmond would like that. Let me get a look at you, Halas." With Tormod and Garek's help, Halas hobbled to the bed and put his feet up. Tormod knelt by them, looking closely. He went to his chest and withdrew a rag and some bandages, along with a vial of a thin, watery liquid. "Drink this," he said, and began to dab the cloth at Halas' feet. Halas popped the stopper off the vial and sniffed. It smelled awful. "Drink it. It's medicine," Tormod said again.

Halas downed it in one go. It tasted funny; not at all like whiskey, as Garek thought it to be.

"What's it do?"

"You'll heal faster."

"Oh."

"Let me see your arm."

Halas looked first, and he realized that there was a long cut there, bleeding into his tunic. He pulled the shirt off, and Tormod examined the wound. He whistled. "That's a big splinter," Garek whispered. Tormod reached into the cut, but Halas didn't feel a thing. The pain was there, he realized, but it was distant—worlds away, in fact. Tormod's hand came free, covered in blood and holding a splinter that was several inches long. Halas looked at the cut again. It spanned from his wrist to his elbow. He blinked, then echoed Tormod's whistle, then laughed.

"That is a really big splinter!" he said through laughter. Tormod cleaned and bandaged the wound. As he wrapped it, Halas pressed his head back against the wall, looking at Garek out of the top corners of his eyes. "Hello. Hell… lloo." Blinking rapidly, he looked at Tormod. His vision was fading; the big man appeared blurry. "Wha's so big about 'chou? Wanna make…want cold to…hungry…me yeah…oh…"

———

When he opened his eyes, he was aware of the stinging in his arm and feet, though it still felt very far away. He was in his bed, looking up at the ceiling. Drool puddled at the corner of his mouth. "Tormod said it's a normal reaction," Desmond said. Halas looked up; his friend sat in a chair beside the bed. Halas saw two Desmonds for a moment before they came together. His head swam.

"What happened at Garek?" he blurted.

"He's asleep," Desmond said.

"Good. Sleepy Garek." He giggled, suddenly finding that thought enormously funny.

"How are you feeling?"

"Dunno. Little…little hungry, I think. Yeah, hungry. There's food?"

"Tormod said he would bring some sandwiches in a bit. He was just in here."

"Oh. He's real nice."

"Yeah, he is."

"I'm going to need a lot of water. Real thirsty. How's your arm?"

"Pain went away almost immediately." Desmond raised the arm above his head and spun it in a little circle. "See?"

Halas tried to follow the motion, but found it made him sick. He clamped his eyes shut.

Tormod shook him awake, and he looked around. Garek dozed in the bed next to him, Desmond across the aisle. "How are you?" Tormod asked. Halas felt like he'd been set on fire multiple times before being brutally stamped out. He groaned in response. "I brought food and water. Figured you could use some."

Halas sat up. His mind swam about in his skull, making his thoughts sluggish and painful. "Thank you," he said. "How is Garek? Desmond?"

"They'll be fine."

"Good." Halas reached over and devoured the two sandwiches, draining almost the entire pitcher of water. Tormod waited until he was finished before speaking.

"I thought I would check your bandages. Your injuries should be mostly healed by now. What I gave you works wonders."

"What was it?"

"Something very special," Tormod mused. He unwrapped Halas' arm and feet, looking them over. Apparently satisfied, he crumpled up the wrappings and tossed them into the bin. "You'll have some scars and some pain, but aside from that, everything looks just fine."

"Thank you," Halas said again, lying back on the bed. "Where is the prince?"

"He is in our cabin, sleeping. It is almost morning; the storm passed a few hours ago."

"And the men? Those who went overboard?"

"They are fine as well, and also resting. I have to say, you really gained some credit with Brennus; you and Desmond were the only two to seriously injure themselves trying to bring up his men. He is impressed. He came by once during the night, but you were both asleep."

"I suppose I should be happy, then." He felt guilty; it had been Garek they had injured themselves for. He hadn't the heart to say otherwise.

Tormod smiled wistfully. It was like he knew. *But he can't know, it's impossible. Wasn't he in the river for everything?* "I suppose so. Do you need anything else?"

"No, thank you, I'll be all right. I think I might like to walk around a bit."

He was still wet when he left the cabin, struggling to fit into his boots. The ship was surprisingly clean, with no significant damage to speak of. Halas picked up a handful of weeds and tossed them over the side. Martarey stood nearby, rubbing his face and looking off toward the horizon. Halas nodded in greeting.

"How's yer arm?" Martarey asked.

"It hurts, a little. You all right?"

"Yeah. Nearly drowned last night, down in the hold. We had to patch the hull in several places with hot tar and swollen rope. My bones are stiff. I tell you, I ain't never see a storm quite like that, not in all my years. It's bad fortune."

Halas nodded again. It was rather awkward, but he wasn't going to be the first to walk away. Martarey relieved him, limping toward some of the men. Halas leaned on the rail, looking off into the now calm waters. Prince Aeon was next to him when he turned. Halas jumped.

"My apologies," the prince said. "I did not mean to sneak up on you."

"No worries."

It was a while before the prince said anything. Then, "Thank you...for helping save Tormod. I do not know what I would do without him. He is as a father to me, you know."

"What of your own father?" Halas blurted.

Prince Aeon shook his head. "He was not often around."

"And your mother? What of the queen?"

"Nor was she. I have not seen my mother in almost three years."

"I'm sorry," Halas said.

"Do not be. My father said that she would try to hurt me; it is why he sent me away. I told him that I would sneak off in the night, but he told Tormod to take me, and Tormod booked passage on this ship. Even my father does not know of my whereabouts. Both of them are worried that my mother's men will come after me. I do not know why; I do not think she would do such a thing. She is my mother." He shook his head again. "No more about me. Tell me about you. Who are your parents?"

"My mother died when I was a child. My father is Halbrick Duer." Prince Aeon cocked his head to the side. "Is something wrong?"

"I know that name, though I do not know from where. Who is he?"

That is a very good question, Halas thought. "A farmer. My family owns a quarter-farm. Potatoes."

"Oh. Perhaps I was mistaken, then."

"Perhaps." Neither one thought so.

———

Things were better. Word traveled fast on *The Wandering Blade,* and when the sailors heard that two of the draftees had been injured while trying to bring their comrades to safety, the men softened. Not a lot, but enough. Halas no longer had to watch his footing around the crew. He no longer felt their spit, no longer was pushed. No one tampered with his food. Only six members of the crew felt any continued hostility toward the three friends, and those were Absolon's best boys. None of the draftees had ever learned their names, and the boys were certainly not forthcoming with any information. In light of the upcoming trial, the boys had been set free from the ship's brig to sort out their defense. Whenever Halas saw one, the boy would scowl and glare until one or the other passed out of eyesight. It became a battle of wills, a question of who would back down first. Halas had no intention of losing that battle. Their trial was brief. Brennus held it on the deck at noon, three days after the storm.

Brennus stood at the captain's wheel, his back to it. *The Wandering Blade* was anchored. Every man in the crew stood on deck. Beside Brennus were four others: Cloart, Flanagan, Absolon, and another sailor whose name Halas didn't know. They were to be the judges. Between them and the crowd sat six of Absolon's best boys. He had ten. The four who had not involved themselves in the violence sat off to the side, watching nervously. Garek and Tormod sat with the boys. Halas stood at the head of the crowd, Desmond on his left and Aeon on his right. Everyone wore his full uniform. Tormod and Aeon had no uniforms, so they were dressed in a drab grey.

"Let it be known," said Brennus, "that Garek Duer and Tormod Farn are not on trial. This is the trial of six crewmen. They are the best boys of Absolon Bayard, Head Chef to *The Wandering Blade*. The names of the defendants are as follows: Bartholomew Hadric, Hector Solem, Ferris Solem, Daniel Alfred, Kayne Rom, and Olan Rom."

Halas did a double take at the final name. He glanced at the boy in question, wondering if it had been Olan all along, following his friends in secret. But no, it wasn't him. That didn't make sense, in any case. Why would Olan attack Garek?

"The charge of this trial is grievous assault of a crewman. Boys, do you understand the charge?"

Murmured agreements. Brennus continued. "Good. Because you serve so closely under Chef Absolon, my first act of this trial will be to dismiss him from the court. Absolon, do you agree?"

"I agree," said Absolon. "Though it pains me to do so. Go easy, Brennus?"

"Step down, please," Brennus said. Absolon nodded and took his place in the crowd. "In his stead, I appoint Crewman Pullman Knox to the court. Crewman Knox, do you accept?"

"I do," said a man in the crowd.

"Come join us, please."

The man made his way to the head of the crowd and moved to Brennus' side.

"Let's begin. Garek Duer, please address the court."

Garek rose and approached. He stopped at the bottom of the stairs. "Sir. Captain."

"Garek Duer, please give your account of the event."

"Gladly. Someone made…a mess…on the aft deck, behind the passenger cabins. I went to clean it. I was alone. These six jumped me. They said they didn't like me because I was a draftee. They said that if I cried out, they would throw me over the side. So it took me a while to cry out."

Halas stiffened at his brother's account of things. He felt so helpless about the whole situation. If only he'd known, he would have been able to help Garek. Garek was decent with his fists, and Halas was even better. Between the two of them, they could have easily handled Absolon's boys.

"They hit me for a while," Garek continued. He stared holes in his boots. "One of them did. I thought, uh, that I was going to die. I got so angry with them. I felt so humiliated. Then Tormod came, and I guess he worked them over like they had me."

"I see. Thank you, Garek. You may be seated. Tormod, please address the court."

Garek took his place. Tormod offered him a reassuring smile as he approached the stairs.

"Tormod Farn, were these the boys you found assaulting Garek Duer?"

Tormod nodded. "They were. Kayne and Olan Rom were on lookout. The Solem boys held Garek's arms. Daniel Alfred had him by the hair, keeping his face exposed. Bartholomew did the hitting."

"And what did you do when you saw this event transpiring?"

"I stopped it."

"How did you stop it?"

"Violently. The Roms were closest, and in my way. I dealt with them quickly. The Solems, too. They dropped Garek and tried to attack me. Their mistake. Bartholomew Hadric went last."

"Do you think your behavior was a little extreme, Tormod?"

"Not at all. I have no tolerance for those who torment and brutalize the helpless. You're a man of honor, Captain. If you had seen what I did, you surely would have done the same."

"Did anything else of note happen, Tormod?"

"No. I carried Garek to the infirmary and some of the crew helped the boys."

"Very well. You may be seated."

Tormod went back to his seat. Halas tried to catch his eyes, but could not. Garek refused to look up.

"I think it is fairly clear what happened here. Does the court agree?"

"Aye," said Cloart.

"Aye," said Flanagan.

"Aye," said Knox.

"Aye," said the final officer.

"Very well. Boys, stand and approach the court. You've been tried with the grievous assault of a crew member, and convicted of this charge. Normally, the penance for such a charge is lashings…"

"No!" Bartholomew wailed. "You're only siding with him because he helped pull some men up from the storm! He's not even part of the crew! You didn't even listen to our side of the story! That's *unfair!*" His voice cracked and wavered with each word.

"*Be quiet!*" Brennus commanded. The boy ceased his whining at once. "I would hardly call six on one a fair fight either, or even four on one. As for your little tantrum, I'll ignore it. As I was saying, the normal sentence is fifteen lashings, but I must take your age into account. You will not receive the whip, but I will double your shifts and lower your allotted rations from three meals a day to two. When we reach Earlsfort, we will be in port for fourteen days. You will spend those days in the city jail. When we depart the city, you will be back on standard duty. Your pay will be docked by half. Does that seem *fair* to you?"

Bartholomew hung his head. The other boys said nothing. Bartholomew whispered, "Yes sir."

And so they traveled down the Inigo River.

———

The sun smiled on them, and there were no more storms. Rain fell gently on occasion, but at nothing more than a drizzle. The winds were warm and relaxing. Brennus announced that they had reached a more easterly vantage, and were at the halfway point in their route.

With less time spent worrying about the crew, Halas' thoughts turned more and more to home. Halbrick. Conroy. Cailin.

The forest.

As much as he pondered over the forest, no answers occurred to him. *Father is probably in there right now.* Halas felt a sharp pang of worry settle into his gut. He wondered what could drive a man into such darkness. All his life, Halas' father had always moved with a sense of purpose, and Halas assumed it was this purpose that kept him on the wrong side of the Treeline. But what purpose? What possible reason could Halbrick have for going into such a dangerous place, and going alone, nonetheless?

Nothing sprang to the forefront of his mind. Conroy was involved. Halas thought of the man's gracious offer to take Halbrick in over the winter, and he knew it was a lie. Halbrick likely hadn't left the forest, if even he was still alive.

A true puzzle, and Halas had never been one for puzzles, especially ones with so very many pieces. How did everything fit together? The draft? The mysterious letters Conroy had tried to decipher? Were those connected? Halas wanted to believe that the draft was just that—a draft, but he could not. Conroy himself had said it was a rarely used practice, and for obvious reasons. Really, what were the chances of it happening just as Halas was getting what Halbrick may have deemed 'too involved?'

Thinking never led Halas down any pleasant roads. He swore, swatting his forehead and resting his palm there. Conroy was a friend, and his father was, well, his father. Neither would send Halas away in such a crude manner.

Or would they? Halbrick had behaved similarly before. Halas remembered when he was a boy of only seven or eight, and Halbrick had decided he was ready to learn to use a bow. Garek had wanted to try as well, but he was too young. He very well may have just shot himself, rather than the straw man Halbrick had erected in the yard. He denied the boy, but Garek persisted, until eventually Halbrick sent him into Cordalis with several detricots and some friends. Halas' father often sent his boys on errands when he thought they needed to be clear of the farm for one reason or anther. Perhaps this was simply a more extreme scenario. And then there was Conroy, who shunned Halas so totally when Halbrick had first gone missing.

He supposed there were really two options. Option one: Halbrick and Conroy decided Halas was becoming a bother and needed him out of the way. Option two: they thought he might be in danger. Nothing in their behavior throughout Halas' life gave him any reason to suspect the former, but his own imagination claimed that idea as the most likely and simply ran with it, logic be damned. Halas spent many sleepless nights pondering that particular gem, but as much as he thought about his father, Cailin dominated his mind twice as often. He'd sit at the rail as the sun fell, watching it, wishing she were in his arms. He imagined her to be at their knoll, curled up against a stump and watching with him. The idea gave him comfort; she'd not forgotten their love.

He supposed that was the root of his problem with being away from her: that she might drift away. His heart burned with a want, a need for her touch, but he also thought that maybe, just maybe, she would find someone else. Memory of Halas would fade, and then some other boy would wander along and sweep her off her feet. Perhaps even one of Halas' friends: Gale, or Olan, or Rufus. Cailin was beautiful and amazing; she would certainly never hurt for suitors.

No hurt that Halas had suffered so far compared to that thought. Cailin, who Halas loved and cherished above all else, may very well forget about him. More than that, she would forget about him and make off with someone else.

That's not to say he didn't trust her; he did, more even than he loved her. But who was to say what was happening in Cordalis? As the days went on and *The Wandering Blade* sailed along, these thoughts became more and more graphic in their detail. Visions of Cailin waiting patiently at their knoll turned to much darker fantasies. He saw her with Olan—more often than not it was Olan—lying in the grass, two sweat-covered bodies rolling about. Her legs wrapped around his, his hands in her hair, their lips entwined, their bodies writhing in pleasure. Halas did all he could to quell these visages, but it was no use. He may as well have tried to stop the wind from blowing.

Cailin had very nearly come of age. If Halas' estimation of the date was correct, there were but thirteen days until her twentieth birthday. Anything could happen. Her mother could take up match making, or her boorish father could take the more direct route and sell her outright. Why not? He was more monster than man, it seemed, more than capable of selling his own daughter for pennies. Halas envisioned Cailin being carted off to a rich family somewhere in the hills. He would return to Cordalis and she would simply be gone.

Nothing more to it. And there was nothing Halas could do.

Four months.

The days continued as normal. Halas went about his daily routine with a growing disgust. He despised farming for the very reason he despised being on the ship: monotony. Each day he would rise, wake Garek (Des was already at work in the kitchen), and go down to the galley for breakfast. It was his meals that differed the most each morning; one meal he would be served eggs, the next it was oatmeal. Mostly it was oatmeal; if they had more of anything than *spódhla*, it was oatmeal, whole barrels of the stuff. The eggs were a rare occasion, as *The Wandering Blade* was down to just five hens.

After breakfast Halas set to work cleaning (swabbing, the sailors called it) the deck. Sometimes he whistled as he worked, though with each day this lessened. After swabbing it was time to clean the kitchen, which he'd finish doing just in time for lunch. Lunch was *spódhla*.

He loved his afternoons as he hated his mornings. After lunch, Halas, officially off duty, would visit Tormod and Prince Aeon. Garek and Des would accompany him more often than not. Aeon smiled more and more around the three draftees, and soon they were chatting like old friends. Prince Aeon told Halas of life in the palace, fencing and riding and hunting game. He was a very adept hunter, he'd tell Halas, and Halas could listen eagerly to these stories all afternoon. Each word was a new adventure, better than the books because Aeon's stories were *real*. The prince did not often leave the castle and had no siblings, so he was kept entertained by his governess, Tessa, whom he'd been with since the crib. Halas wished he had had a governess; Aeon's sounded like a very fun woman. When Aeon was a baby, she would put him on her shoulders and run around his bedroom, laughing and making horse noises. Aeon confided in Halas that he missed Tessa more than anything.

In turn, Halas would talk with Aeon about the joys and pleasures of farming. He tried to embellish these tales, to make them more interesting than they were. Aeon smiled politely and nodded with each telling. After nearly a week of this, Halas burst into laughter.

"What's the matter?" Aeon inquired.

"Perhaps we should stick to your stories, my lord. I fear mine are very dull."

"No, that's not…"

Halas waved his protests away. "I see it in your eyes, Prince Aeon. You are uninterested. It's all right; I hate it as well. You have your lances, I have my potatoes."

Aeon laughed. "Very well then. Let me tell you of the time I first attended my father's court."

They traveled down the river for several weeks unmolested. A few times Halas could actually see land, in the form of towering cliffs, miles and miles away. Halas learned to welcome these sights, however faint they might be. He yearned for land more than he yearned for Cailin or his father. To be able to set his feet on solid ground would be to make everything right in his life. He wanted the world to be steady. On the ship, everything rocked gently to and fro, back and forth, left to right. It was constant, and occasionally still made Halas' stomach churn. Garek was often sick, and it earned him only scorn from the crew.

On one of these occasions, Halas stood behind him, patting his back. Garek leaned over the side. The ship heaved from side to side in a harsh gale. It wasn't nearly equal to the storm of their second month, but it certainly was no romp. The rain battered their backs and the wind made sure footing impossible. Halas clutched the rail tightly with one hand as he comforted Garek with the other. His mop was clenched firmly in his armpit. He decided that using the tool would be fruitless this day.

Captain Brennus approached. "Captain on deck!" someone yelled, and everyone currently unoccupied turned to face him. Brennus waved his hand appreciatively.

"I have good news!" the captain said. "We are well on our way to the end of November, and if my calculations are correct, that puts us at Earlsfort within this next fortnight." At this, the men cheered, Halas and Garek not least among them. Halas realized just how much he needed to set foot on dry land. He needed off the ship. Two weeks seemed like an eternity, but he would have to bear it. He smiled at Garek.

"Hear that, Gare? Just a fortnight."

Garek grinned, but it was a sad grin. "Yes. Two weeks."

He leaned over and was sick again. Halas breathed a single laugh and went back to his patting.

———

Desmond's reaction to the news was a happy one. "That's great!" he yelled, pumping his fist into the air triumphantly. "I cannot wait until we are in Earlsfort. I hear the place is bigger than Cordalis! Imagine all we can do there."

"I can imagine," Garek moaned. Des was perched on the edge of Halas' bunk. Garek sprawled on his own, a pillow over his face. Halas occupied the room's single chair.

"I think I may actually kiss the dirt," Halas said.

Des scrunched up his face in a look of amusement. "We've been on this boat three months, Hal."

"You mean to say you aren't excited?"

"Oh, I'm certainly excited. This place is boring. I was hoping for something of the sea serpent variety, perhaps a dragon or two. Storm was nice, though." He swept his hand over the scar on Halas' arm for emphasis. Halas rolled his eyes.

"You're here for the wrong reasons, Des."

"Fun is never wrong, Halas. Never." His tone was so somber and serious, his expression so straight and stern, that Halas laughed until tears ran down his cheeks.

———

The rain poured continuously for nearly four days before ending just as suddenly as it began. There was no gradual runoff, no lessening. One second it rained, the next the sky was clear. Halas marveled at the sun; it felt good against his skin. Warm.

Some of the men stripped down, lavishing in the heat. Halas peeled off his shirt. It was soaked with rainwater. He slung it over one shoulder and closed his eyes, taking everything in.

Suddenly, he wanted to be with Cailin more than anything in the world. The rain had been miserable, and now it was gone. The voyage had been miserable, but now it was almost at an end (Halas forcibly omitted the fact that they were only to be in Earlsfort for two weeks). The sun was out, he was drying off, and life was good. The only thing missing was Cailin, and her absence put a hole in his heart bigger than he knew. His chest tightened and his legs felt faint. He wanted her so badly, to feel her skin, smell her hair. Halas sat down on the deck and looked at the sky.

"Oh, Cailin," he whispered. He held a hand up to shield his eyes, and imagined that somewhere, possibly on their knoll, she was doing the same thing.

For the rest of the voyage, Cailin never ceased to occupy his thoughts. She danced through his mind throughout the day. As he cleaned, she cleaned with him. He did not, could not, listen to Aeon or Tormod as they told tales that normally kept his rapt attention. He never even wondered about his father and the forest. Nothing except Cailin.

So when Halas first heard the 'land ho' from the crow's nest, he was roused from his daydream. He rushed to the rail but could not see much, only a black speck on the horizon.

Nevertheless, it filled him with hope. They'd reached a major milestone in their journey, and it was now almost halfway done.

"In another few hours we'll be at Earlsfort!" Captain Brennus cried, and several of the men hooted a response, stomping on the deck and cheering. Halas cheered right along with them; he couldn't wait to set foot on dry land. He'd had enough of boats to last a lifetime. He went back to the cabin to tell Garek and Des the news. They were as happy as he was, Garek jumping into the air and laughing.

They went back on deck, all three suddenly impatient, wanting their leave to begin. Though it was only two weeks, setting foot on land was going to be wonderful. Halas couldn't stop smiling. "Wait!" the man called from the crow's nest. "There are ships behind us, closing fast!"

"What?" Captain Brennus walked to the aft of the ship, lifting his spyglass. "They hold the banner of Queen Anaua, and a strange serpent I do not recognize."

Beside Halas, Prince Aeon whispered, "Oh, no." Tormod hurried to the captain. "We must flee," he said.

"What? Flee? From the queen? That's absurd!"

"Yes, Captain, it is, but we must." He was whispering now, so the others could not hear. "The boy I have with me is in mortal danger."

"I told you you'd bring this down upon me! I'll have you skinned, you rotten bastard!"

"Calm yourself! If we make Earlsfort before those men catch us, the boy and I will leave your ship and never return. We'll be out of your business forever, and you may do whatever you like."

"Do not tell me what I can and cannot do on my rutting ship!"

"Captain, please. We have to run. We must. If those ships catch us they will do unspeakable things to your crew and to your ship. If you allow them to catch up, they atrocities committed would be on *your* hands, not mine."

Captain Brennus glowered, but he was stuck. "Fine," he said through gritted teeth. "Full sails, boys! We run! Everyone into your uniforms! Any man not on duty should arm himself." He spun to face Tormod. "It will be nightfall before we reach Earlsfort, even going full speed. They may very well be upon us by then."

"Then we'd best be ready to fight."

———

Halas had his father's sword; Garek had the plain iron broadsword; Desmond had a small hand axe. They stood in the belly of the ship, watching as the sailors who were unarmed proceeded in a line to the armory, taking a sword here and a spear there. Everyone aboard wore their silver uniforms, though many only wore one piece of it. Halas followed his friends up to the deck. Tormod stood stoically at the rail, watching the fast-approaching ships. "They will be here shortly," he said. He hefted his enormous sword. "I want one of you to wait by Aeon's door, guard it. I will do my best to be nearby, though I may not be able to. The other two stay inside with Aeon. Who will be out?"

"I will," Halas said, before the others had a chance to volunteer. His stomach immediately went cold, and he felt it travel up his gullet until it perched just under his throat. His chest clamped shut, trapping it there. Tormod clapped him on the back.

"Right then. Des, Garek, get inside."

Desmond put a hand on Aeon's arm, but the prince stiffened in place. "I can fight!" he said.

"I know you can," Tormod said. He knelt in front of the boy and put a hand on his shoulder. "You're good with a blade, and even better without, but we both have our duties, Aeon. Protecting you, keeping you safe, is mine. We're near enough to Earlsfort that we may dock before all of this is over. If victory is in any way uncertain, you have to promise me you will get clear of this ship."

"Tormod, do not say that. Everything will be all right."

Tormod nodded. "It will be. But if it *isn't*, you get off this ship and disappear. Promise me."

Aeon looked like he wanted to argue. For a moment, he appeared to be two people: one, the noble prince who would risk anything for his subjects, and two, a scared little boy. Halas felt very uncomfortable watching the prince's face. "I promise," Aeon finally said.

"Thank you. Now get inside. Halas, stay close."

When the door was securely fastened, Tormod set about helping the sailors mount a shield wall on the rail. Halas waited by the cabins. Tormod never went far, helping the sailors with their weapons or those few that had it with their armor, a strap here, a buckle there. Halas could see the ships now. There were four of them, rapidly gaining on *The Wandering Blade*. Martarey and two other sailors manned a nearby ballista, and were already taking aim.

"Do not give an inch! They will not take this ship; they will not have our home!" Captain Brennus cried. He wore his full uniform, with a silver hat and cape that identified him as captain, and walked up and down the deck, touching or consoling his men where it was needed. *He's a good man,* Halas thought.

Making sure that Prince Aeon's door was locked, Halas turned to face the approaching ships. They were close enough now that he could clearly make out the ravens on each banner. A whole host of them, it seemed. *They may as well be an armada,* he realized. He didn't want to be in a battle. The thought of it terrified him, made him ill. The day's food was ready and waiting in his throat. He choked it down. Was the prince's door locked? Halas checked again and found that it was. What were battles like, anyway? He imagined them from the stories to be orderly things, where lines of men charged at each other in neat little rows and killed each other in neat little rows.

Facing the prospect now, he knew it would be far more tumultuous than that. Sure, there might be neat rows at the start, but how could chaos not ensue from such a thing? Upwards of a hundred men, running to and fro, hacking each other to pieces, fighting for their lives. Their friends.

It nagged at him now that Aeon's door may not be locked. Halas turned back to jiggle the handle.

What if he himself was forced to take a life? Could he do it? Did he have it in him? There had been people he'd said he wanted dead, but had he meant it? Nolan Dooley. Absolon's best boys. Garek, a time or two. Death was the ultimate end to everything. All thoughts of any sort of afterlife left him then, standing beside Tormod on the deck of *The Wandering Blade*. There would be no paradise, no White, no Inferno. Just blackness. Endless, empty blackness.

Aeon's door was securely locked. Halas was almost certainly going to die here. Only looking at the tower of a man that stood beside him stilled such thoughts.

At least Tormod was here.

————

The sun set and the world was red, the water the color of blood. The queen's ships were almost upon them, almost within range for the ballistae. Sailors were running up and down the line with buckets of water, ready to douse any fires that would be set upon them. "Prepare arrows!" Captain Brennus shouted. All down the line, archers stepped forward, placing their bows between the notches in the shield wall. "Loose the ballistae!"

Only two of the ship's ballistae faced the oncoming attackers. The tips of their arrows were wrapped in canvas and carefully doused with oil. After this was done, the canvas was set aflame, and two giant missiles sprang forth from *The Wandering Blade*, only to splash harmlessly into the river. Halas' heart sank, but it didn't seem to faze Brennus. "Load!" the captain yelled. "Loose!" One hit home this time, dragging across the side of an enemy boat, leaving a trail of fire in its wake. Immediately, the men began pulling at the crank, resetting the ballista. They loaded it, Brennus gave the cry, and then they did it all over again. Moments later, the scorpions let fly.

Queen Anaua's ships were closing. Halas could see the banners now, and that peculiar black serpent. There were at least five ships representing each. The largest of these was pulling away from the rest. A woman's voice shouted from the deck. *"Captain Brennus! My name is Raazoi! You have what I want! Give us the boy, and none of your people shall come to harm!"*

Halas felt confused. The ship was close, yes, but still an impossible distance for voices to travel. Brennus stood nearby, gripping a cane tightly in his hand. Its head was silver and heavy. Halas thought the cane concealed a sword. He recognized the type of weapon from Conroy's museum. Standing nervously beside him, Cloart whispered something. The captain shook his head, raised his hands to cup his lips and called back. *"Not a chance! You shall not have him!"*

The woman, Raazoi, did not respond. Instead, a massive bolt shot across the water, skimming the surface and splashing down just yards from *The Wandering Blade*. Halas jumped. "Loose! Martarey, strike them down!" the captain screamed, and the *Blade* returned fire.

"Sink the bastards!" Flanagan yelled. Several of the men echoed this cry. Halas looked around. He did not see Cloart.

Arrows began to shower the deck. "Loose arrows! Loose at will!" Brennus cried, and the sailors shot back. A ballista round scored the deck near Halas with a tremendous *crunch*, and he nearly threw himself down to be at the mercy of the queen's men.

It certainly didn't sound like a bad idea.

No, he thought. *Don't do that. Stay and fight. Stay and fight!*

An arrow whizzed past his head, embedding itself in the prince's door with a heavy *thunk*. Halas turned to stare at it, perplexed. It quivered in the wood. He reached out to touch it. Nothing seemed real. The arrow was a mirage, surely. Halas was at home, sleeping. Dreaming. Yes, this was all a dream. He smiled.

Tormod ruined everything, grabbing Halas by the shoulder and shouting his name, snapping him from his reverie. *Well, shit*, Halas thought.

He drew his sword. The ships were close now; two were circling around to the front. Halas didn't know what to do. "Do not let them board!" Brennus screamed. On the closest galley, Halas could see men on the masts, holding ropes, ready to swing. They landed on the deck of the *Blade*, behind the line. Sailors turned about to fight them. Halas shrank backwards, pressing himself to Prince Aeon's door. The arrow fletching scratched at his ear, but he ignored it.

They were laying down boarding planks now. Tormod grabbed one by the lip and pushed. "Help me!" he yelled. Halas thought Tormod was talking to him, but his legs refused to cooperate. Luckily, Brennus was there. He rushed to Tormod's side, and together the two pushed it into the water, along with the soldiers who were attempting to cross. Halas could hear them screaming as they floundered in the water, and that gave him hope. Every little bit counted, right?

But there were so many. A soldier jumped down next to Tormod, only to have his head crushed. Tormod lunged for that gangplank, pushing it into the water. More soldiers poured on to the *Blade*. They wore jet black chainmail. Gustava limped away from the fight, a bloody arrow in his side. Tormod pushed him aside, swinging his sword to keep the soldiers at bay while the sailor moved further from the battle, cutting down a man who landed near him.

A soldier came around the back of the cabins, holding a small crossbow that fit in one hand. He raised the weapon and fired. The bolt stuck in Tormod's shoulder, eliciting a growl that sounded to Halas very much like it came from a bear. Halas skittered toward Tormod, but the big man waved him off. "Door!" he cried, and rushed past Halas, toward the man who'd shot him. The soldier, previously untouchable, turned frantic as he saw that his bullet hadn't downed the giant. Tormod scooped him up and hurled him over the side. He took the man's weapon and pointed it back toward Halas, loosing the bolt into the chest of another soldier, one Halas hadn't seen. Was it really that simple to lose track of yourself?

With that thought, he'd lost track of Tormod. Panic set in. They came from all sides, wielding finely made swords and, in some cases, shields. Halas raised his blade to block an attack from the left. He moved toward where Tormod had gone, but the soldier wasn't keen on letting Halas escape. He pressed his advantage, swinging wildly. Halas picked off each attack, and with each movement he grew more confident. He was not just some farmer, as he'd previously thought. No, Halas Duer had trained under some of the best.

But it wasn't enough. Halas had training, yes, but this attacker was a soldier, a professional. Halas stumbled and nearly fell, barely bringing his weapon in line. He felt like the man was playing with him, enjoying the scene. There was a crazed smile on his face, a smile that belonged well away from here. Halas moved forward, trying to get in close, but the man lifted his elbow high and slammed it into Halas' chin, dropping him. The world blurred, but only for a moment. Through sheer force of will, Halas brought things back into focus.

The soldier stood above him. He kicked aside what Halas thought might have been a shield and might have been a head, and lifted his blade. Halas mirrored the man and kicked wildly, catching his gut and leg and forcing him away. Halas grabbed Silvia and lurched to his feet, but the soldier was gone. Halas shook his head. He'd lost track of someone again, a frightening prospect. He still couldn't believe it could be so easy.

The Wandering Blade was a madhouse. People ran in all directions, flashes of black armor and silver clothing. Halas saw Absolon load an enormous crossbow with several arrows and jettison them into a crowd. He watched Flanagan fend off four men at once. He saw Brennus, holding his left arm weakly at his side, fencing a soldier. Halas moved to help him, but three sailors took the duty, grabbing the man who dared wound their captain and tearing him apart.

Where was Tormod? Halas wanted to call for him, but was afraid he would cry if he opened his mouth. He glanced around. Surely Tormod had only been gone a few seconds. How long had Halas' fight with the soldier taken? Not very, he thought. Tormod would be back.

And he was. He came around the back of the cabin shortly afterward. He smiled at Halas. "Are you all right?" Tormod asked.

"Yes. I think so. A man tried to…"

"Good." Tormod ran past him again. Halas saw that another soldier had attempted to take the position, and Halas had once again failed to notice. Tormod dealt with him in short order. "Be more careful," he said to Halas.

"I will."

"You are doing quite well."

Tormod was a whirlwind of destruction. Where he went, soldiers died, and where he wasn't, they overwhelmed the defending sailors. He never strayed far from Halas and Prince Aeon's door. Though he was in such a frenzy, Halas feared for the outcome of the battle. There were just so many soldiers! He was not alone in his worry; evidently Tormod shared it. The sheer number of them moved him into places he did not want to go, forced him away from battles he would have otherwise dominated. Halas wanted to help, but wouldn't he just get in the way? This was he, his father, and the forest all over again. *Let Sea do his work,* he told himself. Tormod was such a fluid fighter. There was a grace about him, but at times it looked to Halas like he was simply flailing in all directions. Swordplay at its finest?

"Get them down below!" Tormod ordered Halas. He was engaged to a man clad entirely in black, with little armor to speak of. Both fought with animal ferocity. Halas grabbed the handle to pull the door open, but of course it was locked. He pounded on it.

"Garek, Des!" he said, "we've got to get down below. Come on!"

The door opened, revealing three bewildered young men. Desmond pushed past Halas suddenly, grabbing a soldier's arm and shoving him against the railing. The soldier tripped over his boots and fell sideways. Desmond raised his axe and brought it down with all the force he could muster, splitting the man's nose open at the bridge and burying it into his face. The man flopped weakly. Desmond's weapon came free with a noise that Halas never could quite get himself to remember properly. Halas looked at him, meaning thanks, but Desmond was already moving on. He led the way to the trapdoor. Halas took up the rear, desperately watching for soldiers. There were none nearby, only bodies. He didn't know where Tormod was.

He followed Desmond across the ship, and they could see the trapdoor when Absolon's best boys decided to finish things.

There were six of them. They were all armed, and they quickly surrounded the four in a semicircle. Desmond's eyes widened. Halas was amazed, but it was Des who spoke. Screamed, rather.

"*Is this a good time!*"

"It's the best time," replied Bartholomew Hadric, the boy who had done most of the hitting when they'd ambushed Garek. "You've caused us tremendous embarrassment, and there may not be another."

"And you are concerned…with us? The battle rages all round, and you wish to beat us up. Don't you realize how incredibly *idiotic* that sounds?"

"No. We've decided against the beatings. This time, we plan to kill you."

Desmond stomped his foot and blinked rapidly, positively overcome with rage over the absolute stupidity of the situation. Halas thought his poor friend might actually explode. He looked from face to face, searching for some sort of sympathy or agreement. "Am I going mad? Are you boys *that* dense? This is not a good time for an argument!"

Hadric stepped forward, a sword in his hand. "Drop it," he commanded.

"You sound ridiculous," said Garek. "Like a child who has finally stumbled upon his father's tools. Desmond is right; this is not an appropriate time at all to have this out! We'll have our spat later, but for now, there are more important things to deal with, don't you agree?"

Garek advanced toward the trapdoor, keeping his weapon ready. From behind him, Bartholomew gripped his sword tightly. Evidently he did not agree. Giving a shout of rage, the boy lunged. Halas saw this and threw himself forward. Halas was quicker. The best boy swung his blade at Garek, but Halas grabbed his wrist, pushing Hadric away from his brother and twisting him to the ground. The boy kicked at Halas, and Halas dodged away out of instinct. Instead of crying off, the boy charged. Halas spun past him and pushed forward with Silvia. Bartholomew gave a weak gasp, looking stupidly down at the weapon in his gut. Halas came back into reality and shook his head. A sort of battle-rush had fallen upon him, but faded just as soon as he'd plunged his father's sword into a child's stomach. He was sad and terrified. This was different from the soldier. This boy was innocent. Stupid, but innocent.

And Halas had killed him. He tore the blade free with disdain. "Leave us be!" he commanded to the others. The boy stumbled, fell to his knees, stared at Halas. The story of his life was one for the books, and he was surely immortal in it. Aren't all the greatest heroes?

The cooking boys disbanded, slinking away and avoiding the battle. Halas thought it miraculous that they had not been attacked during the little confrontation.

He made the mistake of glancing at the dead boy, seeing his face, a face locked in a silent scream of pain. There were clear rivers in the grime on his cheeks where he had cried. Halas tore his eyes away as easily as he had his sword, and they went below.

"Where now?" Prince Aeon asked.

"Infirmary," Halas suggested. His voice cracked. Bartholomew Hadric's blood was hot on his skin. They hid under the beds, the only noise coming from the battle up above. Soon, even that was silent. Halas was alone with his friends and the best boy's haunting gaze. He heard the door swing open, and saw two pairs of feet enter. None of the four in hiding moved. Were these friend or foe?

That question was answered a moment later. "There's nothin in here worth takin," said one. The boots stopped by the far wall, and Halas heard the sound of something being rummaged through. Then there was a crash.

"What about the kitchen?" asked the second voice. He knelt, and for one petrifying second, Halas thought that they would be discovered. But the man's back was to them, and he was only picking up a small package. The man stood up quickly.

"Where is the kitchen?"

"Well I don't know! It must be around here somewheres; let us find it before the others do and spoil all the food."

"Idiot! Can't you think with anything but your stomach?" The two men stormed out, leaving the door open behind them.

———

That was it. *The Wandering Blade* was lost, but were any of her defenders still alive? Halas hoped so. But there were more pressing matters: how many of the queen's soldiers occupied the ship? Certainly there was no way the three friends could fight their way free, even with Prince Aeon helping them. "We should surrender," Garek whispered.

"No!" came Prince Aeon's voice. "We cannot do that."

"And just why not?"

Silence. Halas had his back to Aeon, but he could tell the boy was trying to find his words. Then, "Tormod and I are on a mission. We cannot let these men take me; Aelborough itself hangs in the balance. We must sneak away."

"While that is an easy prospect to speak of, it shall be much harder to accomplish," said Garek.

Going against all of his better judgment and common sense, Halas crawled free of the bed, crept to the door and peered into the hallway. It was empty. "Then we had better move now, and be quick about it."

"There's another way out, rather than the trapdoor," Desmond offered.

"What's that?"

"Another door near the cargo hold."

They followed Des, and sure enough, there was the door. Halas opened it a crack and looked around. This side of the deck was empty. The night air was pleasantly warm on his skin. They clung to the shadows, each one doing his best to keep his footfalls silent. Eventually, they stopped behind a pile of crates, strapped down underneath the stairs that led to the bridge. The ship was anchored not ten meters from the closest pier, and a long plank had been stretched to reach it.

The smell was overwhelming. The last of the battle had been fought only minutes beforehand, but already the stench of death was heavy in the air. Halas wondered how anyone could stand it. The smell combined with the thick, hot air made him want to hurl his lunch over the side. He didn't, of course.

There were indeed some survivors. A dozen sailors, all lined up and on their knees, surrounded by a host of soldiers. Tormod was among them; Prince Aeon let out a little gasp. Halas also saw Captain Brennus and Cloart.

Pressed up against his side, Halas felt Garek tense up. "What is it?" he whispered.

"That's him."

"Who?"

"Nolan Dooley."

Halas looked. Sure enough, there he was: Nolan Dooley, Thief Extraordinaire, the man who had stolen over half of the Duer's money from Halas and Garek. What was he doing here? There was a woman next to him, with black hair and yellow eyes. Her eyes…they were unlike anything Halas had seen, like gemstones, or brilliantly gleaming stars. She was the most beautiful woman Halas had ever laid eyes upon, and yet, there was a certain foulness about her that he could not quite grasp. He knew he had seen her before.

Recognition dawned on him then—she was the woman from his daydream. The girl he had originally mistaken for Cailin.

She walked to Tormod. Tormod turned his head to the captain and offered a weak smile. "I'm so sorry," he said, and that was all. Brennus looked into his eyes for a moment, and cast his gaze back to the deck. The girl put a hand on Tormod's forehead.

"You belong to me now. *Cadelegh*." A mist formed and swirled around the girl, surging down her arm and into Tormod. He grimaced at the final word, but for a moment, nothing happened.

That quickly changed.

Tormod blinked his eyes and scrunched his nose, as if confronted by a horrible odor. A trickle of red formed at the corner of his left eye. His hands, plastered white to the bloody deck, began to shake. The rest of him quickly followed suit. Tormod's teeth chattered together as if it weren't a sweltering summer evening. Nolan bent down and put his face inches from Tormod's. The big man's eyes were wide with fear and pain. "Why—?" was all he managed to say before he bit down on his tongue.

And then, Tormod's eyes exploded.

Someone screamed. Blood squirted over Dooley's face; the former thief and current madman seemed to relish it. Halas' own eyes were rooted to the scene, as were those of his friends. Unfortunately, it was not over. Tormod reeled backwards like a fish out of water, landing hard on his shoulders. Halas heard the sound of bones cracking as the big man thrashed amidst the blood of the crew of *The Wandering Blade*, screaming in uncontrollable anguish. Aeon uttered a little squeak.

Immediately Halas lurched backwards, wrapping both arms around Prince Aeon's head and bringing him to the ground. They saw no more, but they heard. Tormod's strangled cries echoed out over the whole dock for what seemed like an eternity. He was suffering an agony that was incomparable with any agony suffered before. His sounds were unearthly, wretched.

"We have to get out of here," Garek croaked when it was finished. Halas saw that he was trembling.

"I've got an idea," Desmond said. All the joy was gone from his features. His face was pale in the moonlight, and his eyes were red. "Wait here. Move on my signal. I'll find you."

"What signal?"

"I'm sure I'll figure something out."

Desmond stole away, disappearing over the side of the boat.

"Raazoi," Nolan Dooley said, "was that really necessary?"

"Yes," she said seductively over her shoulder, "it was."

Nolan Dooley shrugged. "Would anyone else like to try that?"

The sailors were silent. Captain Brennus spat. "Cloart," Raazoi, the woman, said. "Please stand."

Cloart did so automatically. He did not look afraid, but deeply saddened. He stared at Tormod's body, and his hands grasped repeatedly at nothing. He did not seem to be aware of the gesture. Prince Aeon was sobbing into Halas' sleeve.

"Cloart," she said, "you have done terrible things. You betrayed your friends to us in return for your safety. What do you say to this?"

"Why are ye tellin' them this? Please, speak no more."

"I gave you sedatives that would let this end without blood, yet you did not use them."

"I couldn't poison these men! I couldn't do it." He was weeping.

"Please, please be silent. Please."

"You had yet another opportunity when those boys attacked the draftee. The prince was alone. You were to steal away in the night and deliver him to me."

"There was no time!"

"And then, last night, I told you to break into his room and slit his throat."

"I could not kill a boy..."

"He is most certainly dead now, and if not, he shall be soon. Your failure to act cost you the lives of everyone on this ship.

"I tell you this, because I want your dear friend the captain to decide your punishment."

"What? No! Ye promised ye'd let us go!"

"Did I? I remember no such thing." Nolan cackled. "Well, Captain Brennus? Have you decided?"

Captain Brennus shook his head. "Cloart, how could you do this?"

"She was to spare me, both of us! She promised me. She swore!"

"Get out of my sight, you disgusting little rat. I am ashamed to have ever been friends with you." He appeared to be finished, and two soldiers took Cloart by the arms. Before they could take him away, Brennus continued speaking. Raazoi stalled the soldiers with an uplifted finger.

"I helped you! And you betray me? Why would you do such a thing? These men are my family! You were a part of that family, until you did…*this*. You make me sick! I hope you suffer a million deaths in the Inferno! You are truly worse than even Nebi." To say that one is worse than Nebi the Forsaken is the most terrible thing to say to a man. Even the worst of enemies never utter such words. But Brennus, former captain of *The Wandering Blade*, said them, and they appeared to strike a chord deep in Cloart's heart.

The two soldiers dragged Cloart away. He made no move to stop them, staring sadly into Brennus' eyes, tears forming at his own. They moved out of sight. Halas released the prince, who lay still, quietly sobbing. He was worried about Desmond; the soldiers dragging Cloart moved in his direction. "How deliciously evil," Nolan was saying. "Can I do the next one?"

He took a crossbow from one of the soldiers. A dozen more stepped up, raising weapons of their own. Halas wanted to scream, but there was nothing he could do. These men would die regardless, and this seemed merciful compared to Tormod's end, which had shaken him to the very core. Halas felt numb. He could not get the noises his friend had made out of his head.

"Look!" someone cried, pointing. Everyone did, including Halas. A plume of fire sprouted on the dock; one of the storage sheds was burning. The crowd of citizens that had assembled for the scene started to panic.

"We have to help put that out," said a soldier. His voice wavered, and Halas realized that even the soldiers were bothered by the manner of Tormod's death. Raazoi smirked. Halas was hopeful. This could be the distraction they'd been looking for. *Brennus and the rest of the surviving crew might actually be able to make it out of this!* Halas was starting to climb to his feet when the witch dashed his hopes completely.

"Kill them first!"

The bows sounded and the sailors fell bleeding to the deck. Brennus' eyes were empty before the arrow struck. That quickly, he had gone from a proud captain to a broken man. Just as quickly, he had gone from a broken man to a corpse.

"Put it out!" someone shouted, and then more than half of the soldiers raced down the gangplank toward the fire.

"That'd be Des," Halas whispered. "Get him up." He wished in his heart that Desmond had been just a few seconds quicker. Perhaps the sailors could have mounted some kind of attack, and they could have survived.

And there was the witch to think about. How could anyone fight against such powers? For that matter, how could anyone escape from under her nose? Halas and his friends had to run across the bulk of the deck to escape, right past the girl. His chest tightened at the realization.

Things happened quickly. Garek helped Prince Aeon to his feet, and they made ready to run, but Nolan saw the movement. Dropping the crossbow, he drew a slender sword and came into view. "Do I know you?" he asked, momentarily confused. Halas took advantage of the pause, stabbing clumsily at him, but Nolan parried. Garek moved at the soldiers. He kicked one in the chest and knocked him into the water. Two of his mates dove in after, and a third engaged Garek. Halas' momentum carried him forward; he and Nolan hit the deck. Halas rained down blows with his fists. He grabbed his sword and stabbed Nolan in the gut. Nolan coughed blood, but Halas was already moving, dragging his brother, Prince Aeon, and his father's sword down the gangplank. Behind them, Nolan stumbled over the edge of the ship.

"We must go back!" Prince Aeon said. "We must go back for Tormod! Please, please! *Please*, Halas, we have to go back!"

As much as Halas wanted to, he knew they could not. There was nothing they could do for the poor man; Tormod was gone. Desmond, dripping wet from head to toe, barreled into them, and Halas nearly stabbed him, but held back in time. "Damn it, Des!" he shouted.

They saw a line of spears in the air, running down the pier. The soldiers were giving chase. Halas led his friends around a group of confused citizens, trying to put out the fire and help the soldiers at the same time. It was the chaos caused by these citizens that saved Halas and his friends that night. Halas pushed through a small cluster, making sure his friends were still behind him as he cleared the dock. They were. The four ran into the street. The world seemed to shake around him, as if he were still on the boat. But the boat was gone.

Behind them, *The Wandering Blade* was burning.

Sub Chapter Six

Pale dawn had risen, making his eyes ache along with everything else. "You okay?" someone asked.

Do I look it? Nolan wanted to say, but he held his tongue. Instead he groaned. The physical pain was the least of his worries—seeing that girl, being on that ship, all of it just seemed like too much. The man scooped him up and made his way down the street. "What's your name, son? Talk to me until we get home. It'll keep you awake. What's your name?"

"Nolan." He coughed. "Nolan Dooley."

"How'd you get like this?"

"Carriage."

"Carriage? Painful things, those."

The constant bobbing and weaving of being carried made Nolan feel ill. He leaned away from the man and wretched. The man kept going. "Not far now," he said. "How long you been out here?"

"Don't know," Nolan said. His vision was starting to blur.

"Here we are!" said the man. Carrying Nolan, he stepped into a large room and approached the counter. "Boy's hurt," he said. "Says he got hit by a carriage."

"Ouch," said a raspy voice that Nolan couldn't see. "Put him in the sicky corner. It's empty."

"A small mercy. A man deserves to heal in private."

"Then take him home with you," the raspy man suggested.

There was a brief silence, and then the man who'd rescued Nolan carried him into the corner, laying him down on a mat on the floor. He pulled a blanket over Nolan's chest. The raspy one appeared next to them. "Ten detricots covers bathing, feeding, and basic medical care for a week."

"Yes, I'll pay. Assuming the boy can pay me back."

"I'm...pay you," Nolan whispered. He was dipping out of consciousness. He didn't have ten silvers, but they wouldn't be difficult to obtain once he was healthy.

"Good. I'll be back to check up on you in a few days," said the man. He turned around and left. The raspy one looked at Nolan for a while before whispering, "You're lucky," and departing, snapping shut a curtain before departing.

Nolan slept.

———

He awoke feeling strange. It couldn't be called better, but it was certainly less bad. He found he could sit up. "I think I preferred the girl, honestly," he said. It hurt to speak. "Hello?"

His corner was large enough for maybe six people to lie side by side. What had the man called it? The sicky corner. *Seems appropriate.* The man in question pulled open the curtain a moment later. "Ah, you're awake. How are you feeling?"

"Wondrous what a good night's sleep does for you. Can I have something to eat?"

"I'll get you something here in a bit."

"Thank you. Where are we?"

"Common house. My name's Leon. Yours?"

"Nolan."

"I'll get you some food, Nolan."

He left. Nolan didn't like Leon; the niceness he exuded seemed very artificial. Leon brought soup, and Nolan ate it. He wasn't as badly hurt as he'd thought the previous night. He could eat, he could move, he could bathe and dress himself. On the second day Nolan decided to try and walk, and found he could, albeit with a limp. He hobbled across the commons and asked Leon for lunch.

So Nolan spent the next week in the common house, getting better little by little. He devoted a few hours each day to walking, working out his injured muscles. At the back of his mind there was always a plan. Or the beginnings of one, at least. Dar had had him beaten within an inch of his life, and he would pay for that.

Somehow. Nolan was still a bit fuzzy on the details.

On the fourth day, as Nolan made his way from one end of the house to the other, he met Leon in one of the back hallways. "What's the matter," he asked, "no customers?"

"Funny," Leon said. Since Nolan had been brought to Leon's care, he'd seen two actual patrons. Both had since left.

Nolan winked at him. "I thought so."

"How are the legs?"

"Better, thank you. Still painful. Have you ever been set on fire?"

"Regretfully no."

"Ah, shame. It feels a little bit like that."

"Is that what happened to you?" Leon asked. "Did someone set you on fire?"

They walked into the main living area. Leon steered their course toward the kitchen, something Nolan found he approved of. Walking was hungry work.

"Something like that."

Leon looked at Nolan, his eyes full of disapproval. That was irritating. What did this man have that made him think he could be disapproving? Leon owned a second rate inn that made less money a day than the beggars working the Cordalis slums. Nolan decided then and there he wasn't going to pay him his money.

"Nolan, you can tell me." Leon coughed into his hand. Nolan frowned.

"I lost a fight. That's all there is to the story. Can we just drop it?"

"All right, fair enough." The proprietor reached into his pocket and withdrew a packet of self-rolled cigarettes. Nolan declined his. He didn't feel like smoking.

———

The man who'd rescued Nolan from the gutter was called Bors. A week had passed, and neither Nolan nor Leon had seen him. Nolan was beginning to wonder if he were ever going to come to collect his payment. Not that Nolan had anything to pay him with, of course. Cheating Leon was easy, but he felt he owed Bors a debt. The man had fished him out of pretty deep water, after all. Nolan figured that he'd include Bors in his plans, somehow. First he wanted to actually speak to the man.

He'd figure it out later, but now it was time to leave the common house. Nolan was as healthy as he was going to get, and each day spent lingering was money down the drain.

Unfortunately for both of them, Leon was far from stupid, and he had no intention of letting Nolan out of his sight. Nolan didn't necessarily want to hurt the man, but he wasn't going to give him what he wanted, either. One way or another, Nolan fully intended to walk out of this place up to his eyeballs in a debt he would never pay.

At first he tried to be innocuous about it, suggesting he would go out for a walk, or run a few errands if Leon needed it. But no, Nolan wasn't allowed to leave, and Leon had an errand boy. Nolan had never actually seen this boy, and soon began to doubt his existence.

His second plan was just as simple. Nolan would wait until nightfall, until Leon was asleep, and stroll right out the door. It was Wednesday, the longest Wednesday of his life. Nolan was remarkably impatient about the whole thing. He wanted out. Fresh air, a warm breeze. Good food. He puttered around the commons all day, whistling quietly to himself and watching Leon, who, of course, was watching him just as sharply. When night fell, Nolan settled on to his cot and closed his eyes. Leon's heavy footfalls wandered around the building for a while as he closed up shop. Then the creaking of a mattress. The time had come; Leon would soon pass out and Nolan would be free to leave.

Then Leon started whistling.

Nolan woke up the next morning and swore.

Chapter Seven

Jaden Harves

Halas had to stop running. He held Aeon's hand. The boy's eyes were blank, and silent tears streaked his cheeks. Garek followed listlessly. Of Halas' three companions, only Desmond looked alert. They ran from the dock, from the soldiers and the mob, from the witch. Halas dragged them down several cobbled streets, passing over a bridged canal, hurrying by a couple out for a stroll, and finally ducking into a cramped alleyway.

He gulped for air, looking around, but there was nothing to look at. Earlsfort was an alien city. They may as well have been on the moon, for all the good it did them. Nothing was familiar, nothing looked friendly. Around every corner was danger. Halas put a hand on his chest to steady himself. He still held his father's sword. Panting, he sheathed it. It was an awkward gesture.

"Is everyone all right?" he asked.

Aeon looked at him as if he were crazy, and immediately Halas felt ashamed. Of course they weren't. They were only alive because of Tormod's disturbing death and Desmond's quick thinking. And freak chance, of course. Garek stared at the far wall, and Desmond waved Halas away. He crouched near Garek. "Garek, we've got to keep moving, okay? Hang in there. You with me?"

Garek looked up at Desmond, saw the earnestness on his face. He slowly nodded. "Yeah. Yeah, I'm with you."

Desmond clasped his shoulder. "All right. Up you go, come on." He turned to Halas. "What do we do now?"

Halas wondered that very thing. Surely there was an inn nearby, but Halas wanted to be as far from the dock as possible before they stopped. Raazoi and the soldiers would be searching for them. They would be wanted fugitives. Nowhere was safe. They had to get out of the city.

But how? From his vantage, Halas could see two streets, and both felt identical. What he had seen so far of Earlsfort had been no better than a maze. He did not wish to wander that maze bloody, terrified, and exhausted, especially not in the dark. And all the while they would be pursued. He pursed his lips and finally spoke. "We have to find an inn. We must risk it. In the morning, we'll figure out a plan."

Desmond nodded. He looked concerned, but did not voice any dissent. That was good.

"I will go out," Halas said, "have a look around. Stay here with them, will you?"

"Are you sure that's a good idea?"

"Not at all. But we have to find our bearings somehow, don't we? I can avoid the soldiers."

"Okay. Come back soon. If you're not back in five minutes, I'm coming for you."

"Ten. I'll be back in ten."

Desmond frowned, but acquiesced. "Ten it is."

Halas scurried out of the alley. Once in the street, he doubled back, examining the hiding spot. His friends were not visible from the street. Good. Halas set off, trying to look in all directions at once. Several buildings sported signs; Halas read these eagerly, thanking every god he could think of that he knew his letters. Conroy's tutelage could quite possibly have saved his life that night.

There were few pedestrians on the street. The hour was late, and word of the battle must have spread quickly. All around him, doors were locked and windows shuttered. He passed a blacksmith and a tanner's shop. Both were battened down securely.

He was beginning to get a sense of the area. Halas had always had an excellent sense of direction, and even now that was taking hold. He knew exactly how to find his friends in the alley, and did his best to memorize the street names as an added safeguard. The structures around him were wildly varied, some made of wood, some of stone, some of what appeared to be sand. Halas saw squat stone houses neighbored with grass huts. From within several he could smell roasting meat. It made his mouth water and his stomach grumble. He patted it.

A small contingent of guards hurried across the street in front of him. Halas froze, hands clasped into fists, heart hammering to escape his chest. He had his sword, but against six it was as good as useless. These men would take him, torture him until he gave up his friends, and then kill the lot of them. Halas resolved not to tell them where to find his friends. The soldiers did not even look his direction, however, and terror slowly released its grip. Halas stood, rooted to his spot, and watched a while longer. He wished more than anything for normal clothes, anything but these blood-stained silver uniforms. They were so painfully obvious, Halas could have been identified by a dead man. A woman walked by, eyeing him curiously. Halas squinted, blinked his eyes and rubbed them. When he opened them again, the woman was gone, and Halas felt ready to move.

A few minutes had passed. He would have to turn back soon if he wanted to reach Desmond in time. Poor Desmond. He was holding up remarkably well, under the circumstances. Halas wouldn't have guessed he'd had it in him. And, of course, Desmond had managed to save Halas' life yet again. At this point Halas would be very hard-pressed to repay his friend. He wondered again how he could ever have disliked the young man, and why so many back home shared the sentiment. Desmond was the most loyal friend anyone could ask for. Someday, Halas knew he would be a great man, if he wasn't already. Glass shattered somewhere in the distance, echoing in Halas' head. More soldiers?

He didn't want to find out. It was time to go back to the alley. He found his friends much as he had left them, huddled together in cold silence. The rain had picked up just before, but it was already diminishing. "Anything?" Desmond asked.

"No inns. Houses and shops, mostly."

"What about soldiers? Did you see any?"

"A few, but they passed right by me. Hopefully our uniforms will not be easily identifiable in the dark."

Desmond looked down at himself and plucked at the shirt. He uttered a desperate laugh. "Hadn't thought of that."

Halas glanced at Aeon, finding it extremely unfortunate that he, too, wore the silver outfit. The boy had not even been given one initially, but Tormod scrounged together the necessary clothing before the battle, not wanting Aeon to be confused for anyone but a crewman, cut down by his own side on the field. It was the first time Aeon had donned the uniform. Halas thought it would have been nice to be with someone in plain clothing, but unfortunately it was not to be.

"Hey, I know ya boys," said a voice in the darkness. Halas nearly jumped out of his skin. He drew down on the voice, not noticing Desmond, Aeon, and Garek all do the same.

A small boy stood at the other end of the alley, no more than a waif. He wore tattered burlap rags, and only one shoe. His hair was thin and scraggly. The boy scratched his belly, seemingly unafraid of the brandished weapons. "Yer from the boat, yeh? The burned boat?"

Halas, still feeling the panic, forced himself to lower his blade. "Who are you?"

"Names are for chumps, mate. Ain't never got one, did I? And I ain't a chump."

"Do you know about the boat?"

"Saw it burn. Burned nice, it did. Yer'd be on the run then, huh? Maybe I give you in."

"What do you want?" Halas asked.

"That's a nice sword."

"What else do you want?"

"Got any money?"

Halas reached for his pockets. There had been no time to grab any supplies, so he wasn't likely to have much in the way of money. He found two crumpled bills, and no coins at all. Garek offered up his own wad; together, they produced eleven detricots. Garek tucked the remainder of the wad away, and Halas offered the bills to the waif. He reached for them timidly, like a stray animal offered food. Once the boy held the money, he skittered backwards. "What's this? I said money, not shit! You mess with me? I ain't no chump!" And with that, the boy ran off, clutching their money and wailing for the guards. Garek moved to go after him, but Halas grabbed his shirt.

"No time!" he said. "Just go!"

They took off in the opposite direction, running again. They had had time to recover, and now all four moved with determination, even Prince Aeon. Halas thought he could hear the stomping of armored boots close behind, but he did not dare look. If he did, he would almost certainly trip and fall, and then they would be on him. He led his friends to a staircase dug into the side of a hill, and sprinted up it, rushing up and over several houses. They came parallel to a rooftop, and Halas scrambled over it, dislodging shingles with his boots. True to his nature, he slipped, and slid down the incline and hit the street hard, landing roughly on his hip. Desmond landed next to him, stumbling into the wall. Garek and Aeon came down more gracefully. They helped Halas up, and all four were running. Someone shouted, warning them to stop, but they ignored him, ducking into yet another alleyway. They burst into the street on the opposite end. A group of men and women on horses trotted past, sparing them looks. One woman raised an arm as if to say something, but thought better of it. The horses disappeared around the corner.

"Slow down," Desmond gasped.

Halas did, although every part of him wanted to burst into a run again. He felt as if the soldiers of Queen Anaua were closing in from all sides, moving in for the kill. Still, they could not very well sprint from one end of Earlsfort to the other. They were suspicious enough in the uniforms. Halas forced himself to a walk, gripping his brother's arm tightly for support. Garek allowed it. They walked a ways.

"We should find clothes," Desmond said when they felt more or less under control. "Anything to be out of these uniforms."

"How much money is left?" Halas asked, cursing the boy who robbed them. He himself had none. Garek produced twenty-two detricots. Desmond had four. Aeon had ten.

"This should buy us a room, right?" Garek asked.

"As long as prices here are not outrageously expensive," Halas said. "We should be all right. I think."

"If an innkeeper will even accept detricots," Aeon whispered.

"What do you mean?"

"Why wouldn't he?"

"We are about as far from Cordalis as it gets, and detricots are not universal. Many vendors throughout Aelborough prefer money order notes, or coins. Out here, currency is about as varied as skin tone. Of course, Earlsfort is an Agerian province, so I believe our money will be sufficient, but it is something to look out for."

Once again, Halas tried to blink away the confusion, rubbing his temples. This was getting to be ridiculously complicated. It had to be a dream.

But when he opened his eyes, they were still in Earlsfort. He groaned.

"So how do we find clothes?" he asked. "I do not see any open vendors, and we're nearly broke." For the first time, it occurred to him that they ought to seek out Halbrick's friend, Jaden Harves. Halbrick mentioned him just before the boys left. But as lost as they were, Jaden Harves was just as out of reach as Father himself.

Garek stared at his boots, his face flushed. Desmond stared at Halas, unblinking. It took Halas a minute, but he finally realized what his friend had in mind. He slowly shook his head. "No, that's..." He trailed off. Halas' father was a man of honor and principle. Stealing was something he'd discouraged in his children since birth. Halas felt sick at the idea of it, but he also felt Halbrick would understand, under the circumstances.

Stealing was wrong, but then again, Halas had also killed two people less than an hour before. His stomach turned, remembering their faces. Bartholomew crying as he died, Nolan stumbling over the edge of the ship.

Desmond spoke. "We'll find a clothesline. There's got to be one around here somewhere."

"Not likely," Aeon said. "It has rained seven times since we arrived in the past hour. Seven times. These people must be used to this kind of weather. Would you leave your laundry out in these conditions?"

Garek groaned. "Well then, what would you suggest?"

Halas took over the conversation, glad that he would not have to steal. He wanted to steer the discussion far from that particular topic. "We go as is, take our chances in the silver. We find an inn, and we sleep. In the morning, we can figure something out."

So they walked. It took roughly half an hour, but they found what was almost certainly an inn. Desmond took Halas' arm. "They'll be looking for four of us," he said. "So book a room with a bed for two. Act as if you've hired a woman, and are embarrassed, or something."

"Bad idea," said Garek. "Avoid suspicion, I say. Pay for the room as quickly as you can."

Halas didn't like how he had somehow been elected to get the room. Scowling, he crossed through the inn.

It was unlike any he had ever seen. The common room was outdoors, warm under the stars. There was no fireplace, but a pit in the center of the area. He made his way to the bar and signaled the man behind it. He did as Desmond suggested, booking a room with a large bed under the name of Darius Conroy. "How much would that cost?" he asked, trying to sound excited and nervous. It was not difficult. He still expected the soldiers to descend from all directions and attack.

The barman scowled, looking over Halas' bedraggled appearance. "Not cheap. Fifty a night."

"Fifty?" Halas looked at the roll of detricots in his hand. His heart fell. They had only thirty-six.

But fortune was on his side. At the sight of the money, the barman's face turned to a smile. He put a hand on the bar. "Fifteen of those will do."

Halas raised his eyebrows. "Fifteen detricots?"

"Fourteen's as low as I will go."

"Fifteen is fine. Here you are."

"You're all right, kid. Even if you are squirelly."

The barman took his detricots, handed over a key and directed him. From his position at the bar, Halas could see what he thought were the rooms—straw huts that looked like they'd collapse if you even leaned against one. He returned to his friends briefly. While Garek, Des, and Aeon went to their room, Halas stayed out in the commons to order supper. He ignored the din of the other citizens. Everyone seemed to be talking about what had happened at the docks. Luckily, no one knew much. Stories ranged from a potential invasion to a dragon attack.

Halas stood at the bar, waiting for the barman to come down so he could order. A group of well-dressed men and women sat at a table nearby. They, of course, were debating the night's events. Halas gleaned that they had narrowed it down to two possibilities: a Western Isles invasion and a riot. "What do you think?" one of the women asked. Halas kept his back to her, but when she took his elbow he had to acknowledge the question.

"He doesn't know," a man at the other end of the table whispered. "Look at him, he's a mess."

"And just look at his *clothes*," murmured another.

"I've not heard much," said Halas. He wanted badly to tell these people everything, to wipe the arrogant looks from their faces, but that would arouse suspicion, even if it would make him feel better. It was bad enough that he was in full uniform; he had to hope no one would identify it as such. "I know that there was a fire. Do you think the Islanders could be invading?"

"I think it's certainly possible," said the woman. "At least some people in this town have common sense! You'd best be getting home, my young friend. If it *is* the Islanders, your family ought to be made aware."

Halas forced a smile. "Thank you, ma'am. I'll be sure to let them know."

But she had already turned back, and he was lost to the crowd, just one more impoverished face to be utilized and then discarded. Shaking his head, Halas caught the attention of the man behind the bar and ordered.

Each hut looked the same, and none appeared to be numbered. Halas found their room with some difficulty and sat down across from Garek and Des. Prince Aeon slumped against the wall, staring into nothing, his eyes red and swollen. The shaky feeling persisted, and would for many days to come.

"What do we do?" Garek asked.

"Father spoke of a friend before we left. He said his name was Jaden Harves. Father told me that he could help us if we needed it."

"Did he say anything about where we might find him?" Des asked. He stood above the washbasin, wringing pink water out of his shirt. He did it as easily as he would clean dirt and grass stains, seemingly unaware of the fact that this was blood, that this had been pumping through a man's veins a mere hour before.

"Not a word."

"I suppose we could ask around town. Someone here must know."

"Would that be wise?" Garek said. "Those were soldiers of Queen Anaua back there. Should we broadcast our whereabouts? It's likely that we are wanted fugitives."

A knock came at the door, and all four tensed. Des knelt down beside the basin, his hand closing around his hatchet. Halas walked to the door. "Who's there?"

"I've supper for Darius Conroy and...consort."

Halas looked back at his friends, signaling them to hide. Garek shrugged. Desmond and Aeon disappeared behind the bed, and Garek slid under it. Halas cracked open the door. Before him stood a gnome, carrying a large and heavy tray. Halas took it and the gnome waddled away, saying something about the bill. Halas closed the door. He had ordered a roast chicken and a large wheel of sharp cheddar cheese. It was the best he'd eaten in years. Even Prince Aeon had something. They said not a word until every morsel was gone.

Prince Aeon reached to his lap. A discontented look passed over his face. After a moment, he reached up and wiped his mouth with the back of his hand, then turned to Halas. "Surely Earlsfort has an information directory."

"A what?" Halas asked.

"An information directory. Cordalis has one. My governess used to take me there. It is an archive of sorts, not quite a library, where you can find addresses and dates and such. Perhaps this place has one as well."

"Perhaps. We'll go looking in the morning," Halas said. "For now, we should get some rest. It has been a long day."

—·—

Garek and Aeon took the bed. Garek had long since fallen asleep, as had Desmond. But Halas and Prince Aeon lay awake for most of the night, neither knowing that the other was up, both thinking about the fate of *The Wandering Blade*. Halas remembered the gripping fear he had felt, like a cold hand closing around his heart, causing it to beat faster than it had ever before and somehow not at all.

He closed his eyes and shook his head, trying to clear his thoughts. He thought of the two he had killed, the twisted looks on their faces as they realized that they were breathing their last breaths. He thought of their warm blood on his hands. Looking at them now, he realized that he hadn't washed, that he had eaten a full meal with his hands coated in dry blood.

Halas ambled over to the basin and scrubbed until his skin was red and raw, but clean. Prince Aeon rolled over on his side and watched, bleary-eyed. Halas knelt by his bed and touched his shoulder, intending to give some sort of comfort, some bleak condolence that would help the boy sleep, but he could find no words. What could be said?

Could Halas go through that again?

He'd have to; he knew that much. As much as he wanted his journey to be over, he knew that it was not so. Halas knew that he would have to fight many more battles before he could go home. Aeon's eyes said that the young prince knew the same. The very thought caused Halas to choke, but he drove the fear away. It was for his brother, his friend, and—what exactly was Prince Aeon to Halas? He was more than an authority figure; in fact, Halas had not even thought of the boy as an authority figure until now. At first, he had been a mystery, and then somewhat of a nuisance. But what was he now? A friend?

A friend. That would do, for now. Satisfied, Halas nodded to Aeon, who nodded back. Halas returned to his spot on the floor, but he didn't sleep. He couldn't sleep.

Before he knew it, the sun was up.

———

Of the four, three of them had the ability to read. Garek knew a few words, but hardly enough to help in the search for Jaden Harves. So, leaving Desmond and Garek at the room, Halas and the prince set out to look for the information directory. They left the inn shortly after breakfast. As they passed through the common room, Halas saw that it was just as packed as it had been the previous night. The fire pit had died down, and the conversation was low, but everyone seemed to be accounted for.

The walk was soothing, and Halas got a better look at the city. Earlsfort was a tropical place. Palm trees waved in the warm air. Sand had scattered from the many beaches into the streets. The people were dark and dressed for the climate, in shortened sleeves and trousers. Halas was painfully aware that he and Aeon were dressed strangely for the area, in their silvery uniforms. None of them had thought to bring spare clothes; their escape had been far too harried.

Fortunately, only the shirts displayed the symbol for the Agerian Navy, so Halas and Aeon stripped those off. Most of the men outside were barechested, and while Halas and Aeon certainly looked peculiar in their matching silver pants, they were no longer recognizable as a uniform. Their hair was different, but they could have passed as brothers.

But that was not the only issue at hand.

"We may have a problem," Halas said.

"Yes?"

"What if they recognize you? Your face may well be known throughout the realm."

"We will just have to trust in distance, I suppose. Back home, I rarely strayed from my father's keep, and when I did I was often concealed in a litter. I would not bat an eyelash if the people of *Cordalis* did not know my features. How could these, so far away?"

"I would not bat one if they did."

"Well, yes, there is our luck to take into account." Aeon managed a weak smile. "Trust in distance, my friend."

"We will see."

They found a man walking the streets who pointed them in the right direction, and soon found the directory itself. The man did not recognize the prince.

The archive reminded Halas of Conroy's manor, his study in particular, though on a much grander scale. Books and scrolls stacked well above his head, cabinets bursting at the seams, a general musk in the thick air. Unsurprisingly, the feeling that overwhelmed him was an unpleasant one, but surprisingly, it was not claustrophobia. It was homesickness. An old woman sat behind a counter, cleaning her spectacles, her gray hair wrapped in braids and beads down to her hips. "Should we ask her?" he asked the prince.

"About what?"

"Addresses, I suppose. They've got to be organized…somewhere." Halas looked around, but it all looked the same to him.

"Madam?" Prince Aeon said apprehensively, going to the counter. "Excuse me, madam. Where are the addresses logged?" The corners of his mouth tugged with nerves; now was the ultimate test. If anyone were to know the prince's face, it would be this woman, this librarian.

"Over there," she rasped, pointing a thin, bony finger. "Any address in particular you seek?" Halas and Prince Aeon, masking sighs of relief, looked warily at each other.

"We're looking for the house of Jaden Harves," Aeon finally admitted.

The librarian pondered into her wrinkled hands for a moment before looking up. Halas choked when he saw her eyes had changed to a very dark black. They were cold and dead. Maggots wriggled through gaps in her teeth. He gasped and stumbled, but when he looked back the woman's eyes were pearl-blue, and her smile was kind. Aeon had a worried hand on his shoulder.

"Are you all right?"

"Yes. I'm all right." *She's just an old woman. Surely I'm only imagining things. It's been a difficult day.* "Do you know Mister Harves?"

"I'm afraid not. But as I said, the addresses are logged over there." She pointed again as if they'd forgotten, and the two friends followed her direction. The area looked exactly like the rest of the archives.

"Well," Halas said. The prince coughed.

Try as they might, neither could figure out if the archives were organized by name, number, or some other category. They spent hours pouring over thick book after scroll after thick book, scanning them page-by-page. It made no sense. 'Ato Joel' was before 'Delbert Renward,' and then came 'Eldece

Bannock.' Halas put his head in his hands, and then went back to work. He glanced over at the old woman. He didn't want her out of his sight. Many times the oppressive heat forced them outside into the open air, where they waited for their sweating to abate before returning. Halas wondered how the old woman tolerated the climate, but she appeared to be none the worse for wear, smiling politely each time they reentered the archive.

"What brings you to Earlsfort?" she asked Aeon sometime during the day. Halas was just coming back inside from a short walk. He paused in the doorway.

"Jaden Harves is a friend of my father's. Herb and I," he said, gesturing to Halas, "wish to pay him a visit. Unfortunately, father is quite ill, and…" he choked. Halas moved to his side. Aeon's tears were very real.

"Mister Harves is father's dearest friend, and since our mother passed, he has had no real contact with anyone. We wish to find Jaden, before…before it is too late."

"I see," said the old woman. She looked somberly over her desk at the two, studying them for—what, exactly? She was suspicious of their story, but it was solid, and Aeon's grief was, again, quite real. Halas was once again stricken with dislike for her. Could she be an agent of Queen Anaua? His vision before had seemed so real. After encountering the witch on the boat, Halas felt more inclined to trust the things that floated through his head. "I am sorry for your father, boys. I only wish there was something I could do. Would you like something to eat?"

"No, thank you," said Halas. "We'd rather just get back to our search. It is terribly hot in here."

"Is it? Hm, I hadn't noticed."

After hours of pawing through documents, when Halas was beginning to think he'd skipped over it by mistake, he found the address. He found it by sheer luck, but he found it. 'Jaden Harves,' sandwiched between 'Allan Ladyblossom' and 'Linford Croft.' "172 Kingston," he said. "172 Kingston. Ennym, please memorize this in case I forget. 172 Kingston."

"172 Kingston," Aeon echoed. Halas didn't think he'd even noticed that Halas used the name Tormod had given him.

They moved back to the librarian's desk. She was watching them out of the corner of her spectacles, and smiled when they approached.

"I have one last question, ma'am," Halas said. "Do you know where Kingston is? We've found the address."

"Kingston's a big place, dear. Where in particular?"

Halas and Aeon exchanged a worried glance, but it lasted barely a second. "Nevermind," Halas said. "Do you have a map?"

"Of course I do. Kingston?"

"Yes, please."

"That will cost you four squashes."

Halas frowned. "Squashes?"

"Coins," Aeon whispered.

"You young people! Most folks nowadays use those detricots, but I find coins far easier to handle. You can't ruin a squash in the rain, am I right?"

"Of course," Halas said, laughing nervously.

"We do not have any squashes," Aeon said. "I'm afraid we don't use them in our village."

The old woman smiled sadly. "Then this one is on me," she said. She bent over the desk to get closer to them, and winked. "I won't tell if you don't."

Halas grinned. Perhaps their fortunes had reversed after all. The old woman had seemed suspicious at first, but that seemed to have been a mistake on his part. At least, Halas hoped it had.

The woman ducked back into another room for a few moments, and returned with a map case. She pried off the cap with some difficulty and removed the old, yellowed parchment, flattening it on the counter. "Take your time," she said. "Where is your village?"

"I'm sorry?" Halas asked, stalling for time, and not cleverly. It seemed an innocent enough question, but was it?

"I asked about your village. Is it far?"

"Not far at all," Aeon said. "We live to the west, in Ponce. It is but a few hours away on foot."

"I see. I hear it's lovely there. And they really don't use squashes?"

"No, madam, we do not use currency at all. Our people barter extensively. It is truly crippling when one wishes to travel the outside world."

At this she laughed. Halas and Aeon knelt over the map, and Halas quickly realized he had no idea what he was looking at. He'd seen maps during Conroy's lessons, of course, but he'd never really cared for them, and thus never paid much attention. Once again, he counted himself incredibly lucky that Aeon was there, because the prince scanned it expertly. It took him seconds to find Jaden Harves' home and memorize the route.

"That will do," Aeon announced, surprising Halas and the woman, who both thought it would take longer. "Thank you, madam. Our father is a chef, and has taught us many recipes. Do you like fruitcake?"

The woman laughed. "Oh, you're a dear child, but that will not be necessary."

Aeon smiled. "I'll see to it you get a cake. Thank you for your aid."

"It was my pleasure."

They each bought a bowl of baked nuts from one of the many kiosks on the street and went back to the inn. Halas remembered the way, though he more than suspected that Aeon did as well. Walking toward the building, Halas laughed.

"What was that bit about fruitcakes?" he asked. Aeon grinned from ear to ear.

"I felt it made our tale more convincing, don't you think?"

"Prince Aeon, grand master of lies. What else are you not telling me?"

Aeon's face clouded over, and he took Halas by the arm. All the mirth had gone from his features. He drew close. "I have another secret. Would you like to hear it?" Halas nodded, so caught up in the moment he didn't notice the corners of Aeon's lips twitching.

"I'm actually the prince of Ager."

Halas paused, looking quizzically at Aeon. Aeon responded by bursting into uproarious laughter. He clapped Halas on the back. Halas caught up with the joke, and laughed as well. He hadn't expected such a thing as a joke from the boy, but it was good to hear.

So they laughed, doubled over in the street unfamiliar and frightening to both of them, and cried tears of laughter. Men and woman passing by gave them a wide berth, those curious children in odd clothes laughing like fools, but neither Halas nor Aeon cared. They laughed until their sides hurt, and Halas straightened, wiping his eyes. As he did, he felt a weight lift from his chest. Halas felt relieved, he felt good. About father and the forest, Cailin, the ship, everything.

He almost felt at home.

Halas started walking toward the inn. Aeon was still laughing. They drew a few curious eyes from the common room as they passed through it. It was getting late, and the streetwalkers were about. As Halas and Aeon passed, one leaned over to her buyer and remarked, "Children. Hmph! Who needs em?"

"We found him," Halas announced when they had returned to the room. Garek and Des looked up. They had been playing with a deck of cards they'd found somewhere. Halas noticed that more than half the deck was missing. There was a plate of chicken on the floor.

"Good," Desmond said. He licked the tip of his finger and flipped a card up, sticking it to his forehead. "Garek and I figured you'd been captured. We were about to mount a rescue operation. As you can clearly see." The card fell off and fluttered into his lap. He frowned.

"Where does this man live?" Garek asked, ignoring Des completely.

"172 Kingston," Halas said, as if that meant anything.

"It's just a short walk," Aeon added.

"Should we go now? The sun is setting."

"We shall try," said the prince.

———

Earlsfort continued to impress Halas. The house of Jaden Harves reminded him of Conroy's, as had the information directory, but much larger, and grander. Rows of wooden pillars lined the drive, leading up to two great stone doors. Halas was cold. His friends had all stripped off their uniform shirts, and Halas could see mounds of gooseflesh on Garek's arms. Desmond alone had had the foresight to wear layers during the battle, a light cotton tunic and black trousers that ended at the knees. Without his uniform, he looked colder than the rest, nearly shivering. It had been warm the previous night, but now a chill breeze twisted through the streets.

Halas took the brass knocker and brought it down three times. There was an echo inside the house, and then silence. Halas, suddenly sure that they had the wrong address, thought the silence would never end, but then the doors opened with a bit of a creak. A gnome stood before them, wearing a very loud green suit.

"Who's this then?" he asked, squinting and standing on his toes, inspecting Halas closely. "No solicitors!"

Before he could shut the door, Halas grabbed the edge and stepped forward. "We aren't selling anything," he said. "But we need to see Jaden Harves."

"Who's *we*?"

"Halas Duer. My father is Halbrick Duer; he and Mister Harves served together in the army."

"Hang on a moment."

The gnome shut the door. Halas could hear his footsteps for a few moments, and then things were silent again. He looked between Garek and Des. Garek was chewing on his lower lip. What if they *did* have the wrong house? What if Harves didn't wish to see them? What if Harves was working for the queen? Not long after that thought came, Garek said it aloud.

"What if Jaden Harves works for the queen?"

Halas shook his head. Aloud, it seemed silly. "Father told us to see him. If Father thinks he's safe, then he's safe."

"But Father didn't know things would be this bad," Garek said.

"Didn't he?"

Garek frowned. "What are you on about?"

"Forget it. Father would not send us into enemy hands. He knows his friends."

"You said they served together," Aeon mused. "But under whom? My mother and father have kept separate courts for longer than I have been alive."

Garek ignored the prince. "We should go."

"But we came all this way," Desmond argued. "It hasn't been all that long."

"It's a big house, Garek," Halas said, but he wasn't sure he believed himself anymore. Garek's angst was beginning to spread. "He'll come."

"And what if he doesn't?"

"He will," Desmond said. "I promise."

That, Halas found he could believe. "If we're going to trust him, then we must trust him. Aeon, tell him your entire story, all right? Leave nothing out."

"I was planning on that. We cannot lie to this man. If he is to help us, then he must trust us. Tormod taught me that."

They must have waited for several minutes, watching the sun sink steadily into the horizon. Sudden rain fell for a brief instant before stopping. Back home, the rain had come gradually, but here Halas was already starting to see an uncertain state of mind in the weather patterns. Rain was just as fitful in Earlsfort as it had been on the Inigo, and it was always powerful. A while after the rain stopped, the door opened, and the gnome returned. "Come on in! Make yourselves comfortable."

They did, settling in a room filled with bright red sofas. Earlsfort was a strange place. "Would you like something to drink? Eat?" They declined.

They didn't have to wait long for Jaden Harves to arrive.

His skin dark and his head bald, Jaden Harves was an impressive man. Though his body was lean, Halas could tell that it was not weak. His brown eyes told Halas that he was not to be trifled with, even though the man himself likely had no idea he was giving such a message. He beamed down at them and extended a hand, pointing with a single finger.

"Don't tell me," he said, "let me guess. You and you, you're Halbrick's boys."

He pointed at Halas and Garek. Garek grinned. "We are," he said. "We've heard quite a bit about you."

"Bah, you're lyin. Ole Halbrick never reminisces."

"Oh not at all, he spoke very fondly of you."

Why is he lying? Halas had never heard the name 'Jaden Harves' in his life, at least not before he left on the *Blade*. *Had Garek? Had he and their father actually talked, been friendly with one another?* Still, it seemed to please their host. Jaden eagerly shook hands with all four friends, introducing himself to Des and Prince Aeon. "A prince?" he said. "In my humble home? I think you should explain yourselves. Tom, please fetch us some tea. And by the gods, get them some clothing."

"Right away, sir," said the gnome, hurrying out.

"I do beg your pardon boys, my liege. You all must be terribly cold."

Halas was shivering, but he fought it down. "Thank you. You're too kind."

"In fact, come with me. You all could do with a good bath, I think. I'll have them drawn up. Tom!" he called, leaving the room. Halas glanced at his friends. Again, Garek shrugged.

"I like him," he said.

There were three washrooms in the manor. Halas waited outside Desmond's door. Desmond finished quickly, and when Halas went in he'd found the bath freshly redrawn. He nodded thanks and quickly undressed, slipping into the basin. It was wonderful. Halas never wanted to leave, but he found himself compelled to after only a few minutes. He wanted to explain himself to this man Harves. He felt exposed. He wanted to know if Harves could be trusted.

Jaden Harves waited patiently for them to finish. He had laid out towels and large, ill-fitting robes. Jaden and Tom lived alone, and as such there were no clothes on the estate that would fit their guests. He poured tea and handed out squares of sweet bread before he allowed them to speak. And then they did.

"My father is King Melick," Prince Aeon began, "and my mother, Queen Anaua. They have been fighting over Cordalis for the better part of my life now. Cordalis, and myself. I've lived with my father for as long as I can remember. Recently, however, he decided that I was in danger." He sneered. "In danger, from my own mother. Ha! However foolish it was, he was convinced. So he sent me away. He booked passage with *The Wandering Blade*, a surprise voyage for Captain Brennus and the crew, who were none too pleased.

"But they had no choice, and soon we set out."

From there, Halas took over, detailing from the time Garek had been drafted to their escape at the docks. At times, Garek and Des would interject, making the story sound much more exciting than it actually was, but Halas did nothing to correct them. *Let them exaggerate,* he thought. Neither he nor Des said anything of the forest. Through it all, Jaden Harves sat quietly, watching and listening. His tea was untouched when the account had finished.

"Well," he said after a while, "that certainly is an interesting tale. Are you all right?"

"For the most part," Garek responded.

"And you're wanted by the law."

"Yes, sir."

"Hm."

"Sir," Halas said, "we don't mean to bring down any trouble on you. We just need help. We're in a bad way, and we are unsure of how to proceed. Please, do what little you are comfortable with and we will be on our way as soon as we are able."

"There was never a doubt in my mind that I would help you," said Jaden. "Anything for Halbrick. He's saved my life too many times to count, and he's a dear friend besides. I don't know what I would do with myself if I tossed his boys out in their time of need. I'll show you to your room. Tom, cook us up a supper please. Come along, boys."

Even the guest bedroom reminded Halas of Conroy's manor. It made him sad to think of home. He shouldn't have volunteered to come on this journey.

But then, what would have happened to Garek?

It was curious how Jaden Harves treated his gnome. In Cordalis, they were servants, property made to cook and clean. Just like children and dogs, gnomes were not to be mistreated, but their place in society was unmistakable. Tom was different. Jaden asked him to prepare food and the like, yes, but he never once ordered. He was kind, and thanked Tom for everything. He spoke to the gnome as a friend. Halas thought it odd. He reflected on it while watching Tom cook a small roast. Along with it were a dozen different fruits, most of which Halas had never heard of. He was especially fond of the banana and the mango. The pineapple, he found, was not very good at all.

Something came over him, and he found himself asking Jaden if he had any potatoes. "I've not had any since before leaving home," he explained. Jaden laughed.

"I'll do you one better—these are *sweet* potatoes."

And Tom the gnome entered, carrying a bowl full. Halas tried them, but found that they were far too sweet, as the name would imply. He much preferred the normal stuff.

Garek, however, loved them.

Night fell. The four friends retired to the rooms Harves had laid out for them. Halas pulled the covers up to his chest, and very nearly fell asleep. He roused himself completely when a shadow appeared in his doorway. It quickly disappeared. Halas rose and followed.

The person descended down the spiral staircase and turned a corner. Halas kept low, suspicious. *Who would be creeping about at such a late hour?* As he moved down the stairs, he heard a crash, and froze. Then Aeon cursed. Halas hurried the rest of the way, turned the corner, and saw the prince.

Aeon had wrapped a cloak around himself. The boy knelt on the tile floors, stuffing something back into his pack, which he'd evidently dropped.

"What are you doing?"

Prince Aeon didn't look up. "I am leaving. I wanted to start before I fell asleep."

"What? Where? Why? You cannot leave now!"

"Why not? I've still business, up north."

"Business? What business? Please, my lord, tell me. What are you on about?"

"Halas," said the prince, finally looking up, "I think we are past 'my lord,' don't you?"

"Well, what business?"

Aeon stood and slung his pack. "I've business in the mountains. My father did not send me away only to keep me safe. He sent me on a mission. You have heard of the Temple of my namesake, I am sure. I must go there and stop a great atrocity from taking place."

"What atrocity?"

"Someone seeks to destroy the Temple, and the wards within it. Without that Temple, the Burning Desert will no longer contain the Ifrinn."

"Ifrinn?"

"Some people call them Infernals: the demons that Aeon the Great gave his life to defeat. Many years ago, my father saw it in a dream. When he awoke, he was ill, and blathered about three from another world and a half-Infernal." He scoffed again. "Another world. Why would someone leave their world for *this*? I would gladly forsake this world for another."

"Would that we could."

Aeon snorted. "It took many days for him to be well again, and when he was, he remembered nothing of the dream, not until very recently. He told me that if I should fail, I should seek out the Shifters, for it is often said that they are not from this world, and that they will be able to fulfill his dream. But first I must go north, and do what I can."

"Why do you go alone? Surely you cannot do this by yourself."

"Tormod and my father both gave explicit instructions for me not to trust anyone."

"Then why are you telling me?"

He smiled thinly. "I'm making an exception."

Halas smiled back. It had been seconds, but he knew what he had to do. He understood now what drove his father through life, that strong sense of purpose Halbrick had found. Now Halas had purpose as well. He had to help the prince. "I won't let you do it, you know," he said. "You cannot go alone."

"I have to, Halas."

"No, no you don't. You have friends. I will go with you. *We* will go with you. Please, Aeon, do not do this alone."

"I *have* to!"

"If you leave tonight, I will go straight to Garek and Des, and we will follow. We're going with you; it's just a matter of how you like your company."

"What if they do not come with us?" Aeon asked.

"They may not, but that won't stop me from doing it. Besides, they will. Well, Desmond will. Garek may not like it. Perhaps it would be better for him to stay here anyway." But in his heart, he knew his brother would be with them for the trip.

———

The four friends sat around a small table, with Jaden Harves and Tom. They'd slept long into the day, and awoken to find fresh clothes, purchased that morning. Harves had also found several maps of the area around Earlsfort and the area around the Frigid Peaks. "Where is the Temple?" he asked.

"Here," Aeon said, putting a finger on the map. "Beyond the Stoneacre Crags, in what they call the Arctic Wasteland. Tormod…Tormod once told me that the wasteland is miles of empty tundra, and that the Temple will be easy to spot from anywhere past the crags."

"That's about as far north as it gets, my lord," Jaden said.

"Yes. I imagine my namesake wanted it that way."

"I hear the crags are dangerous. Miles deep, some, and just as far across. The stories tell of terrible beasts that live at the depths, creatures that feed off the very darkness."

"Nothing we can't handle," said Des. "Terrible beasts and eternal darkness are some of our specialties, right Halas?"

He nudged Halas with his elbow. Halas grinned, but in his mind he was frantically trying to rid himself of images of a bloodthirsty great wolf, mysterious cabins, and buzzing lights that somehow took pleasure in pain. *Bastards.*

Meanwhile, Desmond continued. "I assume you won't be going with us?"

"I am sorry, but no. I am old, and cannot go traipsing across Aelborough, even with company such as yourselves and a mission so important. Besides," he grinned, "someone has to throw the soldiers off your trail. However, I will do whatever I may that will make your journey easier. You'll all have horses, maps, fine weapons, and as much food as you can carry. I am preparing a cover for you as well, most likely with a caravan. With," he added, "your leave of course, my lord."

Aeon nodded. "A good idea."

———

They spent a week with Jaden Harves, studying geography and even a little weapons training. True to his word, Harves had horses to spare for them. He led Halas to his: an old brown gelding named Owain. Owain took a handful of oats from Halas' hand and nuzzled his shoulder affectionately. "He's real good with people," Harves said. For Des he had a brown and white paint horse, and a young mare for Garek. To Aeon he gave a magnificent white stallion. Aeon stroked the horse's muzzle; the horse neighed.

Jaden Harves taught them to ride as best as he could. Halas and Garek had been taught as children, and remembered much. Aeon was an accomplished rider. He claimed to have even competed in tournaments. Halas remembered one such event in the previous year, held at the fairgrounds north of Cordalis. He did not remember the prince participating.

Desmond, however, was lousy. The Duer brothers laughed at Des as he took one embarrassing fall after another; they felt it sweet comeuppance for his cooking prowess. "If a grizzled old man like me can learn to ride in just a few days," Jaden said, "so can you. Just keep at it."

Desmond complained, but he kept at it. Halas, Garek, and Aeon led him around the grounds, and once he began to show proficiency in actually staying *on* the horse, their rides spread to the surrounding town.

One afternoon, when Halas, Garek, and Des were out riding, they came upon a group of children playing in an alley. The children had sticks in their hands, and were engaged in a series of mock sword-fights. Halas slowed Owain to a walk and then stopped.

Aelborough had no shortage of great heroes, and all children dreamed of them, of being Aeon the Great or a member of the Candlewood Trio or even Onath Cullough. They played in the dirt with their sticks and rocks and pretended they were legends. In their minds they fought wars, slew dragons, scaled high peaks, all while being sorcerers and warriors of great repute. Halas had seen it before, even participated in the game times without number, but now it was painful to watch. The children thought nothing of pretending to kill each other, but to Halas, it was too much like the things he'd witnessed on *The Wandering Blade*. He looked away. Garek looked on with his brother, hands on his thighs. Desmond watched them solemnly.

The children saw the horses and instantly brightened. Suddenly, the brave warriors had their cavalry. Shouting, cheering, they ran toward the horses. Halas forced a smile and rode away, and the children gave chase, laughter filling the streets.

Halas had no interest in playing. He wasted no time in leading Desmond and Garek away. When the children had been left behind, he could not help but sigh. He felt deeply saddened.

"Those children...." he whispered.

The day had been sunny and bright, but now it began to rain, pounding down on their heads. "I know," said Desmond. "I understand."

"Perhaps we should visit the dock," said Garek. "Just to see."

"See what?" asked Halas. "A burning ship that still smells of the corpses of men we knew and lived with? No, I would not see that again."

"Then let us steer clear of it," said Desmond.

———

The episode with the children put an end to their leisurely rides, so Halas took to watching Aeon, wandering about the garden or the house in a daze. Having found a temporarily safe haven, all humor seemed to have left the boy, and now he was just trying to cope. Though Jaden tried to cheer him up, Aeon never seemed to warm to the man. He spoke in depth only of the mission, telling Jaden very little personal information of himself or Tormod. Halas volunteered nothing more than Aeon had, and let him be.

Garek and Des seemed no worse for wear; in fact, Garek seemed to be happier than Halas had seen him in a long time. He and Jaden were getting along wonderfully. Garek followed Harves around like a lost puppy, eating up every story, every word with never a second thought. Jaden, to his credit, seemed to enjoy the attention.

Desmond occupied a happy middle ground. Halas had the impression that his friend liked being in Earlsfort. Des spent much of his time just wandering the city, taking in the sights. "I think I like the air the most," he said one day. "It's fresher than that at home."

Halas just laughed. "What a strange thing to pick up on," he said. Des grinned.

"What about you? Our lovely traveling companions are at either end of the spectrum, I'd say. Where does Halas see himself?"

"I'm not sure," Halas said. "Earlsfort certainly is a peaceful place, and Jaden is a wonderful host…but I don't think it compares to home."

"What makes you say that?"

Halas shrugged. He'd thought the answer was obvious. "Well, Cailin's there."

Desmond rolled his eyes. "Oh, grow up."

"I can't tell you how much I miss her."

"But not for lack of trying, right?"

Halas pushed him. Desmond knocked the hand away and lunged. Laughing, they spilled over the porch, into the yard. Halas wrapped his arm around Desmond's neck and held him there. Desmond tried to pry free, but Halas pushed him away and sat against a lemon tree, holding his hands out in submission.

They sat like that for a moment, the sun beating down heavily. Desmond tried to shield his eyes from it with a hand, but finally had to turn so that he sat next to Halas. "She's a great girl," he said. "You're lucky to have her."

"She is," Halas said. "You know I never got to say a proper goodbye? On the sixteenth, when we found out we weren't to leave yet—I never spoke to her after that. I went around Cordalis that night trying to find her, but I could not."

"I remember. Her father set the dogs on you?"

"Yes, he did."

"Write her a letter. Ask Jaden to send it."

Halas started. The thought of writing her a letter had not occurred to him. *It's so simple!* How had he not thought of it?

"Don't kick yourself. You'll see her again, when we're finished with this whole Temple business. I promise."

"And what makes you say that? This is…, Desmond, this is dangerous. We'll undoubtedly see Raazoi again, if even we survive the journey itself."

"We will. And if we see Raazoi, we'll kill her. Then we'll be legendary heroes and become rich. You'll return home in a parade and Cailin will fall instantly into your arms. Possibly naked, depending on how large the parade is. Pun most certainly intended."

Halas laughed. "I wish I had your confidence, Des. How are you so certain?"

"Because," Desmond said, "Nothing's going to happen to you, or Garek. I won't allow it."

Halas didn't know how to acknowledge that. Words seemed too little. Any thank you or a response in kind seemed petty and insincere. Halas nodded, clapped Desmond on the shoulder. Petty or not, he had to say something. "Desmond, you know I'll do the same for you." He instantly regretted speaking. The words were bitter in his ears.

"I know."

A bird called sharply from down the coast. Halas tried to sit there, enjoying an afternoon in the sun with Desmond, but he could not bear it. After only a few minutes, he rushed into the house and sat down with a quill and paper, scribbling like a madman. Halas was used to writing with a simple pencil, so the quill was difficult to use, but after twice spilling the ink he decided to take it slow. Cailin wasn't going anywhere. He dipped the quill carefully into the inkwell and began anew, on a fresh scrap of paper.

Dearest Cailin,

I am so sorry that it took you so long to hear from me. I feel stupid. I've been missing you so dearly I cannot stand it. Finally, Desmond told me to write to you. How could I have missed such an obvious answer? It seems silly! I don't even know where to begin, Cailin. So much has happened. I should start by saying that I am all right, though I once again am so sorry you haven't heard from me. Our ship was attacked by Queen Anaua. Apparently, Prince Aeon himself was onboard. He's on a mission, you see. Someone seeks to destroy Aeon the Great's Temple of Immortals. Garek, Des and I managed to get the prince clear and we're living with one of my father's friends in Earlsfort. We're outlaws!

I know I told you I would be back in six months, but this may not be the case. Aeon's mission is to protect the Temple, and I'm going along with him. I miss you and I want nothing more than to be with you right now, but I have to go. I cannot turn my back on something so important. I pray you understand, and you know I don't pray often.

You're going to start hearing rumors soon, if you haven't already. It would not be wise to reply to this letter. Can you tell father and Conroy that we're all right? I suppose Desmond's family would like to know as well. Don't believe the rumors. They're lies. We have not kidnapped the prince. We are not murderers, or traitors, or spies. I do not know what they're saying about us, but I'm sure it is colorful. It is fun to make up stories about people. Do you remember?

That's all I can say for that subject. I miss you, Cailin, so much. I love you more than anything in the world and I cannot wait to be back in your arms. Every day we are apart is a day ruined. I will come home as soon as this business is resolved. I love you.

Forever Yours, Halas

He slipped the letter into an envelope and went downstairs. Jaden sat in the room with all the red sofas, deep into a book. Halas sat across from him.

"Hello, Halas." Jaden spoke without looking up.

"Hello."

"Something I can help you with?"

"I'd like to send a letter home. I think things are going to start getting bad there if this whole situation should come to light. I want my family to know I am safe."

Jaden laid his book down in his lap. Try as he might, Halas could not read the man's expression. "Halas, do you know how dangerous that could be?"

Halas nodded. "Yes. But I want her to know I'm all right."

Jaden's face immediately changed, brightened, into a smile. "Her?"

"Yes, her."

"Can you trust her?"

"I can."

"All right. I know the pains of young love. Frankly, I'm surprised you're not running hell-bent for Cordalis instead of continuing with this mission of yours. Your father would be proud."

Halas shrugged. He wanted to go back to Cailin, certainly, but this Temple business seemed so very important. The thought of her thinking Halas was dead, or worse, chilled him. She deserved to know, and Halas knew she would keep it a secret.

"But we cannot trust a normal messenger with this, not when you're so highly sought after by the authorities."

Halas had an answer for that as well, but he was hesitant to bring it up. He could see Harves being angry at the suggestion. Still, there was nothing for it. Cailin had to know. Anything less was unacceptable. "Would Tom go?"

Jaden's smile faded. He lowered his head and sighed. "I was thinking the same thing. He would if I asked him, and I've been looking for a reason to get him away from the house should this whole mess come crashing down on my head. I suppose it would be for the best."

Relief filled Halas, who had expected an argument. He looked at Jaden, who did not seem to mirror the feeling. No, the man appeared to have gained five years in the time it had taken him to decide to send his friend away. Halas looked at his knees, ashamed, but it wasn't his decision to make. It was Jaden's.

"Yes, I'll send him out. He's loyal; he'll get it there no matter what. Can you go find somewhere to be, Halas? I'd like to continue reading, if you don't mind."

"Of course."

Halas left the room. He tried to put himself in Jaden's position, but found he could not. The only gnome Halas had any close proximity with was Conroy's, and that gnome was an unpleasant, bitter creature. He could not imagine trusting one with such an important thing as Cailin's letter, nor could he imagine such bitter remorse at the idea of separation.

But if Jaden felt he could trust Tom, then Halas could too. He felt comforted that Cailin would know what was happening, but he wondered what would happen next. Soon they were to leave, abandoning all feelings of safety and security with Jaden Harves. But after his conversation with Des, Halas was beginning to think that wasn't entirely true.

———

There was little planning that could be done. Jaden searched for caravans, but so few moved about this late in the year. Halas couldn't hope to assist him with that work; it was entirely local and relied on Jaden's own friends and connections. This left the four friends with precious little to do. They sparred, they explored, they talked. Every so often Garek would force them into a game of riddling, something he was getting increasingly good at; he'd been learning new riddles from Jaden. Contrary to what he'd said earlier, Halas found he wanted to go down to the docks. He wanted to see the aftermath of their battle, and news had spread across the city that it was indeed a battle.

It frustrated Halas to know that Jaden knew more than he was letting on.

He wanted to spare the boys any anguish they might feel, but Halas craved knowledge on the situation more than anything else, almost even Cailin. Were there survivors? Had they been taken prisoner? What was the status on the manhunt? His only word was from passersby on the street, and those folk were considerably unhelpful. Rumors had taken deep root, and many were still convinced that the bloody Western Islanders were invading.

Halas sat with Garek and Desmond on Jaden's lawn. The heat was too oppressive to be anywhere but in the shade. None of the three had donned shirts that morning, and their trousers all ended just before the knee. Halas felt thankful that Jaden's home was on the coast; he imagined it to be hell further into the city, even wearing as little clothing as possible. Tom approached, carrying several glasses. "I thought you might like some lemonade," he said.

"Thank you, Tom!" Garek said happily. He helped Tom set the glasses down. Desmond smiled politely. Halas watched the gnome walk away.

"Does anyone else think it odd how Jaden treats the gnome?" he asked.

"How do you mean?" Garek said.

Halas drank from his glass. It was delicious. "Gnomes are made to be servants, are they not? Yet Jaden treats his like a friend. I don't really understand it."

"What did they teach you in Cordalis?"

"More than they taught you," Desmond chimed in.

"Shut up," Garek said. "Gnomes deserve all that we do. What makes them so different from us? Mister Harves met Tom on auction. He bought him, set him free. Tom's lived here ever since, of his own accord. He's not a *slave*, as you would like him to be."

Halas raised a hand, more than alarmed at the sudden outburst. He didn't know Garek had it in him. He saw where his brother was coming from, but at the same time, likening a gnome to a human was similar to doing the same to a dog. They were loyal servants, and could be fun on occasion, but friends? Before Tom, he'd never known a gnome to be anything more than background decoration.

"I'm sorry. It's just something I've been thinking about."

"Gnomes have always been lowly beings, in Cordalis and everywhere else," Desmond interjected. "They're painted as lesser creatures, existing purely for our benefit. But when I learned to cook, it was mostly gnomes who did the teaching. My father brought me to the house of Chef Merzio. Merzio was something of a bastard, but his staff was kind. My father had his heart set on my becoming a chef, and the gnomes helped me with that. I suppose I see your point, Garek. Halas, you're an insensitive prick."

"Hey! Let's not all turn on me, here. I was just making a statement."

Desmond was laughing. Garek, however, did not appear to be nearly as amused. "Tell me, would you stop and aid if you saw a gnome in need?"

"Of course I would, but that is different."

"It's prejudice, Halas," Desmond said, "and prejudice is *wrong*."

"You're not helping."

"I think I am."

"Shut up, Desmond!" Garek said. "I'm trying to make a point here. Go away, go inside."

"Your point has been made," Halas said. "Can I drink my lemonade, please?"

"It was made with slave labor, and…"

Garek cut him off. "Desmond, if you don't go inside this instant I'm going to hit you in the mouth."

"Fair enough." Desmond rose and walked inside, taking his glass and Halas' with him. Halas hadn't been finished with his, but he let it pass. Clearly Garek had something on his mind.

"What's the matter?"

Halas looked at his brother. Garek's skin, already tanned from a summer hard at work, had gained some hard color, and Halas figured his was much the same, deciding to check the looking glass when next he saw it. Halas also thought that his younger brother had grown quite a bit, though he was still shorter than Halas, and he had thinned out considerably.

"I like it here," Garek said quietly.

"So do I."

"A shame we have to leave."

"Yeah." He looked at Garek, knowing that silence would be the best tool here. His brother would feel the need to speak if Halas did not. Garek stared into his lemonade, swished a finger across the surface.

Finally he gave in. "I can't do it, Halas."

"What?"

Halas stood and rounded on his brother. Garek spread his arms apologetically. "I can't go with you. I can't do this."

"Of course you can!"

"No, Halas, I can't. I've been talking with Mister Harves, and he said it was all right for me to stay, for me to live here, with him."

Halas' confusion increased tenfold. "Live?"

"I'm not going back to Cordalis, to Father. I can't do that either. He probably doesn't even want me back. He hates me." Garek choked out his words.

"He doesn't hate you, Garek! He just—I don't know—he doesn't hate you."

"Yes he does. You know it as well as I do. But Mister Harves…he is everything I have wished for. He treats me with respect. He appreciates my conversation. He is patient. He *likes* me, and that is far more than I can say for Father."

Halas' mind was clouded. He felt betrayed. "You'll just abandon this, all of this, *me*, for no reason? Why? Please Garek, tell me why, because it doesn't make a bit of sense!"

"Halas, please…"

"No! Don't try to calm me down. You're not going with us, and you're not going home. They will find you! They will find you and throw you in jail. Did you think of that? It isn't safe here!"

"Yes. Jaden has many places for me to hide, and a lot of money, should it come to that. We are both prepared."

"Well," said Halas, "that's just wonderful. I'm so glad that you'll…" But there were no words Halas could find. He nearly screamed. He wanted to hit something, so he hit the table, putting a small hole in it and bloodying his fist. Pain shot through his hand. Halas swore. Nothing good could be salvaged from any of this. Garek was stubborn. Halas knew that he would not see reason. He rose and stormed off into the house. He didn't want to look at his little brother any longer. *Why can't he see how incredibly unsafe it is to stay in one place? And here! They'll be combing the city for us!*

"You won't be safe either," Garek said quietly to his back.

But Halas said nothing, and kept walking. The next morning, Jaden Harves found them a caravan.

Sub Chapter Seven

Nolan hurried down the street, trying to be fast and still inconspicuous. In the end, he gave that up and ran, darting through the back streets and alleys, pushing his way through throngs of people and ducking under doorways, running through buildings, losing anyone who may have been in pursuit.

He stopped at a favorite spot of his, a nook between two buildings with only one way out, concealed by crates, baskets, and a tarpaulin. He was hungry. Hiding in the dark, he retrieved a small box from one of the baskets and devoured the food inside. Poking his head out, he jumped; he was face to face with a beautiful woman. She had sleek black hair, prominent features, and yellow eyes that seemed to strip Nolan bare, revealing even his darkest secrets. He'd seen her before. He could tell this woman anything.

He settled on hello.

"Hello," she said. "My name is Raazoi. You are the one." She said it like it was a question but not.

"That depends," Nolan answered. The girl giggled. She was a year or two younger than him, he saw.

"You will accompany me."

"I will?"

"Yes. You just don't know it yet."

Nolan grinned. "And just where are we going?"

"Have you ever heard of the Frigid Peaks?"

"Who hasn't? Why would you want to go to the bloody mountains?"

"There is something I have to do. Would you accompany me?"

He thought about it for a minute. Less than that. "I would," he said. "I'd be delighted to."

Chapter Eight

Three Days Out Of Busby

"The owner's name is Bernard Claymont, a nobleman out of Galveston," Jaden said. "Thirteen wagons, twenty-eight guards. There's a problem, though."

"What's that?" Desmond said.

"Claymont refuses to go through Nesvizh. He's skirting the border."

Aeon went visibly pale. Jaden nodded solemnly. "What's wrong?" Garek asked, feeling the worst of the chill that had set in despite the burning sunlight streaming in through the windows. Halas wiped the cold sweat from his forehead.

"Those lands belong to the Bandit Lord, Torgeir the Mighty: a self-proclaimed title, but not far from the truth. Torgeir controls that entire strip of country, all across the northern border of Nesvizh. He's ruthless; not many that venture there ever come out, and none of 'em leave with their riches. He's an army of at least a thousand with him, and they hide in the most unlikely of places, waiting for weeks to ambush the next traveler, however wary or armed he may be."

"Then we cannot go with this Claymont man," said Desmond matter-of-factly.

"There's the rub," said Jaden. "You don't have a choice. Not too many people come and go through Earlsfort; it's out of the way. There's not another caravan for—well, until next March."

It was November, a few days before December. Halas put his head in his hands.

"How many guards have signed on so far?" Aeon asked.

"Twenty-two. I paid Claymont enough to keep three positions open until you decide. It's your decision, my lord, but I strongly advise against it. There's no more dangerous a place than Torgeir's land."

"There is no other way," said Aeon. "I have to. Maybe Halas and…"

"Oh don't start that," said Des before he could finish, surprising nearly everyone in the room. Evidently he had joined Halas among the few that didn't seem to look upon Aeon as just a prince.

"We could travel by ourselves then," said Halas. "Cut through Nesvizh, and avoid Torgeir's lands entirely."

"Traveling through Torgeir's country will cut the journey nearly in half," said Aeon. "And I would like to reach the Temple as soon as possible, for our foes are already en route. Tormod and I knew from the start that we would have to go through Torgeir's country. He said that we would make a deal with him: as much of the king's gold as he could load on to a caravan. My father agreed to such terms, but now that I face the road..."

They all knew how Aeon felt, Halas perhaps more than the others. He put a reassuring hand on the prince's shoulder.

"We'll stand by you," he said. Desmond glanced at Garek. "For better or worse. If I can protect you, if I can protect that Temple, than I will. If there is anything I can do to accomplish this mission, Aeon, I will."

"And I," said Desmond. Garek was silent. Jaden took the prince's hand and squeezed.

"This is good to know," said Aeon. "Thank you. Thank you all."

Halas stared at Garek. His younger brother could not return the gaze.

———

Jaden was saddling the horses. Halas , Desmond and the prince stood in Harves' foyer. Halas looked up the staircase, clearly hoping Garek would show himself, to change his mind, say goodbye, or even watch. Everyone involved knew there was a strong chance they would not be coming back from this mission. Why would the youngest Duer not even wish to say goodbye?

They made small talk for a time, but it soon became clear Garek was not going to join them. "I suppose we should go," Aeon suggested. Halas looked at him, his eyes reddened and filled with pain, and it broke Desmond's heart, but he said nothing.

"Yes," Halas finally whispered. "Yes, I suppose we should."

"I'll catch up," Desmond told him. He squeezed Halas' shoulder, and jogged up the stairs, to Garek's room. He found Garek leaning on the bureau, staring hard at his fist. "What is wrong with you?"

Garek turned and stood, pulled from whatever daydream he was in. He placed something in an open drawer and shut the bureau. Once that was done, Garek raised his arms, shook his head, and shrugged. "He doesn't want to see me."

"The hell he doesn't," Desmond said. "Go speak with your brother." Then, quietly, "there may not be another chance."

"I…I know that, but I can't. He doesn't want to see me." Garek embraced Desmond. Desmond had no choice but to return the gesture. Garek was his friend as well, after all, and had been longer than Halas had. Before this whole business with the forest and the Temple, Desmond had long suspected Halas did not like him.

"Take care of him, will you?" Garek asked. "Make sure he's safe?"

"You know I will. Both of them. Goodbye, Garek."

"Des."

And Desmond left. He tarried by the horses for nearly half an hour, but Garek did not come down. Finally, Desmond gave up. There was no time left to wait. They left for the depot from which they would meet the caravan and depart.

Following Harves, they trotted down the horse-lanes of Earlsfort to the depot. There they met Dale Crowe, who was Claymont's bodyguard and representative. Aeon choked; he looked quite a bit like Tormod, with his towering stature and fierce but gentle gaze. Halas could hear murmurs about the three friends. "He's so young!" and "Look at how small they are!" were most common.

"Hello, Jaden," a portly man said from behind Crowe. Halas assumed he was Claymont. He was correct.

"Bernard!" Jaden said. He reached up and clasped the man's hand. "It is good to see you again. How have you been?"

"Tired. Yourself?"

"Roughly the same. These are the men I spoke of."

"You spoke of them as if they were men," Claymont said. Halas bit back a snappy retort.

"We've seen battle, sir," he said instead, struggling to keep calm. "We've fought together."

"What?" said one of the men nearby, "roughhousin with the other kiddies?" He laughed, proud of his own joke.

Halas wanted to groan. He wanted to turn around and leave. Why were so many fixated on his age?

"Listen to me," Jaden said. "These here are good men, solid fighters. They've trained under some of the best swordsmen in Ager, under the Arms Master of the House of the King. And they've spilled blood together. So why don't you treat them with a little respect?"

Halas was glad for Jaden's support, but all the same, he felt as if the words would have been better from his own mouth. They didn't need Jaden to rescue them. After *The Wandering Blade*, he had a feeling that it would just make things worse. Perhaps Brennus had been right to leave the crew to their own devices after all.

No more was said on the subject. Claymont told them to prepare their things. Halas wheeled his horse about to face Jaden. "Goodbye, Mister Harves," he said. "Thank you for everything."

"It was the least I can do. I wish your luck to shine brighter than the stars."

"Take care of him, will you?"

"I will. Don't you worry."

"Thank you."

An hour later thirteen wagons left Earlsfort, due west. Halas briefly thought about how they were traveling toward home, but dismissed the thought. It made him too sad. Why was he doing this? He and Garek *should* be going home, not separating, with Halas steadily riding off into the unknown to battle and death.

The column put Earlsfort behind them after the first day, and picked up the pace when they passed the traffic around the city. Halas rode with his friends at the rear of the caravan. They were assigned to the wagon in what Crowe called 'lag,' what Halas assumed meant last.

"Y'all boys don't hail from Earlsfert, do ye?" said the driver. He had no teeth. That was the first thing Halas noticed.

"No sir," said Aeon. "We come from Galveston."

"Pretty place," said the man. "Never been there. And yer names er?"

They'd prepared identities for the trip. Halas had once again taken Conroy's name. Desmond was Art Mathis, and Aeon's assumed name was Ennym Straub. They introduced themselves to the wagon driver, who said his name was Walter.

"Pleasure to meet you, Walter," Halas said.

"Yaswell. Was it true what you said afore, bout spillin blood?"

Aeon's visage darkened. Halas bit his lip. He didn't want to glorify what he'd done, but he suspected that's exactly what Walter intended to do. "Yes," he answered. "We were in a battle. But it was only once, and it was a long time ago."

"Good ter know I got hardened steel at my side," said Walter. "No matter the age. Glad ter have ye aboard."

Halas smiled. Maybe he'd underestimated this man.

The caravan headed west for several hours before gradually leaning north. They kept course by the mountains, always keeping them firmly to the east. They passed through the foothills a time or two, but it was mostly easygoing, plodding across a low and level road for hours on end. Desmond tried teaching Walter to whistle.

Things were far more lax than they had been on *The Wandering Blade*. Bernard Claymont and Dale Crowe were in charge, but direct orders came few and far between. In fact, things did not go too far beyond assigning a certain guard to a certain wagon. Guards were permitted to roam the column to a certain extent, and when they bedded down at night, little was said in the way of keeping watch. Halas found sleep difficult. He wondered if his letter had reached Cailin yet, but of course it had not. He wondered how she was. Did she miss him? If she did, was it nearly as much as he missed her? He worried that his letter would seem too strong. Cailin was surely going to think he'd lost his mind.

Halas sighed.

The next morning they passed through the first checkpoint. Halas sat atop Owain, the sun beating down on him, not moving, wishing he had a hat. Far ahead he could see the front of the column. The checkpoint consisted of a gate and several houses. Halas guessed that maybe ten people lived here, most likely on a rotation. He wondered if the soldiers' families came with them.

Claymont took his time in dealing with the checkpoint officials. There were documents to approve, money to pay, all in all lots of bureaucracy to move a few wagons past a wooden gate. "There's more of us," said Desmond. "Can't we just charge them?"

"Sure are enjoying all this shade," Walter called out from within the wagon. Desmond gave Halas a dry look.

"We'll burn him out if it comes to it," he said. Halas nodded.

"I'll get the matches," said Aeon.

———

They crossed through the second checkpoint four days later. The sun was low, making this one far more bearable. Walter decided to check his wagon's cargo. Halas went around back with him. Aeon and Desmond stayed up front, staring at the checkpoint, willing the caravan to keep moving.

"Hand here?" Walter asked. He'd braced himself under the back of the wagon. Halas hopped off Owain, moving next to Walter.

"Here?" he asked, putting his hands on what he thought was a hatch. Walter nodded. Halas thought it would be more difficult to open, but he could have done it easily himself. Walter smiled, thanked him for the help, and climbed up.

"What are we carrying?" Halas asked.

"Horse feed," Walter answered. "Good lot of it. Don't remember zact numbers, so best if you don't ask."

"Fair enough."

Walter appeared a moment later, dusting his hands off on his coverall. "When you carry feed, you gotter be careful bout mice. They just creep in and eat right through yer load! But everything looks to be in order. Thanks again."

"My pleasure." Halas took his hand and helped him off the wagon. Walter went back up front. Halas mounted Owain. Another half hour of waiting and they were off again.

They drove steadily onward for another three days. On the third night, Crowe gathered all the guards around a large fire. Halas crossed his arms against the chill. It had been a hard day's ride; he wanted rest.

"Tomorrow morning we are going to come to Torgeir's land," Crowe said. "It will be dangerous. We're going to have some rules, starting with a strict watch of six men taking four hour shifts. Torgeir's forces are cunning, but they are only men. Do not fool yourselves into thinking otherwise. They will try and trick you, but I trust the men I've hired are wiser than that." He glanced in Halas' direction at this, and Halas did his best to hold his temper. *This is absurd. I almost hope we are attacked, so that I might show them my worth.* He felt guilty almost immediately upon thinking it. He remembered what had happened to *The Wandering Blade*. Battle was an awful thing. It was one thing to hear it told in books and songs, but to experience it personally…well, that was another thing entirely. No one wrote of how even the bravest of men shit themselves when they died. No one would sing of Tormod writhing in blind agony as his body was twisted by some dark magic. There would be no books written of some stupid kitchen boy who wanted petty revenge.

"Be wary, be cautious. We will get through this if we keep our wits about us. Now get some rest. Tomorrow will be an interesting day."

"Do you think we'll be attacked?" Desmond asked when they'd returned to their wagon.

"Not quite so soon," Halas said. "If ever. I hope not."

Sleep came easily, surprisingly enough. And early the next morning, they came to the border.

———

No one had ever marked it on a map. Torgeir the Bandit Lord had established his country only a year ago, and it was still unofficial. But everyone who knew anything knew that at this spot, fifty miles past the second checkpoint, was where his land began. There were signs scratched in the bark of trees. Most of them were marked 'Get back!' or 'Continue at your own peril,' but then there was a broad wooden gate. It had once been the third, and last, checkpoint, before Torgeir claimed it. Pieces of the gate had been crudely torn apart, and the huts were long since demolished. It was streaked with what Halas hoped was red paint. Tall cages hung from the turrets, filled with the corpses of birds and other animals. It was truly an abomination. On the side of the building was marked:

You are entering the domain of Torgeir the Mighty, Bandit Lord. You are now subject to His Law. Abandon your wealth here and return to your home. You have been warned.

At this both Claymont and Dale Crowe scoffed, but there were murmurs of dissent up and down the line. Halas and Des exchanged glances. They both were afraid, though neither would admit it. "Fear not the words of a coward and a brigand!" declared Dale Crowe. "We ride forth, to the sorrow of any who oppose us."

And so they did, and no one opposed them. After a day the men seemed to be less wary than they were before, though anyone of experience would have known that they were less safe as they went deeper in. Certainly Dale Crowe did. Halas felt just as uneasy as he had watching Queen Anaua's ships gaining ground. Desmond tried to keep in high spirits, but Halas knew his friend was terrified. He was trying too hard to appear otherwise.

Halas rode along, staring at the back of Walter's wagon. The caravan moved steadily into the mountains. They followed a stream for several miles before coming upon a strange sight: a little village nestled in the trees. It was composed of squat, clay buildings, and from their vantage point on the cliffs they could see people walking every which way. Barnard Claymont and his bodyguard conferred for a bit before deciding that they would investigate with a small party. Halas was chosen along with three other men. The cliffs turned into a hard slope near their position, and getting the horses down was difficult, but they all managed. Afterwards they moved at a full gallop toward the village, where they were met by several men with bows and glaives and pitchforks, wearing leather jerkins.

"We told you we'd pay!" cried one of the men.

"Please spare us!"

"We mean no harm!"

Crowe seemed alarmed, but he ignored the begging. "What is this place?" he asked.

At this the men stopped their blubbering and pleas. One cocked his head. "Do you not serve the bandit lord?"

"No," said Crowe. "We are a caravan from Earlsfort. We make for Fort Torrance. I say again: What is this place?"

"This is Busby," said another of the men. He had dark eyes and a gray cloak. Halas thought he looked peculiar, as if he were above the rest of the villagers somehow. He must have been in charge. "What madness possessed you to travel through the lawless lands?"

"Time is short," said Crowe, "and my employer thinks that he can thwart Torgeir's will."

The men laughed. "You cannot thwart the Oppressor," said a fat woman with several children held close. "He rules these lands with an iron fist. If we do not pay him tribute each month, a raiding party rides through and destroys one of our buildings."

"Then why do you stay?" asked Halas.

"This is our home, and we refuse to be routed from it."

"I see," said Crowe.

"Trust me when I tell you this, traveler," said the man in the gray cloak, "but you will not survive. None do, not anymore. Torgeir's lust is no longer for gold but for blood. He has eyes and ears all through this country. I guarantee that he already knows you are here. He will find you soon, I think."

"What do you suggest?"

"It is too late to go back. You have no choice but to continue forward, and hope that your fighters are a match for his. My words bear ill omen, but I would lessen that, if I might. I would like to accompany you."

The villagers looked alarmed. "Why?"

"If you do intend to strike a blow at the Oppressor, I would like to aid such a cause. I know these lands better than Torgeir's best scouts; I can guide you."

"Very well," said Crowe. "We will return in one hour with our wagons. Be prepared."

"Of course."

"What is your name?"

"Elivain. My name is Elivain."

"Well Elivain, until we meet again."

"Indeed."

Claymont was not pleased with the idea of taking another man onboard, but Crowe assured him it would be well worth it to have a guide and extra warrior, and the nobleman eventually conceded. They met Elivain just outside Busby. He wore a light chain-mail shirt under his jerkin, a bow across his back, and a fine sword at his hip. He carried a bundle in his left hand. A spearhead protruded from the blankets. Halas saw that his boots and clothes looked worn, in odd contrast to his weapons. A small crowd of men and women were there to see him off. One woman wept. Her husband, a stout, tired-looking man, put his arm around her shoulders.

"Goodbye, Elivain," he said. "Thanks for nothing, you louse."

"Goodbye, Brown," Elivain said. "Should things go as planned, you will no longer need my protection."

"Planned, eh? If you should abandon us in our time of need, us who took you in and gave you shelter when you were desperate, then so be it. We would be better off without your meddlesome intervention!"

At this, Elivain snarled. It was a savage, animal thing. He dropped his bundle and strode the distance to the man called Brown, drawing a hidden knife from the folds of his cloak as he went. "You may think poorly of me at this hour, but know *this*! I do not abandon you; I do not abandon this city! I leave now to strike a blow at Torgeir the Oppressor, and you know that! My skills will be far more effective outside this town than within it, and you know that very well, Brown! So think poorly of me if you will, but do not presume to think that I abandon you!" He stopped roughly five paces from the man called Brown, and lowered his knife. "I would not abandon you, any of you. Seek not the comfort of Talia's bed tonight, Brown, or forever after."

The man called Brown scowled deeply. His wife looked at him, aghast, and pulled away. He glared at Elivain but said nothing.

The villagers did not know how to react to Elivain's outburst. He watched them all. Halas thought he was searching for more confrontation, but there was none. A ruddy-faced child approached Elivain, offering a wrapped loaf of bread. Elivain took the bread and knelt before the child. He muttered something that Halas could not hear, and the child walked back to his mother. Elivain stood and returned to the caravan.

"Shall we?"

They went.

— — —

Elivain's first outing was a disaster. He tried leading the caravan down through a ravine, but the wagons and horses struggled. Wheels jammed in the mud and tangled undergrowth. One of the horses stumbled, going out from under his rider in an instant. When all was said and done, both horse and rider were uninjured, but the caravan had to retreat backwards and take to the road once more. The road led them out of the mountains. Elivain spent much time in the surrounding woods, scouting the terrain. The men suspected that this was to avoid Bernard Claymont's anger, but if they had truly known Elivain, they would have known he feared no such thing.

Each man in the caravan was worried. They all wondered to themselves when Torgeir would strike. Halas woke up every morning feeling relieved. He went to bed every night with his heart in a vice.

— — —

The hours stretched infinitely as they traveled through Torgeir's country, what a man in Busby had so aptly dubbed the lawless lands.

There were no other towns, but they soon came upon the wrecked caravans that had been spoken so fearfully of. The first was only a few hours away from the ravine. A collection of wagon husks that had been long since burned decorated the path in a circle. They had died defending themselves. Corpses of both man and beast filled the husks and road. Halas rode up to one of these corpses, one that was by now more bone than flesh. He looked down at it, biting his lip. One of the caravan drivers swore.

Desmond and Aeon rode up beside him. Somewhere toward the back, Crowe's voice ordered a clearing of the bodies for burial. "Are you all right?" Desmond asked his friends. Halas nodded. He felt as if there should be tears shed for these men who died alone in the cold wilderness, but no tears would come. Halas looked at Aeon. The boy's cheeks were red and his eyes were runny. He wiped them quickly on his sleeve.

"Aeon…" Halas whispered, trying to maneuver his horse closer to the boy to try and comfort him.

"This must be what *The Wandering Blade* is, now, after the battle. They burned it, didn't they? They burned the ship and everyone onboard, survivors or not."

Halas nodded somberly.

Aeon continued. "We were on that ship for nearly three months. It was our home. And now it is a graveyard." He turned to Halas, and Halas could see that his eyes were hollow. "And the worst of it is that it is all my fault."

"No," Desmond said weakly.

"It is! Look into my eyes, Desmond, and tell me that those men would not still be alive if not for my intervention."

Desmond put a hand over his stubbled face. He'd been trying to grow a goatee back in Cordalis, but now it resembled something altogether more feral. "Aeon, that is simply not true. You are not at fault. You cannot help your parentage. As Prince, you stand for something, and they knew that. Those men died defending you, defending their country and ideals."

"Those men did not die for anything of the sort. They died because I was on their boat and I was a target! They fought only for themselves. Do not make them martyrs, Desmond Mallon, for they are not. They are victims. I do not value my life over any other, and I will not have anyone else do as such. Any man who would die for someone like *me* is a foolish man, and foolish was something Captain Brennus and his men were not."

Desmond looked down and quickly rode away.

Behind them, Crowe and Bernard Claymont were having a disagreement. A portion of the men were trying to deal with the bodies at Crowe's wish, but there were just as many who stayed on their mounts, looking uneasily between the caravan leader and his lieutenant.

"Sir, these men deserve a proper burial," Crowe said.

"And we simply do not have the time. We cannot tarry in these dangerous lands, my friend. Torgeir's men may come upon us at any hour, and I would not prolong our stay here for the dead. The dead do not care how their remains are dealt with."

Crowe sighed. "I suppose you are right. It just does not sit right with me, leaving them here."

"I feel there will be many more of these sites to come. You may want to reexamine your feelings."

"Indeed, sir."

Claymont rode away, leaving Dale Crowe thoroughly chagrined. Halas looked back at the scene. For a brief moment, he saw it as it had been, harried men on horseback pushing through Torgeir's lands, cursing and screaming. Despite the fear, there was still mirth, still good. A lute playing softly from inside one of the wagons. Laughter. The clinking of glasses.

And then there was only death.

———

Bernard Claymont was right—there were a great many more dead caravans. Skeletons picked clean to the bone. Eyes peeking out from burnt out wagons. Carrion birds by the score, circling above. The stench was unbearable. To compensate, Halas quickly learned from Crowe himself. The man who reminded them so painfully of Tormod had tied a rag around his neck and covered the lower portion of his face with it. Occasionally he would wet this rag from his canteen. The other men soon followed suit. Claymont hid himself in his wagon and slammed shut the windows.

They passed these awful graveyards each day. Crowe steered the caravan around them, but the sites, it seemed, were unavoidable. Bones seemed as frequent as grass, and what few rivers they saw were stained red.

Two days had passed since Busby when the caravan first heard from Torgeir's men. They traveled through a winding valley, with tall trees obscuring the sun. Halas thought any number of men could be concealed in those trees, or the cliffs above them. The thought chilled him. He kept one hand on his sword.

Halas nearly flew from the saddle when a horn blast interrupted the silence. At the head of the column, Crowe drew his sword. "Ride on! Ride on! I need one rider from each wagon, to me!" he cried. Halas rode forward, gesturing for Des and Aeon to stay with Walter.

Another horn came from further up the bank. It was quickly followed by a third. Halas pulled Owain to a halt near Crowe. A group of riders had assembled. "We're going to clear a path," Crowe told them. "Follow my lead!"

They spurred the horses on. Halas managed to keep pace with a barrel-chested rider he didn't know. They moved ahead, passing swiftly through the valley. As they reached the end, nothing came of it. No men could be seen. There were no more horns.

It was all a farce.

Elivain, sitting atop his horse near Halas, swore. The barrel-chested rider echoed his statement. "The bastard's playing games with us, isn't he?"

"Dwell on this not," Crowe said. "Torgeir's men will come, and when they do, we will be ready for them. Do not fear his tricks, for they are harmless."

"I should hope so," said a man Halas thought was called Porter.

But to Halas, Crowe sounded uneasy. And still, they wondered when Torgeir would strike.

It happened three days out of Busby. It had been almost a full day since they'd passed the last boneyard, but evidently there were fresher corpses near at hand. Elivain returned to the wagons, dragging a half-dead man in one hand, his other holding a bloody knife.

"Scouts!" he said. "Tell them what you told me!"

The man laughed, stopping only to cough blood. "You'll all be dead soon," he yelled. "Every one of you!"

Elivain growled and slashed the man's throat. Halas put an uncomfortable hand on the hilt of his sword, looking around. The woods were still, and now that he paid attention, that scared him most of all. In death they were alive.

At once, Crowe set to work. "Circle the wagons," he ordered. "My Lord Claymont, please get inside. All caravan guards to the front line. Circle the wagons!"

Twenty-nine horses formed a rim around the wagons, the crew and passengers hiding inside, many of them constructing barriers to protect them from stray arrows. Halas was between Des and Aeon. He gulped. What if they made it no farther than here? What if they failed in their mission? He found himself missing Garek, wishing he could dash back to Earlsfort and take his brother home, wishing at least he could have said goodbye. But most of all, he found that he missed Cailin. He missed her smooth hair. He missed her face that was beautiful even when covered in dirt. He missed her soft voice.

They were in a field, surrounded on two sides by tall, threatening trees.

All was silent.

A single arrow arced through the air, striking a caravan guard in his chest and throwing him from his horse. Elivain's bow twanged, his arrow launching for the woods where he knew to be a bandit. At once, the other archers in the caravan followed suit, and soon the battle was joined. Halas wished he had a bow. As it was, he could only hope that no stray arrows hit him.

When seven of the guards were dead and two wounded, the fighting stopped. A host of men rode from the woods to ride in circles around the formation, prodding them with long and sharp spears. Halas still did not draw his sword, knowing it was useless. The horsemen jeered at them, spitting and taunting. Every so often one would dart in, exchanging blows with a guard and riding back to his friends. But there was no real desire to kill the men of the caravan, Halas saw. They were just toying with them.

Perhaps the killing came later.

———

The bandits stopped. They were twice the number of the caravan guards, forming a circle around them. They quarreled viciously amongst themselves, even drawing down on one another in some cases. One rode to the front. "Who is in charge here?"

"I am," said Crowe, sitting up straighter on his horse. He was wounded in his shoulder.

The man rode up to him. "In the name of Torgeir the Mighty, I demand that you surrender your riches, or your life is forfeit," he declared.

"Then my life is forfeit!"

The bandit raised his eyebrows. He spurred his horse, and they trotted closer until the bandit and Crowe were nearly face-to-face. "I give you one last warning, fool. There shall be no others."

But Crowe was still. "Very well then," said the bandit, and he drew his sword. But before he could raise the weapon, Aeon moved to say something, but Halas saw this and beat him to it.

"Wait!"

"Halas!" Desmond hissed.

The bandit turned to regard him, and laughed. "What do you want, boy?"

"We have no treasures with us."

The highwayman laughed again. "Am I to trust the silly words of a child?"

"I am not a child, and you did not let me finish. We do not have any treasure with us, because we've hidden it."

This piqued the man's interest. "Oh?"

"Yes. I know where it is, even, but I will only take you on one condition: Torgeir himself must come with me. Alone."

At this, the man laughed even harder. He rode to Halas. "You are in no position to be making demands. You will take me to your hidings. Torgeir does not deal with His subjects."

"Then he is a poor king!"

The bandit took Halas by the neck. This seemed to upset Owain, who, with a great whinny, reared up on his hind legs. The poor bandit was still holding on to Halas when it happened, and was thrown from his own horse. His fellows looked on in astonishment, and several made as if to shoot Owain. But the man stilled them with a wave of his hand. He was laughing again.

"I like that beast," he said. "And I find myself liking his rider. I will agree to your conditions then, Brave Rider. I am Torgeir the Mighty. Let us go now. Vir! Take his sword."

"Very well," said Halas. He looked at Des and shrugged, trying to appear casual, though he was barely able to keep himself from shaking. Two men rode forth and took his sword. Torgeir mounted his horse, and Halas led him off, back toward Busby.

Of course, there was no hidden treasure, and Halas knew that. But a plan had been formulating in his mind. He had the bandit lord alone, and unwary. That plan had ended the moment Torgeir ordered him disarmed. Now he was worried. What was he to do? There was a knife in Owain's saddlebags. No more than a letter opener, but it was something.

He just had to get to it.

Perhaps he could offer Torgeir the deal Aeon had spoken of: as much of the king's gold as he could carry. If that didn't work, well, Halas supposed he'd just jump on the man and have at it.

"I'm afraid you have me at a disadvantage," said Torgeir, breaking the silence. The caravan was out of sight. "What's your name?"

"Halas." His eyes widened—he'd broken his cover!

"Everything all right?"

"No. Well, yes. No. I suppose not."

"Why's that?"

Halas pondered a moment. He decided that the king of a group of thieves and murderers cared little for Agerian lawbreakers. "Are you going to kill me?"

"That depends. Are you taking me to your treasure?"

"Of course."

"My men have watched you since you passed my borders. When did you have time to bury your things?"

"We did it under cover of night, from beneath a wagon."

"Ah."

They rode for some time. At length Torgeir spoke again. "How far?"

"Not very."

The path had gone into a natural ditch, lined by two ridges just above their heads. Halas was the first to see the danger. Two tigers leapt from one of the ridges like streaks of dark fire. Their fur was the color of the night sky. He marveled at this for a moment before he cried out, steering Owain clear and spurring him on. The first tiger missed Halas, but the second landed squarely on Torgeir, carrying the bandit out of the saddle and to the ground. Owain stumbled and Halas fell, hitting the ground with a hard thump. The horse stopped and kicked at the dirt, as if he were trying to tell Halas to get back on. Torgeir's horse screamed.

Halas rolled over on his belly and saw the tigers. Both were on top of Torgeir, who was fending them off with his bracers and knees. Halas scrambled to his feet. He turned back to Owain and dug madly through the saddlebags. His hands closed around the hilt of the knife. There was no time to think.

Torgeir yelled. The first tiger's jaws had clamped shut around his arm. Halas rushed at them, driving the knife into the top of the beast's head. It released Torgeir and roared, turning to Halas and bearing him to the ground. Halas kicked it in the teeth, knocking a few out, but only succeeded in angering the creature further.

Halas glanced at Owain. The horse moved toward the fight, but then his fear caught up with him, and he moved backwards. The tiger on top of Halas roared again and collapsed. It felt to him as if a house had been dumped on his chest, and suddenly he was gasping at breaths that were devoid of air.

Then the weight was moved. Torgeir heaved the tiger off of Halas with a strained grunt and sank down against the natural wall. Both men were breathing heavily. Halas saw that the second tiger was dead. There was a dull, throbbing pain in his leg where the bulk of the beast had landed.

"Thank you," Halas said. Torgeir grunted again. "Are you all right?"

"Actually, Halas, I believe I am slightly drunk, as luck would have it! This was fate, and you saved my life," he said, "though I would have taken yours. I am in your debt. Should we ever meet again, I will do my best to pay that debt. And I give you one favor that you may ask of me. Think hard, for it will only be one. And should I refuse, you will not get another option."

Halas did think about it. There were a few obvious choices. He should ask Torgeir to renounce his kingdom and cease his highway robbery. But what if he refused? He would, for sure. Owain nestled his head on Halas' shoulder; Halas stroked his muzzle.

What if he didn't? What if he agreed to give up his country? The chance was slim, but it was there. Torgeir was clearly a madman; there was no telling what he would agree to. Halas could free Busby and the countless other villages under Torgeir's control, as well as make the region a much safer place for travelers.

But what of the mission?

If Torgeir refused, Halas would not get another favor. What if he didn't allow them to continue? Halas wanted to curl up in a ball and sleep. He did not wish to make this decision.

But Aeon's quest was crucial. There was nothing of more importance, not even their own lives, Halas realized. He didn't like that, but he knew it to be true. Torgeir would not give up his domain, and Halas couldn't believe how incredibly naïve he had been to even think it. He felt silly.

"I would like safe passage," he whispered, "for my caravan and I."

Torgeir pondered for a moment and then said, "Very well, though I am afraid I must claim your treasure as my own. Policy, you see."

"There is no treasure," said Halas.

Torgeir frowned. His hand drifted down to his sword. He then realized that the blade was buried in the neck of a strange blue tiger, and instead deftly plucked the letter opener from Halas' fingers. Halas made as if to take it back, but Torgeir grabbed him by the throat and pushed him against the bank, placing the weapon against Halas' cheekbone hard enough to draw blood. "You lied to me."

"Yes, I did. You were going to kill us." His voice rose in pitch with each word until he was nearly squeaking.

"I don't like being lied to."

"And I'm not fond of being *murdered*, now that you mention it!"

For a moment the two men stared at each other, and then Torgeir laughed. He stood, tossed aside the knife, and helped Halas to his feet. "Let us return to our people, Halas Who Is Not Entirely of the Truth. My men shall hinder your path no more."

Halas, thinking he'd probably never quite get his breath back, climbed on to Owain with a little trouble, for his leg still hurt. But soon both men were mounted, and they rode off, back toward the caravan and Torgeir's bandits. It had begun to rain when they reached them, little drops here and there. A cold wind blew, and Halas wrapped himself in his cloak.

"What happened?" asked the men.

"Return to the wood, soldiers!" Torgeir cried. "We shall bother these fine gentlemen no longer." He glanced at Dale, though Halas knew that the bandit lord was not really looking at the grizzled old warrior, but the twenty-year old farm boy. "Good day to you, sirs. Pleasure doing business!"

Torgeir turned and rode off. His people followed a moment later. At once, the men of the caravan burst into cheers. The men ignored their dead comrades and clapped for their own survival. They were alive; someone had saved them, and that was all that mattered. Halas felt disgusted.

Des and Aeon raced to his side, but Crowe arrived first. "What happened? What did you do?"

"We were attacked," Halas said. "I saved his life. We have safe passage to Fort Torrance."

"I wish you had not done that," said Elivain. "Torgeir is most certainly a man this world would be better off without."

"I know."

"Then why did you save his life?"

"I don't know."

"Are you all right? Are you injured?" Desmond and Aeon asked. Crowe brushed their questions aside.

"What attacked you?" he asked.

"Two tigers. They were…blue. I don't know where they came from."

"Blue tigers?" said Elivain.

"That's…strange," Aeon said.

Elivain continued. "It sounds to me like you have help, my young friend. Outside help."

Halas did not like the sound of that, and he was beginning to dislike Elivain. Crowe nodded his appreciation. "You did a good job," he said, and rode off.

Des tried to give Halas a hug, but his horse refused to cooperate, and so he had to settle for a clap on the shoulder. "Are you all right?" he asked.

"I think so. One of the beasts landed on my leg."

"Can you move it?" Aeon asked.

"Yes."

"Good."

———

The horses were tethered. They stood at the far end of the field, under light guard, eating grass and drinking from the stream. Meanwhile, the others buried the bodies. Seven men had died in the initial attack, and another had succumbed to his wounds shortly after.

Halas, being both injured and responsible for saving the caravan, was not required to participate in the dig. He sat on the grass, kneading his sore leg, and watched Desmond and Aeon, Des in particular. He seemed deeply saddened by the losses, though Halas felt strangely empty. These men had looked down upon Halas and his companions, much as the crew of *The Wandering Blade* had, and now, they shared their fate.

Too many people had died. Halas, sickened with himself at the thought, realized that he was growing accustomed to it. He was on a very important journey, and men died during such things. In all the stories, men died by the score. Of the monks who had waged war on the Mad Lord Nenner in Springdell, three had survived the final battle. Aeon the Great's party left a scant few. Death was a natural part of the journey, Halas thought. You only survived if you were truly dedicated to the idea of it. Death could come, but Halas wondered if maybe, just maybe, you couldn't keep it away through willpower alone.

Desmond, bless him, did not seem to share Halas' feelings on the matter. Halas could see that his friend's cheeks were wet with tears, and he was putting every ounce of effort he had into digging. The men were making a large grave for all eight of the fallen, and Desmond had disappeared from the waist down in one section of the hole.

Halas realized he was crying. Elivain sat down next to him. Halas started; he'd not heard the man approach.

"It is all right, I mean you no harm, and I bear you no ill will, for that matter. You did what any naïve child would have done."

"I am not…"

Elivain silenced him with a waved hand. "Calm, I also mean no disrespect. You *are* naïve, Halas Duer of Cordalis. I expect you thought to ask the Oppressor to forsake his land, even." He chuckled at the thought, but Halas did not think it particularly funny. A moment later, he realized what had happened.

Elivain knew who he was!

"How do you know me?" Halas asked. So far he'd done a *fantastic* job of keeping to his assumed name, and he knew he had to proceed carefully.

"I know many things. I have wandered far during my years, and met many interesting characters. For instance, I once dealt with a gnome who seemed to think he was a goat. I also knew your father; I fought briefly with him once, long ago."

"You knew my father?"

"I fight with you, Halas Duer. Remember this in the coming days."

Elivain slid to his feet and walked away, toward the trees. Halas looked after him, mystified. Not long after he left, Halas received his second visitor: an old man, one of the caravan drivers. Halas thought his name was Ragley, but he was unsure. Ragley laid a kind hand on Halas' shoulder.

"Service is starting," he said.

"Thank you."

The men laid the bodies side-by-side. They then covered them up, and made a tall marker. Crowe, standing at the front of the assembly, drew his sword. "Draw yours as well, men, and salute these brave souls who have passed on, defending you and yours."

Halas took the hilt and pulled, but his sword did not come free. He realized with a start that he hadn't cleaned it since *The Wandering Blade*. Suddenly very worried, he gave it a good yank. The sword came free. Halas inspected it. There was a thin red crust around the edges, but nothing more. No rust, no stains. He scratched off the crust and saluted the men.

When the funeral was over he cleaned both sheath and sword in the stream, making sure to dry them well. Night had fallen, and though they had Torgeir's promise, they kept a heavy guard. Still, the others were awake well into the night, clutching weapons.

They set out early that morning, indeed before the sun had even risen, and went at a fast pace, racing across the fields and through the forests. Halas took no notice of anything that went on at this time, though he could see Aeon and Desmond speaking fervently whenever they were together. Claymont drove them on through the night, and they stopped for a brief rest after the sun rose before taking off again.

It was a grueling pace, and they saw no sign of any bandits. Elivain, despite his earlier words, did not seem pleased with Halas, and spoke not a word to him through the rest of the journey. Eleven days after Halas killed the tiger, the spires of Fort Torrance came into view. The men forgot their sorrows; they laughed and cheered; they were safe.

But it was an altogether different feeling for the three friends. It dawned on Halas then that they were wanted fugitives, and here they were, riding straight into a military fortress.

Aeon's words reverberated in his mind: *Trust in distance, my friend.*

Trust in distance.

Sub Chapter Eight

"A ship!" cried the lookout. "There's a ship on the horizon!"

Raazoi strode to the bow, staring off into the distance. She smiled. "It's them."

"How do you know?" Nolan asked.

"Trust me."

Raazoi was the new captain of the ship. She had a falcon sent to the others in their little fleet, ordering them to be ready for battle. "Today, you avenge your Admiral King," she told those near her. They smiled and readied their weapons.

The Wandering Blade came on strong. Raazoi ordered ballistae to be fired; she ordered the ship to be stopped. "But Prince Aeon is to be saved," she said. "You may do with the others what you wish."

When the craft were within yards of each other, Raazoi disappeared into their cabin, leaving Nolan to command the battle. "Charge!" he yelled, and leapt across the small path between the ships. He was met by two sailors in bright silver uniforms. He cut them down.

Laughing maniacally, he charged another group, slaughtering them as well, relishing the feeling of blood on his hands. His sword shone brightly in it. He took no wounds, and eventually, came face to face with a giant of a man.

Tormod hefted his sword angrily. Nolan snarled. Everyone around them instinctively knew to avoid, to stay clear. This was between the two men, two men who hated each other with a passion and did not know entirely why.

Nolan met Tormod head on, leaping into the air and slicing downward. Tormod, big though he was, was agile. He parried with total efficiency, driving Nolan off-balance as he landed. Nolan told himself that he would not underestimate this man again. He darted in, stabbing, probing the defenses. Tormod was tired and heavy. He was also wounded; there was a gash that ran down his left thigh.

Nolan danced around the bigger man, just out of his reach, slapping his sides with his cutlass. It took only seconds.

He kicked the big man's wound.

Tormod toppled.

Nolan stabbed him in the back, pushing past the tip of the blade. He knelt down beside Tormod's ear, and smiled.

"I win," he whispered.

Tormod sagged.

The battle was over. The bodies of the dead were mixed with those of the nearly-dead, crying out for help and gods and families. Nolan took pleasure in ending them. But there were prisoners. Raazoi walked delicately across the gangplank, smiling at Nolan as he stood, drenched in blood. He smiled back.

Chapter Nine

Escape From Fort Torrence

Fort Torrance, though far out of Ager, was an Agerian Fortress ruled and controlled by King Melick. A general was in charge of the fort itself. His word was law. Five such castles existed in Aelborough, and Conroy had once told Halas the names of all the generals. He'd since forgotten them.

Desmond rode beside him. "Aeon and I have been talking," he whispered. "We've got to leave."

"I was thinking the same thing, but how? There's no cover for a mile; anyone on the wall will be able to see us."

"Aye, that's what worries me. We're going to have to wait until nightfall. Aeon says that we'll ride out tonight as soon as we can."

"There may not be any shelter until we reach Bakunin." He glanced at the mountains, looming ominously above them. Snow capped the peaks and had begun to stretch downward. Traversing those mountains was going to be very unpleasant. "It's going to be a very cold walk. We'll need food, and furs."

Desmond's face was resolute. "We'll steal some. Are you all right with that?"

"I don't suppose I have much choice."

"Sorry."

"Don't be." Halas offered a smile. Desmond was doing his best.

They rode to the gate. Claymont showed his papers to the guard, and they were allowed in. The horses were stabled and the men led inside. They were sat at a long table. Claymont and Crowe followed two guards deeper into the castle. A captain addressed the rest of the men. "You must be hungry, and weary," he said. "Please, allow us to aid you. Do any of you require medical attention? No? Excellent. Food shall be brought to you soon."

It was cold. Halas and Des sat together while they waited, and after a minute Halas spoke. "Do you ever think about the forest?"

"All the time. I wonder what Halbrick was doing in there."

"I hope he's all right," Halas lamented.

"I'm sure he's fine. He strikes me as the type that can take care of himself, you know? And the way he handles that sword, he's a right genius, I reckon. You should not worry about him."

There was a rich feast of hot soup, stiff meats and juicy fruits and vegetables. There was bread enough to fill everyone's stomachs, with actual butter to go with it. Halas tore into the food with a fevered intensity. Some of it was less than grand, however. Halfway through the meal, Walter bit into a potato, and immediately began coughing and hacking. Halas saw the potato—it was black and green: rotted. He grimaced. "Can you believe this shit?" Walter asked. "First tater I get in months, and it's got the rot."

"It's perfect for you," said Porter, several seats over. Walter laughed and threw it at him.

Throughout the feast, when he was sure no one was watching, Des would slip a fistful of crabapples or berries, a carrot, or a slice of wrapped ham into the pack at his feet. Aeon leaned over to Halas. "Did Desmond tell you the plan?"

"Yes. Let's hope we are quartered together."

They were given the option of their rooms, and the three friends chose one with four soft beds lining the walls. The guard who took them was an older man, who glanced at Aeon several times as they walked with the look of someone who has seen what he believes to be an old friend. Aeon shied away, uncomfortable with the man's gaze.

They knew it was too much to ask for a fourth man not to join their room, and Halas hoped dearly it would be Walter. Walter would understand their leaving, but it was not to be. Not two minutes after entering the chamber, Elivain sauntered inside, laying his kit down beside the fourth bed. He nodded curtly to Halas before going immediately to sleep. Halas sat on the edge of his own bed. He wondered how he was going to prevent himself from falling asleep on the thing; it was like a cloud.

———

It was his leg that kept him up. Once the excitement had died down, Halas noticed the dull throb. As he lay in the soft, oh so soft bed, the pain gradually worsened. Twice Halas had to look at it, expecting to see a deep gash, but saw only purple bruises up and down his thigh.

Late in the night, Elivain's snores told Halas that the man was asleep. He sat up, dressed, and slung his pack, creeping across the room to Aeon's bed. The prince was already awake, so Halas went to Desmond. Desmond was sound asleep. He rolled over and hiccupped. "Des!" Halas hissed. "Des, wake up. Des. Des!"

"Not now…" muttered Desmond.

Halas shook him roughly. He bolted upright with a shout.

Halas cocked an eyebrow. "Sorry," Desmond said, "dreaming."

"Get a move on then, we've got to hurry."

"Right."

Des got up, but nearly cried out as someone grabbed his arm. It was Elivain in the next bed over. Aeon took hold of the man's wrist, spun it around, and flipped him over the side of the bed. Elivain rolled to his knees, pushing the prince away. Halas, the pain in his leg momentarily forgotten, grabbed Aeon by the arm and moved for the door, but Elivain skipped over the bed and barred the way.

"Not so fast! Where are you three off to in the dead of night?"

"Just leave us alone," said Aeon. "You won't understand."

"I think you'll find that there is not a lot that can surprise me, Prince Aeon."

If Halas could see in the dark, he would have seen that Aeon's face went stark white. Elivain knew who they were, but was he friend, or foe? *He said that he was not an enemy, but how am I to be sure?* "How…how do you know who I am?" Aeon asked.

"I am older than I look, and well-traveled. I remember when you were born; I was in Cordalis at the time. Now, tell me, where is it you are off to?"

The three friends looked between each other. "Tell me," he continued, "or I will alert the guards, and you two will be off to the jail. What'll it be?"

Aeon took a wary step back. Halas put a hand on his shoulder. They had to tell Elivain. There was nothing else for it. *And besides, he claims to have fought with my father. That means he can be trusted, to a certain extent.* "We make for Aeon's Temple," said Aeon. "My namesake."

The room seemed to grow even darker. "Then the old words are true," Elivain said. "There is one who is half-Ifrinn, and he seeks to free his people."

"She, actually," said Desmond. "The half-Ifrinn is a woman. A witch."

"This seems a worthy cause," said Elivain. "I would like to assist you."

"No," said Aeon.

"No?" There was a hint of amusement in his voice. Halas was reminded of Conroy denying them weapons. It seemed so long ago, in another life. If only Conroy could see him now. Since leaving Cordalis, Halas had done things he never would have dreamed himself capable of.

"It is out of the question. We do not know you. How can we trust you?"

"I suppose you'll have to. As I said—I'll call the guards. Besides that, I've been to Bakunin. I know the way through the Frigid Peaks. Can any of you say the same? How do you expect to navigate such a place without a guide?"

"We hadn't thought of that…" Desmond said. Halas shot him a glare.

"Exactly. Now, I suppose we'll need supplies. I'll sneak down to the larder. Meet me at the West Gate. There is a way through the wall there. Stay in the shadows, and stay quiet. Should any of the guards notice us, your quest will be over before it even begins."

With that, he left the room, leaving the three friends surprised, scared, and, in Halas' case at least, severely irritated.

"Should we trust him?" Des asked.

"He was right," said Halas. "We don't have a choice."

"We shall have to be wary," said Aeon, "as we do not yet know his true intentions. Let us go down to the West Gate. Soon we'll know if he means to alert the guards or not."

They snuck quietly down the corridors, nearly getting lost, but luckily Halas remembered the way outside. From there they made along the wall until they were at the correct gate and hunkered down behind a few barrels. A guard patrolled nearby, twirling a club in his hands and whistling. He stopped on the corner to exchange words with another guard. Halas couldn't hear either of them, but the second guard burst into uproarious laughter before moving on.

They waited.

The streets were narrow, and frequently they were passed by one or more patrolling guards. The men came far too close for Halas' liking. Each time the three pressed against their cover and prayed the moonlight would not give them away. Halas was terrified they would be discovered. It would be difficult enough to explain being out at so late an hour, but trying to tell a guard why they were so blatantly hiding would be impossible.

"He isn't coming," Desmond whispered after they had waited an eternity.

"No, but the soldiers don't seem to be on alert," Aeon replied. "I think Elivain's been captured."

Halas' blood ran cold. "He knows who we are. He knows our mission."

"Elivain doesn't seem the type to give us away," Desmond said. "But all the same, we should escape before anything happens."

"Do you know what the penalty for thieving in a military fortress is, Desmond?" Aeon asked.

"No."

"It's death. By dragging."

Desmond shook his head and fell into thought.

Halas spoke. "We don't have enough food, only a little of what Mister Harves gave us and whatever Des stole at supper. We have to go back, at the very least for that. Besides, if we manage to free him soon, maybe he won't have talked yet. Perhaps we can still get away."

"It doesn't seem like they're expecting any of us to be up and about," Desmond said. "Let's do it."

Aeon stopped them. "Do you know where they're keeping him?"

Des coughed quietly.

"No. But I mean to find out. We'll grab the next guard. He'll tell us."

Time stretched on as they waited for another guard to come by. When he did, luck was with the friends—the man was alone. Halas fell over one of the barrels, stumbling across the alley and into him. Aeon and Des grabbed the guard and pushed him roughly against the wall. Desmond struck him across the face. His sword was in his hand. He put it to the man's neck. "Where's your thief?" he demanded. "Tell me where he is or I'll run you through!"

"Des!" Halas hissed. "We can't do this, you ass! We can't kill anyone here."

"I mean to," said Des, "if he doesn't show us the way. And you can be sure of it if he cries out."

The guard turned. He was young, young as Halas and Des, certainly. His face was covered in the pimples. A curl of scraggly blond hair peered out from under his helmet, and his upper lip quivered. The poor boy looked on the verge of tears. It was likely he'd never experienced anything so violent. "Follow me," he said, his voice shaking.

They did, and soon they came to a tall, dark tower in the corner of the fortress. Halas had a coil of rope in his pack. Shivering from the cold, he tied and gagged their hostage. The boy didn't struggle, and Halas felt absolutely miserable about the whole thing. Desmond crept along a low wall toward the tower door, where another soldier stood watch. He whistled, and when the guard went to investigate, Des smashed him in the back of the head with the hilt of his sword. The guard collapsed. He tried to rise, but Desmond pressed the point of his blade against his throat.

"Be quiet."

They tied him to the boy. Halas was first to the door. He turned the handle gently, and looked to his friends. "Ready?"

"Ready," they said.

He threw open the door. There were four men in the room. Elivain was one of them; the other three were guards. They had Elivain tied to a chair, and while two guards rifled through his things, the third struck Elivain repeatedly in the face and stomach. Halas, Des, and Aeon each took a man. With no time for a plan, they acted instinctively, each trusting the other to do what had to be done.

The man who stood over Elivain turned toward the door, a blank look on his face. He was fully engrossed in his task. Halas saw a small spackling of blood that likely wasn't his as he barreled into the man, bringing him to the ground. The guard's head connected firmly with the floor as they landed. He gave out a grunt and fell silent. Desmond took on the man nearest to the door. His sword was still buckled at his hip. Desmond pressed his own blade to the man's cheek. "Hands," Des whispered.

Aeon had more trouble. As he cleared the room, the third guard managed to re-act, drawing his sword and getting into position. Aeon came on wildly, swinging in what looked to be a reckless manner but was actually a maneuver Tormod had tried to teach Halas aboard *The Wandering Blade*, designed to overwhelm an opponent of average skill. It did its job, but Aeon was not able to subdue the guard peacefully. They exchanged blows before Aeon overcame him, sweeping the man's head off his shoulders with little effort. Halas saw this as the guard he'd tackled tried to get to his feet. Halas hit him under the arm and pressed his face to the ground.

"Not a word!"

Aeon moved to Elivain next, slashing the bonds that held him. Wordlessly, Elivain took his sword from the counter with his things and slit Desmond's prisoner's throat. The man fell backwards, grasping at his neck. Desmond tried to catch him, but then stepped back, unsure of what to do.

"Elivain! What are you doing?" Halas cried.

Elivain pushed him aside. Halas couldn't find it in him to truly resist. He looked away as Elivain drove his weapon home. It was all too familiar. All he could see was the face of Bartholomew Hadric. "They will give us away otherwise. Quickly, help me put my things in order. We cannot stay here."

Elivain had three packs, his cloak, and his belt. Halas began stuffing bits of food and supplies into the first pack, distracting himself from looking at the bodies on the floor. The other bags were untouched. He put on his belt and cloak, slung the packs, and together, the four ran back to the West Gate. Elivain showed them a low door and they ducked through it, disappearing into the shadows. Open plains stretched as far as Halas could see.

"How are we going to get clear?" he asked.

"Therein lies the trouble," Elivain said. "We're going to have to run for a while." He led them along the wall. They faced west, but had to go north. Above them, Halas could hear guards on watch, laughing and fooling around.

"What about the horses?" Halas asked, feeling a pang of guilt. He'd grown to like Owain. Elivain shrugged.

"They are in good care here. A pity to leave them behind, but what's done is done."

They sprinted across the fields toward the distant mountains. Halas' thigh was on fire by the time they reached the first bit of cover, in the form of a low ditch. The four slid in and made themselves small. Halas went to work then, rubbing and kneading the muscles. He didn't want his leg locking up, not while there was still so much walking to do. Elivain dropped his pack and took a long draught of water.

"What did you manage to get?" Des asked. Still drinking, Elivain gestured for him to open the bag.

Desmond groaned, for the pack was filled with *spódhla*.

———

Garek watched Jaden Harves pull up the drive and come into the house. He ran downstairs, already wishing that he had said goodbye to his brother. He missed Halas more than he would have thought possible. "Hello, Garek!" said Harves. "What's for supper, then?"

"We've got some pork left over."

"Are you all right?"

"Of course I'm all right. Why wouldn't I be?"

"You were angry with your brother."

"Still am."

"You should have made up before he left."

"I know." At that moment, Garek started to sob. He hadn't felt it coming on, there was no buildup, but before he knew it he was on the floor. "He wouldn't even be here if not for me. He only volunteered to go on that blasted ship because of me. If something happens to him, it's my fault. I feel terrible."

Harves sat beside him and put his arm around Garek's broad shoulders. "That is not so, Garek. You were drafted—there's nothing you could have done to prevent that. Halas only went along because he is your brother, and he loves you. Both of you are in the wrong for not saying goodbye, however, but what's done is done. There's nothing you can do about that, either. He'll be back soon, I trust. Theirs is now a much shorter journey than your trip up the Inigo. It will seem like no time has passed at all."

Garek smiled sadly. "Thank you."

"It is my pleasure."

Garek felt very much at home, sitting next to Jaden with the man's arm over his shoulders. He felt like Halas must have felt quite often back in Cordalis. Acceptance, comforting love. And what right did Halas have to be angry, anyway? Did Garek not deserve to have a father? Was it so wrong that he'd found his own place to call home? It wasn't, not to Garek.

"How is Tom?" he asked.

"Tom went away this morning. I cannot believe it's going to be almost a year before I see him again."

"I'm sorry."

"Do not be. He and I agreed it was for the best. Tom will be safest out there, as long as he keeps to the road. I do hope he keeps to the road."

"I'm sure he will."

"I have no doubt that…" Jaden paused, and looked up. His eyes glazed; the man was listening intently for something.

"Hide!" he hissed. He pushed Garek toward the stairs, but as Garek crossed the foyer the front door was kicked in, showering him with splinters. Jaden sprang forward, grabbing Garek by the shoulder and flinging him away. "Run!"

"Jaden Harves!" one called. "Give us the boy! He's a wanted fugitive, and I will have him in my custody!"

Jaden had a knife in his hand, standing between the soldiers and Garek. He made no move to surrender, but Garek, frozen with fear, made no move to escape.

"Very well," said the captain. "By order of the queen, I, Lord Gilroy of the Agerian Military, place both of you under arrest."

The soldiers moved in, and set manacles around their wrists. They were cautious with Harves, but in the end, when he saw that there was no escape for Garek, he relented. Gilroy leaned in close, a wicked smile on his face. "I think you'll enjoy Crumman," he whispered. "I think you will enjoy it very much."

Harves took a step back and began to thrash in his chains. One soldier stumbled away as he was kicked. "Garek, run!" Jaden screamed. A soldier cuffed him on the chin, but Jaden kept fighting. Garek didn't know what Crumman was, but he knew the very mention of it terrified Jaden. This time he did try to run, but it was just as fruitless as before. Several soldiers bore down on him, and soon he was unconscious.

Chapter Ten

A Very Cold Walk

They knew that they would be followed, so they made a quick pace. Elivain cautioned against running, but Aeon wished to get the Temple quickly, and they had at least a hundred miles to cross, nearly half of that mountainous. So they ran when they could, taking short rests in between sprints. This began to take its toll on Desmond first.

"I can't do this anymore," he said, sitting against a tree, breathing heavily. They were in a small copse of trees, old and new leaves coating the ground like a crisp blanket. Elivain lit a fire.

"Sorry Desmond, but we have no other option. Our master drives us at a slave's pace."

Aeon didn't hear the remark, but Halas did. It troubled him; their journey was dangerous enough without inner squabbling. They should never have taken Elivain along. Still, they did need a guide, and he claimed to know the way.

But how can we trust him? What if he leads us into a trap?

Halas frowned; this way of thinking would get him nowhere. They had no choice but to trust Elivain, but they could still be cautious. He trusted his father, and that would have to be enough. In the meantime, it would do Halas no good to dwell on it. As they ate a meager lunch, he wondered about Walter, and Crowe, and the others of the caravan. What had become of them? Had they been punished for taking in fugitives? Halas surely hoped not. Walter especially had been kind to them, and Halas had nothing but the utmost respect for Dale Crowe.

"We have to move," Aeon said. "We'll run until we have to stop. Up you go!"

Of the four, all of the running was hard on Halas and Desmond, especially poor Des. He was a merchant's son, and not used to intense physical activity. Though Halas was, the running was too much. Eventually, even he had to rest. His injured leg was humming with pain. He thought that cutting it off would be for the best. Aeon and Elivain were fine, though the latter man was grouchy.

"We cannot keep up this pace! They'll soon collapse of exhaustion, and then where will we be?"

"That is indeed a risk," said Aeon, "but it is one we must take, for the soldiers at our backs will surely have horses and we did not have much of a head start, if indeed we had one at all. You've also made them angry. You should not have killed their friends."

Elivain brushed off the rebuke. "That is certainly so, but we can only keep this up for so long. I will find a place to hide."

Elivain went off, and returned soon after. He'd found a natural culvert, a tunnel buried deep within a hill. Halas, Des, and the prince crawled inside, while Elivain covered the entrance with leaves and sticks. He finished from within, scooting back down the narrow tunnel to join the three friends.

It was dark, incredibly so. Only a few patches of light shone through Elivain's cover, and those did not go far into their tunnel before disappearing. Halas and his friends huddled in the dark with Elivain. Evening came on; it was chilly. Halas was awake, though he was unsure if anyone else was. They'd all decided not to speak.

Suddenly, Halas heard faint voices outside. He put his hand on the hilt of his sword, but even he knew that to try to fight would be a useless gesture. Beside and behind him, he felt Desmond stiffen. Outside, the sound of voices was getting closer, accompanied by hoof beats and the sounds of metal grating against metal. Armored men were close by.

The dim patches of light disappeared suddenly; Halas realized that there was someone just outside. He was holding his breath.

"You see something?" came a voice.

"Not rightly sure," said a louder one, most likely the man outside their hiding spot. "I smell something, though."

"Maybe they came by here."

"Maybe. Ride on!"

The light returned, and Halas could feel vibrations at his feet and head, which was braced against the ceiling of the tunnel. There were horses above them. *Wonderful,* he thought. *After such a close call, a horse is just going to break through the ground and crush us!*

But that did not happen, and soon the world was quiet again.

"We will rest here for tonight," Aeon said, "and make our way cautiously to the mountains. Elivain, how far are they?"

"About a day's march," Elivain said. "Moreso, if we're creeping about. Still, I am glad that we hid—those men were very close behind us."

"Yes, they were."

Things were quiet again, until Desmond began to snore. Halas was later sure that the rest of his companions were likewise asleep, and had to laugh. Elivain's breathing was quiet; he didn't snore.

The whole thing at Fort Torrance had been an act. He shook his head, and eventually drifted off.

They rested for a few hours before setting out again. Elivain took the lead, and Aeon let them go at a slower pace, though not much of one. The soldiers were now in front of them, and it would not do to catch up. Even still, he worried about reaching the Temple ahead of those who would seek to do it harm.

———

It was rough going. The ground had begun to slope noticeably upward, and soon the four were climbing steep hills, granted only minor reprieves in between. The grass thinned and the air became colder. After one such hill, Des flopped down. "We have to rest," he moaned. Aeon rounded on him.

"Get up! We cannot rest, not here, not now. We must reach the Temple of Immortals, and we must do it soon."

"Aeon," Elivain said, "I'm afraid that such a thing is impossible. Even at the fastest run, Bakunin is still several days from here. After that, the distance is far greater. We are in for at least a fortnight of walking, and it will not do for us to collapse out here!"

"We must!"

Elivain growled. "You wanted me to guide you to that blasted temple, but I will not run all the way there! If you continue this, I will simply turn around and go home."

Aeon's hand drifted to the hilt of his sword, as did Elivain's. Halas' eyes widened; he stepped forward, waving his hands empathetically.

"Stop this! Stop! Both of you are right. It is true that there are people on the way to our objective, and we must beat them to it. But we cannot go at these speeds, Aeon, my friend, not while we traverse such dangerous ground."

"Halas," Aeon said, "stop defending him!"

"He is right! You drive us too fast, and there is much ground to cover."

"Do you not see the significance of this journey?"

"I do."

"Then why would you seek to hinder us?"

"I would rather get there late, but alive, than die out here in the cold!" Halas was beginning to get angry. Why did this boy not see?

Aeon hung his head. When he looked up, Halas saw that there were tears in his eyes. He immediately softened. "Halas," Aeon whispered, "I understand that. I just…I just…we have to get there, and we must outrun ships who have likely had an incredible head start. Tormod…Tormod would have done the same."

Halas understood now. He put a reassuring hand on his friend's shoulder. "We will make it," he said. "And you will accomplish your mission. Tormod would be proud."

"I shall set the pace," said Elivain. Aeon nodded dejectedly. It was only later that Halas realized what had happened. Elivain had made a bid for leadership, and he had won.

They cleared the foothills, making it a little ways up the mountain before encountering any snow. But soon it was cold, and soon the frozen stuff was everywhere, whipping around their faces in a vicious frenzy, trapping their feet with every step. Elivain distributed furs, and they wrapped them tightly about their bodies, trudging onward.

The road was hard to find, but Elivain managed to keep them tight to the path, at times crawling through the snow on their bellies, slipping on ice every few steps. Halas' face, peeking out through the fur, was frozen. He felt as if he could snap his nose off, or his ears. His eyes were dry, and every breath came ragged, the cold air stabbing his throat like a million little daggers. He could only see a few foot-lengths in front of him.

After hours of misery, Elivain veered sharply to the right, and Halas, close behind, had no choice but to follow. He hoped that Aeon and Des were behind them, and a quick check ensured that they were. Elivain disappeared suddenly, and then the snow, too, was gone.

They were in a cave, Halas noted with relief. It kept the wind out, but the floor was covered in a thin layer of ice. Halas felt the chill leaving his bones a little at a time. Elivain was laying down several blankets.

"Glad we brought those," Desmond said, and Halas agreed. They slept back-to-back, and slept long.

Halas awoke sometime in the night to see Desmond struggling with a fire. "Here," he said, "let me help you with that." Between the two of them, they soon had a meager blaze going, on which they cooked a sausage each. "There's only a little of the real stuff left," Halas said sourly.

"Don't remind me," said Des, wrinkling his nose. "But the longer I go without eating any of that *spódhla*, the happier I'll be.

Halas snorted laughter. "How are you?" he asked.

Des shrugged. "Aside from the biting winds and piles of snow high enough to bury me three times over? I'm just lovely. How are you?"

"About the same."

"No, that's not what I meant. How are you?"

Halas had thought he didn't want to talk, or even think about Garek, but right then he supposed he did. And who better to discuss it with than Des? He looked outside. He couldn't tell if it had stopped snowing. Dark clouds blanketed the moon and stars, making vision impossible. "I don't know," he said after a brief moment of thought. "He's safer with Mister Harves, isn't he?"

"I suppose so. All the same, I wish he were here."

"As do I. These two aren't much in the way of company."

"You're one to talk."

Halas grinned, Des winked.

"I do pity the boy—the prince—Aeon, I mean. He's really warming up to us, I think, but if it took losing my mentor and closest friend? I'd choose to stay an ass, thank you very much."

"You don't have a mentor."

"No. My father doesn't know Conroy." Another grin.

"Never gets old, Des."

"Oh, I was being facetious."

"I know."

<hr>

Elivain woke them before the sun was up, and they skipped breakfast. His morning goal was a mountain pass, about a mile over a few ridges, which turned into hours of grueling climbing and pushing through snow that was hip-deep. Elivain walked at the front, brushing aside drifts of it with his spear, floundering forward inches at a time. The spear made for a terrible spade, but it was better than nothing. Halas sank into one of the piles, and Desmond turned to face him. "Can't stop now," he said, and helped him up. They continued on.

The day was clear, and because of that, the night was frozen. They had no cave, so Elivain cleared a space and set to work constructing a shelter from the snow. "I was hoping to travel ahead of this weather," he grumbled as he worked. Desmond watched, interested. Halas and Aeon sat off to the side. Aeon scanned the hills around them. Halas crossed his arms over his chest and wished he were back at home.

Elivain's shelter scarcely left room for the four of them. They hid their gear outside, high in a tree. Halas worried about the bags; what if they were blown away in the night, or carried off by some animal? But he needn't have worried. The next morning, Aeon climbed up and found their stuff precisely where they'd left it.

As they pushed deeper into the mountains, Halas wondered if he'd ever see Cordalis again. Things here were so cold, so barren, he felt as if he'd come into an entirely new world, one from which there was no returning. His leg alone burned, but the rest of his body was filled with a cold so deep he knew he would never be rid of it.

The next few days were much of the same. The snow was unbearably deep and the air unbearably frozen, and Halas soon thought he would lose his fingers. Aeon was quiet and sullen, but Halas and Des never seemed to run out of things to talk about, trying desperately to keep their spirits up. Elivain pushed everyone grimly on. The days were bad, but to Halas, the nights where he huddled awake long after the others were asleep, alone with his own thoughts, were even worse. They rested whenever they found a suitable spot, usually a cave, though more than once Elivain was forced to build another shelter from the snow. Then, one by one, they would drift off, leaving Halas to himself. He thought of his father and Conroy's betrayal, of Cailin and Olan. The more he dwelt on such things, the more he became convinced everyone in Cordalis wanted him never to return. They were better off. It was silly, he tried to convince himself, but the idea stayed.

And so, thinking such thoughts, Halas would finally sleep, and dream uneasy dreams.

On the fourth morning, Halas woke to find he was alone. The cave was empty, yet he saw bedrolls and furs. Had something taken his companions? Grabbing Silvia, Halas stumbled from the cave and into the light.

Desmond, Elivain, and Aeon stood a ways away, huddled over something. Halas shivered and crossed his arms across his body. Already the tips of his fingers were turning blue. Feeling very foolish, he sheathed his sword, dressed, and joined them.

"Hello, Halas," Desmond said. He had three crabapples in his hand. He tossed one to Halas. Halas nearly dropped it and took a quick bite. It was bitter, but it was food.

"Morning. What's the matter?"

Aeon gestured toward the ground. Halas looked, and saw an enormous paw print, big enough to stand in twice over. "Bear, I think," he said.

"This is no bear," Elivain said. "I thought you were a hunter."

"I am. But what else could this be? It looks like a wolf's paw, but no wolves grow to be that size."

"Some do," Elivain said.

Aeon narrowed his eyes at the man. "Do not play games, Elivain. Dire wolves have long been extinct."

"So you say. But I think you will find a lot of things in these mountains you believe to be extinct. Dire wolves, goblins, trolls. Things thrive here, far from civilization."

"What is a dire wolf?" Desmond asked. Halas thought he already knew the answer.

"Legends say that they are the souls of evil men, punished by Santrum and the Forces of Equilibrium to maintain the body of a giant wolf," Aeon said. "A counterpoint to the forces of good."

"Legends say that of all beasts," Elivain scoffed. "In the old days everything was about the *Equilibrium*. But beasts are beasts. Monsters are monsters, and demons are demons. Dire wolves are just great big wolves, demonic only in size and with no special abilities of their own. We should ware them as we ware all predators, but pay them no heed beyond the norm."

Halas looked at Desmond. Aeon began to argue with Elivain, but Halas' mind was on other things. "Des," he whispered, "does that sound familiar to you?"

Desmond nodded. Halas noticed he'd unconsciously reached up to touch the scar on his arm, left from when they had been attacked in the forest outside Cordalis. One wolf had nearly killed both of them back then. Now, they were four, and well armed, but would that make a difference?

They met no beasts, or monsters, or demons during the remainder of their walk. Indeed, Halas felt completely alone in the desolate mountain range. The landscape all looked so similar, so on the cusp of their first week out of Fort Torrance, it was a considerable surprise when the four stumbled into a village. There were no boundaries of any sort, just a wooden house sitting there in the snow, a delicious smell emanating from within.

"Well," said Elivain, trying to mask his alarm, "here we are."

"You mean to say that this is Bakunin?" Aeon asked.

"Indeed it is. Let's find the inn, shall we?"

Coming around the side of the house, they startled a rather large woman relaxing on her front porch. She jumped to her feet with deceptive agility, putting her hands to her chest and giggling. "Oh! Hello there!"

Elivain tipped his hood toward the lady. "Hello, my dear. How do you fare?"

"Supper's cooking and the air is crisp. It is a fine day. And yourself? You'd be new here, I expect."

"We've just arrived. Would you know where we could find affordable lodgings? It has been some time since I was last here."

"Oh, you've been to Bakunin before, have you? And what would you go by?" the woman asked. Halas thought she seemed genuinely interested. He guessed these people didn't see outsiders too much.

"I am Elivain, of the south."

"Well, Elivain, I think you'll find that most everything is of the south." She smiled warmly. Elivain returned it. Halas found himself liking the woman.

"Where I come from is," Elivain said. He paused, thinking, very south.

"What is your name, madam?" Aeon asked, stepping forward.

"He speaks, does he? And he has manners!" She squealed with delight, clapping her hands together. "I am Miriam. My husband is Harden, and our children are Hild and Carth. Here in Bakunin my husband is the mayor, though I myself am content to weave baskets from bark. We shall have to have you all over for supper while you are here. How long are you staying?"

"Not very long, though we shall be back," Elivain said.

Aeon interjected. "We have an urgent errand up north. I would love to take you up on your offer upon its completion." He bowed low. "It would be an honor."

"It would indeed! And what would you go by, young man? It's not often that folks from out of town are so polite!"

"I am Ennym Straub. These are my friends, Darius and Art. We come from Cordalis."

"And what is your errand, should I ask?"

"Perhaps I will tell you when we return. We are under orders from King Melick of Ager himself. I pray you understand."

Halas didn't see much point in using their false names if Aeon was going to detail their mission anyway, but he said nothing. Elivain would sort things out. Miriam nodded balefully. "I will hold you to it, my new friends. In answer to your first question, there's only one inn here. Marrok calls it Little Sayad. He's a tricky fellow; his prices are low, but they do add up. Be wary."

"We will, madam," Elivain said. "Thank you for your time."

"It was my pleasure! I know you do not have time for supper, but perhaps you would like to meet my Harden? As mayor, he likes to greet new arrivals, you see. Views it as part of the job."

"Of course. Is he in?"

"He is. Just a moment." Halas expected the woman to go into her home and return moments later, husband in tow, but she did no such thing. Still watching the four travelers, Miriam opened wide and called in the most unpleasant voice imaginable, "*HARDEN!* Harden Graves, come outside this instant! We have visitors!"

Des snickered, but thankfully managed to keep it at that.

196

The door swung open, and through it came a bearded man with very little hair otherwise. He held a rag in his hands. "Visitors? At this time of night? Tell me, folks, are you loony? Have you any idea just how cold it is out there?"

"Some," Elivain said.

Harden Graves beamed. He stepped forward to shake Elivain's hand. "You a family, then? New here?"

"I'm afraid not. We're only passing through."

"They're on a mission from the Agerian *king*," Miriam attempted to whisper in her husband's ear.

"A mission, eh? What would that be?"

"A secret one, I'm afraid. My apologies. My friends and I need but a few days to rest and gather supplies. Then we shall be on our way."

"Nonsense," Harden said, ignoring the expression. "Town's plenty big enough for four decent looking folk such as yourself. Stay as long as you need, you won't hear any complaints on my end. Although, fair warning, some of the town might just nag your ear off." He made eye contact with Aeon and tossed him a wink.

"Thank you," Elivain said. "Miriam was kind enough to direct us to Bakunin's inn, and we are very tired. We'll let you get back to your meal."

"If you're sure," said Harden. "Come by tomorrow to speak with me, Mister Elivain. Anyone on business from the king would have my full support. Anything I can do for you, just ask."

"I will, but for now I think we're willing to settle for lodgings and a hot meal. A pleasant evening to the both of you."

"And you."

As soon as they had left sight of the house, Elivain jabbed Aeon harshly on the chest. "Do not do that again," he said.

"Do what?"

"I don't care how important it makes you feel, if you continue to speak about our mission to everyone we meet I'll have to tie you up and lock you in a cellar!"

"This is not *our* mission, Elivain. This is *my* mission. If not for us you would be sleeping in a bed in Fort Torrance, wondering bitterly how to get back at Torgeir."

"And if not for me, *you* would all be frozen corpses. I think we come out even, don't you?"

Aeon's scowl grew. Before the argument could escalate, Desmond stepped forward. "Would you both stop crying for a minute and realize just how bloody cold it is out here? Elivain, we hired you as a guide, so why don't you guide us to the damned inn so we can rest? I swear, if I have to listen to this debate anymore I'm going to fling myself off a roof."

Elivain looked at him as if he'd sprouted a third head and flown off into the sunset, but Desmond held fast. Eventually, their guide relented.

"That sounds fair to me."

More structures soon came into view as they trudged further into the village. The snow had been shoveled away from the main path, to the extreme gratitude of the four. Walking became easy, though they found their limbs sluggish and tired. Patches of brown grass peeked through the blanket. The buildings all looked to be run-down, though a closer inspection would reveal them hardy dwellings that had lasted for decades and would continue to do so for many more to come. They formed a sort of square around a large pavilion, with a fire pit in the center, frozen but for a few lasting embers. Halas could see several other structures past the square. There was a tall steeple in the distance, and briefly wondered if that were the temple they sought, dismissing the idea quickly.

That would be too simple. If his luck were anything to go by, the Temple of Immortals would be only accessible through a special route through fire and torment, and likely a thousand more miles of traveling. Halas wondered where the Temple received its name. Maybe it was guarded by beings that could not be killed? That would be only par for the course.

Halas shook his head. He was too tired to think. A thin and stretched dog lay underneath a musty porch, gnawing on a bone. He regarded the travelers with a passing interest before going back to his meal. A group of children ran past Halas, laughing and swatting each other. They ran to a party of seven or eight men, bearing two stretchers piled high with meat. Even cold and raw, it looked delicious. Having lived off naught but *spódhla* for a week, the three friends and Elivain couldn't help but stare. There was a large rack of antlers on the skull of whatever beast they had killed. "Excuse me," Halas said to one of the men. He was darker skinned than most, but lighter than Jaden Harves. "But what's that?"

"Moose," said the man. He stopped, and the others bore their load into the building with the dog underneath. It followed them inside. "You're new here." A young boy his color stood next to him.

"Indeed we are, sir," said Halas.

"We come from Busby," said Elivain.

"Busby? Never heard of it. In any case, welcome to Bakunin. My name is Marrok; I own the inn here. She is my pride and joy, aside from my son." The kid laughed. "Come on in and have a drink or two, please. I brew my own fireale, and my wife's cider is spectacular. For visitors to Bakunin, the first glass is always on Little Sayad." He thumped his chest for emphasis. Marrok's frame looked to be as thick as his accent, though it was hard to tell through the layers of heavy fur. His beard hung low and shaggy over his chest.

"We would be glad to," said Desmond, before anyone could say otherwise. The six went in. Immediately Halas started itching, but it was a good itch, the kind of itch that meant he was warming up, and soon after the four travelers were seated in a comfortable booth, Desmond nodding off to sleep.

———

Marrok didn't charge much for anything, so they ordered heaping plates of food and ate every bite. Halas hadn't thought about it until now, but for obvious reasons, they hadn't been paid for either *The Wandering Blade* or Claymont's caravan. Elivain had little in the way of money. Fortunately, Jaden had given them quite a bit, more than Halas thought they would need. The three friends had left Earlsfort with bags stuffed full of copper, silver, and paper. Desmond danced several coins across his knuckles, though as he fell deeper into his cups, the movement became more clumsy, and the common room was filled with laughter when he banged his wrist on the table and scattered pennies everywhere. Aeon showed the innkeep's boy a silver coin, and handed it to him when he was sure Adrian's father wasn't looking. Halas thought back to home, to the coin his father had once given Garek. It seemed unlike him, to give such a sentimental gift to the younger Duer, and more unlike Garek to cherish it as he did. Halas wondered where Garek was now.

Soon Halas noticed his friends tiring, and the burden of entertainment shifted from the visitors to the locals. Several of the townspeople wanted nothing more than to share their tales with fresh ears, most of which consisted of great and false deeds.

There was Brahm, who had once served directly under King Melick's father, King Formic, as his personal bodyguard. Martin, who was responsible for slaying not one, but two dragons with only a crossbow. Horace claimed to have bedded over half the women in Galveston. Lo, a foul-mouthed woman roughly sixty years of age, who had once been the personal mistress of King Melick. She was, in fact, mother to a secret prince, a boy imprisoned in the bowels of the castle to prevent embarrassment to the throne, and one day she would return to Cordalis to free her son and rule as queen. Aeon himself smiled at this but said nothing.

There were many more. Had the stories contained even a single grain of truth, every single man and woman in Bakunin was a great hero worthy of song. Halas decided that he didn't much care for their falsehoods. He wanted to talk with Miriam again; Halas liked her. She'd been just as grandiose as the rest of them, but only in mannerisms. At least she was honest. The moose was delicious, so he busied himself in that. It came from the last stores of the previous hunt, Braham said. Marrok had cooked it with spices he never shared with the other villagers.

"Go ahead," said Brahm, "take advantage of the place. The innkeeper's a Sayad; he'll do anything to keep a customer."

"He's the only tavern in the village," said Elivain. Unlike the boys, he had kept to just one drink, and nursed it throughout the evening. Halas himself was rounding on seven, and Marrok's fireale was stronger than much of what he'd grown used to in Cordalis. True to its name, the ale left tendrils of fire curling in his throat and belly, and the burning taste remained on his tongue well after he'd swallowed. Aeon did not appear to be drinking at all, and Halas had long since lost track of Desmond's total. Even after everything they had been through since leaving home, it was nice to know that his friend still drank like a fish.

"Yeah," said another man, who was just as fat as he was drunk, "but he's a bloody Sayad! Nobody wants to eat with one of them."

"Bout thirty years back," explained Brahm, "a small group of the things came up here, started living in the north corner, keeping to themselves mostly. But last winter, the old tavern burned down, and poor Weston didn't make it out. So Marrok started this place up. Some folks think he did it, burned down the old place."

"Which is a load of bollocks," said thin, nasally woman.

"Sure it is!" boasted the fat one. "If Marrok didn't kill old Wes, I'm King of Aelborough!" He hiccupped.

There were eight rooms in the hotel, and all eight were available. The four travelers were put in separate lodgings, for eleven detricts a night. Halas found himself wishing he were quartered with Des. He laughed the thought away. It would be nice to have some time alone. He arrived in his room to find it not yet done up. There was a woman there. A Sayad, like Marrok. She was pulling a sheet tightly over the bed. "Hello," she said, bowing her head slightly. "I will be out of your way shortly."

"No worries," said Halas. "What's your name?"

"I am Jassia; I am wed to Marrok. You must forgive my slowness with your room. It is not often we have patrons here."

"Perfectly fine." He settled into a chair by the door and yawned into his hand. His head felt heavy, and his legs thin.

"You are very kind, sir. Is there anything else you require?"

"A hot bath would be wonderful. I injured my leg on the road, you see, and it has been many weeks since my last."

"I will see to it." She smiled at him, a provocative smile that she wore well.

As Jassia went about the room, Halas found himself watching her. She was beautiful. The room around her swayed, but the woman herself was clear to him. He saw the way her hair met her skin as she walked, the way her curves moved beneath her thin gown—he shook his head tiredly. Such thoughts never led to anything good, especially concerning married women. "How long have you lived here?"

"All of my life, sir. Marrok and I were wed when I was but thirteen years of age, and he fifteen. Our parents arranged it."

"They allow that?"

"It is customary of my people, sir."

"I see."

"I understand that you think it odd. Most everyone here does. They do not look upon Marrok and I, or our poor boy, as equals. We decided to give our son a more common name to help him blend in. Adrian. Though many of the other boys still taunt him."

"I'm sorry to hear that." He was nodding off. *Oh dear.*

"The truth is that Marrok does not usually help to put these rumors to rest. He is loud and obnoxious, and often drunk. He is not pleasant when he is drunk."

"Sorry," Halas repeated, attempting to stifle a yawn.

"No, no," said Jassia, "I am sorry. I should not trouble you with such matters."

"No!" Halas said, getting to his feet as she went for the door. "No, it is all right. I've simply had a long day, and am very tired. May we speak more of this tomorrow?"

"I would like that," she said, "but cannot. Sorry. Good night, sir. Your bath will be drawn whenever you wish it."

She left. "Good night," Halas muttered down the corridor, but he was too tired to be bothered. He barely made it to the bed before falling asleep. It took a warm bed to realize just how tired he was. He slept for almost a full day.

"Do you believe that Marrok killed the old innkeeper?"

It was Desmond who spoke. He and Halas sat in Halas' room. Desmond had brought his breakfast up, most of which Halas had hungrily devoured.

"I don't know," Halas said between bites of Desmond's bacon. "An accidental fire in the middle of winter? Such a blaze would be difficult to come by, I imagine."

"These people are sheltered. Far more than anything we've known in Cordalis." A lump rose in Halas' throat at the mention of their home. He stifled it. "I entertained a group of men earlier this morning with a tale of how we are on a holy pilgrimage."

"Perhaps you should tell them that we're brigands, on the run from the law."

"I was going to scream it from the top of a mountain later." Still, Des looked embarrassed; despite Elivain and Aeon's near constant arguing since their arrival, he hadn't thought of that.

"If he did, Jassia would know. She and he are betrothed, and she's not fond of him. She tells me that Marrok is a drunk and a liar. It wouldn't surprise me, judging by the other folk here."

"We should speak with her," Desmond said. Halas agreed.

They left the room and turned toward the stairs. As they walked past Elivain's room, a rough hand grabbed Halas and stopped both of them. It was Elivain, looking surly and annoyed, as usual. "Just what do you think you're doing?" he asked.

Des jerked a thumb toward the stairs. "Going to see Marrok," he muttered.

"Do not lie to me. Do you think it wise to call notice to yourselves? You would leave this village in shambles and then depart. This is not our concern. Do not start trouble if you have no intention of seeing it through."

"If this man has committed murder, he ought not go free. We should expose him," said Halas.

"As you did with Torgeir?"

At this Halas' face went red. He looked at his feet, suddenly angry but unsure of what to say. "So what do we do?" asked Des.

"We shall slip away from the village as soon as the sun is gone. I've sent Aeon for provisions. You two should go help him carry everything back. I imagine it's all quite heavy."

"Sure it is," said Des, but they both got the message. They wrapped up and tromped across the tightly packed snow toward the building they had figured to be the town's shop. A group of townspeople had assembled at the fire pit, busy piling on fresh wood. Among them, Halas recognized Mayor Graves and Brahm, from the night before. Graves steadied two heavy looking logs while Brahm and another man pushed a third into place beneath them. Graves offered them a wave. The pyramid they were constructing buckled, and he quickly returned his grip to the logs, breathing a sigh of relief when everything didn't come toppling down. "Mornin, boys!" he said.

"Good morning."

"What's the occasion?" Desmond asked.

"Having a gathering tonight. Something Miriam likes to organize in her spare time. Lots of women and old stories and the like. You fellas interested in joining?"

Brahm stood up from his task and walked past Halas and Des, whispering, "Get out while you still can," under his breath.

"Don't listen to him," Harden said. "Brahm's an old softy. Likes the gatherings more than most, I figure."

"I can imagine," said Desmond.

Halas felt saddened that Elivain wanted to leave that night. Though he thought most of the people of Bakunin to be pompous braggarts, the thought of sitting around a roaring blaze with them sounded appealing, relaxing. "We may stop in for a bit," he said, meaning it. If nothing else, he would glean more life stories to tell Cailin. The Bakunin folks were far more entertaining than those who crowded the Cordalis Gate courtyard. "Do you know where we can find the shop?"

"Right over there," said a man who had somehow managed to stuff two bundles of chopped wood under each arm. Halas had never seen someone with such unusually long limbs. It was impressive. The man pointed at one of the buildings from under his bundles. "First on your left, with the hole in the awning."

"Thank you."

Halas found the store easily. Standing directly under the awning, he could see a ring of clear blue sky above his head. Desmond joined him. "Think they'd have this fixed by now," he said.

"Desmond, when you repair your own porch, maybe you can have a go at this one. Until then, no talking."

Desmond went inside.

Aeon stood before the shopkeeper, a counter and list between them. The shopkeeper noticed their entrance before Aeon did.

"Quite the outfit you boys are building up," he said. Halas nodded. They walked to Aeon and said their greetings.

"What do we have here?" Halas asked.

Aeon laid out what he'd so far purchased. They needed more and better-fitted furs, and plenty of food. They also needed a large supply of fuel, and the shopkeeper said that it would not hurt to keep their own firewood. There was good news: with all the snow, water would not be hard to come by; they would not have to carry any, only skins. "What are those things?" Desmond asked. He pointed to the wall; on it were a pair of balloon-shaped objects, with holes cut out of the wide end in a checkered pattern and a rough handle.

"Those? Those'd be snowshoes," the shopkeeper said. "You wear em on your feet in deep snow. They're supposed to distribute your weight more evenly, so you don't sink in, get stuck."

"How much for four pairs?" said Halas.

———

An hour later they had everything they would need. The shopkeeper offered to keep it all in a back room in the store, but Halas declined. It made him nervous to think that someone might know exactly when they left, and between the four rooms they had at the inn, there was easily enough space to store it all. So, carrying heavy loads on their backs and in their arms, they marched back. With Elivain, they divided up the gear into what they would carry, and spent the rest of the afternoon packing.

When Halas finished, he felt like finally having his bath. Pain burned brightly in his thigh. Elivain wanted to leave just before dawn, and it was already dark. Likely the party had already started outside. Halas wanted to join them, but a bath sounded, quite honestly, like the best thing in the world. He found the boy, Adrian, loitering about the common room and asked him to draw it. When the boy was finished and departed, Halas peeled off his clothes and stepped toward the basin, already relishing the warm feeling on his skin. He slipped into the tub and actually found himself sighing. It was as if all the pains and burdens of the journey were washed away instantly. Halas relaxed his legs against the end of the tub and let himself go under the water. Layers of grime peeled themselves away, but that was the least of it. Halas allowed himself a moment to pretend that he was back home. He would surface, to find himself in Cordalis, with Cailin waiting, and his friends and family just outside. But it was not to be. *This is all happening,* he told himself one last time, *there's no escaping it. I will get home, but for now, I'm stuck. Just have to deal with it.*

Someone knocked on his door. That was odd; his three companions would just come in. Feeling suddenly vulnerable, Halas sat up in the basin and wished he had a weapon. "Come in," he said.

The door opened and Jassia glided in. She wore a red gown, and put a finger to her lips, closing the door behind her. She knelt at the edge of the tub.

"You remind me of a lover I once had," she said. "He was tall, handsome, and brave. He and I were happy together." She leaned in and kissed Halas on the lips. He started, jumping up and backing away. The rim of the tub caught his knees and he tripped, hitting the floor hard on his injured leg. Water sloshed over the sides of the basin. Halas scrambled up, to the far corner. This seemed to crush Jassia. "You do not wish to share a bed with me?"

"Well," Halas stammered, very surprised. "No. My heart belongs to another. What happened to your lover?"

Jassia's smiled sadly. Still kneeling by the basin, she placed her hands on the rim and swirled a finger across the surface of the water. "My husband is a jealous man. We were not yet even wed."

"Oh. Sorry."

"Do not be. Just, please, do not deny me some degree of happiness. I am a lonely woman."

She came at him again, but he backed farther away, pressing himself up against the wall. "No, Jassia. I cannot. I am sorry, so sorry, but I cannot." He looked at her body, and almost changed his mind. *No! Remember Cailin,* he scolded, upset with himself.

"If you are worried about what my husband would do if he found out, he will never. Only you and I would ever have to know. Marrok is with the others, by their fire. Your own lover would never discover us. We are safe."

He was in a corner, and very suddenly aware of the fact that he was completely naked. She pressed herself up against him, stroking his arm gently with her finger. She was so warm, so soft. Her skin was smooth. Halas tried to contain himself, but was hard-pressed. Their lips came together, but only for a moment. Halas pulled away, hating himself both for doing so and for not doing it soon enough. He took Jassia's shoulders and held her at arm's length.

"I can make sure Marrok does not bother us again," the woman pleaded. "I know things about him, things he's done. He murdered my lover, and he murdered the former innkeeper. It was he who set fire to the inn."

"How do you know?"

"Myself and several villagers saw it, but Marrok is a terrifying man, and he threatened us. They all have families. I have Adrian. But I am not afraid anymore. I can speak up; I can get the others to cooperate. Just give me tonight. Please."

She wrapped her arms around him, but he slipped out from between her and the wall, stumbling over to his clothes. "Do so," he said. "Expose him for his crimes. It is the right thing to do. But we cannot be together. Goodbye, Jassia." Gathering up his things, he stumbled naked to his room and dressed. He felt alone, and alone he would be vulnerable to the woman's charms, so he took his share of the supplies and moved to Aeon's room. Desmond was likely asleep.

Chapter Eleven
Another Hasty Departure

Elivain roused them. It was still dark outside. Halas looked at Aeon. "You ready?" he asked.

Aeon nodded. "I am. Thank you, Halas," he said when Elivain left the room. They embraced; no other gesture seemed to do.

"Lead on, Prince." He grinned.

The four stole out of the inn, passing the still smoldering fire pit. Halas felt a pang of regret as he remembered the gathering. He'd been too afraid to leave Aeon's room the previous night, worried Jassia would be about. The surrounding buildings were dark, still but for a few lazy columns of smoke from a chimney. While the bulk of the village's inhabitants lived in the area around Little Sayad, Halas found that the village itself was a lot larger than he'd thought. Most of the buildings were abandoned, but as they made their way north, they saw farmhouses and shops and little sheds. Many of them had been stripped bare, disassembled for firewood or repairs to places that remained occupied.

Their packs were heavy and their layers thick. It had snowed again during the night. Even with the snowshoes, the stuff came up several inches above Halas' boots. He trudged on, just behind Elivain and beside Desmond. The wind blew sharply, and they were glad they had bought masks and goggles to cover their faces. But the stuff somehow managed to get around their protective layers and sting horribly.

After a few hours, Elivain held up his hand to silence the three friends. They stopped. Elivain crept ahead. "There is a farm here," he said, "but I see no one within. We should go around."

He straightened up. There was a harsh *twang*, and an arrow thudded into the tree next to his head. They all spun around.

A soldier stood above him. Three more appeared at his side. Halas saw a bowman in the trees.

They'd been caught!

"I'd lower your weapons, if I were you," said a voice. "I believe you boys are lost."

———

Bale son of Bale was a soldier, through and through. He was ten years old when he killed his first brigand, a wimpy lad just older than himself. He'd returned with the boy's head, and would remember his father (a captain of the Agerian Guard) beaming at him, his few remaining teeth glistening with red wine as he spoke to his son.

"I'm so very proud of you," he'd said.

From then on, Bale son of Bale was a soldier. He'd joined the military shortly after his fifteenth birthday, after his father had died of stomach rot. His mother had persevered for almost a year before succumbing to the same, and Bale son of no one was left with a brother of three and a meager position in the army. He'd risen through the ranks quickly, making corporal before his seventeenth year. Bale had killed bandits, thieves, murderers, and even a pack of organized raiders that terrorized some of the southern communities.

A full-fledged captain at twenty, there was not a single thing Bale could not handle, except Digby.

Where Bale had his sense of duty, Digby had an entirely different perception. Duty to Bale was doing the right thing no matter the cost, protecting the innocent and the royalty above all others, upholding the righteous and quashing the evil.

Duty to Digby was following orders.

As luck, or most certainly the opposite, would have it, Digby had been put into Bale's unit, despite the deep dislike and mistrust the two had for each other. They had set out of Fort Torrance a mere two hours after the fugitives who had kidnapped the as-yet-unnamed-important-person, as Bale's superiors had identified him, and now they had them. The party was staying in Bakunin, the little hole in the ground that was the only sort of pseudo-civilization this side of the mountains.

They had orders to keep things quiet and not disturb the village, so Bale had moved his soldiers quietly around the outskirts, setting up camp within an empty farmhouse whose owners had been given to the winter. Bale's informant, a dirty Sayad if there ever was one, had said that the kidnappers planned to go to the tundra. This news had set unease in the pit of Bale's stomach, but not Digby. Digby held his bow roughly and shook his head.

"Do your duty," he'd said curtly.

"Are you not curious?" Bale had asked.

"Not in the slightest," Digby had responded. "Our orders are to take these outlaws in, and kill them if we have to. We cannot deviate from our orders."

Bale, who was where he was precisely because he had deviated from orders (his decision to do so had saved nearly forty lives at the expense of his captain's, and thus no one ever knew he had broken the chain of command) had shaken his head and arranged his men around the farmhouse. Their informant had told Digby that the men planned to leave that very day.

Now, as Bale watched his breath crystallize in the air with bored fascination, he heard footsteps and faint voices.

"There is a farm here," said a gruff voice, "but I see no one within. We should go around."

Bale peered through the branches and observed their enemies. Three of them were children, his age, maybe a little younger. Bale, having achieved so much at such a young age, paid them no disrespect for what would have been considered by many as a disadvantage.

The fourth man, the man in the lead, was the oldest, and he frightened Bale. His cool green eyes seemed to see everything from under his hood, and his voice was steadier than stone. His sword was finely crafted, as was his bow. Yes, that one was certainly the most frightening of the four. Bale felt the dread in his gut deepen. He did not know that this man was the one who would help usher both Bale and Digby into the land of the dead, but he certainly suspected something was amiss.

Digby was off to Bale's right. On Bale's signal, he fired an arrow into the tree near the party. It thudded solidly into the wood, quivering for a bit before coming to rest. Bale signaled to the rest of his men, and stepped into the clearing.

"I'd lower your weapons, if I were you. I believe you boys are lost," he said.

"We are," said the boy with what was once the ragged remains of a goatee, and now was something entirely unrecognizable. "Can you direct us back to town?"

"Amusing. Stay your hand and lay down your weapons. We have you surrounded by bowmen. If you should make even the slightest movement, you shall be shot down where you stand." His gaze dropped to the youngest of the group, with hair that dangled in front of his eyes and a cocky stance. Looking at that boy, Bale former son of Bale choked.

The boy was Prince Aeon.

"My liege," he breathed, and found himself dropping to one knee. His soldiers were silent, but one by one, they too knelt. Digby tensed by Bale's side. "Is it really you?"

"It is I," said the prince. He strode forward and drew his sword, holding it in an awkward salute. Bale drew his own steel and returned the gesture. "Men of Ager," he announced to the clearing, "you have done well in fulfilling your duties, but you have been given them in falsehood.

"I am not a prisoner. I travel with these three men of my own volition; they are my friends. We are on a mission of great importance. Of this mission I can tell you little, but know this! We are not to be hindered any further. You will return to Bakunin and await my return. Once my errand is complete, I will surrender myself to your custody and allow you to transport myself and any who wish to go with me back to Cordalis. Of this you have my word."

"Surely," Bale said quietly, "you cannot expect us to take you for your word. You are under duress, my lord. What is your mission?"

Prince Aeon sighed. He glanced at the blond-haired boy, who nodded almost imperceptibly. The prince looked back to Bale. "You have heard the tale of the Temple of Immortals, correct?"

"Of course."

"Then you know that if that Temple is destroyed, there will be nothing to prevent the Ifrinn from returning to Aelborough."

"Of course." Bale's arms stiffened at the mention of the Ifrinn. Every boy and girl in Aelborough knew that tale. Depending on the region, they had different versions of it, of course, but the gist was the same: there was a Temple in the arctic that warded the gates to the Infernos of Hell.

"Someone seeks to destroy this Temple. My friends and I journey to protect it. Every second you dawdle here brings our foes closer, and creates a further disadvantage for us." Prince Aeon's voice took on a sudden harshness then. "Stand aside! Return to Bakunin, and disturb us no longer!

"*Stand aside!*"

For a brief moment, the clearing was silent. Then the captain stood. He whistled sharply to his men. "We shall obey the prince's word," he said. "I deem him to be telling the truth, and I would not have us be the cause of his mission's failure. I would not have that mission failed at all. Prince Aeon, I would be honored if you would take me into your service. With my men, we…" he was cut off by the arrow that was lodged in his throat. Halas registered the bowman's movements, but it was Elivain who acted.

The bowman off to the right was attempting to notch a second arrow when Elivain drove his home into the aggressor's eye. Just like that, everything stopped. There was silence for another moment, and then Bale formerly of Bale began gasping for air, writhing in the snow. Soldiers and the four travelers ran to his side.

"There is nothing we can do for him," said Elivain after a cursory examination. He laid a hand on the dying man's chest, and muttered a soft prayer. The man's eyes locked with Halas'. For a moment, Halas wondered if he should put him out of his misery. *No, that would be barbaric.* He cursed himself for thinking such thoughts.

The poor man. His eyes were already dead, half-glazed and pale white, but still scared. They were wide, and he was trembling. Halas realized that he was too. He touched the soldier's hand, searching his brain for any sort of prayer or verse that might help put him at ease. But Halas was not a religious person. He wondered what was colder, the man's breastplate or his flesh.

Bale gave one final wheeze, and was still. One of his men cried out in anguish. But then all the sorrow was forgotten, and the soldiers brandished weapons against the four travelers. Elivain reached for another arrow; Halas drew his sword.

Aeon simply held up his hands, a look of solemn regret on his face.

"Let us not fight," he said. "Enough blood has been spilled this day. Return to the village, I command you. I *beg* you."

Looks were exchanged between the men, but gradually they began to sheath their swords and lower their bows. They picked up their fallen leader and, one by one, trudged back toward Bakunin.

They'd left the bowman behind. When the rest were gone, Desmond looked at the body. "Reckon we should bury him?"

"No," said Elivain, his voice as cold as the tip of Halas' nose. He knelt by the dead soldier and took up his quiver. "Let's keep moving."

———

As the land stretched upwards, the trees thinned out almost completely. The three friends and Elivain crested one final ridge. Before them was a great expanse of tundra, stretching as far as the eye could see. Halas started forward on what he thought to be the last legs of their journey. The snow was thinner here as well, almost nonexistent, and he cast off the snowshoes, strapping them to his back. They were cold even against his layers.

No one spoke, disturbed as they were by the episode with the soldiers. They just walked solemnly forward, each step taking them closer to their destiny. Days passed, a week, two. Elivain shot a deer. There was no time to harvest the whole animal, and they left more than half of the carcass behind. Every morning, Halas awoke ready for anything. He told himself each day that this could be the day they found the Temple, and Raazoi. He told himself each day that this could be the day he died. Could he face that? He'd have to. He knew he ought to savor every moment, but he could not. The days were cold and slow, and on the tundra nothing ever seemed to change, making it appear that they were making no progress. Each day was the same.

Halas walked until his feet were dragging, and still he was in the lead. Elivain would tell him if he was going the wrong way, if Elivain even knew. Halas wondered why they'd taken the man along.

At least they should have left him in Bakunin.

He was so deep in thought that he didn't notice the ground as it began a sharp decline. His toe jammed into the dirt and his leg flared in pain. He fell forward and was suddenly falling, sliding in the snow. Desmond and Aeon cried out; Des jumped for his friend and grabbed on to his boot. Both continued to slide. Elivain took hold of Aeon's hood and yanked, barely managing to pull the boy back, as Halas and Des went over the edge of a cliff.

Chapter Twelve
Deyrey Baaish

A groan. Halas opened his eyes—at least, he thought he did, he was unsure if they were open or closed. There was nothing but darkness and pain. Waves of it surged through his wounded leg. Halas reached for where it hurt and hissed through the pain. He groaned again and looked around. Nothing. Pitch black. Darker even than the forest. Where was he? He felt the area around him, searching for—for what? Desmond. There had been some sort of cliff, or a hole, and Desmond had gone after him.

Halas opened his mouth to speak, but could not. His throat was a raw mess, and the darkness was oppressive. Halas did not wish to reveal himself to anything that could have found a home within it.

"Des?" he asked cautiously.

He heard the sound of someone shuffling away, and a very distinctly human gasp of alarm. "Desmond!"

There was silence. Halas nearly called out again, but Desmond finally answered. Incredible relief hit him at the sound of his friend's voice. "What? Bloody hell, Halas?"

"Yes. Get back here."

"Where?"

"Follow my voice. I'm here. I'm here. What happened?"

He felt Desmond's hand on his own, but was suddenly struck with a thought. *What if it isn't Desmond?* There could be all manner of creatures down here with them. He closed his eyes and drew in breath. It would be no good to panic. "What happened?"

"You fell, you dolt. I jumped after you. I remember a...a tunnel, I suppose, of ice. Then I fainted until just now."

"Sounds like you're the dolt."

"I'll remember that next time you decide to jump off of a cliff. I thought you'd seen it, honestly. The hole was very large."

"Thanks."

"Do you have your matches?"

"I hope so. Check for yours, too." Still sitting for fear his leg would explode again, he groped for his pack; he still wore it, but the fabric had torn in several places. He pricked his finger on something. One of the snowshoes. The wires had snapped. Halas was careful to take them off and toss them aside. He set his pack on the ground, wishing his eyes would adjust to the darkness. His hands found the flap, and he reached inside. It was wet. Had the water bottles been destroyed?

There were three. Two were torn to ribbons, but the third was intact. Halas unscrewed the stopper and took a sip. He'd have to save it. "How much water do you have left?"

"All three bottles. *Spódhla?*"

Halas felt the offered stick of meat press against his arm. He took it, chewing thoughtfully. What would they do? Where was Aeon? Had he gone after them as well? Had he and Elivain continued on? He figured Aeon would have spoken by now, unless he was injured or worse.

Oh no.

He felt furiously for his matchbook. The matches were wet, forcing him to expend two, cursing himself for the waste all the while. He managed to strike the third, barely illuminating the area around his hand. He looked around.

They were in a cave, that much he could tell. He lowered the match to the floor, moving his arm in a slow arc. Yes, they were definitely in a cave. Desmond succeeded with his matches on the first try. The light reminded Halas of the orbs in the forest. The orbs that had almost killed them. "I'll look for a way out," Desmond said. Halas agreed. The match burnt his finger, and he dropped it with a curse. He lit another one; it took two tries.

Desmond's light disappeared shortly after, and he lit another match as well. *His must be dry,* Halas thought with a little envy. Fortunately, he could see no sign of anyone else, only bits and pieces of Desmond as their lights hit just right. Des was moving in a circle around Halas. Finally, he spoke. "Only one way," he said from far away. "Follow my voice."

"Just give me a minute," Halas whispered.

"What's the matter?"

"My leg. I must have landed on it."

"Your leg?" Desmond asked. "From the tigers? It's still bothering you?"

"I'm all right. I just want to be sure the thing still works."

There were shuffling footsteps in the cave and then Desmond put a hand on his shoulder. "Here," he said. Halas took his hand and Desmond helped him up. Halas stood on his good leg for a moment before testing the waters, prodding the ground with his foot. The pain was there, but relatively distant. Manageable.

"All right," he said. "I can walk." His voice was steady, but he could hardly contain his relief. To be stranded down in this pit was bad enough, but to be crippled as well? Halas didn't want to entertain the thought, but as always, he could not help himself. Desmond would stay with him, would carry him if need be, but what then? The two would be forced to wander blind until death took them both. For a while they made small talk, neither one wanting to speak of the Temple, or Aeon, or this cave. They both agreed that they would wait for their eyes to adjust, but they never did. The darkness was complete.

Desmond spoke. "Give me a snowshoe. I cannot find mine." Halas back-tracked, groping blindly. He stumbled upon one of the shoes, and walked back to Des by the sound of his voice. Desmond took it, and Halas heard the sound of ripping fabric. Then nothing. Then Desmond lit a match. He'd fastened a shirt to the snowshoe and set it aflame. It glowed around them, at least two foot-lengths in each direction. The globe of light nauseated Halas somehow, and he turned away, blinking his eyes to keep away the tears.

"Put it out," he muttered.

"You don't like it either?" Des asked. "Thank the gods. It makes me sick to look at."

"And I."

They sat in silence for a while.

"Shall we keep moving?" Halas finally asked.

"I suppose so."

"Come to the wall."

They did, and Halas clutched his friend's hand almost desperately. He and Desmond felt around the outside of the passage that may or may not lead out of this place of perpetual darkness. It was small; they would have to crouch. That worried him, with his leg. Still holding Desmond's hand, Halas started to move. He heard Desmond's awkward footsteps behind him. That and their breathing were the only sounds, and they cast terrifying echoes in the void.

Suddenly he was holding nothing at all. He froze, refusing even to breathe. "Des?" he whispered.

"I'm here." Hands on his back. Good. "There's got to be a better way to do this. These gloves make things hard to hold, and I don't reckon we'll be able to remove them anytime soon. There's a rope in my pack."

Halas heard Desmond stepping, turning around. When he stopped, Halas opened the flap, reaching blindly into the thing. He was reminded of a prank Gale had pulled on him when Halas was twelve and Gale fourteen. He'd showed up at the Duer cottage one day with a plain wooden box. Inside the box, he'd said, was candy. All Halas had to do was reach beneath the shroud and take it. Halas had not been completely taken in, but in the end he'd relented.

His hands had gone into the box, felt past the shroud, and instead of candy, they had closed around a snake. The snake bit him. Halas had jumped free (thirty feet in the air, Gale still maintained to this day), the snake still attached to his thumb. He's smashed it against Garek's bed, screaming all the while. Halbrick had stormed in. He'd clouted Gale pretty hard across the ears and sent him home before tending to Halas' wound.

Reaching into Desmond's pack now, Halas could not help but be reminded of that box. The snake bite had once been Halas' most painful injury to date. He thought that once it hadn't been entirely bad, but the pain inflated with memory. Now, with his leg, it seemed paltry. Halas decided there were more important things to dwell on. Still, he cursed Gale quietly, and Des, who loved telling the story as if he had actually been there, chuckled.

Finally he found it. For a split second, Halas thought he'd grabbed a snake, and he bit down hard on his bottom lip. But it wasn't a snake—it was a thin length of rope. He yanked it free of the pack and closed the flap. He tied the two ends into lassos and looped one end around his waist, the other around Desmond's. He cinched the loops tight and gave a good tug. There were about six foot-lengths between them. Desmond gathered the loose coil in his arms, reducing that to just over one.

They set off one miserable step at a time. With the passage so constricted and the complete absence of light, they only made a few foot-lengths each minute. Their legs cramped every so often, sending fiery bursts of agony through Halas. He ignored it, but eventually they had to stop. Halas discovered that he was thick with sweat. Desmond squatted down in front of him.

"At least we can breathe," he mused.

That changed soon after. The air became muggy and hot, and they both had to take deep, labored breaths through their mouths. Nose breathing had become impossible. Sweat poured from their skin in gallons. Halas' hands were slick against the rough surfaces. And worst of all, it was still dark. Desmond had stopped talking several hours before. Halas felt the rope tighten, and he stopped. "What is it?"

"My legs are cramping. I need to stretch."

"All right."

So they walked. When they grew tired of walking, they rested. When they finished resting, they walked. It was a cycle that Halas feared would continue until their deaths. He tried to remember the opening that had brought them here. Perhaps they should have searched for that when they'd originally woken up, but they would never find their way back now. There had to be another entrance. *There has been one, so there must be another, right? An entrance means an exit.*

His palms ached from the constant contact with the rough-hewn walls. He curled them into fists and kept moving. Unfortunately, it took only seconds for him to come down just a little too hard, tearing the skin from his knuckles. He hissed at the sting of it.

"What's the matter?" Desmond asked.

"I think this cave is determined to take me apart piece by piece."

"Sorry. If it means anything to you, I nearly took my head off a while ago."

"Such great comfort."

Desmond grunted. Halas had to smile. For his own sake, he was glad Desmond had gone after him. But for Desmond's…Halas couldn't say.

He woke to Desmond shaking him. "We should keep moving."

"Right."

He had no idea how long he had been asleep, or how long they'd been down here. Time becomes meaningless when one has no way of measuring it. He had no idea what Aeon and Elivain were doing. They had only been a few days from the Temple, according to Jaden's maps. Had it been that long? Halas doubted it, but there was absolutely no way to be sure.

His mind drifted back to something Elivain had said when Halas and Desmond wanted to expose Marrok for his crimes. He'd warned them not to start trouble when they couldn't see it through. Halas had said Marrok should not be allowed to go free, and Elivain's response was, "As you did with Torgeir?"

At the time Halas had been chastened, but now he thought of Elivain as a hypocrite. It occurred to him that Elivain had started some sort of campaign against Torgeir the Mighty, but he'd abandoned it just as quick as can be when they left Fort Torrance. Halas wished he'd made mention of the fact. Now that he'd thought about it, the whole exchange bothered him.

His hand slipped on the ceiling and he fell on his face. Desmond spilled after him, landing on top. "Get off!" Halas grunted. Desmond rolled to the side, stretching the rope, pulling it taut. It dug painfully into his stomach. He yanked Desmond closer.

"Can we stand up?" he asked.

"I dunno. I can't reach the ceiling. Let's try it."

Halas rolled on to his stomach, pushing off against the oiled stone. He got to his knees and then stood. Reaching up, he felt for the ceiling, but it was too high. He felt a rush of elation, and smiled. It wasn't much, but it was something.

"Halas, you hear that?"

"Hear what?"

Something was breathing.

———

They had no choice but to keep moving. Desmond struck a match, taking a few careful steps forward, scanning the darkness. "This way," he said. The breathing had disappeared, but if Halas concentrated hard enough, he could just barely make it out. Whatever the thing was, it was definitely following them.

Halas had no intention of dying. Not here, not now. He had a life to get back to. Cailin. Forcing thoughts of the creature out of his mind, Halas touched the rope and followed the light until it dwindled into nothing. He felt along the wall. Suddenly, the texture beneath his hand changed. He jumped back, nearly knocking both of them to the ground. "What is it?" Desmond asked.

"Wood! It's wood."

They both explored with their palms until they were sure that Halas was correct; it was indeed wood. "It's a door," he muttered, finding the latch. It was hot to the touch. He pulled, and the door swung open, its hinges creaking. Halas spun around, putting a hand on his sword. He listened for whatever was out there. It had to have heard the creak.

After a time, Desmond put a hand on his shoulder. "We should go through that door."

"Right, the door. Do you hear it?"

"No, not anymore. I think it's gone."

Halas wasn't so sure, but there was nothing for it. He had to duck to get inside, and Desmond reached for another match. Halas shut the door behind them. It jammed, but he gave it a good shove.

And then a voice cut through the darkness, a voice that did not belong to either of them.

"Who's there?"

———

Halas felt Desmond's hand close tightly around his forearm; he froze. The voice was rough and low, as if it had not been in use for a while.

"Who's there?" it asked again. "I know someone is there, I can see you both! Who are you? Answer me, before I take my hammer to your skulls."

"My…my name is Halas. This is my friend Desmond. Who are you?"

"Gilshenn Sidoor, if you please. Tell me, how did you get past Deyrey Baaish?"

"The what?" asked Desmond.

"Deyrey Baaish—the king's old pet. Tools of the gods, does that abomination still draw breath?"

"What is it?"

"Forgive me for my rudeness. When I said the king's old pet, I meant to say: the old king's pet. There's not been a king down here for many years. There's not been anything but me for many years. If She was right, anyhow."

"Who are you? What is this place?"

"Orhill Caverns," said Gilshenn. "Or the Mines of Orhill, according to you people, however you please. It all started with that damned captain. His people found the southern entrances. We were more and happy to trade with new folk, but they gave us more than we bargained for. They brought plague. Plague brought famine. I used to be a potter, but my shop went under. No one was buying anything. I could not feed myself, and I fell ill and dreamt of a beautiful woman. She told me to come down here—this is the prison, where Deyrey Baaish lives—and lock myself in this room with food and water and tools. I do not know who She was, but I did it. I did what She said. She told me I'd sleep for years, until the king was dead and buried. I was told to wait. For you, I now assume.

"Tell me, how long has it been?"

"I've not heard of this," Halas said. "I apologize. What captain do you speak of?"

"The man who brought you all over here: Captain Aelworth!"

Halas was stunned. "Surely you jest."

"I do not."

"Gilshenn…Captain Aelworth died over two thousand years ago."

———

For a while there was silence, and then they heard a heavy thump, followed by coarse growling. But it wasn't growling. Gilshenn was sobbing. Halas wanted to reach out and comfort him, but he knew that to move even the slightest was a bad idea, with no hold on the walls.

"Sorry," Desmond offered weakly.

"My people?" Gilshenn asked meekly. "Are they…I knew what She meant, I just…I just never, never thought that it was real." His sobs were heavy. Halas' legs were weak when they stopped. He'd have to sit soon.

"Gilshenn?"

"Yes, I'm here."

"Are you…well, could you lead us out of here?"

"This is to do with that thrice-damned Temple, isn't it?"

"What do you know of the Temple?" Desmond asked.

"Only what the woman told me. I can lead you out. I've followed Her orders thus far, it would be a shame if I decided to stop that now." A pause, followed by a sniffle. "Indeed, it would. Right then, first we'll need to kill that monster out there."

"How?"

"How indeed."

"Do you have torches?" Halas said. "We cannot fight it if we cannot see. How can you see?"

"We used to live both above ground and below it. I lived here, closer to the best dirt. When you've been down here for as long as I, you learn to adapt. So no, no torches. I possess my hammer and bow, plenty of food, water and alcohol, and clothes. I suppose I did not quite believe Her when She told me I would sleep most of the time."

"Can you see well enough to fight it?"

"Aye, but I cannot do it myself."

Halas' mind was rapidly formulating a plan. It was simple, but it would work. He told it to Desmond and Gilshenn. "Aye, that'll do," Gilshenn said. "Good on you."

They spent several hours cutting up Gilshenn's clothes, ripping and tearing them into long strips. Gilshenn supervised, and when they were finished, he stole into the corridor, rolling a small keg out before him. He returned shortly after. "It's set," he said. "Let's go wake the bastard up."

Gilshenn led them into the corridor by the hand. He stopped suddenly. "This is it," he said. "Here he comes. May death not befoul us with His presence."

———

They waited then. Before long, Gilshenn began shouting. "I'm here! Come and get me, foul creature! Bring your ugly face to me! I'm here!"

Footsteps like those of a giant. Halas drew his sword. He kissed the blade without realizing. Memories of the day he'd gotten it rushed back to him. There had been tears in Halbrick's eyes. Halas had asked for a blade for Garek, but he'd never thought to go to Conroy. Fresh guilt came with that thought, and then doubled when he remembered he'd left his brother in Earlsfort. "Are you sure you laid it out correctly?" he asked.

"Certain."

The footsteps were closer. "*NOW!*" yelled Gilshenn. A match sparked in Desmond's hand, and he tossed it to the ground. Where it should have sizzled and died, it roared to life in the alcohol-drenched cloth. It shot down the path assigned, fire blazing up tall, crackling with warmth and light. Halas' eyes watered. He yelped in alarm, but he could see.

The Deyrey Baaish towered above them. It had thick muscles, limbs like tree trunks, and the head of a bull. Its horns were razor sharp. Halas was not afraid, and the realization brought a grim smile to his face. The beast was trapped in a prison of flame, roaring in pain and anguish. Tall and imposing though it was, Halas found he was not afraid. He could see the beast; he saw that it had a head, it had a heart. The beast was a living, breathing being. It could be killed.

Halas hefted his sword.

Gilshenn drew back his bow and shot it in the chest. It roared louder, plucking the shaft from its flesh as if it were no more than an insect bite. The Deyrey Baaish charged forward, and Gilshenn shot it again. This time it braved the fire, leaping through the barrier and at the three friends. Halas and Desmond were tossed aside like tissue paper, Desmond missing the fire by mere inches. The beast went straight for Gilshenn, who picked up a heavy hammer and brought it down on the creature's knuckles. It screamed, picking him up and pinning him to the ceiling. Halas *was* afraid then, but he found it manageable.

"Yeah, you've wanted this for two millennia! Come and get it!" Gilshenn snarled, biting and scratching. Despite his efforts, the Deyrey Baaish was going to squeeze the life out of him. Halas rose and sunk his sword into its thigh, driving it in halfway down the blade. The creature roared, dropping Gilshenn and swinging around, causing Halas to lose his grip. He took the brunt of the blow and careened into the wall.

It turned to face Gilshenn once more. Gilshenn took up his hammer. Halas had only a moment to examine the man. He was short, very short, and wore a thick beard down nearly to his boots. It had been growing for centuries; Halas expected it to be even longer. The beast tore Silvia from its leg, snapping the blade in half and dropping it with a loud clatter. Desmond stood while Halas dove for his sword. The monster tried to stop him, but Desmond had circled around behind. He slashed downward and cut a deep wound in its shoulder. It whirled to face him, ducking its head low, trying to gore Des with its horns. That was a mistake, for Gilshenn moved in and cracked his hammer across its neck. With a terrible roar, the thing grabbed Gilshenn and squeezed. Gilshenn bit down hard on its finger. The Deyrey Baaish waved him at Halas. It stumbled away, toward Gilshenn's cell. Its heavy head looked every which way with frantic fervor. The monster turned away from the fire and started down the hall, still holding Gilshenn.

But Desmond was there, again drawing deep red lines into the creature's back. The Deyrey Baaish screamed, turning to take on this new threat, but Halas stabbed it in the side. It dropped Gilshenn. Gilshenn grabbed his hammer, smashing it into the side of the creature's kneecap. Halas heard a tremendous crunch, and the beast fell. It scrambled away on its hands and knees, unwittingly toward the fire. Gilshenn brought the hammer down once more, on to its toes.

It toppled headfirst into the flame.

The fires caused the beast to convulse and roll deeper into the prison within a prison. The Deyrey Baaish screamed, really *screamed*, wrapping itself in the shrouds and crawling down the tunnel. Halas was horrified but somehow enticed by the spectacle. All the while, Gilshenn Sidoor cursed and yelled insults, jeered and shot arrows down the corridor, until finally the flames were extinguished beneath the creature's massive weight.

The Deyrey Baaish was dead, and the tunnel was once again cast into darkness. Halas felt sick.

———

"That is the end of that," said Gilshenn after he was done whooping. "I think my old eyes are bleeding."

"It's been quite a while since you've seen light like that, I reckon," said Desmond. "Maybe they are."

"Laugh it up. You want out of here or not?"

"Of course I do. I was merely being facetious."

"I'm afraid I do not know what that means."

"Sarcastic. I'm sure your eyes are fine."

"Oh. Well, shove off."

Gilshenn's voice was distant for a moment, and they heard a sharp crack. *It's another one*, Halas thought with dread. "What are you doing?" he asked aloud.

"I want the horns. I will come back for the head later."

Another snap, and Gilshenn returned. "These things can skewer even the thickest of armor. Damned lucky they didn't catch you. Come on then, let's get out of this place."

———

Gilshenn led them through the tunnels, though doors and archways, across bridges and up long slopes with stairs carved into them. Once out of the prison, the tunnels once again became small and cramped. Halas and Des had to stoop, and occasionally they were forced to crawl. Halas found that, while crawling played havoc on his back, it was heaven on his wounded leg. Every so often, one of them would step on something that crunched. Gilshenn made nothing of it, but Halas was sure they were walking on the bones of the dead. Their skeletons must have been remarkably preserved in the stiff air.

As they went, Gilshenn served as a tour guide. Here was the refinery, here was the churchyard, here was the officer's quarters, here the armory. Sometimes he couldn't talk; when they tried to elicit a response, he'd sniffle or choke, and they left him alone. Halas wondered how such a broad city could be built inside such small conditions.

Gradually the halls widened, and the air cooled. Halas stopped sweating when he felt something glide across his face. Desmond laughed—it was wind!

Bits of light shone through cracks in the ceiling. They were close now. Gilshenn led them to a staircase and helped them up. Halas felt the chill rush of air before he saw it. They were in a cave. Brilliant sunlight shone from the mouth. He and Desmond raced for it, forgetting their aches and pains, laughing and dancing and cheering, leaving the bones of everyone Gilshenn Sidoor had ever known behind.

Halas and Desmond collapsed into the snow. The beautiful, wonderful snow. Halas tackled Des and pushed his head under. It was as if they were children again.

They were in a glade, surrounded by fir trees, their branches stark white with glittering crystals, the kind of look only taken after a fresh and copious snowfall followed by a deep freeze. Halas didn't care that he wasn't bundled, that his fingers and toes were already red, that his leg protested every movement, that his father's sword was broken. He laughed and laughed, so happy to be out of those caves.

"These trees were planted in my youth," Gilshenn lamented. "I remember when they were small. I remember it took all of the king's power to get them to keep."

Halas realized that though there had been light during their battle, he'd not really seen Gilshenn until now.

"You're a gnome!" he said. And he was. Around the beard were rosy cheeks and a thin, pointed nose. Gilshenn's bald, rounded head stopped right above Halas' waist. His hands were pudgy. Gilshenn smiled, and then did something that surprised Halas.

Gnome or human, two millennia old or a mere two decades, there was no mistaking the gesture that could mean a million things at once or nothing at all.

No, there was no mistaking a shrug.

"Up here!" Desmond hissed before Gilshenn could respond further. Halas looked. Their glade was at the base of a small hill. Desmond had crawled to the top. He gestured for Halas and Gilshenn to stay low, and they did, shimmying up through the snow. Halas looked at where Des was pointing.

The hill leveled out into tundra. A few dozen yards away, Halas saw Aeon and Elivain, on their knees, surrounded by armed men.

And before them stood Raazoi.

Chapter Thirteen
Daylight

"Where is it?" she demanded, slapping Aeon across the face with the back of her hand. He fell on his back, red lines drawn across his cheek. Blood trickled into the snow and turned it pink.

"I do not know!" he spit.

Raazoi did not bother to wipe it from her chin. "If you do not tell me what I wish to know, things will become very unpleasant for you. Where is the bloody Temple?"

Aeon shook his head. Three of the soldiers were wounded from their fight to subdue the two travelers, and Aeon had a large red mark covering the lower portion of his face that had already started to bruise. Raazoi walked to him, getting to her knees and closing the distance.

"I can make things unpleasant if you refuse to cooperate, and yet, I can please you in ways you have never been pleased, my young prince." She took him in hand, and he drew in a sharp breath. "I can show you things."

Elivain growled. He propelled himself to his feet, lowered his head, and charged. He struck Raazoi squarely in the midsection, and whatever power she had momentarily gained over the boy was lost as she crashed to the snow. One of the soldiers lunged, yanking Elivain up by his hair. Elivain jerked free and struck this man as well, using only his head to fight someone who had both weapons and armor. A second soldier pushed his friend aside and bashed Elivain with the pommel of his sword. Elivain toppled. The blow had opened up the skin of his brow, and blood trickled down his cheeks and the bridge of his nose. Aeon moved to rise, but two soldiers clamped mailed fists down on his shoulders, driving him painfully back down.

Climbing to his knees, Elivain stared icily into the eyes of one of the soldiers, the man who had hit him. The man blanched.

———

Halas could hear their voices now. He, Des, and Gilshenn snaked their way across the tundra. Halas was several foot-lengths ahead of the gnome, but he could feel Desmond's breath on his exposed ankles. He took yet another fistful of thin grass and pulled himself forward. He was tired, cold, and wet. He wanted to go home. As he crawled, he worried about Aeon. The prince had a vague idea of where the Temple was, but Raazoi seemed to want exact coordinates. What would happen if he didn't tell her anything?

What would happen if he did?

Halas cursed quietly, forcing himself to think about other things. Cailin flashed into his head, smiling and laughing. It made his eyes cloudy. He thought of Halbrick, of Conroy. He thought about his cottage. His bed. His soft, comfortable bed.

His fingers were cold and stiff. He tucked them into his sleeves and crawled with his elbows. He wished more than anything he could massage his aching leg, but there was no time to waste.

That was when Aeon screamed. It was a piercing, shrill wail filled with anguish. It carried across the tundra, echoing off the distant mountains. Halas could not endure it anymore—his friend was in trouble. He had to move now.

So Halas stood, and drew his sword.

At that moment, absolutely everything went wrong.

His fingers were frozen. He was able to hold his sword until it came from the sheath, at which point he was suddenly no longer gripping the weapon. He simply could not feel his fingers. The sword bounced off of one of the soldiers, and the momentum of the action carried Halas forward, tripping over his own feet. He cried out as he hit the ground. The soldiers swarmed him in moments. Halas could hear them bearing down. Cold, metal hands gripped his jerkin and hauled him up. Suddenly he was face-to-face with the ugliest man he'd ever seen. The soldier had even fewer teeth than Walter, and his breath smelled of stale onions. He coughed in Halas' face. Halas tried to pull away, but another man had grabbed his shoulder. He fought down the waves of terror that threatened to drown him, and thrashed in their grip. Halas kicked out, and was suddenly free.

———

Desmond saw his friend go down and leapt to his feet, his own sword glinting in the pale sunlight. The soldiers were grabbing Halas. Desmond pitched into them, swinging his blade at the nearest soldier's helmet and knocking him into the others. Another soldier threw out the butt end of his spear, knocking Desmond's legs out from under him. He sprawled on his back, but managed to bring his sword up in time to parry the man's spear.

"Desmond!" Elivain yelled. "Raazoi is the threat! Attack the girl!"

Desmond sprang nimbly to his feet. He spared a glance at Halas. His friend had regained his ground and was scrambling for his sword. Des wanted to go to him, but Elivain was right; Raazoi was the threat. He cleared the wreck, twirling the blade and leaving Halas and Gilshenn to deal with the men. The witch smirked at his charge. He lifted his blade above his head, roaring louder than he thought possible.

That was as far as he got.

Raazoi smirked, lifted her hand and wiggled her fingers. Desmond realized it was a spell a moment too late. His arms and legs were suddenly heavy; he couldn't move them, it was as if they were encased in stone. He fell forward but rebounded back into place like a reed in the wind; his feet were firmly rooted to the dirt. The sword fell. Raazoi ran her tongue across her lips, and then Desmond couldn't breathe.

———

So occupied was she that she didn't notice Aeon. The prince's hands were bound behind his back. Despite this, he threw himself forward, tackling Raazoi with his shoulder and bearing her down. This woman had killed Tormod, and she would pay dearly for that. Aeon wanted nothing more in that moment than to hurt her.

Desmond came free of the spell almost instantly. He scooped up his blade. "Untie me!" Elivain hissed. Des complied.

———

Halas reached his sword just in time. He rolled on to his back and parried a spear thrust that would have eviscerated him. The man stumbled and would have crushed Halas, but Halas rolled away. The soldier hit the ground. Halas climbed over him and attacked his comrades. Two of them moved to face him. He slashed wildly, trying to get a better measure of their fighting prowess. The onion man batted away Silvia with his shield. Despite being half a foot-length shorter than it ought to be, Halas' sword held up remarkably well. Halas expected it to be no better than a stick, but that was not so. He lunged again. Neither man took their eyes from Halas. Onion circled around, trying to get behind him, but Halas retreated.

The first soldier grabbed his trouser leg. Halas screamed. The soldier had lost both sword and shield in his fall, so Halas not expected him to get back into the fight from the ground. He had drawn a nasty looking dagger from a sheath on his hip. Halas kicked the man's gauntlet away and stumbled. The three came on strong, spear and sword and dagger flashing in the sunlight. Halas parried the first few blows, but he was being forced ever backward. Where were his friends? He saw Gilshenn, swinging his hammer at two of the soldiers. They were undeterred.

Onion man bashed his shield against his chest and barked laughter. Halas was desperate. The men were fast and well trained, and they outnumbered him. He parried for his life, unable to press an offense. There was no way he would win this fight. He tripped over his own feet, and was once again on the ground.

That was when Elivain entered the fray. He dove in from seemingly nowhere, wrapping his arm around Onion's neck and dragging him away from the fracas. He'd managed to push the soldier's helmet up and to the left, blinding him. Onion staggered away, trying to dislodge Elivain. He screamed for assistance, and suddenly Halas was fighting only one man, a man still laughing as he charged. *And why shouldn't he laugh?* Halas thought. *He fights a gnome, a boy, and an unarmed man. On top of all that, he has a witch at his back. It's a miracle we aren't all dead already.*

He threw himself forward, smacking the soldier's dagger with enough force to knock it out of his hand. The man reached for it, but Halas pushed in close, driving his jagged chunk of steel into the gap between breastplate and helmet. The man choked and fell away with a spray of blood. Halas shuddered as it struck him, pleasantly and shockingly warm. He stumbled, feeling numb to the whole experience. Everything was a blur. Desmond and Aeon stood over Raazoi. Elivain had stolen a soldier's spear and killed three of the men. He and Gilshenn were closing in on the fourth. They finished him quickly. With Elivain involved, the men had never had a chance. It had lasted seconds, and just like that, Raazoi was alone, and she was surrounded.

"It's over," Elivain declared.

"Halas, Des," Aeon said, "you're alive!"

Desmond nodded. Halas, his breath hard in coming, offered the prince a weak smile. In truth, he was glad to see him, and overjoyed that they had arrived in time. He put a hand on his chest, could feel his heart pounding beneath the surface.

Raazoi's eye was already swollen. Bruises dotted her face and neck. There was a series of cuts from where she'd scraped her cheek on hitting the ground. Her dress was torn in several places, revealing shapely leg and stomach. Halas forced his eyes upward. She looked at Gilshenn. "You. You know where it is. Tell me."

"Are you mad?" he snapped.

"We should kill her," said Elivain.

"I agree," said Aeon. He bent down and took up a sword, cutting himself free as he did so. An uneasy rumble came up from Halas' gut. Now that the fight was over, he found himself thinking again. Raazoi was in their custody. They could not kill her.

"No!" said Halas. "She's harmless. We take her back with us."

"For what?" Aeon demanded. "To stand trial for her crimes? She has my mother in her pocket! For the love of Aelborough, Halas, she has to die. She is far too dangerous to be left alive."

"I don't care. I will not murder an unarmed woman, and neither will I let any of you."

As they argued, Raazoi stared at Gilshenn. The gnome was silent. Dropping his hammer, he put grizzled fingertips to his forehead. One of the nails cracked and flaked off. There was no blood. "My head," he whispered.

"You are very old," Raazoi whispered. "The last of your people. Why don't you roll over and let them go?"

"He is not the last!" Halas snapped, pointing his sword. "Do not listen to her, Gilshenn. Your people live side-by-side with mine all across Aelborough."

"Heed not the words of a snake," Aeon whispered through gritted teeth.

"He is the last. The last free gnome. His descendents were made as slaves."

"You lie," he whispered.

"My people suffered a similar fate. But we fought. We fought against the unjust, the corrupt, the tyranny of man, and that is why we were banished.

"Well, I must thank you, Gnome."

"For what?"

She disappeared.

—⋅—

Elivain lunged, but she was already gone. Gilshenn fell forward. Halas rushed to his side, rolling him over. He was bleeding from his eyes and mouth. For the first time, his skin showed signs of age. Gilshenn's already gray hair turned an unhealthy black and fell from his scalp in patches. Wrinkles cut through his cheeks and chin like a lance. His forehead tightened. What few teeth he had left began to follow his hair, cracking, breaking, and falling into the back of his throat.

"Dammit!" Elivain screamed. "We should have killed her!"

"Gilshenn? Gilshenn!" Halas shook him gently. He was suddenly aware that the gnome's body was very old, very fragile, and Halas had no wish to hurt his new friend further. "Gilshenn, please. Where is the Temple?"

Gilshenn coughed. "It is my time," he croaked. "That girl was right. Time to sleep, Gilshenn Sidoor. Good night."

"No! Gilshenn, where is the Temple?"

Gilshenn closed his eyes. Halas shook him again. "Gilshenn!"

"Let me sleep, boy."

"*GILSHENN!*"

"What!"

"Where. Is. The. Temple?"

"It's—oh, you're making this complicated. Come here, take my hand."

Halas did, tentatively. He didn't know what Gilshenn was thinking, but he suspected the poor gnome was simply delirious. "What are you doing?" he asked.

"Just hold on. This is going to feel odd. It did for me, at least."

Gilshenn was right. It did feel odd.

———

The world went black, and then changed. Gone was the snow, the cold, the smell of blood. Gone were his friends. The harsh tundra was replaced by a familiar and wonderful scene. Halas Duer had been transported from the arctic wasteland to the site he had often shared with the love of his life. Their knoll.

And *she* was there with him.

Cailin curled up in the crook of his arm, warm against his side. She smelled of daisies, her favorite flower. She ran a light fingertip up his chest. Halas' flesh prickled at the touch, even through his tunic. He sighed, but then everything came upon him in a rush, a physical blow that made him reel. Halas jolted to his feet and whirled around. *What happened? What is going on?*

"Halas," Cailin asked, straightening, "are you all right? What's the matter?"

"I'm…Cailin, how long have we been here?"

"Forever."

"I have…" he stopped. Forever? "What?"

"You and I began here, and we will end here. This place is forever. You know that."

"Cailin, I'm not supposed to be here right now. I haven't been here in months."

"I know. This isn't real, and it's not a dream. I don't know what to call it, frankly."

Halas was warming up already, but his blood froze as she spoke. "You aren't Cailin, are you?"

"I'm afraid not. Would you like me to be someone else?" Cailin's body shifted then. Her skin darkened, her breasts filled, her legs lengthened. He knew this to be some illusion, but felt a pang of regret nonetheless as she disappeared. "Jassia, perhaps?"

He took a step back. If he hadn't seen the transformation himself, he would have believed this to actually be Jassia. It was a perfect replica. "How do you do that? Who are you?"

Jassia sighed. "I'm a lot of things. Once you've been through what I have, you pick up a few tricks. Trust me, you wouldn't want to look upon me as I truly am."

"Try me."

"No. Your mind would explode. Literally. Humankind cannot behold me."

That seemed to be an acceptable answer. Halas took what Jassia said as truth, solid fact. He didn't know why, or how, but he knew that whatever this thing was, it wasn't lying. Perhaps it *couldn't* lie. That seemed to make about as much sense as anything else.

"I am a servant of Equilibrium. Do you know what that is?"

"I have heard of it."

"Good. Without us, without stability, there would be nothing, chaos. Good or evil, no one desires this. Chaos would mean the end of all things."

"Are you a god?"

"No. I am more than that. Aren't you listening?"

Suddenly Halas was in the Gate pavilion. The people around him were wraiths. His father stood, clear as stars in the night sky, at the wall, a proud statue. Fire spewed above his head. Jassia appeared beside him. "There is much in store for you, Halas Duer. Gilshenn Sidoor was my pupil, the vessel from which I operated on your plane. He was loyal, obedient. He will be missed, but I have made a place for him in Heaven. He shall be happy there. My people are fairly rewarded. You will be one day, too."

"Gilshenn—is he dead?"

"Not yet, though he will be soon. We haven't much time, and all the time in the world. Things are funny here."

"Do you have a name?"

"Many. None you would understand. Let us stick with Jassia, or would you prefer someone else?"

Jassia began to change rapidly before his eyes. She became Halbrick; Halbrick became Desmond; Desmond became Conroy; Conroy became Garek. Halas fell to one knee at the spectacle of it. Something was digging at the back of his head. He put a hand to it and felt a lump. Something throbbed and twisted beneath his fingers. Halas' vision blurred, and Garek faded before him. There was a hard ball of pressure building in his skull, like an ever-expanding rat burrowing deeper into his brain. He was sweating. *I'm in the middle of the tundra, why am I sweating?*

"You're not there anymore," Garek answered. "Not even on your plane of existence. I'm sorry about your head. I get ahead of myself sometimes. It happens to the best of us, I'm afraid." Approaching Halas, Garek stopped and chortled to himself. "*Ahead.* Ha!"

His brother laid a hand on his forehead, and Halas' pain disappeared immediately. He stood on shaky legs. Now even his injured left leg felt good, better than it had since before the incident with the tigers. Garek looked solemn. "I'm afraid that won't last," he said. "When you return home, all your aches and pains will be restored. An unfortunate side effect."

And then he was at home, sitting with his brother in their bedroom. The window was an opaque mist, and the beds were made of red, pulsing straw. Halas tested one. "Why am I here? What do you want with me?"

"I didn't bring you here. You were sent."

"Gilshenn."

"Correct. Sidoor chose you to be his replacement."

"Replacement for what?"

"Guardian of the Temple. Aeon's Temple. Anything worth protecting is worth protecting properly, wouldn't you say? And believe me, this Temple is most certainly worth protecting."

Halas' mouth went dry. *Guardian.* What did that mean? Would he be forced to stay here, in the tundra, sleeping as Gilshenn Sidoor had slept?

"Why are you doing this? I thought you kept things in order, good or evil. Why prevent the Infernals from being risen?"

"The Ifrinn are…unpredictable. And *strong*!" Garek laughed and clapped his hands. "Even my superiors cannot foresee what they may choose to do if released from their prison. It's best for everyone if they just stay put."

"Why not destroy them?"

"Are you even listening to me?" Garek stood and gave an exasperated sigh. Halas would have laughed if he hadn't been so utterly confused. "I cannot enter your plane of existence. I cannot interfere directly. Even if I was allowed to, the Ifrinn are strong. Their leader, Tharog the Warbrood, is stubborn. Let's say you come across a spider of a particular potent venom. The only way to contain this spider is to seal it shut in a box of indestructible metals. You do this, but the spider is still there. How would you kill the spider?"

"You would have to open the box."

"Well, maybe you're not completely hopeless. The only way to kill the spider would be to open its prison, and then it would be free to do whatever it wants. You could risk it, of course, but there's always the chance the spider may be expecting a trap. You may crush it with a thumbnail, or it may escape. It's all up in the air."

"And we can't have that."

"Don't be sarcastic. It's unbecoming of you. I want to get one thing clear: if I had been given the choice, I would not have chosen you. You're too… fogged. Your future is clouded, but it is clear even to lowly peons such as myself that you have much to do. Gilshenn Sidoor was the perfect guardian. He was a nobody, an out-of-work potter in a dying city. Gilshenn was a loser."

Halas had never heard that term before, but he found he didn't much care for it. "Gilshenn is my friend. Do not speak of him like that."

Garek rolled his eyes. "You knew Gilshenn for but a few hours. His memory will fade. In time, you will not even recall his face. I'm sure he was a fine character, but that is not for me to judge, nor do I care. He served his purpose, and you will serve yours."

Halas stood and walked forward until he faced his brother eye-to-eye. It took longer than he would have thought. The room seemed to expand with every step. "You listen here," he said, "I am no man's puppet."

"Correct. I am no man. Hell, I'm not even in charge. We are both puppets here, Halas Duer, marionettes held by powers greater than we can comprehend. It has been my lot in life since Creation, and now it is yours. I'm afraid you're going to have to get used to the cold, Halas Duer. It's going to be a long time before you may leave. You are going to give me everything."

"No. I'm not going to give you anything. I won't," Halas stammered, suddenly nervous. He could think of no fate worse than that. He would never see his father again, his home, Cailin.

"No, I'm afraid you will not. They will not know where to find you. Your lives are short, and your bodies difficult to preserve. Gilshenn Sidoor had his chamber, and you will have yours. It's tough to face, I know, but the Orhill Caverns are your home now. Get used to it."

Halas shook his head. "I won't do it. Find another man. You cannot ask me to do this."

"Lucky for both of us I am not asking, then, isn't it?" Garek's face twisted into a snarl. "I'm getting bored of this, Halas Duer. I've given you sight, I've given you knowledge, and I've given you your orders. Now do as I say, and go save the Temple!"

Sight? What does he mean by that? It was all too much to take in. Halas felt a strong urge to turn and run the other way. He'd find a way out of this world, and flee all the way back to Cordalis. He would not, could not, accept this creature's offer. That was just too much.

He pivoted, but Garek was impossibly fast. Halas didn't even register the thing masquerading as his brother move, but suddenly Halas was face-down on the ground, his breath violently driven away. The world changed again. His face no longer pressed on stark wood, but cold stone. Halas rolled up into a sit. They were on the pinnacle of a tall stone tower. Below them sprawled a castle keep. Peasants and soldiers milled about far below. Halas climbed to his feet.

"Would you *stop it*?" Garek whined. "Keeping this world in place is taxing, you idiot. I just want to go home."

"I know the feeling."

"Listen, if you do not acquiesce, I'm going to have to resort to something drastic. Accept my offer, fulfill your role, or I will kill every form I've taken since we met. All of them."

That did it. All the fear left Halas then. His face twitched, became something of a scowl. He marched right up to his brother and poked him in the chest.

"You said you cannot interfere. There's not a thing you can do to force me to play your little game, is there? You may hold all the cards *here*, but where I come from, you're nothing more than an insect. You're not even allowed *in*. I'll save your bloody Temple once, this once, but after I plan full well on going home. And there's not a thing you can do to stop me! Find another guardian! And if I ever find a way to get back here, I'm going to find you, and I'm going to kill you.

"Do you understand me?"

But Garek was gone.

Chapter Fourteen

The Temple Of Immortals

Halas shook his head. Desmond stood over him, looking concerned. He sat up and nearly vomited as a result. A thick, salty taste filled his mouth. Halas leaned over and spat. What came out was milky and yellow. Desmond put a hand on his shoulder. "Halas, are you all right?"

Halas looked blankly at his friend for a moment, trying to force down the nausea. He still felt worlds away. "I'm fine. What happened?"

"Gilshenn touched you and you fainted. Are you all right?"

"Gilshenn—where is Gilshenn? Is he alive?"

"I think…"

"I must speak with him." Halas tried to stand, but his legs were water. Desmond grabbed him before he could fall. "Help me."

Leaning heavily on Desmond, Halas hobbled over to his friends. The gnome coughed. "Halas. Do you understand?"

"I do," he lied. "They gave it to me."

"It?" Elivain asked. "What do you mean, it?"

"What's he talking about?" That came from Aeon. Halas ignored them both. He and Gilshenn were in their own little world, almost literally.

"Save it, please," Gilshenn said. "Save it so everything I did wasn't for nothing."

"I will. This once, I promise I will. But where is the Temple?"

"You know. Just close your eyes. You'll know."

Halas closed his eyes, and found he did know.

He knew exactly where to find the Temple of Immortals.

"Thank you. Good night, Gilshenn Sidoor."

"Good night."

Gilshenn slowly withered away. His bones turned to ash, and the ash was blown away in the wind. Halas stood up; Desmond patted his shoulder. Halas nodded. "Let's go," he said, and set off.

"Go where?" Elivain demanded. "We haven't the foggiest idea of where this thing may be."

"I do. The Temple of Immortals is beneath us. We have to back into Orhill. We have time; Raazoi will not know quite how to get through the wards. The Temple is a lot hardier than even she can give it credit for."

"How do you know that?"

"I'll explain it all later. When you thought I fainted, I had some sort of vision. I've had a lot of visions. I promise I will tell you everything later, when we have time, but for now we have to run."

He turned back toward the entrance to the Orhill Caverns, but Desmond grabbed his arm. "Halas, it's bloody dark in there. Even if you somehow know where to go, how will we see?"

Halas thought he knew the answer to that, too. "Just stay close to me."

And with that, he ran. His leg began hurting almost instantly. That thing—Garek, Cailin, whatever it had been—was right when it said all his pain would return. It seemed worse, somehow, like broken glass in his left thigh. The gods had deemed it necessary to melt that glass down by his knee, but below that the pain subsided into a low, warm ache. His chest heaved; it felt like he had been kicked by a horse, making every breath a dagger in his throat. He thanked the gods that there was little snow to encumber his boots. They slid into the dell, and Halas did not hesitate in plunging into darkness.

But there was light. It felt as if a slick filter slipped over his eyes, and suddenly he could see, clear as day. He reached behind him and took Desmond's hand. "Stay close, follow me, and do not let go of one another. These stairs are treacherous."

They descended down the stairs with surprising ease. "Halas, what happened?" Des asked.

"Later, Des. After this is all over."

Desmond said nothing, and Halas led them through the caverns. They were marvelous to behold. The ceilings were high, incredibly so by gnome standards, and the halls wide. Curiosity picked at him as he passed closed doors, the wood rotted away to almost nothing. This place was so new, so unexplored. How much history lurked in these halls? How many stories? Conroy would love it, he knew.

"Halas!" Aeon called. Halas turned. The prince stood a few paces behind Desmond. Elivain clung to his shoulder. Halas frowned. It was strange being able to see when he knew his friends could not, almost frustrating. He doubled back, took Aeon's hand, and placed it in Desmond's.

He knew where to find the Temple. It was as if there was an audible map in his head. *Turn here,* it would say, or *through that door.* At times the voice sounded remarkably similar to that of Harden Graves, the mayor of Bakunin, and other times it sounded like his father. Halas pressed on. He had to stop several times to retrace his steps and keep his friends from getting lost, but he checked on them over his shoulder almost constantly, and they never fell too far behind.

That door is locked, his voice said, *but you must pass through it.* "Hold here," Halas told his friends. One kick and the door shattered into a million pieces. He led them onward, into a dining hall. Tables that had once been great littered the place. Now they were rotted. The ruins of ancient tapestries hung from the walls. Everywhere Halas saw the signs that Orhill had once been a bustling civilization, but there were no bodies. However this place had ended, Halas thought it had not been violent. But what had they stepped through earlier? Halas had been sure Orhill was a crypt.

Deeper they went.

"Where are we going?" Elivain asked.

"The Temple. Just a little further."

Elivain grumbled something that Halas did not hear. Shortly after, Desmond lost his grip and Halas had to reorder everyone. These incidents were taking time, time Halas thought they didn't have. He knew Raazoi would have trouble with the wards leading up to the Temple, but a witch of her caliber would not be delayed long. He had to hope she was not laying traps behind her, but he didn't think she was. *Does she even know we are coming? She can't possibly.*

To his left, a section of wall fell away when Halas put his hand on it. He recoiled. Desmond yelled. The four had gotten tangled up again. "Stop!" Halas said. No one had their packs, meaning there was no rope to tether them together, as he and Des had traveled earlier. He sorted them out. "I need you to *hang on,*" he told them. "We haven't much time."

"Hanging on wouldn't be a problem if you would not walk so quickly," Elivain said. "How do you even know where you're going?"

"For the last time, I just do. You must trust me."

"Fine."

You're almost there, the voice said. *Not long now. Take the passage on your left.* Halas took the passage on his left. There was a terrible humming at the back of his mind, but he had ignored it up until now. It was growing louder. "Do you hear that?" Aeon asked, as if on cue.

"I do. It's the Temple. We are very near."

"What about the witch? Is she here, too?"

"I don't know." He didn't, but she had to be. Where else?

"How are we to fight her if we can't see?"

"I can see."

"So you'll fight her alone?" Elivain snapped.

"If I must. Please, just trust me. We have to get there before she can do anything."

The corridor took a sharp right, and then dipped left. Halas felt they were descending deeper into the earth. There would be a few more twists and turns, and then a doorway, and then stairs.

And then they would be at the Temple.

He thought they had passed through some of the wards already destroyed by Raazoi. Where they had been, the stones gave off a twang that was almost musical. The half-Infernal woman was powerful indeed.

Halas felt above himself. He'd said he would try and fight the witch alone if it came down to it, and he'd meant it. He was a warrior, trained by some of the best, weathered through battle and hardship, watched and chosen by powers beyond even his comprehension. Had the thing that had taken Garek's form been what had sent the blue tigers to kill Torgeir? It had to be. How many blue tigers were there in Aelborough? Precious few, he thought, but that was beside the point. Halas knew he could stop Raazoi. He *had* to. She could not be allowed to let the spider out of the box, at any cost.

They came to one final doorway. *You're here,* his father's voice said, and then fell silent. The door in question had been splintered, and not by conventional means. It looked like the entire hallway had exploded. Black scorch marks scoured the walls. The floor was gouged and littered with wood splinters. This door had been the final ward, and the strongest of them, but it had given Raazoi no pause. Halas didn't know how he knew this. He could see her clearly in his mind's eye, could see her torn dress push back as a wind erupted in her hair. She lifted a hand, and the door blew apart as if made of paper, and then descended into darkness.

But it wasn't dark down there. As Halas crossed the threshold, the filtered scales fell from his eyes. They were a physical membrane, he was surprised to find. Without thinking, he reached up and caught them on his palm, where they quickly dissolved. Halas' stomach rumbled at the sensation. It was unpleasant.

The Temple of Immortals was blue.

They were in some sort of tower. A winding stone staircase led down. Nearly half a mile below them was the Temple. Halas could see it well enough. It was made up of a single shrine in the center of the room, ringed by broad stone obelisks that curved into blunt scythes. The altar glowed blue, a hue Halas had never seen before. Enthralled, he stumbled toward it, and nearly fell off the stairs, but Des caught him.

"Watch out," he whispered.

"I have to get down there."

Aeon stepped up beside him, gaping. It was the most remarkable thing any of them had ever seen. So simple, yet so beautiful. So important. How could the something so crucial consist of but a few stones?

Elivain was already running. He took the stairs three at a time, silent as a cat. Halas turned to his friends. "Ready?"

"Ready," they said in unison, and they went.

The stairs wrapped around the wall of the tower. As they descended, Raazoi came into view below, half-concealed behind one of the pillars. She chanted in a whisper, but her words echoed up to reach Halas' ears. He could not understand a thing she was saying.

They caught up to Elivain at the base of the stairs, on his haunches. Raazoi had her back to them, but Halas thought she knew they were there. "Can she see us?" Aeon asked.

Halas stepped onto the main floor, and was met with an immediate sense of overwhelming power. His skin prickled in gooseflesh, his heart pumped furiously, his hair stood on end, his trousers tightened. He swallowed and nearly fell. Des took his arm. Elivain eyed him curiously. Halas blinked rapidly against tears. "Can you feel it?" he whispered.

"What?" Desmond asked. His voice was high, strained with worry. "Halas, feel what?"

The details of the Temple leaped forward into Halas' vision. He saw the altar, clear pictograms were etched on its surface, an owl and a moon and a snake and an island; written on each of the outlying pillars was a name, each was different, and none were legible; pale ghosts of men and women stood by each, stoically watching the events unfold, their gazes stern but their stances slumped, almost defeated; the stone beneath their feet pulsed and trembled with light and music and power; the blue glow from the altar was alien, born from another world Halas could never see or even conceive, a world where colors and other visuals blended with the other senses, senses Halas would never know existed. The words Raazoi spoke came from this world, he thought. Her voice was not entirely her own, assisted by some unknown entity. Did it belong to her, the magics deep within her own body? Or did Raazoi have help? Halas reached at this idea, and began peeling away the layers of her words, digging, trying to discover the second voice, completely unaware of what he was doing or how he was doing it.

And then the river of power began to recede. Already it seemed faint. His mind reached out, trying to grasp at what weak tendrils remained. It had felt so *good*, so *strong*. With the power of the Temple of Immortals and Aeon the Great, Halas knew he would have no trouble defeating Raazoi—if it didn't kill him first. He sighed as the last of the power rushed out of him. The experience had lasted maybe two seconds, but they were the best two seconds of his life. For two seconds, Halas Duer had been more than just a man, more than just a twenty-year-old farmer from Cordalis. He'd been a higher being. He shuddered.

"I'm all right," he said. The power was gone. The wraiths were gone. The stone was silent. Before them, Raazoi continued to chant. The words she spoke were nebulous, almost complete gibberish. Had they been familiar before? Aeon lifted his blade.

"Can she see us?" he repeated.

It was Elivain who answered. "I don't know. I'll go left, you all go right. Halas, up the center. We take her at the same time. I don't…" But he was interrupted. Raazoi's voice hitched deeply, and a chunk of rubble above the staircase broke free. It cascaded down toward Halas, who watched, rooted to the spot. There was no time to react.

But the Temple saved them. Forty feet above their heads, the rubble erupted into a million little bits of gravel to rain down harmlessly with no more force than mild hail. Halas realized what the witch had in mind; she was going to bring down the Orhill Caverns and crush the Temple.

"Go!" Elivain hissed, and darted off. Halas followed suit. He couldn't remember drawing his sword, but it was in his hand, gleaming in the blue. Raazoi turned to regard them, calm as can be. They may as well have been trying to make polite conversation over tea and cakes. Elivain hurled his spear like a javelin. It skipped out of his hand and splintered. Elivain crashed to the ground and skidded to the altar. Desmond swung his blade, but it burst into flame and exploded, searing his palms. Des screamed. Halas' heart wrenched at the sound. Aeon moved to charge, but Halas put a hand on his chest.

"Don't. She'll kill you."

"He's right," Raazoi said. "I will. You've no idea how much power this place is imbuing me with. I've never felt anything like it before. You cannot stop me. No one can."

"We can," Aeon said.

"Bringing down this tower will do you no good," Halas said. "The Temple is protected. Can you not feel the barrier?"

"All barriers can be overwhelmed. Even this."

"You cannot do this." Halas looked at Elivain, by the altar. The man was stirring. Halas just had to stall until he regained his senses. If anyone could get them out of this, it was Elivain.

His boots were suddenly wet. Halas stepped back toward the stairs, but it was only water, seeping up through the stone at his feet. Halas had never seen anything like it. It trickled down the walls from above. *We must be near the ocean. Are we underwater?* Then, *I've traveled from the southernmost edge of Ager to the northernmost. Wouldn't Conroy be proud?*

"If you do this, you'll die too."

She closed her eyes and clenched her fist. Halas could feel the power radiating through her in waves. "Possibly, but I can think of no better cause to die for. This is the salvation of my people. Now shut up and let me finish."

"No!" Aeon exclaimed, genuinely taken aback by the nonchalant tone of her command. Before Halas could stop him, the boy crossed the room and swung his blade. It shattered, blasting metal splinters back into his body. He cried out and fell. Halas screamed and ran to his side, sliding in water that was already over his boots. He lifted Aeon's head out of it, and looked for his friends. Elivain was on his hands and knees; Desmond had sat up against the altar, cradling his hands weakly before him.

"This is what you fight to protect, princeling," Raazoi said. Her mouth did not move, and the voice seemed to come from all around. "This is how you end."

"Why are you doing this?" Halas asked. It was weak, but he felt he had to say *something*. Never had he expected to fail so miserably. He'd felt the power of the Temple, but it was gone before he could make any use of it. All the time spent on this mission, all the lives lost—and *this* was how it ended? They'd not even been able to put up a fight.

"For my people. We've been prisoner to you for long enough, and now it is time to turn the tide. It is time to break from our cages, to overthrow you pigs and establish our own kingdom. Humanity is over. We shall purge this place of your kind, and we shall live in peace. No more shall we be plagued by your ignorance and bigotry. No more shall we be tortured and killed for no *purpose!*"

Her voice deepened, and she seemed to grow taller. An angry wind came suddenly and whipped her gown about her knees. "We did nothing to you! Yet you hunted us wherever you could! You're animals! Dirt!" She spit; the water sizzled and steamed where it landed. "You burned…murdered…" She seemed to fade then, and fall. Her voice came out in bits and pieces as she continued her rant. Halas could not understand what she was saying. He glanced at Elivain, who groaned. A chunk of rubble struck the barrier, and this time more gravel came through than before. The flash of light was weak.

"I did not do any of this," he said. "My friends did not. *No one here has done your people harm!* Surely you cannot harbor us any ill will, for Aeon the Great lived two thousand years ago!"

"Aeon the Terrible," she corrected. "He was a scourge for my people. All of you were, but for one man. You killed my Nolan, human swine! I loved him and you took him from me!"

Raazoi lunged at him and dug her fingers into his face. He screamed. Instantly, thoughts of gold and jewels came into Halas' head. Riches beyond his dreams. Immortality. Raazoi writhing in ecstasy. A towering palace of crystal and ice. The gold haze surrounding these visions turned a deep purple. He saw Nolan, drifting in the water. Conroy resting in a field of flowers. A friendly voice cackling with malice. A crowd of worshipers as far as he could see, all chanting his name. A mountain of diamonds.

Then he saw Cailin. The haze melted away. She was sitting on a stump at their knoll, her hands pressed between her thighs. The sun illuminated her beauty, turning her hair a beautiful dark brown that made Halas' heart leap. She looked up and smiled at him, and her teeth were pearly white. "Hey there," she said. She held up a strange looking object, almost like a melon, with a warped face carved into it. "I got you this. Neat, huh?"

And then she died.

Halas saw a blade pierce her gut. He watched her eyes flicker and go dark. The creature that stood behind her was taller than a man, encased entirely in black armor. "NO!" he screamed, and snapped back into reality.

Raazoi stood before him, her face twisted impossibly with rage. Halas' vision turned red. Blood trickled down from his eyes. He tried to pull away, but could not. He kicked, splashing weakly in the water, helpless in her grip. *Is this how Tormod died? Please, do not let me suffer that same fate.* He clawed at her arms. She was so strong. How could someone her size be so strong? He coughed, spraying blood. His mouth was filled with it. One of his eyes had swollen shut. She leaned in closer, and whispered in his ear.

"I will make this come to pass."

Halas snarled. He reached up, took a handful of the witch's hair, and yanked her down.

Right on to Silvia.

Raazoi inhaled sharply. She tried to pull away, but Halas held on, twisting the broken blade, moving it back and forth inside her belly. He was on fire then, and he flew back, skidding across the chamber. The others were simultaneously released from her spell. Elivain kicked Raazoi in the knee, but she did not fall. Halas seemed to be in a stupor. Everything moved slowly.

He watched Aeon rise. The prince stumbled toward Raazoi, growling through his teeth. He pushed aside her arms and wrapped his hands around her neck. Halas noticed how small they were: like a child's hands, because the prince *was* a child. He was but fifteen years of age. Halas tried to get up to assist his friend, but could not. Aeon, still growling, squeezed. Raazoi reached up and took him by the wrists.

The world was black then, quickly turning several colors at once before going back to jet. The blue of the Temple changed to white, two pure silhouettes wrestling in the newfound brightness. Raazoi let out a bloodcurdling shriek that made Halas' head hurt, right down to his teeth. Rock fell from above, and Halas could see the sky. Lightning flashed. The water churned. It was up to Halas' chest. He pulled through it, found Desmond, and dragged him to his feet. They clung to the altar. A storm appeared, seeming to be centered on the conflict between prince and princess as they wrestled over the gleaming broken blade that had once belonged to Halbrick Duer.

Aeon cried out and fell. Raazoi gripped Silvia by the handle and tumbled backward, into suddenly still waters.

Her body made no splash. "Desmond, are you all right?" Halas asked. Des nodded. Halas pushed off and yanked Silvia free. The blade was clean and the hilt was hot. He jammed it into its sheath.

"We've got to go!"

The water was pressing him down, but he fought, grabbing Aeon under one arm and Des with the other. Desmond pushed him. "I've got it!" he cried.

But when Halas touched the prince, he stopped moving. Everything was a blur, but only for an instant. The next second, Desmond struck him across the face. Halas fell backward into the water, dropping Aeon. He reeled. Des pulled the prince above the surface. Halas grabbed him.

"Stairs! Get topside!"

Confused, Halas struggled against the current, toward the stairs. Aeon was a heavy burden, but he would not drop the boy, even though he was likely dead. *No, don't think that. Do not think that!* "Hold on, Aeon. Just hold on." He didn't know he was speaking. He could not hear himself over the roaring water.

They reached the stairs and fell into Desmond and Elivain's waiting arms. Elivain hauled the boy up and out of the water. They hurried up along the wall. A piece of the stair chipped under Elivain's boot, but Des caught him before he could fall. Halas tried to get a good look at Aeon as they ran. He didn't know if the boy was alive or not. Was he breathing? He could not be sure.

The water was far below, but rushing quickly to meet them. Elivain led them through the door, but Halas grabbed his arm before he could continue. "You have to wait here," he said.

"What do you mean?"

"I'll only be a minute." He spared Aeon a pained look, but still could not tell if the boy lived.

But there was no time. He smiled at Des, turned, and hurled himself into the water.

———

Already frozen, the sudden impact did little to hinder his progress. He could not swim, but he would not have to. For this final goal, Halas Duer only had to sink. He angled himself toward the dull blue glow and pulled himself down. He had to know if the Temple of Immortals had been destroyed. He could see the glow, but it wasn't enough. If the Temple was gone, then everything had been for naught. Tormod, Brennus and the crew of *The Wandering Blade,* Dale Crowe...Aeon. Many men had given their lives for this thing, and Halas was not going to let their sacrifice be in vain. He sank like a stone. A wicked numbness spread through his body. From what he could see, his hands and forearms were a blistered red.

For the first time since he set out, Halas realized that there may be no rescue.

But still, he swam. Waves and ripples in the water fanned him along. He came to the Temple. The stone pillars beckoned him like a welcoming hand. Halas tried to grip one, but his own hands were frozen and useless. He kicked along, but his legs were failing. It was all so *cold.* Halas felt a sharp stab in his gut and cried out. An air bubble popped on his chin. He was running out of breath.

The Temple was all right. The stonework around the altar had cracked and splintered, but the altar itself was untouched. It thrummed powerfully in the water, rippling and pulsing, pushing Halas away. The force of the Temple twisted him away from the pillar. He was suddenly disoriented. *Up, up, I have to reach the surface. Which way is the surface?*

He tried to find Raazoi, or the altar, or even the wall, but could not. Everything was beginning to dim. *Is this the end?*

With that thought, he tried to pivot around, to no avail. His limbs had ceased to cooperate. With that came a sort of rising panic. Raazoi had said it best. *If there is anything worth dying for, it is this. The salvation of my people.*

But I don't want to die. Please, don't let me die! I'll do whatever you ask! I'll stay, I promise! Please! He put a foot against something and tried to push up, but could not. He'd seen people swim before, and tried to emulate that, but could not. His body was breaking down. It felt as if his skin was peeling off, bit by bit. The water stabbed at him from all directions, burning with cold fire. He cried out in pain, and suddenly it was in his mouth, rushing down his throat, into his lungs, and he couldn't breathe. He thrashed, trying to push the water away, trying to escape, but all that did was cause him to sink even more, and he was at the altar, clutching it, in more pain than he'd ever been in his life, scared, dying, drowning in the dark.

———

Desmond felt numb. Not because he was cold, but because his friends were falling all around him. Aeon lay across his lap, rasping for breath, breath that came sparingly. When Halas had gone into the water, Des had tried to follow, but Elivain stopped him. "You'll freeze!" he had said, and jumped in.

"But you won't?" Desmond asked the empty air. He went back to Aeon and pulled him close. Now the boy was coughing. Desmond ran a hand through his hair. "It's okay, it's all going to be okay. Just hang in there."

He coughed too; it was infectious. Aeon was shaking. "It's not," he whispered.

"What's that?"

"It's not. I think…I think they passed it to me."

Desmond didn't know what the boy was talking about, nor did he care. But when someone was wounded, you were supposed to keep them speaking. "Passed what?"

"Responsibility."

"For what?"

Someone screamed off to his side. Desmond looked up. Elivain scrambled through the doorway, Halas in his arms. Desmond looked down at Aeon's sullen face. "Responsibility for what?" he asked again, unsure of what to do. Everything was happening so fast; he was having trouble taking it all in.

Aeon didn't respond. He'd stopped breathing. Desmond shook him, but still the boy said nothing. He stood up and went to Halas and Elivain. "Aeon's not breathing," he muttered.

"But Halas is. Come on, we have to get him away from here. These caverns are warm."

"I'm not leaving the prince."

"There's no time! That water is rising quickly. Come on!"

"I'm not leaving him!"

Elivain snarled, and disappeared. Only a bit of light was cast in the tunnel from the wreck up above, but that faded quickly. Desmond, too weak to do anything else, took Aeon's wrists and began dragging him, following the sound of Elivain's footsteps. Soon they had left the roaring of the water behind. Desmond could see nothing, but he kept walking, until Elivain called a halt.

"We shall rest here. Help me warm him."

"How did you get him out?"

"I have my ways."

"How did you get him out?" Desmond repeated.

Elivain sighed. "I took the form of an animal and swam him to safety."

"Oh." That sounded normal enough. So Elivain was a Shifter. Desmond remembered the stories. "Is Halas going to be all right?"

"If we can keep him warm. Here, huddle close."

"What are you going to do?"

"Change."

And Elivain did. Desmond could see nothing, but he could still hear, and the sound of it was terrifying. Elivain crunched and crackled. Skin tore and something wet *squelched*. Desmond could not help but flee. Elivain yelled, but it was cut short. Everything was silent for a time, and then the corridors were filled with deep, animal breaths. It sounded similar to the Deyrey Baaish, too similar. Desmond scrambled away in a panic. The fight with the Deyrey Baaish seemed long ago, but Desmond realized it had only been a few hours before. They'd killed it. This breathing had to be something else. It occurred to him that it was only Elivain. He came back. Des wondered what animal form he took, but it didn't really matter, did it?

He pressed himself against warm fur and fell asleep.

———

Halas opened his eyes, unsure of what had happened. His last memory had been drowning in the Temple. Was this the afterlife? Had the thing that appeared as Conroy whisked him away back to that awful *in-between* world? *No, it cannot. That being is finished with me.* He coughed.

"You're awake!" someone exclaimed. Halas started and reached for his sword, but it was only Des, embracing him. "Oh Halas, I thought you weren't going to make it! Elivain was not worried, but—it's so dark in here, and you were so cold. Don't do that again!"

But Desmond was laughing. Halas embraced him back. He could see Des clearly, and the poor man looked dead on his feet. They sat against the wall, close together. Elivain stood nearby, nearly naked. "What happened to you?"

"Elivain is a Shifter," Desmond explained.

Halas frowned. "Why did you not tell us this before?"

Elivain shook his head. "It doesn't matter. We're all safe now. It's time we got topside. I wish to see the sun again."

Halas looked at his friends, and a feeling of pure relief washed over him. Desmond, his face haggard and low; Elivain, naked but for a bloody cloak, and Aeon—where was Aeon? "The prince?" Halas asked. Desmond coughed.

"Halas...Aeon died. Raazoi killed him."

The words hit him hard. He put a hand to his chest, trying to massage away the tightness that had gathered there. "Dead?"

"I'm afraid so. He…I'm sorry."

"Where is he?"

But as soon as Halas looked, he knew. Desmond had brought the boy's body along. He lay nearby, a tangle of limbs. It took quite a bit of willpower to stand, but once Halas did, he walked to Aeon and collapsed again. When Halas touched him, he could see the boy prince's last few moments, cradled by Desmond, cold and afraid.

"Responsibility," he whispered, and just like that, Aeon had stopped breathing. He did not turn to dust like Gilshenn, he just…stopped. His chest rose and fell one last time. A small gasp escaped his already purple lips. His eyes rolled back into his head and mercifully closed.

For a moment, Halas saw the prince as he would turn out to be. This was not an ugly sight, like it had been with Gilshenn. No, Prince Aeon looked kind, wizened, yet strong and beautiful.

He looked noble.

Halas put his head to Aeon's ruined chest, a chest that had, mere hours ago, been full of life, and wept. He heard Desmond dragging himself through the tunnel, felt his arm across his shoulders. "We won, Halas," he said. "We won."

"I don't care," Halas whispered back. "I just want to go home."

"Then let's go home."

———

Desmond moved to pick up Aeon's body, but Halas stopped him. "It is better if we leave him here."

"What? Halas, no, we cannot. Aeon was our friend."

"And he is the guardian now. It is better for his spirit, if his body remains in the caverns. He will be stronger."

"What?"

Halas had had another vision, this one very brief. He only remembered bits and pieces of it. This time, the thing had taken Aeon's form. He told Halas, on no uncertain terms, what he thought of him. He said that Aeon's spirit would more than serve. He said, "Go to Hell," and threw Halas right back into the Temple to die.

What Halas knew of spirits, he'd learned from Conroy. Ghosts haunted the areas they'd died or were buried. They were more powerful when close to their bodies, as if the tether that held them to this plane of existence was stronger there. Halas thought this was as good a final resting place as any, for a time. He clasped the boy's hand. Aeon had a lot to do.

One day, Halas thought, *I'm going to get you out of this. I'll find a way to free you, Aeon. If Raazoi could not destroy the Temple by bringing the whole ocean down upon it, then I don't know what will. This place does not need a guardian. I'll see to it that you rest in peace. I swear it.*

"Come on," he said aloud. "Let's go."

Halas could still see; evidently the thing had not been able to reclaim what few gifts he'd given Halas. The scales felt perfectly at home over his eyes. He wondered if they would come anywhere, or if they were specific to Orhill. Did it matter? As he led Desmond and Elivain steadily topside, Halas explained everything. He found he knew little. What was the thing that called itself a servant of Equilibrium? Halas didn't know, and neither Des nor Elivain had much to say on the subject.

They came to the final staircase. Sunlight peaked at them from up above. "I hate to be a bother," Elivain said dryly, "but would one of you like to go find my pack? It's cold up there."

Halas smiled, and said he would go. Desmond tried to follow, but Halas made him sit. Halas felt like being alone. He went up the stairs, felt the scales pour away, and went outside.

Chapter Fifteen

Four Went In, Three Came Out

He walked slowly to the bodies of the soldiers. When Halas arrived, there were already a few scavenger birds there, picking and tearing through the mail at the bodies. Halas kicked at one and screamed, and the birds took flight. They stopped a few foot-lengths away, waiting to resume their meal, beady black eyes watching this newcomer with irritation.

He ignored them. He looked around the site. There was where Aeon and Elivain had been. There was where Halas had lost his grip on his sword. He saw the severed bonds where Desmond had cut Elivain loose, and then Aeon's a ways past that. He kicked these lamely aside and approached the bodies again. A different sort of blade glinted up through the horror, one with a silvery sheen. Halas picked it up; it was Aeon's weapon. He found a belt and scabbard that fit him and strapped it on, cleaning the blade and sheathing it at his left hip. He saw Elivain's pack then, pinned beneath a body. Halas took the man by his chainmail and heaved, rolling him over against a second corpse. The soldier's eyes stared up at him, and Halas could not bear it. He flung himself away and retched once, then twice. Nothing came up but for a thin line of bile. It made Halas realize that he hadn't had anything to eat in almost a day. He and Des had only eaten twice during their journey through the caverns.

When he knelt by the body again he avoided looking at it. Halas grabbed the pack and quickly retreated to the mouth of the Orhill Caverns. It was not at the base of the hill as he'd previously thought, but nestled in a bowl, which explained the deep snow. Across the tundra was only a light layer of the stuff, but in here, it had filled, compacted, and tumbled in over the sides. At one end was a hole, the door leading to Orhill Caverns. Between that and Halas was a thin trail of ash. "All that remains of Gilshenn Sidoor," Halas whispered to no one.

The hill was steeper than he remembered it, and after a minute of massaging his leg, he was able to keep his feet as he skidded down. He gathered the ashes in his left hand. Like everything else in this blasted wasteland, they were cold. Halas threw them into the wind, scattering them partway across the frozen tundra and partway into the tunnels.

With that done, Halas went to find his friends. "Perhaps you should come up anyway," he said to Elivain. "I don't wish to dress you." Elivain frowned, clutching the bag across his chest.

"I suppose. Dammit."

Halas led them up, out of Orhill and into the snow. Elivain quickly rummaged through his things and dressed.

Halas hunkered down and looked back at the door, at the caverns. A wan smile played across his lips as he remembered Gilshenn shouting at the Deyrey Baaish. He did not know why he smiled, but it felt appropriate.

His back and knees cracked as he stood up, and he started at the sudden sound. After that, the only noises were those of his feet crunching on the grass and the birds, cawing and pecking behind him. He did not turn back.

He limped a ways from the site of battle and sat down. Desmond and Elivain followed. They'd policed Aeon's pack and Elivain's weapons. "The sun is going down," Elivain whispered. "We'll have to make camp soon." He was looking through the bags, taking inventory of what few provisions they had left. "But there are more soldiers back there that must be dealt with."

Fresh dread came upon Halas. He hadn't even thought of that.

"Can't we just leave? They will not come looking for their companions for some time now, I expect."

"Here we are!" Elivain interrupted, producing a small bottle from the pack. He squirted salve into his palm. "Desmond, give me your hands."

Halas continued. "If we walk through the night, we would be able to put many miles between us and them."

"No, that won't do," Elivain said as he treated Desmond's burns. "You both look fit to drop, and I'm not far behind. I don't want to spend the next two weeks wondering if we're about to be set upon or not. No, best to deal with this problem now." He moved to Halas, and put the stuff over the cuts on his face. It stung. He wished they'd been able to bring whatever Tormod had used for healing. *That* stuff worked wonders. Halas knew magic had to be involved somehow. It must have been a potion. How else could something heal so quickly?

Elivain hefted his spear and stood up, pointing with the shaft. "The Stoneacre Crags are that way. You should reach them before dark. Make camp there. In the morning, cross. Aeon and I marked the route we took with strips of clothing. I…"

"Wait, no. You're not doing this alone. You said it yourself, you're in bad shape."

"I will be fine." He smiled. "I am more than capable of reason. Do not worry. But if I do not return by sundown tomorrow, make haste for Bakunin. Do not come looking for me."

With that, he was off.

———

The Stoneacre Crags were a series of cliffs and drops, each one more dangerous than the last. Halas looked at Desmond. "Can you climb?" he asked, indicating his hands. "We may have to," he added.

Desmond nodded.

The morning sun poked a few timid fingers through the cloud cover, glittering harshly off the snow, but Halas could see the flags Elivain had made. They waved proudly from their places in the drifts. "Just follow the flags," Desmond whispered to himself. Halas nodded. They had slept easily enough, but even now Halas felt on the verge of exhaustion.

The first few jumps were easy enough, just a simple matter of stepping over cracks and hopping across small openings in the ground, but the cracks and openings seemed to become steep drops and gaping maws as the two friends moved along. It became more and more difficult to cross each gap. The crags themselves became wider and the spaces between narrower. Everything was slick. Halas looked over his shoulder at Desmond, half expecting to see Elivain, a black speck in the distance.

My friend, he'd said. Halas heard it over and over again in his head.

My friend.

My friend.

Were he and Elivain friends? Certainly they'd been through much together. But had they been in it together, *really together*, or had they merely been involved in the same situations? It was hard to decide. He remembered a similar chain of thought he'd once had about Aeon, and felt tears coming on. He wiped them clean; it would not do for them to freeze.

The next jump was ten foot-lengths below them. Halas saw that they would have to jump to a low ledge barely jutting out from the cliff, and climb to the top. "There's picks," Desmond noticed aloud. "To grab on to. They really thought this through, didn't they?" He smiled.

Halas saw the picks, embedded to the hilts in the cliff face.

They rested for a time, then took off their gloves and shoved them into their pockets. Halas rubbed his bare (and already cold) hands together before making the jump. He cleared the gap easily, taking hold of the picks. His feet slipped and went over the edge, and he cried out in surprise. For a brief moment, he thought that he was going to fall. His hands would slip, the picks would come free, and he would fall.

But he was not afraid. Instead, Halas gritted his teeth and snarled. He would not die out here in the cold. Nothing would make him angrier than that.

Desmond started, but there was nothing he could do. Quickly, Halas jammed his feet deeply into the snow of the ledge, pressing himself to the cold blue ice that was the cliff wall, clinging tightly to the frozen picks. Relief washed over him, and he muttered a prayer to whatever gods were listening, thanking them, for the hilts weren't slippery. He allowed the grim smile to play at his lips; under other circumstances, some would have considered such a thing blasphemous.

Halas felt that he'd been through enough to be allowed to blaspheme every now and then. "Come across!" he finally said.

"Get off the ledge!" Desmond shouted back. Though they were only about five or six foot-lengths from each other, both felt that shouting was necessary. "Climb up to the top. I will have more room to jump, and if I slip, you can catch me."

He thought nervously for a moment before adding, "You better catch me."

But Halas did not need to catch him. Desmond leapt the chasm, caught the picks, and scrambled up the cliff just as easy as can be. If Des felt any pain in his burned hands, he refused to show it. He climbed up almost as easily as Halas had.

***

It took the better part of the day to cross over, but things were immediately easier once they had. The ground leveled out almost immediately. At the head of the crags, they stood at the mouth of a dark cave, sloping into blackness below. The walls and floor were of blue ice. Halas realized that this had been the entrance to the Orhill Caverns.

"How did you fail to see that?" Desmond asked. He was laughing. Halas laughed too.

It really was hard to miss.

***

They'd managed to survive the Stoneacre Crags, and made camp far away from the edges. There was no wood for a fire, so they wished for one high and bright, and had a not so rich meal of *spódhla*.

And they waited.

Halas wondered if Elivain was still alive. He and Desmond decided without words to wait as long as they had to.

But he did return. Just under a day after he'd left, they heard him calling. The sun set, but Halas had faith in the man. He expertly navigated the crags, passing them and arriving at the camp in but a few hours. It was still dark. Halas noticed that his chin sagged. There was a cut on his cheek that had not been there before. He immediately set to work kindling a small fire with strips of wood and bark from his pack.

"Are you all right?" Halas asked stupidly.

"Perfectly fine, just a few hits heavier than I would have expected. I'm glad to see you made it across. I…" he paused, "regretted leaving you both the moment I did; this is a dangerous place. Forgive me, Halas Duer. Forgive me, Desmond Mallon. I would beg for both of your pardons."

Halas and Des glanced nervously at each other, each one wondering the same thing: *Does he jest?* And then: *What happened to him out there?*

But he was serious. Elivain knelt down and bowed his head. Desmond coughed into his hand. "We forgive you, Elivain," Halas said. Their friend—for he was a friend, Halas had finally decided—looked up with a smile on his face. A smile that was *off*, somehow.

"Thank you. I'd like to rest now, if neither of you have any objections."

They didn't, and he did. Elivain slept for nearly a full day. Desmond and Halas tried to keep the fire alive, but vegetation was sparse and there were no trees. Eventually, they let it die. Halas thought that was only too appropriate. "We should sleep as well," he whispered.

Desmond nodded his agreement. He stood up, crossed the campsite, and laid a hand on Elivain's side. The man looked dead to the world, lying as he was. Desmond went back to Halas. "Just making sure. Rest?"

They laid with Elivain and slept.

———

Halas woke sometime in the night. Elivain was up, naked to the waist, tending to a wound on his arm. Halas sat up and hissed at the sight of it. The wound was large and raw, the skin around it blue. "What happened?" Halas asked.

"Small token of their appreciation. I will live."

From somewhere in his bag he produced a needle and thread, and began hooking it through the cut, holding the thread with his teeth when necessary. Halas looked away. Beside him, Desmond groaned. "Must you do that here?"

Elivain shrugged. The effort of it caused him to hiss in pain and nearly drop the thread. Halas hurried to his side and held his arm. Elivain raised his brow in thanks. Halas wanted to say something, but was again lost for words. He remembered someone saying it was important for a wounded man to speak, so his mind could be kept occupied. Halas didn't know where he'd heard that. Perhaps the *Blade*, but it didn't matter. It felt like truth, so he talked. "What happened to you? When Des and I fell."

There was a pause before Elivain's reply. "The prince grieved. We thought you both to be dead. He wanted to try and climb the tunnel, but I thought better of it. I'm sorry."

"You made the right choice," said Desmond. "Following us would only have endangered Aeon and risked the mission."

"He didn't give a hoot about the mission. You know how stubborn he can be. We argued it for hours. I don't know how I did it, but I found reason in him, and we pressed on. For three days we crossed the tundra. The dire wolf pack returned to us on the first night. I saw one, a great wolf the size of three. Thankfully they left us alone. The next morning we found an arctic bear, starved to the point of madness. Aeon and I slew the thing. Again we argued; he wanted to eat it, but I felt it could be diseased. Animals that size do not tend to starve without reason, especially when game is so abundant. I think the boy knew that, but he fought. Every step of the way, he fought me." Elivain shook his head and put a hand on his chin. "He was very difficult."

Halas offered a small smile. Once again, it was the truth. Aeon was nothing if not opinionated. Strong-willed to some and brick-headed to others, depending on whose side you were on. Elivain continued. "The crags took us near two days. It was no coincidence that the witch's men fell upon us where they did, I think. I've often felt that you've been gifted with divine aid, and this was no different. I do not buy into this Equilibrium nonsense. This is not the work of some lowly servant. This is the doing of the gods. Someone watches over you, Halas, wouldn't you say?"

Halas didn't know what to think. He helped Elivain stitch the cut, dress, and then they were off.

The trees slowly filtered their way back into the environment. Elivain stoically led the way, trudging through the deep snow, sometimes pulling himself along with his hands. He'd given his snowshoes to Halas, and Desmond had taken Aeon's. They wore them with embarrassment, but they wore them.

Eleven days had passed since the Temple, and gradually Elivain's softness and kindness wore off. Halas figured the shock of what they'd accomplished had done it, and he found he had to laugh. They were around a campfire in the dead of night when he did. Halas saw the whole scene clearly; he'd been pleased to discover that he still had the scales. He'd been practicing, and could nearly form them at will. It distracted him from the shame of having broken his father's sword, and his disturbing thoughts of Cailin. Elivain sat across the fire, his knees drawn up across his chest, poking at the base of the coals with a twig. Desmond lay on his side with his head propped against his fist. Their bottles, recently filled with snow, rested against the wall of stones Elivain had built to keep them from rolling into the fire while their contents melted.

"What is it?" Elivain asked.

"It's just—we *saved Aelborough*. We killed Raazoi, protected the Temple, and prevented the Ifrinn from returning. The four of us. We aren't exactly the grandest of heroes, eh Des?" He started laughing again, and laughed until there was a stitch in his side. Desmond joined in. Even Elivain smiled.

The laughter slowed to a stop, and Halas remembered Aeon, how noble the boy had looked in passing. He had been a dear friend to Halas, and now he was dead, and stranded. He'd saved the Temple, hadn't he? It was done. The Temple of Immortals was buried beneath an ocean, but still there were some who thought a need for protection. Protection from what? No one was going to find that place, ever again. Aeon deserved to rest.

Halas knew it was possible to exorcise a spirit and allow it to pass on; Conroy had performed the ritual several times himself. He would learn how, and come back.

Halas would find no true rest until he knew that his friend could do the same.

One morning, Halas awoke to the sound of a dog barking. He sat up in his bedroll and glanced at Desmond, who was similarly awake, disheveled and wild looking. Halas smiled.

"We're almost there, Des."

They roused Elivain. A short time later he stooped over the remains of last night's fire, rubbing a stick between his palms. He looked worried. "Something on your mind?" Halas asked.

"Those soldiers from Fort Torrance are not going to take the news of Prince Aeon's demise kindly," Elivain said.

Halas frowned. Once again, he hadn't thought of that. *We truly are blessed to have Elivain along,* he thought. *How many times would we have failed this mission without him? We'd be dead a dozen times over.*

Of course, that reminded him that Aeon actually *was* dead, and he felt his chest begin to tighten. He'd known the boy for only a scant few months, but he counted Aeon as one of his truest friends. Halas put a hand against his chest and rubbed it, trying to massage the pain away, but of course that would not work. He felt tears stinging at his eyes.

But that wouldn't do. Des put a hand on his shoulder and squeezed. Halas nodded to himself. Elivain made breakfast. They had little enough left in the way of provisions, but he made do. Halas sat, crunching on *spódhla*, deep in thought.

There was much to do. Even Halas knew that it would be more than difficult to sort out their lives. They'd become wanted criminals, fugitives from Queen Anaua. The world thought them to have kidnapped Prince Aeon, and now the boy was dead, lost in the wilderness. Would anyone believe their story of the Temple? Halas didn't know.

An hour's march later, the church spire came into view over the treetops, and that made things better. Bakunin was the first step in going home, something Halas wanted now more than ever. He missed his life dearly. *I'm going to get it back,* he thought. *That thing told me it would take everything, but it was bluffing. It cannot interfere. I'm going to see my father again, my friends, Cailin. I don't care what I have to do to get there.* Halas and Desmond talked all the way to the village. They were overjoyed at the prospect of a warm meal and a bed. They did not know what was to come.

If they had known that, they probably would have turned back.